NO MAN'S LAND

DEBRA DUNBAR

CHAPTER 1

*K*elly stood with her back to the doorway, her hands clasped behind her. Nothing she did helped stem the rising panic. Any moment, someone was going to walk through that door, and then she would most likely be dead.

Breathe, breathe. But no matter how she tried to regulate her breathing and relax her muscles, they continued to tense. It still seemed unreal, like she was trapped in a bad dream. Just yesterday she'd been the manager of a large, lucrative casino, but with one slip of temper it had all vanished. Now she was just one more vampire waiting in a soundless hallway for her death sentence. How many had stood here before her, desperately holding onto their last moments before execution? How many had waited in this deceptively innocuous passage with its textured, brocade-print carpeting, and signed watercolor paintings?

Could be worse. They could have stuck me in an elevator for three hours listening to Barry Manilow instrumentals on repeat, she thought, staring at the patterned blue and gold carpet. Or in the dumpster out back with the rotting food and equally rotting body parts.

It was no use. Every attempt at humor rang false in her mind. How could anyone approach the end of their life with laughter? There was nothing funny about death. Dead. In a few hours, she'd be dead. And there would be no one to mourn her. Vampires didn't grieve; they quickly jockeyed for favor to take over the dead's status and position. There wasn't a single vampire in her family that would think on her demise with sorrow, none that would speak up to save her. Not one.

George. He would have mourned. No, he would have fought to save her, scolded her for getting into this mess, then held her in his arms. She thought of his warm skin, the way his rough shirt scratched her cheek, how very safe she'd always felt when he was near. But George had been dead a long time.

Her hand crept into a small pocket in her skirt, touching the round metal ring. It was all she had left of him, of the only moment of sunshine in her life. Sharp pain stabbed her finger where the tape covering had torn. Silver burned hotter than a flame against her skin, but she refused to let go. The one link to the only love she'd ever had, and couldn't touch it without agony.

A wave of grief threatened to overwhelm her, crushing her panic with its intensity. Her eyes brimmed and she blinked, trying to hold back a sob. Sadness and loss felt worse than the fear. *George. I'm so sorry, George. If only you were here now, if even just to hold my hand.* He wasn't. No one was. She was alone. The panic crept back in, and her legs began to shake. Dead.

I really screwed the pooch this time. Kelly felt her shoulders tighten, anger replacing some of her fright. Her temper had caused her downfall; it was only fitting that she now turn that significant character flaw in upon herself. Not that anger was her only sin. Pride and greed rounded out her failings, although among vampires those were considered attributes to be cultivated. Anger was most definitely not.

Pride. She'd been turned after a mere seven years of being Chosen, been the youngest vampire in her family to be granted New status, risen rapidly through the ranks. Yeah, she had a right to be proud. Everything she touched turned to gold. It had all come with a heady feeling of invincibility — the power of a vampire, the respect for her brains and business skills. What a fairy tale it had been for a penniless bastard previously destined for a short life of squalor. Unfortunately, the fairy tale was ending.

Kelly shifted slightly, hoping the action went unnoticed. The hallway was monitored, and showing discomfort would weigh against her. Her legs ached, her head throbbed, and her back was begging for a change in position. She'd been standing motionless for over three hours. Before that she'd been in a tiny, windowless room; waiting. Dawn had come and gone; she could feel it pulling on her bones like a weight, even as young as she was. It had been dark when they'd put her in the room, but the Master would obviously not make her punishment a priority. She was just a cog in the wheel, one that could wait until after he'd slept through the daylight hours as all the old ones must do.

So very tired. Not that she had to be in a coffin during the day or anything, but the daylight had sapped her strength, and she'd been up for twenty-four hours taking care of the casino. A hot bath would be wonderful, followed by the embrace of cool sheets and soft pillows. Mmm, she'd never wanted her bed so badly. Kelly shook her head with dark amusement, her mind returning to the fate before her. It was ridiculous to be thinking of sleep and aching legs in her situation.

The door opened, and Kelly's heart sank as she saw the vampire. Pierre's malicious grin was almost more than she could take. They all hated her, but Pierre hated her the most. He had always resented that she'd gotten the casino management job over him. He'd argued that she was barely Made, wasn't even two-hundred-years old, that she shouldn't even be let out of the catacombs. Pierre hadn't been the only one pissed about it. There had been twenty vampires in the family in line for that job, and every one of them considered Kelly the least qualified of the lot. Twenty vampires, all waiting for the slightest error on her part. *They'd had to wait almost forty years*, she thought with some pride. Nobody had thought she'd last forty days.

Pierre took her arm and roughly led her into the room. The walk toward the desk seemed to extend for miles, and Kelly wondered if this was how people felt approaching the guillotine. The Master was behind the desk, writing on some papers. He appeared a distinguished man with black hair and elegant tanned fingers, but Kelly saw beyond the illusion he projected. An involuntary shiver ran through her. This was how vampires really looked. This was how she would have looked if she'd lived long enough for the transition to be complete.

Behind the façade of aristocratic wealth lurked something that no longer appeared human. The Master's skin was bluish-grey and stretched tight over bone and lean sinew. Long yellow nails tipped fingers with extra joints. The Master's eyes were solid white as they glanced up from the paperwork on the desk. Kelly hid a shudder of revulsion and willed herself to only see the illusion.

No one ever saw this when they were being considered for the change. No one. It was all about immortality, enhanced strength, the opportunity to be a valued part of a rich and powerful family. The convoluted politics, backbiting and constant jockeying for position and favor, the ever-looming threat of death by a member of your own family — no one discussed those things with Candidates. And no one ever discussed *this*. A hideous appearance, the eventual inability to tolerate the day, the growing loss of interest in any food beyond blood — all those facts were carefully hidden from the humans so eager to trade their lives away.

Would she have done it if she'd known? Probably. It's not like her human life had held any kind of future for her. She'd be long dead by now, forgotten in some unmarked grave. *There are never any good choices, just hard decisions*, she thought.

Pierre yanked her arm, sending sharp pain through her shoulder, and she obligingly picked up the pace. As much as she longed to spout off a snarky quip, cover her fear with sarcastic commentary, Kelly kept her mouth shut. Temper, pride, and greed were enough; she wasn't about to add stupidity to her list of faults. She might be facing death, but if there was a slim chance she could get out of this room alive, she'd take it. Screw her pride. It wouldn't be the first time she'd humiliated herself to survive, and with any luck it wouldn't be the last.

There was another vampire half sitting on the front edge of the desk with his foot dangling casually. Only one vampire would ever be allowed such familiarity. This was the Master's son, referred to as the Prince. His real name was Kyle Fournier. Not that anyone would ever address him by this name. He was 'Born' not 'Made', and that created a huge divide between him and all but the oldest of vampires.

The Prince was Born from a line that could trace their status to the beginning of the species. He, as well as the Master, was a *true* vampire. The rest of them, no matter how old or how valuable their service, would never measure up. Kelly had no delusions of leniency from that quarter. Still, she looked at him, trying to remain subdued and respectful as she checked him out. It wasn't every day you got to see a god. This would probably be the last time she'd see him, even if she lived through the morning.

The Prince was still young enough to appear human without the need for an illusion. He looked to be about late twenties in human years, although Kelly remembered hearing he was just over three hundred. He had the dark hair of his father's illusion, cut fashionably short and gelled into a disheveled state. Faint stubble darkened the edge of his jaw, casting his cheekbones into relief. She couldn't see the color of his eyes, but long dark lashes brushed the cheekbones. His mouth turned up at the corner, and she couldn't quite tell if he was smiling, or if the upturned edges were just the normal position of his mouth. It made him look oddly approachable, as if he found everything in life rather amusing. Of course, with the circumstances of his birth, everything in life probably was amusing.

Her eyes traveled down his frame, and she felt a twinge of annoyance with herself as she admired him. He was muscular without being overly bulky. His light grey suit screamed money. Even the dark socks and the shiny, black patent shoes announced his privileged state. He was good looking, and his aura flowed out like someone ten times his age. He wasn't human, and neither was she anymore. She needed to remember that fact. It was one thing to appreciate his human-looking physical form, but she should never forget what lay inside. These vampires held her life in their powerful hands, and contrary to myth, sex had never had the power to sway a vampire. Confirming her thoughts, the Fournier Prince glanced up at her, his cold, gray eyes holding nothing but boredom.

Neither the Master nor his son said a word as she approached. The Prince returned to contemplating the end of his shoe, and Kelly couldn't help her eyes from tracking there also. It was a nice wingtip, but it didn't appear worthy of such attention. Now, if the Prince had been sporting a pair of bright red suede Zanottis or rhinestone encrusted Lorenzi platform pumps that would have been a different story. Those would be worth more than a casual look.

All too soon Kelly stood before the desk, awaiting The Master's attention. Pierre did the same. Only the Prince remained relaxed, slouched half on the desk edge. Silence filled the room, broken by the occasional scratching of the Master's pen and the noise of silk on silk as Kyle swung his dangling foot.

It seemed like hours, but probably only ten minutes had passed before The Master stacked his papers and set aside his pen to look up at her.

"Kelly Demir," The Master said in a tone of mild interest. "An unusual name. Irish with a Persian surname?"

Any question from The Master demanded answer.

"Yes, my Master. My mother was Irish and my father Turkish." She thought so anyway. Her name had originally been Elizabeth, and she'd quickly changed it after becoming Chosen. Her chest tightened at the memory. Elizabeth was someone she'd been happy to leave behind.

"And you were born a human in England? Eighteen fifteen, or thereabouts?"

"Yes, my Master." Thereabouts was closer to the truth.

"You are quite young to be managing the casino," the Master stated blandly, as if announcing it was raining outside. His sentence was not in the form of a question, so Kelly remained silent.

"Your service and behavior have been exemplary until last night. A few missteps here and there, but that's to be expected with a newly made vampire, especially one so young." He exchanged a quick glance with his son.

"Kelly, do you know why we provide the utmost in hospitality to the demons? Why we uncomplainingly clean up the messes they leave behind?"

"Because their alliance is crucial to our survival," Kelly replied calmly. She was proud that her voice did not waver at all. "Because one day the angels or the elves or the humans will move against us and we will need these allies to ensure the future of our species."

The Master looked at her with his milk-white eyes, breaking through the illusion. It was like being burned, being seared by a branding iron. "Do you believe this, Kelly?" he asked softly.

No, she did not. The angel assigned to negotiate and act as an emissary to them had always been reasonable and pleasant. There hadn't been an elf in this realm in millions of years. The humans were numerous, but they were also stupid and blind to the existence of vampires. Plus they were *food*, for crying out loud. Since when was food a menace? Where was this mysterious threat that meant they had to risk their assets by playing doormats to a bunch of boorish demons? It would have been more beneficial to sic one of the angels on the demons and sweep the place clean. God, she hated demons. They were far worse than the angels or non-existent elves could ever be.

"It is not my place to believe or offer an opinion, my Master," she said instead. "My place is only to serve and obey."

The Master sighed and leaned back into his chair, his hands forming a steeple under his chin as he eyed her with consideration.

"But obey, you did not." He stated this as a fact.

No, she had not. The demon was an ass. They were all asses — crude, demanding, breaking rules and violating other patrons. Every time a demon came into the casino, she held her breath. Kelly had seen her share of demons in and out of the casinos, and something always went wrong. This had gone terribly wrong, but there would be no excuse for her behavior. At the end of the day, she was just another worker, another Made whose death would be insignificant except to serve as an example to the others.

If they had found the money, she would have been doubly screwed. Not that she could be any more screwed than "dead." It's not like the money was going to be of benefit where she was going. Rich didn't do a person much good when their heart was ripped out and their head decorating the lobby on a pike.

Kelly felt the tension in the room build; the only sound the swish-swish of silk. . She glanced over, wondering if she could manage to rip the foot off the Prince's leg before they killed her. That had to be the most annoying noise in the world. Worse than a Barry Manilow instrumental.

"Did you obey yesterday evening, Kelly?" the vampire behind the desk asked.

"No, my Master," Kelly replied.

Well, this was it. Time to face the music. The panic that had gripped her for hours in the hallway returned full force, and she struggled to remain upright.

The Master leaned forward and looked at a few other papers on his desk, making notes on one of them. After a few minutes he looked up, as if surprised to see her and Pierre still standing there.

"Pierre, please take her downstairs to the first floor. I'll send Kyle down momentarily with instructions."

Pierre didn't hesitate to half-drag Kelly by the arm through the door. She knew exactly where she was going. There was a room on the first floor for punishment. It had easy access to the private back alley for disposal of bodies and parts. Hopefully it would just be parts of her going out that door and not her lifeless body.

Kelly stood in the punishment room and tried to maintain her composure. It was no use. She'd begun retching the moment she'd walked in, and although she managed to wrestle her empty digestive system under control, she couldn't stop the shaking that wracked her body. This was so much worse than she'd ever imagined. Everything in the room reminded her that there were things she dreaded more than death.

Pierre stood beside her, no doubt to keep her from killing herself before they had a chance to extract maximum pain and agony. There was one chair in the room, and Kelly refused to go near it. It looked like an execution chair with straps for arms, legs, and even for the head. Fully strapped in, the neck would be open and free. Lots of other parts would be too.

Trays on wheels lined the walls, their silk-draped surfaces filled with neatly lined tools. Picks, saws, hammers, pliers, drills, torches. The padded walls ensured total soundproofing. The smell of the room was even worse than the appearance — bleach and cleaning fluid that did little to cover up the overwhelming scent of blood, vomit, excrement, and fear. Pierre grinned gleefully, fairly dancing in anticipation. There was nowhere for Kelly to look that didn't remind her of what was coming.

The door clicked open and the Prince walked in flanked by two male vampires. He nodded toward her, and she could have sworn she saw a flash of amusement in his bored eyes. The two males grabbed her by the arms and took her to the chair, strapping her in. She didn't resist. It wasn't like she could fight two vampires, evade Pierre and the Master's son, then somehow manage to escape from a resort filled with loyal vampires. Even if she did, where would she go? Better to take her punishment and die with some dignity.

Calm. Calm. You can get through it, girl. You're strong enough to endure anything they do to you. She could do this. There would either be a lot of pain, and she'd live, or a lot of pain and she'd die. Either way, it wouldn't go on forever. Kelly tried everything she could think of to calm herself, but it was impossible when she was strapped to a chair and facing shining torture instruments.

One of the older vampires took a metal apparatus, and gripping her jaw, shoved it into her mouth. The device held her mouth open. Even with her vampire strength, she was unable to move her jaw, the strap across her head holding her immobile. Suddenly Kelly realized what they meant to do. Whatever resolve she'd had fled. She trembled uncontrollably as her heart pounded and tears flooded her eyes, blinding her. Rough, calloused hands pinched her jaw, bruising and digging into her flesh.

"Let me," a deep voice said. Strong fingers gripped her jaw and expertly hit the pressure points. Her fangs snapped down, exposed.

Tears poured from her eyes, and her breath came in fast pants as she felt the scrape of metal on her right fang. White light blinded her. Pain made all conscious thought impossible as the fang was yanked from her mouth. Kelly heard herself scream as if it were another person. Blood and venom from her glands filled her mouth, and she choked and sputtered instinctively to keep from inhaling the fluids. Crimson bubbled and spat from her mouth as she gasped for air. She'd barely had time to recognize the pain when she felt the metal on her second fang.

"No, no, no," she begged as coherently as she could with her mouth pried open and the flood of blood threatening to pour down her lungs. Again the hand held her jaw and she felt the white-hot pain as the fang was yanked from her mouth in one pull. Everything went dark.

She came to, not sure how long she'd been unconscious, and realized they were unstrapping her from the chair. Was that it? They only pulled her fangs? Not that removing her fangs was light punishment. A vampire's fangs were deeply embedded into the bone of their jaw, and nerve endings filled the tooth and canals leading to the venom glands. They were one of the few body parts that wouldn't regenerate. Without them, she would need another vampire's assistance to feed, or face a slow and painful starvation. But that was the future. Right now, she was hoping to survive long enough to face it.

The two older vampires pulled her from the chair and dragged her by her arms out the back door to the private alley. Blood poured from Kelly's mouth, dribbling a trail of red down her clothing and across the floor. Her glands had long emptied, leaving her mouth tingly with a sharp, bitter taste. The empty sockets, where her fangs had been, throbbed with agony. She thought about the day before, when she'd fed on a guest who'd borrowed heavily at the black jack table. His blood had tasted warm and rich with a tang of gin from the martinis he'd drank. She'd never envisioned that would be her last meal.

Pierre thrust open the door into the alley, and the moonlight stung her eyes, the reek of dumpsters assaulting her nose. They weren't just filled with rotted lettuce and banana peels; but also with dismembered body parts. She could smell them; the congealed blood, and the decaying flesh. Everything was so sharp, so clear. It was as the books had said — death brought her surroundings into clearer focus. The two vampires holding her arms spun her around. She caught a glimpse of Pierre's smug face, and the emotionless, somewhat bored expression on the Master's son before a fist in her stomach doubled her over.

Blows came at her from all sides, and Kelly ineffectually tried to deflect them with her hands. It only meant the few that missed her waist and head bruised her arms instead. A kick to the side threw her off balance, and she curled into a ball on the oily asphalt, trying to protect her midsection.

"Get her back up again."

Pierre's frustrated voice sounded tinny in her ringing ears. A hand grabbed each of her arms, one twisting until she heard her shoulder pop and felt a snap of bone. The two elder vampires held her upright, while Pierre, grinning with glee, repeatedly punched her face.

The pain all blended together with the tickle of wet blood from her arm, face, and mouth. It hurt to breathe, and in her blurred vision she saw the Prince standing ten feet away with his arms crossed, his toe tapping impatiently. *Won't get blood on his suit or shoes over there*, she thought through the pain. Pierre's fists left her face, and he drove a hard punch into her shoulder, ripping the splintered edge of her broken arm through the flesh.

"Help him out. I don't have all night," the Prince drawled. One of the vampires that had been holding her upright, kicked the side of her leg, and Kelly felt her knee give way and heard the sharp crack as her thigh bone fractured. The vampire on the other side mirrored his move slightly higher, breaking her other leg. Now she was suspended by her separated shoulder, the weight of her body sagging in agony on broken ribs.

"Kill me," she pleaded, looking at the only man in the alley with the authority to grant her a merciful death.

The Prince smiled. "But that would be no fun at all, and we have a long evening ahead of us. Let's see how long we can make it last."

The two vampires at her side let go of her shoulders, and Kelly collapsed, her broken legs folding like sticks beneath her. Three sets of feet kicked at her, tossing her back and forth like a football with the force of each blow. Thankfully, one to the side of her head knocked her into blessed oblivion.

CHAPTER 3

Jaq held her tall, thin frame absolutely still in the shadows of the propane tank. The three men with the big black car were vampires, and she did not want them to see her — or smell her for that matter. It was a few hours until dawn. If she hadn't been out hunting, she would never have seen them drive silently up to the vacant trailer.

Skirting the patches of moonlight, she darted to the rear of the trailer, assessing this new threat. One vampire would have been child's play, but three? And these weren't just lone scouts or spies; these ones were warriors.

Half crawling, she cautiously peered around the cinder blocks that supported the mobile home. Two warriors, she corrected. They were both old and strong enough to give her pause, but the third one raised the skin on the back of her neck. He seemed an attractive human male in an expensive suit, but the feel of power rolling from him set her on edge. It was a young power, raw and untrained, but it still felt like a fist against her senses. The odds weren't in her favor taking on these three. It would be better to take a hit to her pride and live to fight another day.

"What stinks here?" the large one complained, holding a beefy hand in front of his nose. "Don't these rednecks ever bathe? It smells like a cross between dogs in heat and old ham."

The one in the suit ignored him. Jaq could see by the buzzing street light that his outfit would have cost more than every car on the block combined. It fit well, like it was custom made, and glided in a quiet rustle as he moved. *Silk,* she thought, sniffing the air.

They pulled something out of the trunk of the car bundled in sheets. It looked like a body. Jaq could smell the old blood. Lots of blood. Her nose told her it was a strange mix of human and vampire blood. *Had they killed a human?* she wondered uneasily. If so, she might not be able to let them leave without a challenge, regardless of how it would probably end. Trespassing was one thing, but poaching was unforgivable.

But why was there a faint vampire smell to the old blood? None of the men appeared injured, so it probably wasn't coming from them. Was it a dead human in that sheet or a dead vampire? And why would they dump a body outside their own territory?

The large, complaining vampire tossed the body over his shoulder and strode up the rickety wooden steps into the trailer. Jaq saw a thin white arm dangle loose from the sheet and she caught her breath. A woman? A child? Silently she glided in the shadows back around to the rear of the trailer and peeked through a corner window. The large man threw the body down carelessly, unconcerned that a portion of it landed hard against the coffee table before rolling onto the carpet.

"Take the sheet." The tall one laughed. "Don't even leave her with that."

The large one ripped the sheet from the body, thumping it against the floor and edge of the couch. "I'd take her clothes off and leave her naked if they weren't so filthy with blood," he said in amusement.

The two men left the trailer and Jaq moved to see the inside better through the window. The woman on the floor was tiny, with a cap of dark hair. Her legs and arms twisted unnaturally, and blood seeped out in a slow spread across the carpet.

Her scabs must have been ripped off with the sheet, Jaq thought. She watched the spread of crimson slow to a stop and winced. The poor thing probably didn't have much blood left in her to lose.

The trailer door banged open again and Jaq froze, afraid to move lest the vampire notice her looking through the window. The man wearing the suit came in and stared down at the body. He removed something from his jacket and placed it on the coffee table.

"Ten grand says you don't make it three days," he told the body. "I really like to win my bets, so I'll leave you this gift."

He left the trailer, and Jaq heard the big car crunch its way down the gravel road. Carefully she made her way around to the front of the trailer and in the door, wincing as it squeaked open on rusty hinges. The body remained motionless on the ground.

"Hello," she called softly. The woman hadn't responded from being tossed around the floor, but Jaq wasn't taking any chances.

The body stayed still, and Jaq cautiously approached, leaning down to check the periodic pulse and occasional breath. *This woman shouldn't be alive*, she thought. Legs were twisted practically backwards, bone protruded from a shoulder, and probably from elsewhere given the odd lumps in her clothing. The woman was covered in blood and vomit, urine and some kind of glandular secretion. She smelled of vampire, but that might have been from her attackers. Wanting to make sure, Jaq leaned closely and sniffed, jumping back as the sharp, familiar scent hit her nose. Vampire, but weak and heavily tinged with human odors. Whoever she was, she'd been turned less than two centuries ago.

They'd left this woman here for dead, but vampires didn't die all that easy. She still had her head on, still had a heart somewhat beating in her chest. She'd pull through if she had food and blood to regenerate. If not, then she was in for a horrible, lingering death. Jaq stared down at the battered female in indecision. Vampires were the enemy, but it was hard to see this tiny woman on the floor as anything but a victim.

This was their land, and they'd never tolerated a vampire here, although living in the middle of two fractious vampire clans had its challenges. This woman should die. If she survived her horrendous injuries, she wouldn't survive here for long. Trespassers never did. It would be sensible to kill her now, while she lay helpless on the floor. It would be merciful to end her life now. Jaq had put down plenty of dying animals in her life, and this was no different. Vampire or not, this creature had to die.

But something stayed her hand. "Poor thing. What did you do to deserve this?"

The fragile woman on the floor didn't look at all like the vampires she'd faced over the years. This was no threatening enemy; this was a broken bird on her doorstep, and despite her fierce reputation, Jaq had always had a soft spot for broken birds.

Gently she straightened the vampire's legs and pushed the

protruding bone back through her shoulder. It must have hurt, but the vampire didn't give any indication that she felt pain. Jaq placed a tentative finger against the woman's face, feeling bone like bits of gravel shifting under the skin. *She should heal. She should be fine,* Jaq chanted silently to herself, but she wasn't convinced. The woman had lost too much blood, and the faintly human smell of her led Jaq to doubt that the dark-haired woman had the regenerative powers to come back from this level of injury.

It would be best if she died now, quick and painless on the trailer floor. Best for the Pack, and best for this poor creature. How could she feed it if it began to heal? Would Jaq come home from work one night and find the neighbors drained of all their blood? It would be cruel to nurse this woman to health only to kill her when she recovered and proved to be just as much of a threat as every other vampire that crossed the border.

Taking a deep breath, Jaq looked toward the ceiling of the trailer, as if she could see straight through it to the stars above and the god that she hoped watched over them all. "I'm a fool. I'm a fool for letting her live, and I'm a fool for what I'm about to do."

A white band of light twisted around her left hand to join with a golden one from her right. Jaq guided the light down through the tiny woman before her. It was like diving beneath the surface of another's skin, feeling along muscle, bone, and nerve, but this was unfamiliar territory. The woman's body appeared to be the same as others she'd healed, but there must be differences. What else could account for the fact that when she pulled the light back into her core, the woman remained just as battered and broken as before.

"Well, I tried. I guess whether you live or die is truly up to you, and whatever god looks over vampires." Jaq rose to her feet. She couldn't heal the woman, but perhaps there were other things she could do.

Briskly and efficiently, Jaq searched the small trailer. The electricity and water were on, but the fridge was empty. A few dishes and some silverware lay dusty in the cabinets, but nothing else. There weren't even sheets on the bed. As she stood, contemplating what to do, her gaze drifted to the coffee table. A knife. A well-made filet knife with a carved bone handle and a blade of silver alloy. Why in all that was holy had that vampire chosen to leave this woman a suicide knife? What was wrong with these people? Torturing one of their own, dumping her in enemy territory, and then encouraging her to end it all. She'd never understand them, didn't want to even try.

Jaq picked up the knife, using her shirt edge to guard her fingers against the silver. Walking to the kitchen area, she shoved the knife in a drawer. *No suicide for you, little one.* There was no way she would let that happen, even to a vampire.

Now, what to do about food? Jaq made a quick trip back to her own neighboring trailer, careful not to wake her snoring brother, Mike, as she raided their refrigerator. What could vampires eat? It's not like she had bags of human blood in her freezer, or bags of human anything in her freezer. Ugh. Humans tasted worse than anything in the world. Worse than salad. Although neither she or nor anyone she knew had actually eaten a human. The angels would exterminate them all in a blink if they started feasting on their neighbors. Throwing her hands upward in frustration, Jaq finally grabbed a huge steak Mike had thawed for dinner and carted it back to the other trailer, stuffing it in the empty fridge.

Hoping the vampire had the presence of mind to look for her offering once she awoke, Jaq stared at her, watching the broken body as it began to twitch on the floor. The woman moaned, and Jaq couldn't help but go to her, stroking her torn cheek and soft, silken black hair.

"Shhh. It's okay. I've got you. I'll keep you safe."

This was wrong, so very wrong. By morning others in the Pack would know this vampire was here. Jaq would need to let them know, to provide some sort of protection for the woman until she was strong enough to leave. But leave she must, because their land could never be home to any vampire.

* * *

HIS FATHER KEPT his attention firmly rooted to his paperwork as Kyle approached. It wasn't the first time that the Master refused to acknowledge him. The distance had been growing between them over the last few decades, foretelling the future when they'd go their separate ways, when they'd become adversaries instead of allies. It was the way things were. He may be his father's flesh and blood, his only son, the only Born he'd sired in his very long life, but when a child reached a certain age, all fatherly instincts went out the window. Territory, status, dominance were survival, and a young, powerful Born son threatened all of that.

Kyle knew he was strong. He'd proven himself to be an excellent leader. His staff both loved and feared him. *You're not ready,* an uneasy inner voice reminded him. *You're too young to control a large vampire population, to hold a territory.* Maybe not, but he could tell his father was on the edge of a decision — throw him out, or lock him away where the son could no longer be a threat to the father. Either way, it would be sink or swim — carve out a place of his own, either from a rival or his sire's territory, or perish in an eventual bloody fight for dominance.

Kyle dropped into a chair and propped his feet on the desk, purposely pointing the bottom of his shoes toward the Master. He didn't want to appear a weak clingy son that his father needed to throw out of the nest. Better to be seen as insolent. Better to turn his subtle challenges overt. It was time for him to get his own territory, time to leave the family before the things between his father and he turned deadly and split them all down the middle. He wasn't ready yet, but some things couldn't wait for a person to be ready.

"It's done," Kyle told him, his tone emotionless as befit a vampire of his stature. "I doubt she'll survive the week."

"Where did you dump her?" the Master asked in an equally emotionless tone.

"Outside Ranson, West Virginia."

The older man gave a short bark of laughter, and Kyle shrugged with nonchalance. West Virginia was beyond the southern edge of their territory. There wasn't a vampire around for a hundred miles of there. If she didn't starve or go insane from exile, one of the Kincaid scouts would execute her. Or worse. West Virginia was home to a particularly vicious pack of werewolves. There wasn't much in the state worth defending, but the brainless idiots guarded it like it was the Garden of Eden.

"Stacking the odds pretty hard against her, are you?" the Master asked, his voice light with amusement.

Kyle shrugged again. "It's a ruthless world. She screwed up."

They sat in silence for a few moments.

"You'll be heading up to New York now?" the older man asked.

Kyle tensed. He'd been given Delaware, Maryland, and Pennsylvania to manage. Did his father's comment suggest that his sections were stable enough that he could manage them remotely from Manhattan, or that he was too incompetent to handle the states and should crawl back into the womb? Talking with the old man was like playing a never-ending game of chess.

"No, I'm heading back to Baltimore," he said, brushing a speck of lint from his pants.

"You're not strong enough to move against Kincaid, my boy," the ancient vampire told Kyle, his words coated with cloying affection that rang false in Kyle's ears. "Give yourself time to mature a bit more. Go to New York. I've got some lobbying work I need you to do. I'll send Durand down to Baltimore."

His smile was cool as he turned his attention back to the paperwork on his desk.

A crackle of power filled the room, although Kyle's expression remained bland. He stood, bowing deeply to his father as he left with a casual pace, clicking the door shut quietly behind him. His calm demeanor remained in place as he strolled through the casino, got into his car and drove south.

CHAPTER 4

*E*very inch of Kelly ached. She was lying on something hard and cold. In fact, the air was cold. She was damp. Her mouth throbbed; her eyes throbbed; her chest hurt with every shallow breath; her extremities felt like someone had been whacking them with metal rods. Carefully she forced her eyes open and looked at what seemed to be the legs of a chair. Dirty vinyl flooring stretched in front of her face in a plaid pattern of olive and beige. With blurred vision, she could see a table, and the cloth skirt of what presumably was a sofa.

Where was she? Everything in her mind jumbled together in a crazy mosaic. The casino, the demon, Pierre's grinning face, it all combined with dusty human memories of her standing on a stool to reach the tabletop, her small hands rinsing a cup in a bowl of water. She needed to be careful, or it would break — shatter like the legs twisted under her body.

Something brushed along her hair in a soft rhythm, accompanied by a caring whisper.

"Shhh. It's okay. I've got you. I'll keep you safe."

George. *I'll keep you safe.* Except this was a woman's voice, and the hand on her hair was lithe, its touch light and gentle.

The pain receded into the distance, and Kelly focused on the touch. How long had it been since anyone had soothed her? Again a boy's face swam out of her memories. The thought of his quick grin and laughing blue eyes was more painful than the agony that lanced her body.

No. Kelly crammed the memories back into the recesses of her mind. That was long ago. The girl she'd been had died, and there was nothing to be gained from giving that tiny portion of her life the slightest thought. Kelly closed her eyes and felt the rhythmic stroking of her hair and cheek. It lulled her away into darkness.

When she came to again, Kelly could clearly see the battered table legs and shredded fabric edges of the sofa. Underneath stretched a thick layer of dust and a crumpled packet of cigarettes. Where was she? No rooms in the casino had such shabby furnishings, let alone this level of uncleanliness. She tried to lift her head and thought better of it as everything started to blur again. Best to lay here a moment.

Everything hurt worse than last time she was conscious, but at least she felt like she could think properly. The gentle stroking against her hair, the comforting whisper had disappeared, and she wondered if she had imagined it. Carefully, Kelly moved arms and legs. Her shoulders had been dislocated, but they were now back in their sockets and healing well, as was the broken arm. Four broken ribs, a broken hip, every finger broken, both legs broken, and some internal injuries. Everything healing slowly, but healing. She didn't even want to think about her face. Or her fangs.

Kelly pulled herself into a sitting position, reclining against the coffee table to take the pressure off her cracked hip. Nausea heaved her stomach upward, and the room swam before her, but after a few moments the pain dulled to a manageable level, and her vision cleared, allowing her to check out her surroundings.

A trailer. They'd dumped her in a trailer, and not even a clean one by any standard. The hideous sofa was covered in floral upholstery that sagged in the middle, tufts of stuffing poked from randomly placed slashes, as if the former occupant had frequent violent battles with the cushions. The table to her left was equally battered, and the mismatched appliances in the kitchen looked like they had seen the hard end of a fist. Whoever the owner was, Kelly hoped he didn't return before she managed to heal enough to defend herself.

Where was she? One moment she'd been facing a painful death next to a dumpster, and the next she was inexplicably in a dilapidated trailer. The only bright spot in all this was that she hadn't come to strapped into the torture chair. One encounter with that thing was enough, and as nasty as this place looked, it didn't appear designed for pain.

Nausea rose up again in her throat, and Kelly gagged — the action like a knife through her lungs. Every inch of her hurt, and her few moments of visual exploration were the most she could manage. She glanced toward the bedroom, knowing she'd never be able to manage the distance in her current condition. The bed was out of the question, but she couldn't bring herself to just slump back down on the filthy floor. Bracing herself against the coming pain, Kelly dragged herself closer to the sofa and attempted to pull herself up. It was no use. Her bones just hadn't healed enough yet.

How long had it been since they'd dumped her here? How long had it been since she'd been beaten? Vampire healing prioritized itself by critical area, so damaged organs and essential bones would repair long before more cosmetic injuries, but she was New and wouldn't heal as quickly as the older vampires would. Still, she did heal fast. More than a day? She was guessing it might be around thirty hours or so.

Her head ached trying to think of these things, and the sofa was clearly out of reach. Giving up for the moment, she pulled the ugly cushions to the floor and rolled onto them, gratefully embracing the darkness.

Kelly awoke this time to find the trailer pitch black. Eventually her night vision took over, outlining her surroundings in a brownish grey. The broken bones in her hands had knitted together, although they were stiff and puffy from lack of motion. She wiggled her fingers and heard them pop and creak in protest. Gingerly she rose to her feet and tested her limits.

Everything critical except for her fangs had healed, but that didn't mean she felt spry and ready to roll. Her chest throbbed with each breath, and every movement was slow and painful. She'd have bruises and cuts for a few more days at the very least, and the ones she was sporting were extensive. They wouldn't heal at all if she wasn't able to eat. Her stomach growled, and she realized that the continual nausea wasn't from her head injury but the lack of food.

Great. She was starving, in a trailer in God-knows-where. What she wouldn't give for a human right now, although feeding without fangs would be a problem. She could cut her victim open with a knife and lap the blood like a dog, but it would be a struggle. The venom in her glands had been more than a numbing agent and an anti-coagulant; it was also a narcotic, giving the human a rush of ecstasy followed by mild short-term memory loss. Without her fangs, feeding would be a violent affair, and she'd probably need to kill the human afterward. Not that there were any humans within grabbing distance. Besides, she was in no condition to wrestle her meal to the ground and hold them still as she dined.

They hadn't killed her, and although this wasn't exactly the Hilton, it was a reasonable shelter. Maybe her family had also left her some food. Kelly made her way slowly over to the fridge and opened it, blinking as the light temporarily blinded her. It was empty except for one item; a raw steak.

Steak. Kelly frowned at the meat neatly wrapped in plastic on a Styrofoam tray. Were they taunting her? A packet of fresh human blood would have meant all was forgiven and that she was to wait here for them to eventually bring her back. But a steak? Vampires ate solid food for hundreds of years before the need for it tapered off, but she required human blood in order to properly metabolize this food. She'd been so injured that she wasn't even sure she could digest this without a few pints to wash it down. Animal blood would help, but there wasn't enough of it in this package to kick-start her healing. And animal blood wouldn't hold her for long. Did they intend for her to starve to death? Was this a sign of eventual forgiveness, or a cruel reminder of a short, agonizing future?

Taking the Styrofoam and plastic-wrapped package from the shelf, Kelly looked at the date. It was fresh by human standards, not fresh enough by vampire standards. Her heart sank, but it was no time to for an internal debate over the meaning of this strange offering and whether she'd ever be welcomed back into her family. Right now, this steak was all she had.

"Beggars can't be choosers," Kelly said out loud, slurring the words with her mangled mouth as she ripped open the package.

She ate the steak raw, wincing as bits jabbed into the empty sockets where her fangs should have been. The thing had been slaughtered months ago and frozen since. It was horrible, but it was the only food in the house. Finishing the two-pound steak, Kelly carefully poured the blood from the plate into a glass and licked the plate clean. She had no idea where or when her next meal would come from.

She eyed the glass of blood thoughtfully. Saving the blood

in the fridge would allow her sustenance for later, but there was a good chance it would be undrinkable by tomorrow. She picked up the glass and threw the blood as a shot down her throat. Normally the taste filled her with peaceful satisfaction — a flood of flavors, warm and sensuous on her tongue. This stuff was cold and congealed. Nasty, but it would keep her going.

Kelly rinsed the dishes then carefully peeled off her bloody clothing, washing it in the sink as best as she could before draping it across the counter and the chairs to dry. She freshened up a bit in the bathroom then collapsed into the lumpy bed, convinced she'd be covered in bed bug bites by morning. Reasonably full, and with throbbing pain from the empty holes in her mouth, she drifted off to sleep.

CHAPTER 5

*B*ang, bang. Bang, bang, bang.

Don't hit me! I'm sorry, please don't hit me! Elizabeth cringed, covering her head as Cook flung another pot at her. It hit the table, ricocheting off the wall behind and onto the floor. She'd be blamed for the dented pots too. Double the beating, although beating was preferable to some punishments. The two days she'd spent locked in the cupboard without food or water had been far worse.

The cook screamed, her English failing in anger as she ran around the long wooden table, this time brandishing a knife.

I'm sorry, I'm sorry! The little girl darted under the table, thankful for once that she was tiny and quick.

Not quick enough. A fat hand grabbed her ankle like a steel manacle, throwing Elizabeth face-first onto the stone floor. The grip around her ankle tightened painfully as the cook dragged her from under the table. A sob of terror caught in the girl's throat as she frantically tried to pull free.

You'll be sorry soon enough, dirty little bastard.

Bang, bang, bang.

Kelly's mind rose with the sound, jarring her from the unpleasant dream. She wasn't a human anymore; she was a vampire, and far away from that dingy kitchen. What was that noise? Was someone throwing dining trays around her manager's suite? Why did her bed feel like the mattress was stuffed with acorns? Why was she so sore? She felt starved, as if she hadn't eaten in days. And why did her down comforter itch and scratch like cheap polyester?

"Hellooooo," a cheerful female voice called. "Are you ok in there, sweetie?"

Memory flooded Kelly, and she opened her eyes to stare at the faded, teal-striped wallpaper and lacy curtained window a scant foot from her bed. She was sore with tight muscles, like she'd run a marathon in the night, but thankfully the only pain was from the throbbing in her mouth.

Bang, bang, bang. "Hellooooo."

Daylight. Judging from how sluggish she felt, it had to be early morning. It sucked to be up during the day. She'd always tried to pawn off early casino duties on a subordinate vampire.

The banging echoed again through the trailer, and Kelly grumbled. This person wasn't going to leave until she answered the door. Maybe whoever it was had a bloodmobile parked out front. Probably not, but a girl could have her fantasies.

Kelly squirmed to the end of the bed and stood, wrapping the itchy blue comforter around her naked body and shuffled to the door. A female face peered through the window, disappearing only to reappear at the door as she opened it.

"I'm so glad y'all are finally awake," the human woman said with obscene cheerfulness. "I saw you moved in last week, but you never seemed to be home when I came 'round. I peeked through the window this morning and saw you sleeping and just *had* to come by and welcome you to the neighborhood."

The woman appeared to be in her late forties. She was stout, but not obese, her figure at a horrible disadvantage in black leggings and a t-shirt that barely cleared her midriff. Her blond hair showed a hint of dark roots, and her make-up was carefully applied.

Kelly stared at her with fascination. She'd had very little interaction with humans for nearly a century. Sure, she saw them all the time in the casino and spoke with them somewhat before biting them, but she'd not actually had a conversation with one in longer than she could remember. Others handled most of the day-to-day dealings with the humans. She'd been too busy, and there hadn't really seemed to be a point to engaging them in any kind of social interaction. One didn't talk to one's food.

The woman pushed by her into the trailer, and Kelly realized she was carrying a container of some sort. She smelled the warmth of the woman, heard the thud of her pulse. Had she said it had been a week since she'd arrived? A week with only a two pound steak to keep her going after all the blood she'd lost and all the damage she'd needed to heal. No wonder she felt so weak and bruised. Her body was probably refusing to heal further until she ate. If she'd had her fangs, she would have jumped right on this woman and bled her dry. Normally a pint would do it, but Kelly felt like she could drain a whole football team to empty husks and still not be satiated. Her stomach growled.

"I'm Melody Cramer, and I live in the next place down. I brought you over a nice tuna casserole. You don't seem to have a microwave, but you can warm it up at three fifty for about twenty minutes and it will be wonderful. My heavens, it's cold in here! You really need to turn up the heat."

Placing the container of tuna casserole on the counter, Melody walked to the thermostat by the door and adjusted it.

"There. Now I'll just put this casserole in your fridge here. You can bring back the container when you're done. No hurry at all. My goodness! You don't have a lick of food here beyond this steak!"

Steak? Kelly had eaten the only steak in the fridge. How did there come to be another one in there?

"I noticed you don't have a car. I can pick you up some staples when I run into town. Or maybe you can come with me. If not, the nineteen bus stops right at the end of the road four times a day, and you can catch that into town."

Melody's words faded to a buzz as Kelly stared at her. Blood. Blood. She envisioned sinking fangs into the woman's neck, or her wrist, and the crimson liquid filling her mouth — warm and salty, with that lovely metallic tang. Kelly, in cruel anticipation, swallowed the saliva that filled her mouth and realized that Melody had stopped talking. The woman was looking at her expectantly.

"Oh, sweetie! Here I am babbling away and you probably don't even have any coffee. I can't imagine putting my brain in gear in the morning without coffee. I'll be right back."

Melody whisked out of the trailer with unexpected speed given her chubbiness. It seemed like the door had barely slapped on its hinges before she was back carrying a plastic tub of Folgers and a handful of coffee filters. Grabbing the stained and slightly melted coffee maker off the counter, she efficiently started a pot brewing. With a steady stream of conversation, she ransacked the little kitchen, looking for who knew what.

"Ah here, you've got a couple coffee cups and glasses and some dishes and silverware. One saucepot and one fry pan, and your coffee maker. And this crazy knife. Goodness knows what that will come in handy for. Maybe home protection." She chuckled.

Kelly looked at the filleting knife. It was the only new thing in the trailer. It was high quality, sharp, with an intricately carved bone handle. It was silver. No doubt it had been specifically left in case she got too desperate, reached the end of her rope, gave up. It was a kind gesture. One she hadn't expected.

Suddenly the door flung open and a tall, thin woman burst through. Kelly instinctively crouched in a defensive posture, which was ridiculous given she was naked and wrapped in a cheap polyester bedspread inside a ramshackle trailer. The woman seemed out of breath, whipping her blond hair from side to side as she looked frantically from Kelly to Melody and back again.

"You're alive," the woman informed Melody, as if she had expected to find the opposite. Kelly frowned.

"Well, of course I am, Jaq," Melody chuckled. "Although I wasn't sure I would survive that Shrimp Lo Mein last night. Why Joe insists on getting take-out from that place, I'll never know. The man has a stomach of iron."

The blond woman, Jaq, didn't seem to be paying any attention to Melody; instead, she had turned her pale gray eyes to Kelly, looking her over as if she'd expected her to be dead as well. Kelly stared back, more out of irritation than any particular interest — another human whose pulse beat tantalizingly out of reach. Jaq was ridiculously tall, towering almost a foot over Kelly, with hair the color of sand escaping her ponytail and flying in wisps around a freckled face. The woman was covered with faint spots, as if she were part jaguar.

"You okay?" the woman asked Kelly, her voice soft.

No, Kelly thought. *I'm starving to death and you smell so good. Even better than the round woman in the yoga pants.*

"Fine." The words came out garbled as she forced her swollen, damaged mouth to form the sounds.

Melody scurried around the tiny kitchen in the background as the other two women stared at each other. This Jaq woman didn't look to be a threat. Not that Kelly could do much if she was. It was just the way she looked at the vampire, as though Kelly were a wounded animal in need of care — a dangerous wounded animal. The whole thing made Kelly feel uncomfortable — and hungry.

"I'll just move these clothes and we can sit down. . .." Melody's voice trailed off as she picked up the dry shirt from the back of the chair.

Kelly's blood turned to ice, knowing exactly what the woman had seen. Laundry in a sink, in the dark, without detergent had not made a dent in the dried, caked blood staining the shirt. The skirt was black and hid the stains better, but her shirt had been white with grey pinstripes at one point. It was now pink with grey pinstripes and huge crusted smears of blood.

The tall woman looked away from Kelly toward the shirt and tensed expectantly, a look of alarm coming over her face. Yeah, it looked like Kelly had been slaughtering goats in her spare time. Or had bled out all over her clothing and risen from the dead to find herself in the middle of nowhere in an ancient mobile home.

Would they call the police? Kelly might be able to take on a small group of humans and win, especially if she didn't have to worry about leaving them alive, but there were probably hundreds of them in the area. They'd eventually overpower her, injure her faster than she could repair herself. Plus, she was in no physical state to battle even these two women, and she sensed no vampires nearby to come to her aid. Suddenly she understood what the elders had always told her about the humans, why vampires chose to live in the shadows and feed with secrecy. There was power in numbers, and the humans far outnumbered even the largest vampire family.

Did she even have a family anymore? Fear and loss poured through her. As adversarial as relationships were among family members, vampires needed each other. They bonded together to support and work toward common goals. It was disconcerting to be in this chilly trailer, facing two human women as they eyed her bloodstained clothing with undecipherable expressions flickering across their faces. Kelly tensed. What would they do?

Uncharacteristically silent, Melody placed the shirt into the sink and moved the chair back to the dining room table. Gently, she took Kelly by the shoulders and pushed her down to sit on the worn sofa. Kelly glanced up at Jaq, who shook her head in warning. Then she looked back at Melody. The woman was so close, leaning over her slightly. The warmth of her body washed over Kelly, and the vampire was painfully aware of the strong heartbeat so close to her face.

Melody scrutinized Kelly's face for a moment, the sadness in her expression hardening into a steely anger. Kelly heard the woman's teeth grind as she got up and stomped into the bedroom. The sound of drawers and doors opening and shutting filtered into the hallway as the woman worked her way through the bedroom and on to the bathroom.

"Don't bite her," Jaq whispered, her voice somewhere between steely and pleading.

She knew. Kelly met her gaze and realized that the blond wouldn't hesitate to come to Melody's aid if she tried to feed on her. Jaq was all arms and legs, a tall, gangly woman, yet Kelly got the feeling she was stronger and quicker than she appeared. Not that the other woman had anything to fear at the moment.

"Bite her with what?" Kelly replied bitterly, her words slurred by the swelling in her mouth. "They pulled my fangs."

"Haven't they grown back yet? I mean, your legs and arms have healed, I just assumed. . .."

"They won't grow back. Ever. I'm too young." Too young to starve to death. Too young to die in this trailer. But why was she bothering telling this woman her pitiful story?

Jaq's eyes softened, and she made a brief motion, as if she was holding herself back from physically comforting the vampire.

"You have nothing? Nothing?" Melody asked from the bathroom, the sound of tears choking her voice.

She walked back into the main room of the trailer, oblivious to the undercurrents between the other two.

"You didn't even have time to pack a bag?" Her voice caught, and she sat down on the sofa, taking Kelly's hands in her own. "That bastard. That bastard! I saw you'd been punched around a bit when I first came in, but round here that's nothing new, and lots of women don't want no one to interfere. All that blood on your shirt though . . . he must have damn near killed you. I'm so glad you got away, dear. None of that stuff you left behind is worth your life. Me and the girls in the neighborhood, we'll get you started with some supplies; we'll help you get a job when you're ready. Don't you ever go back to him, honey. No matter what he says, how sorry he is, next time he's gonna kill you."

Kelly glanced over at Jaq. The blond woman nodded, clearly urging her to confirm Melody's story. So much for the powerful, up-and-coming vampire; she was now a de-fanged, battered spouse. Kelly hated being portrayed as a victim. And why did she keep looking to that Jaq woman for guidance?

"It was a car accident," Kelly said with difficulty, realizing too late that it sounded like the lie it was.

Melody winced. "You hush, sweetie. Just sit here and I'll be right back. Jaq, you put some of that tuna casserole in the oven for her and get her some coffee. Don't just stand there — make yourself useful."

The door slammed as Melody raced out. Kelly looked up at Jaq, wondering whether the woman planned to attack her. Instead, she slid the casserole dish into the oven, turned it on and came to sit beside the vampire. Kelly couldn't help scooting away slightly, feeling oddly guilty as her motion triggered a hurt expression on the other woman's face. Sitting this close to a human . . . it was weird. And they all smelled weird here, too. The whole place reeked of dogs and ham, yet this woman so close beside her smelled oddly sharp and clean, like a pine forest after an ice storm.

"Are you strong enough to leave?" Jaq asked. "You need to go home. Get outta here and back to your family."

Kelly shook her head. It wasn't just her physical state; it was the word *home* that worried her. Where was she? Her family hadn't killed her, but had they banished her? Did they ever intend on bringing her back, or was she supposed to die out here — wherever *here* was? The only hope she had was to stay put for as long as she could and hope someone contacted her, hope someone reached out to her with an opportunity for redemption and a chance to rejoin her family.

The blond woman scooted closer, and Kelly found herself trapped against the stained, upholstered arm of the sofa. "I saw them dump you here. Do you even know where you are?"

"New Jersey?" Kelly asked hopefully.

"West Virginia."

Cold despair poured through her like freshly melted snow. West Virginia. It was the buffer zone between her family and the Kincaid vampires to the south. She was isolated, abandoned, and she felt an acute sense of danger sitting so close to this tall, freckled woman. Kelly shifted nervously, wanting nothing more than to get away from Jaq, from the cheerful chubby one who would probably return any moment, to get away from the whole state. Scouts and spies that tried to enter Kincaid lands through West Virginia usually didn't come back, or sometimes pieces of them were found on the border. She'd always assumed the rival family to the south had done it, but there had been rumors that vicious werewolves called this place home. Werewolves didn't take kindly to vampire trespassers. Now she not only needed to worry about starvation, but that a Kincaid patrol crossing the border would end her life, or that the furry barbarians who lived here would come after her. Kelly eyed the woman beside her. An equal danger was that the humans would band together and kill her, or jail her until she starved to death in a cell.

"They'll come back for me," she said, hating the soft note of desperation in her voice.

Jaq jerked backward in alarm. "They'll come back to kill you? How many? Who?"

The blond woman jumped from the sofa and paced, her long legs taking barely four strides from the kitchen to the hallway. Kelly watched her, perplexed. Jaq seemed angry, and . . . protective?

"No," Kelly corrected. "I'm being punished. They'll give me a chance to redeem myself, and then I can go home. I just need to stay here and wait for them."

She hoped so, anyway. Maybe they just dumped her here to slowly starve to death or be killed. Kelly shook her head, trying to rid her mind of the depressing thoughts. Her offence hadn't been *that* bad. If they hadn't killed her outright, there must be some chance to return. It would take forever to work herself back up to where she'd been, but in a few centuries all should be forgiven. The pessimist that always lived inside her told her otherwise, but she shoved it aside and refused to listen. It would all be okay. Just wait, and then do whatever they asked.

The door flung open, and both women jumped. Melody blew through the trailer, stuffing more food in the fridge, checking on the casserole in the oven and scolding Kelly for not drinking her coffee. Before the vampire could take an obligatory sip, the woman left, threatening to return in a few seconds with more 'stuff'.

With a rush of coming and going, Kelly found herself bundled on the sofa in a much softer polyester blanket. There was a small stack of sweat pants, jeans, and t-shirts on her bed, and assorted toiletries in her bathroom. Melody continued to ply her with coffee and tuna casserole, then left to return again with a battered, red milk crate from Butler's Dairy. Milk, a package of bologna, bread, and processed squares of cheese went into the fridge. An assortment of cans went into the cabinets.

"We all scrounged up what we could, but we'll bring you more as we can. Jaq, I know you and Mike have got a bunch of venison and other meat in your freezer. See if y'all can spare some steaks or sausage."

Jaq nodded, and Kelly shot her a quick look, realizing that the beef steaks in the fridge had come from this benefactor and not her family after all. She'd hoped the meat had been a sign of forgiveness, but instead it was a human taking pity on the injured vampire. The thought should have depressed her, but all she felt was a wary sense of gratitude. This woman knew she was a vampire and had kept her secret. More than that, she'd brought her food. That was more than anyone had ever done for her. Anyone except for George.

"I'll be fine," she assured them. The food was important, but it wouldn't do her any good if she didn't get fresh blood soon. Once again she looked longingly at Melody, only to see Jaq frown and shake her head.

Melody ignored her protests. "I told the other girls not to be pestering you until you've had a while to settle in and get over the shock. We're all here for you though, sweetie. We'll watch out for you. You're safe here. If that bastard tries to come here and get you back, I'm gonna give him the hard end of a baseball bat."

Jaq snorted a laugh, slapping her hand over her mouth as Melody glared at her. "Oh, like you wouldn't do the same! Or blow him to kingdom-come with your shotgun."

"I'm fine. Really," Kelly said. "I won't be here long, I promise."

The last part was more for that Jaq woman, but Melody shook a menacing finger at her. "Oh no. You're to stay right here. You're family now. You ain't going nowhere."

With that rather alarming pronouncement, Melody encouraged her to get some rest and left. Jaq peered out the window until the other woman vanished into her trailer then went to work chopping up the steak from the fridge and carefully draining the blood into a glass.

"Sorry it's cold. Do you want the steak cooked or raw? And do you want some more of this tuna?"

"Yes, please. Raw is fine."

She was reluctant to tell the other woman that she needed warm, fresh blood, that she needed *human* blood. Vampires didn't rely on other species to help them. That's what family was for. The less this Jaq woman knew about her, the better though, so she smiled and wolfed down the tuna and raw steak, chasing it with the glass of cold, previously frozen, cow's blood.

"Thank you, I'm so much better now," she proclaimed, realizing how wooden and false her voice sounded. "I just need to get some sleep. I'll be good as new in the morning."

The blond woman looked at her with narrowed eyes. Kelly held her breath. Would she leave, or was Jaq going to be some kind of warden, ensuring she didn't harm any of the neighbors? After a few moments, Jaq nodded and walked to the door. Kelly carefully let out the breath she hadn't realized she'd been holding.

"I'm the trailer to the left of you, me and my brother, Mike. Come see me if you need anything," Jaq told her with a shake of a finger. "Anything. We like blood too, so I've got a lot of it in the freezer. All kinds. Just don't go hurting anyone and I'll get you anything you need. Okay?"

Kelly nodded, astonished. Humans liked blood too? When had that happened? Huh.

The freckled woman left, carefully shutting the door behind her, and Kelly looked around the ramshackle trailer in amazement. This was an unexpected and rather bizarre turn of events. At least she'd have food in her stomach and clothes to wear that wouldn't result in her being hauled in by the police.

She glanced at the doorway, remembering Jaq's warning. Unless she was intending on slashing someone in broad daylight and licking the blood from their wounds, human blood would be out of the question for the moment. She'd have to make do with whatever she could get her hands on for now, and then find a human to kill after dark. Jaq might not want her to eat the neighbors, but she could hardly keep her eye on every human in a five mile radius. Kelly would need to be careful, but someone was going to meet with a bloody accident before dawn, guaranteed.

Kelly collapsed on the sofa, filled with a sudden sense of inertia. The situation was surreal. To wake up injured and discarded outside of her family's territory was disorientating enough, but to promptly be invaded by a tuna-casserole-toting human, and another who recognized her as a vampire, completely threw her off stride. The whole place smelled off. Even Melody had a faint odd odor to her. And that Jaq — what the heck was she? She looked human, but Kelly's nose told her otherwise.

Maybe when they'd pulled her fangs, they'd damaged her other senses too. Perhaps all the unusual smells were an olfactory hallucination stemming from her injuries. Either way, she had to deal with her most pressing — starvation in her very near future if she couldn't find out a way to secure human blood without getting caught. Filthy and naked in a blanket wasn't conducive to planning and strategy. First things first — shower.

Musing over her options, Kelly practically moaned as the warm water hit her skin. Her hair was a ball of grease, and the water ran a red brown as she carefully scrubbed the blood from her body. It felt so good to see the red water turn pink, then clear, washing the nightmares of the past down the drain. Bathing had always been one of her favorite things. Each time she left the tub feeling as if she had been given a fresh new start to life, like a baptism. Twice, sometimes three times a day she'd submerged herself in the huge marble tub in her manager's suite, the water so hot it practically scalded her skin. The warmth of it on her skin was so different from when she'd been a child.

Kelly slid the soapy washcloth down her legs, remembering the dreaded baths from her days as a human. She'd always squirmed and wiggled, trying to escape the rough hands and rougher cloth that smelled like wet garlic and moldy cheese.

Oww. Don't.

Hold still, you little brat. I won't have a filthy urchin smelling up my kitchen. Clean up or into the gutter with you.

She'd frozen, terror over Cook's threat overcoming her dislike of the monthly ritual. Holding her breath and squeezing shut her eyes, she'd prayed Cook would make quick work of it. The odor still crept into her mouth and lungs, the cloth cold and slimy on her skin. The wool dress she wore would itch for days after this makeshift bath, prolonging the torture.

Kelly shook her head and pushed the memories down, locking them safely away. That was a long time ago, and she wasn't about to let herself dwell on her short life as a human. Right now the water was warm, and even though it wasn't as hot as she would have liked, Kelly was grateful.

All too soon, she shut off the shower and climbed out, regarding herself in the mirror attached to the back of the bathroom door as she dried off. Under the harsh glare of the fluorescent lights, the bruises all over her body took on a greenish-purple glow. They should have vanished days ago, along with the scabs where she'd apparently been dragged across the pavement. Slowly she turned, cataloging injuries that she thankfully had no recollection of receiving.

"Well, you're no beauty queen, but at least everything is functioning," Kelly told her reflection.

Melody had been absolutely thorough in her collections. There was shampoo, conditioner, soap, razors, toothbrush and toothpaste, comb and brush, and soap, as well as washcloths and towels. Beside the sink was a deodorant stick and a small tube of lipstick.

The clothes Melody had stacked on the sofa were big, but at least they were clean. A wave of dizziness hit Kelly as she rolled up the cuffs and rolled down the waistband. Time to go. It was too much to hope for that she could find someone to feed on now — a drunk in a dark alley who wouldn't scream too much as she slashed his throat. If not, Kelly hoped to at least find a promising spot to return to after dark.

She slipped on her bloodstained flats and grimaced. Not exactly good shoes for hunting prey. She'd need to find a belt somewhere, and some sneakers or boots. Digging in her black skirt, Kelly found a twenty-dollar bill she'd stuck in her pocket, what seemed like years ago, back at the casino. She caught her breath. If that was still in her skirt, then maybe. . .. She practically ripped the waistband trying to shove her fingers in the little pocket. With a sigh of relief she touched hard metal, felt the welcome pain as it burned her fingertips.

It was silly to be fighting for her survival and worried about a ring she couldn't even wear. She pulled it from the pocket and put it on the table, sucking her burned fingers. Plain silver, covered with frayed clear tape. Silly, but losing the ring would be like losing a part of herself – the only part that hadn't become a selfish unfeeling monster.

With a deep breath, Kelly turned her back on the ring and

went back to searching her skirt pockets. No identification. Of course if the police ever questioned her, identification would be the least of her problems.

The lack of money was a concern. She'd need more than twenty dollars if she was going to survive long enough for her family to return for her. Oh the irony to have several million in embezzled money stashed away up in New Jersey that she dare not access. They may have tossed her into a trailer in West Virginia, but she'd be a fool if she thought for one second they weren't watching her. If they caught her transferring money and followed the account trail, she'd be dead before she could find an ATM. So twenty dollars it was. That was all she had to her name. Better make it last as long as she could.

Not trusting the pockets in the baggy borrowed pants, she stuck the bill in her tattered bra and made her way out of the trailer, carefully looking to make sure none of the pesky neighboring humans were lying in wait for her. She'd do some scouting around, some reconnaissance during the daylight hours then she'd venture back out at night.

The trailer Kelly left was raised above the ground on cement blocks; a weathered wooden porch and steps rested on top of brown grass. A dirt parking area was right next to the steps, which led the thirty feet to a gravel road. She could see Melody's trailer about fifty yards off to the right, and the edge of another trailer beyond that, half hidden by the trees. There was a similar line of trailers to the left of hers. Behind the trailers stood a dense wooded area with no signs of human habitation through the winter-bare trees. Tall grass and briars in a field lay on the other side of the gravel road. In the near distance were gently sloped mountains, still green even in November, and criss-crossed with scars from the high-voltage electrical line right-of-way. Kelly raised her head and carefully sniffed the air. Fresh water lay a few-hundred yards away —there was no hint of the saltwater smell she'd grown accustomed to.

No humans were in the vicinity, although there was still that lingering old-ham smell as well as the aroma of various mammals, and exhaust fumes from ahead in the distance. Nothing smelled of vampire. She couldn't even make out lingering traces of those that had brought her here. A pang of loneliness speared through her, but there was nothing she could do about that.

Kelly walked down the gravel road heading toward the car exhaust fumes. She might as well keep her eyes open for useful roadside trash. Anything she could find might help her survive, and would be one item less that she'd have to spend her meager twenty dollars on.

Grabbing a plastic grocery store bag caught on a briar bush, she looked around. *Shame there aren't any size-two pants, or a nice pair of Nike's,* she thought. *Or a fresh bag of blood.*

There were no clothes or hundred-dollar bills, but by the time she'd reached the road, Kelly had found a bungee cord and an empty plastic water bottle. The road before her was two lanes wide with shoulders on either side. She glanced north then south wondering which way led to the nearby town. A sign at the corner of the gravel road indicated she lived on Briar Lane. Kelly sniffed, but the smell was pretty much the same either way. She shrugged and turned left.

She felt odd walking down the shoulder of a country road in ill-fitting, cheap clothing, gathering cast off items in a plastic bag like a homeless person. *How quickly I've fallen,* Kelly thought with wry amusement. *Pretty much back where I started as a human.*

A slightly bent ten-penny nail, a nearly full spool of steel wire, about a foot of quarter-inch zinc-coated chain, two wire hangers, and many pieces of nylon baling cord all went into her bulging plastic bag. She'd also managed to collect fifty cents in change. Sheesh, she was like a bag lady, delighting in her discovered riches. Or some kind of vampire McGyver. A cut up wire hanger, ends from a bungee cord, and voila! Instant fangs. She laughed, envisioning herself with bits of wire protruding from her mouth. What a ridiculous idea. She was obviously starting to go loopy from hunger.

The bushes off to the side of the road rustled, and Kelly paused, frowning. It wasn't the first time she'd heard the noise. Initially, she'd thought it was a squirrel, but whatever it was seemed to be following her. The vampire hesitated, trying to remember what wild animals there were in West Virginia. Bear? Wolf? Coyote? What animal would be stupid enough to stalk *her? An animal that wants to be dead*, she thought as she continued walking.

About two miles down she saw a roadside bar with a neon sign proclaiming it was "Dale's". Kelly walked through the deserted parking lot to find the door locked. Where there were restaurants, though, there were humans. This would be an ideal place for her to return to tonight and satisfy her desperate need for blood.

Slinging the plastic bag over her shoulder, Kelly walked around to the rear of the building, scoping out the best place to lurk and pounce on a victim once the sun had set. A huge dumpster sat just outside the barred back door of the bar. Clearly the owners cut corners on their collection service. The thing was overflowing and stank to high heaven. She would have strung her staff up by their toes if they'd allowed the refuse to get to this state in her casino. *Not that it's my casino anymore*, she thought ruefully, shaking her head.

A dumpster like this would attract all sorts of vermin. Yep, she smelled rats. Lots of rats. Some buried down deep in the dumpster, and others holed up for the day somewhere inside the building. Yuck. The very thought disgusted her, but her body desperately needed fresh blood. Fresh, not that frozen old-cow stuff from the steaks.

It was definitely on her agenda to grab a human tonight, but maybe there was something here that could hold her off. With a bitter laugh, Kelly contemplated dumpster diving for rats. The metal container was old and rusted. With her luck, she'd find herself covered in stinky garbage and the rats would escape to safety through some hole. Still, her need for blood was desperate. She wasn't sure she could wait for nightfall. Just when she was about to climb into the dumpster, she saw the squirrel.

It was thin and scrawny with a dull, mangy coat. It was probably diseased. Kelly wrinkled her nose in distaste, but she proceeded to kneel down, trying to slowly edge towards it. The animal took one glance at her and bolted into the woods.

Great. She couldn't even manage to catch and eat a sickly squirrel. Not that she really wanted to. Kelly shuddered, imagining how nasty and tainted the blood would be, if there was more than a mouthful in the thing. It was probably anemic from fleas. Did squirrels even get fleas? Kelly shook her head to clear it. She was so hungry her mind was wandering all over the place.

Every thought since she'd awoken in the trailer had been on survival. Now the reality of her situation rushed at her. She was alone in an unknown place contemplating drinking blood from a diseased squirrel she couldn't bite even if she *had* managed to catch it.

She couldn't feed properly — would *never* be able to again. How long could she go stabbing humans before one got away and made a police report? Or until the human cops traced a series of grisly attacks back to her doorstep? She'd need to constantly be on the move, and there weren't many places to go. The enemy vampires were to the south, and she couldn't go back into her family's lands unless asked. West Virginia wasn't a big state. She'd eventually be caught by humans, by some roving vampire spy, or by werewolves.

And beyond that, she was alone. The old fears from her human life crept back. No one would help her; there was no one to turn to. Kelly had to completely rely on herself for survival, and she doubted she had the skills or strength to make it alone.

Covering her face with her hands, she leaned backward against the rough brick of the building and slid down it to the ground, tears wetting her fingers. The sound of birdsong and the scrabble of climbing squirrels mixed with the ever-present rustling sound from the wooded area next to the smelly dumpster. It gave a strange accompaniment to Kelly's sobs. Curling into a ball, she rocked herself, trying to fight the feelings of fear and loneliness.

George. She thought of his strong arms and lopsided grin. If only he were here now, but George was long dead. She'd gone with the vampires, made her choice. They were her family— she just had to find a way back to them, to do something to prove her worth so they'd bring her back. They hadn't killed her; they must be planning to collect her after an appropriate punishment period.

Finally she gulped the tears back down, wiping her eyes and nose on the rolled-up sleeve of her oversized sweatshirt. When she'd left her humanity behind to become a vampire, she'd mourned. She'd need to mourn her fall from grace too. Even if her family did eventually come for her, she'd be back to menial labor for decades, centuries even. Could she do that? Go back to being everybody's whipping post? It would be like her human life all over again.

Kelly stood and clenched her jaw in determination. Whipping post was better than dead. She'd need to survive until they came for her. What else could she do, a lone vampire in hostile territory, squeezed between two powerful families?

Kelly thought of the silver fillet knife back in her trailer. If things got too bad, at least she had an option to slow death by starvation. But, it was no time to stand here, tear stained and thinking negative thoughts. Time to keep collecting useless, stray items then head back to her trailer and hope to channel the spirit of MacGyver. Crossing her fingers, she hoped that there was at least one drunk wandering outside this bar tonight that no one would miss.

Kelly scoped out the parking lot in a grid pattern, excited to find another five dollars in change and a ten-dollar bill. Evidently, inebriated humans regularly spilled money from their pockets and purses. She also picked up a plastic packet with a handful of large metal washers in it, and another bungee cord.

The noise of car tires on gravel. Kelly looked up to see a small pick-up truck pulling into the bar area.

"Can I help you?" a man asked as he pulled alongside her. His pleasant tone ended abruptly once he got within a few feet. His red nose lifted, and his lip curled up in a snarl visible even through his dark brown beard.

A human, and she was starving. Kelly resisted the urge to jump on him and rip his throat out with her bare hands. Now was not the time, especially with the man clearly suspicious and on alert. Getting mowed over by his truck as she tried to throttle him wasn't a good plan. So instead, pushing the thoughts away, she tried to smile.

"I dropped something the other night and walked back to look for it. I live just up the road," she said. Her voice came out slurred and puffy from her swollen mouth. It took effort to articulate properly.

"You'll have to do better than that," he said briskly. "Your kind isn't welcome here. Get on back home before any of the others see you around. They won't be half as charitable as me."

What was with this stupid state? Leaning closer, Kelly felt a blast of warm from the truck heater — and caught the man's scent. She froze, and her urge to eat him changed to an urge to run. He smelled of smoked ham mingled with an odd canine note. That's what the faint smell from back in the trailer area was. Werewolves. Panic seized her heart. They had to have been everywhere for their scent to be so strong. They were probably living right on the same street as her trailer. She'd never met a werewolf. None had ever been foolish enough to walk into a vampire-owned casino.

Crap. Evidently she was smack in the middle of their territory — solo, injured, with nowhere else to go. How the heck was she going to be able to hunt human prey with a werewolf pack nearby, and that freckled woman, the modern-day Van Helsing, watching her every move?

"I'm leaving soon. I just need to heal up a bit and I'll be out of here," she said, hurriedly backing up a safe distance from the truck.

He looked at her, a flash of sympathy in his eyes as he took in her bruised and battered face.

"That *soon* better be by nightfall, cause that's when I'm telling the Alpha you're here. Got it? And if so much as one human shows up with something bigger than a mosquito bite on em, I'm comin' after you myself. Got it? "

Yes, she "got it". Kelly nodded and hastily headed back down the road toward Briar Lane. Things were going from bad to worse. All she needed now was a demon waiting at her trailer door and she'd know she was truly cursed.

CHAPTER 7

It wasn't a demon, but Jaq sitting on the step outside her trailer. The tall woman had a shotgun with her, held like it was permanently attached to her arm. She stood and followed Kelly into the trailer without saying a word. Inside, there was a large roll of what looked like sausage on the table and a bottle of blackberry wine.

"I brought you more food," the woman said, still holding the shotgun. Kelly wondered what on earth she planned to shoot. Hopefully not her. In her current state, it would probably take her weeks to recover from a gunshot wound. "That's some deer bologna from this fall." Jaq indicated the sausage-like roll. "I also put some venison and beef in the fridge. It's fresh, not the frozen stuff. I thought maybe it would help you heal quicker to have fresh."

"Thanks." Kelly looked intently at the woman, wishing she could read her mind. Jaq had been an odd combination of wary and kind from the moment she'd met her. Why was she being so generous? Was the endless supply of food to keep Kelly from attacking the neighbors, or something more altruistic?

Jaq shifted her weight, her expression closed as she held the shotgun against her thigh. "Do you like liver? I gave you some liver, and a heart. A lot of people don't like that stuff nowadays, but I thought maybe you might. Everyone thinks I'm weird for eating it, but it reminds me of when I was a kid."

Kelly stared. That was oddly personal, given their mutual state of distrust. Should she make some small confession from her childhood in return?

"Ran into a werewolf at that bar down the road — Dale's. I take it this is their territory?" So much for offering a personal revelation. Oh well, she'd never been one for polite chit-chat or dancing around the issue, especially now that she felt the edge of starvation gnawing at her.

The blond woman sucked in a sharp breath. "Yes." Her tone was resigned. "Our pack holds the entire state. I'm surprised he didn't kill you."

Kelly couldn't help a sniff of contempt. A vampire killed by a werewolf. That would be the day. Although she was in no condition to take on a werewolf in a truck. *Or a woman holding a shotgun,* she thought, eyeing the weapon.

"He said he was going to tell the Alpha and that I should be gone by nightfall if I wanted to remain among the living."

Now it was the other woman's turn to sniff, her gray eyes turning to steel. "Not if I have anything to do with it," she snarled. "How long do you need to heal-up? How long before you can go?"

"I don't know." Kelly stared at the woman, bemused. She'd said *their* pack. But Jaq didn't smell at all like a werewolf. Could humans possibly be honorary members? Even so, she couldn't imagine how this human was planning on defending her, a vampire, against a pack of werewolves — even with a shotgun.

Jaq sighed, rubbing a hand along her cheek and across the

back of her neck, as if soothing a tense muscle. "Great. How about a ballpark? Days? A week? Never?"

Never. The thought chilled Kelly and she felt the empty fang sockets with a tentative tongue. Never might be about right.

"A month?" That might give her enough time to prove of service to her family and actually have somewhere to go. Of course, she'd need to live long enough to do that. An unlikely prospect with werewolves and this annoying woman breathing down her neck and keeping her from the human blood she so desperately need.

"That will be difficult." Jaq's expression turned grim, and she seemed to be thinking unpleasant thoughts. Hopefully they didn't involve Kelly's demise.

"If you'd let me take a human, it might be a lot sooner." It was a lie. Kelly had no way of knowing when or if her family would ever allow her back across the border, but at least she'd be healed and strong enough to make a break for it. Maybe even strong enough to fight off a few of these werewolves.

"That's not going to happen. You go killing a human and I won't be able to stop them from ripping you limb from limb."

Kelly felt a surge of irritation. She rarely killed humans anymore, although without her fangs and given her current state of hunger, she wasn't making any promises. "I'm a vampire. I can certainly defend myself if I need to."

Jaq snorted. "Right. You're injured, and from your smell, you're not very old. Plus there are thousands of us in the pack. We own this state, and we know every stone and tree root. Unless you've got an army of your own, you better swallow your pride and just accept the fact that you need to lay low and keep away from the humans until you can go back to your own kind."

She didn't have an army, and in spite of her bravado,

Kelly was well aware she was in no condition to fight anything. Heck, she hadn't even managed to catch a squirrel.

"Were you following me? Was it you in the bushes?"

Jaq's eyes widened, and she laughed. "That was my brother, Mike. I asked him to keep an eye on you. Sheesh, I can't believe you heard him. He must really be off his game."

"And Mike is a werewolf?"

Jaq nodded. "A noisy one, evidently. I'll have someone more quiet follow you next time."

Great. She'd never be able to grab a human with the werewolf babysitters following her every move. She needed to get out of here, but how? She was trapped, and the walls seemed to be closing in faster every moment.

Silence stretched out between them, and, finally, Jaq shifted her gun upward and turned to leave. There was something in her eyes that bothered Kelly — frustration, and an odd disappointment. This woman had been kind, had done more for Kelly than most had. She deserved something in return, some expression of gratitude.

"I love liver," Kelly blurted out, needing to clear the air before the other woman left. "Thank you."

Jaq halted, turning her head to see Kelly over her shoulder. "You're welcome."

The woman hesitated, and Kelly found herself scrambling for words to make her stay. The sun wouldn't set for hours, and although she should be sleeping, the vampire found herself slightly panicked at the thought of being alone. This weird-smelling human, or whatever Jaq was, was better than no one at all.

"Wait. I'm . . . uh . . . maybe you'd like to share some of this with me? Wine and liver, I mean. And stay for a bit? If you don't have anything else to do. I mean, I'm sure you're busy, so maybe some other time."

Crap. She sounded like an idiot. Why was it so hard to

talk to this woman? It had never been difficult before, but then she hadn't really needed anyone before. Just delegate work, bark out some quick orders if they were one of her vampire staff, or bite first and ask permission later if they were a human. And here she was, alone, surrounded by these weird smelling *others*, asking one to hang out and have a drink with her. Good Lord, what *was* the world coming to?

All the tension seemed to fall from the tall, lanky woman as she turned to face Kelly and smiled. It transformed her thin face, turning her from serious to playful in an instant.

"I'll pour the wine."

Kelly went to get the liver from the fridge, her hands shaking slightly. She was so weak she was beginning to feel light headed. She'd expected to find the meat carefully packaged in the sealed plastic the butcher shops used, but instead they were in heavy-duty zip-lock bags. Pulling out the bag with the liver, she examined it in surprise. Usually meat packages only held the residual blood from the raw meat, but this liver was literally swimming in about a pint of blood. The heart was too. It was as if Jaq had added a large quantity of blood to the meat.

"Do you want some of this too?" She asked, pouring the blood into a large glass. It came right to the rim.

Jaq pulled two more glasses from the cabinet for the wine. "Nah. You drink it. I wasn't sure you vampires ate solid food at all when I first found you."

Kelly took a huge swig of the blood and hid a grimace. Cold cow blood. Ugh. At least it was reasonably fresh, though. "We do. It just doesn't metabolize if we don't have blood." Everything would eventually shut down. Her body was probably already beginning to devour itself, and this cow blood would only delay the inevitable.

The other woman nodded, seemingly unbothered by

Kelly's beverage. "I don't really know that much about you all. Hard to tell what's myth and what's real."

Kelly watched Jaq pour the wine and dug a fry pan out of the bottom of the stove. She was tired of eating raw meat, and she assumed the other woman would want it cooked. It had been over a century since she'd actually prepared her own meal, but frying up a piece of liver couldn't be all that hard.

"There's a grain of truth in most of the myths. Don't bother with the garlic, though. That's complete bullshit."

Jaq shot her a quick grin. "Werewolves don't need the full moon to change form."

"And I still wear my cross pendant," Kelly continued. Well, she would have still worn it if it hadn't been silver. The very thought made her cringe.

"Silver bullets," the tall woman added as if she had read Kelly's mind. "Those things burn like the fires of Hades. Grabbed a candlestick once when I was a kid and nearly wound up in the hospital. Hives everywhere, blisters all over my hands. Took me forever to heal. Me! It was bizarre."

It was how the other woman smelled that was most bizarre. "Are you really a werewolf too, then? You don't smell anything like the other guy — the one down at the bar."

Jaq turned to jam the cork back into the wine bottle. "Yes, I'm a werewolf. We don't all smell the same."

Kelly got the odd feeling the woman was lying, although she had no experience with werewolves. Perhaps they did all smell different.

"So what happened that you got turned into a vampire?" the werewolf continued. "Accosted in a dark alley one night?"

More stereotypes. "Humans accosted in a dark alley find themselves dead, not turned. I chose this. We're Candidates for a while and if everything works out, we get turned."

"Can you guys change your minds?"

Yes. And wind up dead. Same with those who didn't "work out". It was another thing the vampires never told anyone, not even in the fine print.

"Of course. Once you're Chosen, though, once you get the venom, it's irreversible."

Jaq took a big gulp of her wine. "How bad is it? The transformation, I mean?"

Kelly grimaced, glancing over at Jaq as she gave the frying pan a quick swipe with a towel and put it onto the stovetop. "Bad. It's like having the flu with non-stop charley horses throughout your body. That's the first couple of decades. You beg them to kill you, even try to take yourself out. It gets better about fifty years in, although the genetic change isn't totally complete for a few thousand years."

Out of the corner of her eye, she saw the werewolf shift nervously. Kelly took a deep breath and dug through the fridge for butter, trying to appear nonchalant about the whole experience. It still shook her — so recent and raw in her memories. Another thing they didn't disclose. The pain had gone on forever, more terrible then even her worst imaginings of hell.

"Why did you do it?"

Kelly turned around, still kneeling in front of the fridge. "Huh?"

Jaq's gray eyes held a mix of sympathy and morbid fascination. "Why would you choose to become a vampire? What was appealing about . . . this?"

The question should have been insulting, but Kelly felt no anger. The glaring fluorescent light from the refrigerator warred in her vision with the soft golden sunlight streaming through the window. Why had she? Kelly couldn't really put it into words.

Human life had always been a struggle, and her future had been . . . bleak. She had grown into a woman cleaning pots and chopping vegetables — the same thing she'd been doing her whole life. The only difference was the men who cornered her in the pantry, squeezing her budding breasts and pressing onion-laced kisses on her lips and skin. She would have become pregnant and been tossed into the streets, or if she was lucky, one of the delivery boys would have proposed to her. Then she would have spent her life working her hands raw and birthing children until one killed her on the way out. So many would have chosen the devil they knew, but Kelly couldn't face that particular demon. Anything had to be better than what her future would have been as a human. Anything.

"I was fifteen," she replied, her voice dry and hollow. "A bastard child, a girl. I worked in the kitchens for as long as I could remember. I didn't want to live and die a nothing. I wanted to feel I had some control over my destiny, even if it was deciding to abandon my humanity."

Kelly turned away, snatching the butter from the fridge and slicing a generous chunk into the hot fry pan. She could feel Jaq's gaze on her back, sympathetic and kind. It was too much. The air was thick with emotion and memories of the past. Kelly rubbed her chest to loosen the knot there and searched for a way to lighten things up once more, to put all the horror and sorrow back into a little box in the back of her mind.

"How did you know that I was a vampire? Have you seen us before?" Her tone was brittle and forced, but it worked. A ghost of a smile crossed Jaq's face.

"Y'all smell funny. And yes, I see far more of you vampires than I ever want to. If I catch them, they all wind up dead. Every one of them."

Kelly shifted, uneasy. There had been an odd connection between them, like two friends chatting about their lives. It was strange to think that the woman she'd just bared her soul to had never said more than a word to another vampire before slicing their head off. It snapped her back to reality, and reminded her that as nice as this werewolf seemed, her loyalties were elsewhere.

"This place is considered the buffer zone between two large families. The only vampires coming through here are scouts and spies. Well, and me."

Jaq nodded. "That's another reason why you can't stay. I'm assuming you're from that family up north. Most of the vampires that come through here are the southern ones. I don't know much about vampires, but I'm guessing they'd kill you if they caught wind of you here."

They would. Kincaid spies wouldn't hesitate to rip her head off. An unaffiliated vampire was a disgrace and would be culled. Kelly put the butter in the pan and grimaced. One day at a time. Just survive. She didn't have the luxury of thinking that far ahead when starvation stood right outside her window.

"Why do you have – ouch!"

Kelly turned and saw Jaq waving her hand frantically, a small silver ring rolling across the table.

"Don't touch it!" With vampire speed, she snatched the ring, shoving it in her pocket. The werewolf's eyes widened. "I mean, don't. . . it's personal. I'm sorry, just please don't touch that."

Jaq tilted her head. "No problem. Are your fingers okay? It was silver."

Kelly nodded, turning back to the cooking liver. Her fingers were red and blistered just from that quick touch. She took a deep breath, getting her emotions under control. Jaq must think she was a complete fool, acting like that over a cheap band of silver.

Within minutes, the smell of cooking filled the small trailer, and Kelly's glass of blood was empty, replaced with one filled with wine. She felt better. Maybe it was the nasty cow's blood, maybe it was the wine. Any alcohol effects would be quickly burned off with her ramped-up metabolism, but the slight buzz the sweet liquid gave her was welcome.

"What's all this?" Jaq asked, sorting through the contents of Kelly's plastic bag of found items. It seemed that werewolves weren't particular about respecting privacy. Coming and going in each other's homes, digging through personal belongings.

"Are vampires like magpies? Are you a hoarder? That would make a great show. 'Vampire Hoarders of the Appalachian Mountains.' I'd watch it."

Kelly paused, spatula in hand, and turned to face the other woman. That little smile had turned up one corner of her mouth, and she wiggled her eyebrows as she waved a bungee cord at the vampire. The woman was teasing her. Teasing. Kelly stood there, speechless, unable to think of a reply — unable to think of anything.

"I know where there are some abandoned cars in the woods," Jaq went on. "Or maybe you'd like that bag of rusty nails just past Melody's place."

Kelly knew she was trying to lighten things up, but her comments just brought home how bleak her situation was. What the hell was she planning on doing with that junk anyway? All the thoughts of vampire MacGyver she'd had while collecting it seemed foolish right now. Accumulating random junk off the road was a futile act. It was a way to lie to herself about her terrible situation, to pretend it would somehow be better. Her eyes strayed to the knife drawer. Perhaps that was the best thing for her to do.

"Hey. I'm sorry. I shouldn't have been making jokes after all you've been through."

In a blink, Jaq's arms were around her. The woman's

sharp, clean sent filled her nose, the pounding of her heart so close to her ears. Could this day get any weirder? Frying liver in a kitchen, being hugged by a werewolf. Kelly held the spatula awkwardly in her hand and remained stiff in the other woman's embrace, wondering what she should do. Hug her back? Beat her with the spatula? Rip her throat out with dull incisors? Just as she thought she couldn't take any more, Jaq pulled away, sniffing the air.

"You're burning the liver."

"Shit! Shit!" Kelly spun around and lowered the heat, fanning the meat with her spatula. Was it burnt? She thought it was supposed to be that dark, although come to think of it, the liver Cook had prepared back in her human days hadn't smelled quite this charred. She looked up and saw Jaq watching her. The woman's lips twitched.

"Maybe I'll cook the liver." Gripping her arms, Jaq led Kelly over to the sofa and pushed her gently down onto it. "You sit right there. I'll bring your drink and finish cooking."

The werewolf relieved Kelly of her utensil and walked back to the kitchen area. Kelly gripped her wine in both hands and watched the tall woman flip the liver once more, expertly sliding it onto a plate. Why had she invited a werewolf to share a crazy dinner of liver and blackberry wine when she should be out trying to find a human to drink from?

"Thank you," Kelly said, taking the plate of liver from Jaq and glancing past her to the window on the other side of the trailer. As soon as it was dark, she'd head out. And in spite of the warnings from two werewolves, if a neighbor had to meet with a bloody accident, so be it.

CHAPTER 8

*J*aq eyed the setting sun with trepidation. Pink and golden rays streaming over the distant mountain range should have filled her with peace, but not this evening. Drat Jonah and his customs. What should have been a quick one-hour meeting had turned into dinner and a tour of his back property. It's not like she'd never been here before. It's not like she didn't see her Alpha weekly.

"There's a vampire one trailer down from me. I'm respectfully asking everyone to keep their paws off."

Jonah turned to her, his ruddy face tightening with displeasure. Interrupting the Alpha was not polite, but Jaq had been more than patient this evening. It would soon be dark, and she'd need to hurry back to make sure her new neighbor didn't start eating the locals.

"Yes, Dale told me this afternoon. He's more upset that you're protecting a vampire than the fact that one has moved in half a mile from his place of business."

"She's injured, and pretty young from her scent. I just

want to give her a chance to heal up a bit, then I'll chase her off."

The Alpha halted and turned to face Jaq, his hands on his hips. "What, like a wildlife catch and release? Seriously, Jaq, this isn't a bear cub for you to bottle-feed then return to the wild; it's a vampire. You've seen what they can do, how little regard they have for any life but their own. What in the world are you thinking to allow such a danger to live?"

"She was severely wounded," Jaq argued.

In truth, she wasn't sure what the heck she was thinking. The broken and bloody girl in the trailer had tugged at her sympathies somehow. Maybe Jonah was right. This was complete folly. Kelly wasn't a little kitten in need of help, she was a predator that would most likely turn on Jaq the moment she was strong enough.

"Severely wounded now," Jonah said, echoing her thoughts. "Give her twenty-four hours and we'll see how quickly she tries to take your head off. They're fast and strong, sneaky with no sense of honor. It doesn't matter that you fed or sheltered her; she'll try to kill you, and you won't be able to take her by surprise like you've done the others."

He was right, but something inside Jaq still rebelled when she thought about killing Kelly. "Her own family beat her almost to death and dumped her here to die. They know we're here, that we'd kill her. What kind of people do that?"

"Vampires do that," Jonah's voice was firm. "And don't you ever forget it. Don't go thinking that this one is different because she's a little tiny thing covered in bruises. Dale told me what she looked like, and said even he felt a bit sorry for her himself. I don't blame you. You've got a big heart, Jaq, and you're full of kindness and optimism when it comes to others, but you've got to snap out of this sentimental crap and face the reality. Kill her tonight and be done with it."

No. Jaq held back the word. The circumstances of her birth had always allowed her great privilege when it came to the pack and the Alpha, but she knew better than to draw a line in the sand with Jonah.

"Can I please have one month? I'll take care of her, be personally responsible for making sure she doesn't break any rules. One month, then I'll drive her back over the border."

Crap, she *did* sound like a child pleading to keep a found pet. *I promise I'll feed it, and clean up if it pisses on the floor. . . .*

Jonah muttered a soft explicative. "I swear, Jaq, if you weren't a First-Born, you'd never have the balls to ask such a thing of me, your own Alpha for Christ's sake. If this gets out, I'll have a riot on my hands. Full-fledged riot, pitchforks and torches and the like. Vampires."

Jaq smothered a grin. He'd spat out the last word like it was rotted possum in his mouth, but she knew she'd won. "How's the leg doing?"

Jonah instinctively reached down to his thigh and rubbed it. He was still young, barely fifty, and with more blond to his beard than gray, but even a werewolf in the prime of his life found it difficult to take down an enraged bear. "Not even a twinge," he replied, gratitude in his voice. "Just a scrape. Nothing compared to what I did to that bear."

Jaq nodded, her eyes solemn. It wouldn't do to have their Alpha bleed out on top of a dead bear. She'd kept his secrets, and he'd kept hers. They'd all kept hers. That's what a pack did. She felt a twinge of guilt for putting them at risk. A vampire — what was she thinking? But then she remembered Kelly, twisted and bleeding on the floor of the trailer, the look of fear and loss that crept all too often into the woman's brown eyes. She didn't seem like a monster. Maybe Jonah was right, but maybe he was wrong. Could there be more to this vampire than a dangerous predator, or was she once again being a sentimental fool?

"One week," Jonah warned her. "One week, then either she goes or she dies."

CHAPTER 9

*D*usk was slipping into night as Kelly looked at her assortment of items and went through the alternatives in her head. She needed to find something tonight, hopefully something alive that walked on two legs, or she'd be in the agony of starvation by dawn. Already she felt it gnawing at her sanity.

Options. Top choice was to grab a neighbor, but Jaq's brother was keeping a close eye on her. She could occasionally hear him nearby, catching a whiff of werewolf in the air. The wiser alternative was to waste precious energy losing the werewolf and head down to that bar. But would that other werewolf from the afternoon be there? Would she have enough strength left to defend herself against one or more of them? It would be difficult to poach a human customer right from under their noses and not get caught, especially with no fangs. No, that bar was almost as risky as snatching one of the neighbors.

But how to get far enough away without a vehicle and without the energy to run a long distance? She could hardly take a bus to and from her hunt. At the thought of it, a laugh escaped her. The number nineteen into town, then back again, covered in blood from her messy dining experience.

There had to be someplace besides that bar down the road. Kelly had no idea how big a territory the werewolves had, or if Mike was fast enough to keep up, but she was fairly certain if she could lose her babysitter, she could be sneaky enough to take one human without notice. Humans went missing all the time — if she chose her victim carefully, they'd never know.

A pang of guilt went through her at the thought. She had never killed a human on purpose before. Outside of that one accident after she was first turned, she hadn't killed any at all. Maybe if she found someone really drunk or high, she wouldn't have to kill them. Or maybe she could find a mass murderer. It wouldn't be so terrible to drain one of them dry, would it?

Kelly wrapped a razor blade and the silver filet knife into a plastic bag then shoved them into her waistband. Like it or not, she was starving. Hopefully there would be some alternative to killing her victim, but she may not have much choice.

The night air bit with the promise of winter. The best thing about cold was that it brought all the scents into sharp relief. Moving quietly with vampire stealth, Kelly ducked into the forest and trailed down along the road. She sniffed the air. Humans, dogs, cars. The werewolf scent had dissipated, and she took a few seconds to prowl by Jaq's trailer. The lights were on, and she could see the television through the window as well as the back of a man sprawled across the sofa. Mike must have gotten bored with her. Kelly chuckled, thinking how pissed-off Jaq would be that her brother abandoned his post for an episode of Breaking Bad.

Feeling a bit like a hunting dog, Kelly distanced herself from the trailers, scenting the air for prey. The closest was a fox. She tracked it by smell, locating the animal with her night vision. The fox looked unthreatened by the vampire woman trying unsuccessfully to sneak up on it, but as soon as she got close enough to lunge toward it, the fox jumped, dashing into the safety of the briar bushes.

Her stomach growled and cramped as she struggled to her feet. There had to be more than one animal in this neighborhood. Forcing down waves of dizziness, Kelly continued to prowl the line of trees between the trailers and the woods. In only a few moments, she'd scented a rabbit.

It hopped along, eyes reflecting the light from the porch of a nearby trailer. Kelly hesitated. It was one thing to drink cold animal blood from a bag, another thing entirely to grab one from the woods. It seemed so uncivilized, and this rabbit was kind of cute. Starving vampires couldn't be picky, though, so she steadily moved within striking distance then snatched it at full speed. The rabbit twisted in surprise, biting down on her hand and digging in with sharp claws.

"Ow, damnit!" Kelly swore, nearly dropping the animal as she transferred it to one hand and sliced its neck with the razor blade.

A wave of shame rolled through her as she frantically tried to get as much of the fountaining blood into her mouth as possible. Pitiful. Drinking from a defenseless animal with blood smeared all over her face and hands. Along with the blood, she tasted fur on her tongue and tickling down her throat. This had to be the most horrible thing she'd ever done. It certainly was the most disgusting thing she'd ever eaten, even including Cook's terrible attempts at kidney pie.

Finished, she dropped the animal and collapsed to the forest floor, panting with relief. Blessed relief. That should keep her going until she could manage to find a human a few safe miles away. Kelly leaned against a tree and closed her eyes, trying to steady her breath. Now she'd only need to dispose of the carcass and clean up a bit then head out five miles or so to find the prey she really needed.

A noise brought her quickly to her feet. She snatched the knife from her waistband and listened, scenting the air. Had Mike come out to check on her and tracked her here? How angry was the werewolf going to be that she'd slipped his watch and snuck out? But the smell that hit her nose wasn't werewolf; it was vampire. Not just any vampire — this was one from her family. She blinked at the tears that sprang to her eyes. Was this horrible nightmare over? Had they sent someone to bring her home?

"I expected to find you dead already." The masculine was filled with horror. "But here I find you chewing on a bunny like a rabid dog."

Kelly tensed as the vampire walked silently from the dark woods, her heart racing with hope and a tinge of fear. He was old — at least five hundred by his aura. She tucked the knife back into her waistband, wincing as the silver briefly burned a patch of skin, and stood at respectful attention. The vampire walked closer and circled around her, inspecting.

"The betting odds were that you killed yourself the moment you came to. Secondary odds were that you'd starved to death by now. Third that I'd find you incoherent and dying on the floor of the trailer. It was really a long shot to find you alive and hunting, although from the look of you, you've only got a couple more days. A bunny?" He shook his head. "Really?"

She stood silent, unsure how to answer that question. The vampire nudged the carcass with his foot. Bending over, he picked up the rabbit gingerly with his thumb and forefinger.

"Good Lord. You practically gnawed the thing's head off." He sounded outraged. "I think this is closer to incoherent and dying on the floor than alive and hunting." He tossed the dead animal into the woods. "Pathetic," he said, leaning close to her face. "You should have just killed yourself. It would have been more dignified. I should kill you right now. It would do the world a favor. And certainly do animal lovers everywhere a favor."

Kelly kept her breathing steady as the vampire encircled her neck with his hands. Damn. All her struggle to stay alive and this guy was going to kill her because he didn't like her eating woodland creatures. Easy for him to talk. He'd probably never been hungry since the day of his turning. Slowly the vampire ran his fingers down her neck and across her shoulders.

"Unfortunately, orders are to leave you alive. I am Rube Mohs, and I report directly to the Prince. The Master has a job for you, Kelly Demir of House Fournier. Plus there are betting odds to consider here, and some people would be very angry if I skewed them in my favor."

Kelly practically hyperventilated in relief. He wasn't going to kill her, and most importantly, he'd referred to her by her family affiliation. She was still in — on the outskirts, but if she did this job, she'd be back in. If she could keep the werewolves off her back, manage to not starve to death, and do whatever this senior vampire asked of her, the whole nightmare would be over.

The man pulled a small bag from his pocket and tossed it on the ground in front of Kelly. She trembled, staring at the package. Blood. She couldn't scent it through the thick plastic, but she'd bet it was human blood. Only a pint or so, but, still, she went weak at the thought.

"We've lost a lot of scouts and spies lately — more in this section than anywhere else in the buffer zone, and I know they've not all been killed by werewolves. I'll be back, and I'll want to know of any Kincaid scum prowling around here as well as plots they may have against us."

"How am I supposed to find that out?" Kelly panted,

unable to wrench her eyes from the packet by her feet. "I have no transportation, no money. I'm still healing from my punishment; I can't feed properly. How am I supposed to roam along the Virginia border searching for the enemy like this?"

From the corner of her eye she saw him shrug. "Not my problem. I'll expect information when I return. And if you don't have what the Master needs, I'll be very happy to relieve you of your suffering, bet or no bet."

He disappeared in a flash of speed. Kelly fell to her knees, carefully picking up the packet with shaking hands. She should take it back to the trailer where she could carefully open and pour it out so as to not spill a drop, but she no longer had the willpower to wait. She sliced a small hole with the razor blade and eagerly drank, collapsing the plastic in upon itself. Done, she lay down upon the dirt and leaves, feeling her limbs grow numb as her body concentrated on absorbing the desperately needed nutrients. All she wanted to do was sleep. This blood would get her through the day — a day she'd now need to spend trying to scout out other vampires instead of fighting for survival. Two competing interests. Starvation still stood patiently waiting like the grim reaper on the horizon, but death would be quick and sure if she didn't do as her family commanded.

CHAPTER 10

Gideon Kincaid looked around, feeling awkward and out of place. These human diners always made him uncomfortable, even though he was safely within his own territory. He never really knew what to say to the employees, or how to treat them. Still, this was a suitable place to hold a private conversation, just south of the Maryland border. He'd been spending a lot of time in the northern part of his territory — more than he would have liked. It was nerve racking, waiting for the inevitable attack from the Fournier vampires. All he could do was gather as much information as he could, and put the right people in the right place to counter a strike.

He'd used this particular diner often to meet scouts and any Fournier vampires he'd convinced to betray their family. It was a good diner. The humans left him alone for the most part, and he liked the pancakes. Gideon glanced down at the nearly empty plate — a sticky mess of syrup and the few bites he'd left uneaten. Fried batter. Fried dough.

An image rose in his mind of ebony hands shaping a circle of dough with practiced ease. Long thin hands, their bones and veins raising the skin as they twisted and turned, flashing nimble fingers and soft pink nails. He remembered those nails. They had little crescents of white at their base, like tiny moons. He used to trace them with his fingers and imagine that she was marked, favored of the moon goddess. It was so long ago that he couldn't remember her face, could remember nothing about his mother but her hands patting out the thin circles and laying them on the hot stones, flipping them quickly with the tips of her fingers to brown the other side.

A hand appeared in his line of vision to grasp the plate. Equally dark, but this one plump and rounded.

"Are you all finished with this, Sir?" a voice asked, soft with a light Virginia drawl.

He looked up at the waitress who smiled, waiting for a response.

"Yes," he replied awkwardly. The woman took the plate and swished off while Gideon thankfully retreated to his paper and coffee. Glancing toward the door, he saw another vampire enter. Wes. The scout he was waiting to meet.

Wes slid into the booth across from him and took the offered coffee from the waitress, smiling as he did so. Gideon envied him his ease with the human woman, but, then again, Wes was a good two-thousand years younger than him. He probably still remembered his human name, the face of the human woman who bore him.

"Report?" Gideon asked, returning his eyes to the newspaper.

"Derrick found a scout just west of Charles Town," Wes said, clearly trying to fight down the edge of panic in his voice.

Gideon frowned at his paper. Wes was just over two hundred and would never rise to more than a borderland scout. There had never been any vampire occupation of West

Virginia because of the sizable werewolf population. The sudden presence of a Fournier scout was no reason to panic. One occasionally came in to Charles Town to look at a business or two there. It was probably just him, checking the border before heading back to Baltimore.

"Did Derrick kill him?"

"No. And it was a woman. She had an older vampire with her, one with an aura." Wes squirmed in his seat, showing signs of agitation.

Gideon sighed in frustration. How this guy ever became Chosen was beyond him. "So? What did Derrick discover? Did he follow them to make sure they left the state?"

"The old one left, but the woman appears to be permanently assigned at the border. Derrick doesn't know how long she's been there or what she knows. She's barely New, hardly smells at all of vampire yet." Wes paused and squirmed again. "And she's not feeding like a vampire. She's living as a human would. We would never have known about her if Derrick hadn't stumbled across her when the older one with the aura was there. He thinks she may have been in place for at least six months, if not longer."

Gideon put his paper down in irritation and gave Wes his entire attention. "He needs to interrogate her and kill her. Make her disappear." He tapped his finger on the rim of his coffee cup, frowning. "What did Derrick glean from her conversation with the older vampire?"

Wes squirmed in his seat. "Derrick had to stay pretty far back and couldn't hear the whole conversation, but he says the older vampire was upset about her eating a bunny."

"A bunny? As in a rabbit? As in cooked it over a spit and ate it?"

"No!" Wes' eyes grew huge. "She drank its blood."

Gideon fought down a surge of annoyance. Idiots, all of them. With scouts like this, he was in danger of losing more than just the northern half of his territory. "Derrick must have misunderstood. No one drinks rabbit blood."

Wes shook his head. "He said that part of the conversation was very clear. The older vampire was disgusted and angry about her eating the animal. After they left, Derrick looked around and found it. It wasn't a clean bite either; she'd chewed the thing's head practically off."

Gideon stared at him. This was ridiculous. He needed information about Fournier's probable attack. When. Where. Not some wild story about perverted blood fetishes.

"Clearly Derrick made a mistake. It must have been a dog that killed it," he told Wes in a dismissive tone.

"No, Derrick said it would have been shredded if it were a dog. It was drained dry of blood. Sucked dry. Dogs don't do that." Wes stared at Gideon with huge eyes. "She's crazy. Insane. Fournier has an insane vampire strategically placed right on our border."

Every vampire family had fighters — those skilled in assassination, bodyguards, fighters trained to attack and protect. Legend was that every now and then one of them would exhibit signs of losing their sanity. Berserker rage, breaking laws and social taboos, amoral actions. They slid into madness, into the realm of the demons, and never returned to rational and civilized behavior. Insane vampires were dangerous and unpredictable. They were always killed. If a Master had the stomach though, he could point them like a missile at his enemies and follow in the path of their destruction.

"She's living on the edge of starvation, keeping her feeding tightly limited so she can appear as a human," Wes said in a hushed whisper. "She's drinking the blood of *wild animals!*"

Gideon restrained himself from rolling his eyes. This had gone far enough. He wondered if he'd have to put these two scouts down, if they'd reached the end of their usefulness. "Wes, vampires do not drink blood from wild animals, especially with an entire neighborhood of humans right within reach. Besides, she'd need to have an aura, need to have been a fighter for at least three-hundred years before even a hint of madness would appear. She's New. She's just a scout. And some dog ravaged a rabbit. Have Derrick interrogate and kill her." With a dismissive gesture, Gideon picked up his newspaper and continued reading.

Wes squirmed in his chair before he got up to leave. The older vampire watched him over the edge of his paper with a feeling of despair. He'd seized this territory almost three-hundred years ago when the previous Master had met an untimely end at sea. For nearly fifty years, the family had been in turmoil as factions schemed and assassinated their way to the top. By the time the dust settled, they'd lost nearly half of their family, and the financial foundations of the territory were in ruins.

The Kincaid lands were the poorest territory on the continent. Each tiny progress he'd made over the centuries was negated through human mismanagement or natural disaster. He had fought for the right to rule, worked tirelessly to rebuild a decimated family and dwindling funds. He was just starting to see progress and wasn't about to give it all up to a Born upstart with a silver spoon stuck firmly in his arrogant mouth.

Gideon glanced out the diner window at the night. A light rain had begun to fall, and he knew it would turn to sleet within the hour. He longed for his favorite home in southern Florida, where the heat covered him like a humid blanket. He was old enough now that the sun was starting to bother him. It blistered his dark skin if he was out too long. He wanted to enjoy it while he still could.

The brown hand once again came into his vision, refilling his coffee. He looked up, and the woman smiled.

"Horrible weather," she commented. "You're gonna freeze not wearing any coat."

The vampire looked at her blankly. Although he didn't feel the cold like the humans did, Gideon disliked the dreariness of it, the way it reminded him of death and the grave — things he thought he'd escaped by becoming a vampire. Now, over two-thousand years later, he felt death on the horizon, in his near future. There was no escaping it, no matter what devil's deal a person made.

"I saw you didn't drive here," the waitress added, looking away for a quick moment. "I can give you a lift home. My shift ends at two."

Was this human flirting with him? It had been so long. It was like having a loaf of bread proposition him. She was food, though, and he was hungry.

"Ok," he replied.

The woman beamed at him and practically skipped away. It was like picking up a ham sandwich, no big deal. This sort of exchange had been going on for thousands of years, although in the early days they hadn't needed to be quite as careful.

He watched as the waitress went about finishing up her shift and thought again about his warm home, the sun that now singed his skin, of a future of darkness. At least he had Monica, he thought fondly. She was older than she admitted and hadn't been able to tolerate sunlight since he'd known her. Of course, if he couldn't manage to hold his territory together, to retain his status as Master of the family, Monica would leave.

CHAPTER 11

At dawn, Jaq knocked on the door of Kelly's trailer. The vampire staggered through the narrow room to let her in, scowling at the light that streamed through the doorway. She'd returned to her bed after downing the small packet of human blood, collapsing in blissful sleep. It had thrown off her rhythm, but even with her long slumber, she still wasn't ready to face the day. The werewolf wore a tan heavy-canvas jumper, her hair, in the usual ponytail, swung from side to side as she bounded cheerfully through the doorway.

"Here," she handed a plastic grocery store bag to the vampire. "You're looking much better this morning. Did you sleep well? I thought you all were nocturnal, but you were abed all night long."

Kelly glared at her, irritated the werewolves were keeping such a close eye on her. Taking the bag, Kelly peered into it to see more meat, and what appeared to be a soup container full of blood. Ugh. If she never tasted cow blood again it would be too soon. Still, it was better than nothing, and she didn't want to appear ungrateful, especially since she now needed more from this woman than her offerings of food.

"We're nocturnal, but we can adjust our schedules if we need to." Well, most of them could. The ancient ones became increasingly locked into sleep patterns and couldn't bear the faintest of sunlight, but she doubted Jaq would ever meet one of *them*. Kelly looked up at Jaq, forcing a smile to her face. "Would you like to come in for coffee? And some of the donuts Melody left?"

Jaq tilted her head, her eyes searching the other woman's. "Sure."

Kelly ushered the woman in, starting a pot of coffee and setting a donut on a chipped plate. Jaq took a tentative bite, and eyed the vampire suspiciously. It was no use. Kelly was a terrible actress and needed to just get to the point.

"Can you tell me about the other vampires you've seen around here? The ones you've killed? What they looked like, where they came from? What they were doing?"

Jaq sat the donut on the plate and slid it onto the table. "Why?"

The vampire took a deep breath, wondering how much to tell her. "Remember when I said that this is a buffer zone between two vampire families? Well, my ticket out of here hinges upon my providing information to my family about the enemy scouts."

Jaq took another bite from the donut and relaxed back in her chair. "They beat you within an inch of your life. They took your fangs and dumped you here for dead, and now you're telling me they'll forgive everything and bring you back for information they could easily gather themselves?"

Kelly squashed the fear that rose within her at Jaq's words. Yeah, information easily gathered if vampires weren't so cagey and there wasn't a pack of pissed-off werewolves wedged right between them.

"They'll let me back. I just need to see how many rival scouts have been coming across the border and to get as much information as I can. This is typical stuff for a disgraced vampire to do in order to redeem themself."

"What's going on? Seriously. We've held West Virginia since before it was a state. There have always been the usual trespassers, but never this level of intrigue."

"There's nothing going on." Kelly lied. She had a pretty good suspicion there was something going on. The whole family had been buzzing with gossip the last five years. "I know you guys keep track of this sort of thing. Help me out here and I'll be out of your hair by the end of the week."

Jaq let out a noise that sounded suspiciously like a growl. "Is your family planning on making a bid for our territory? Did they plant you here to spy on us as well as the other vampires, beating you up as part of your cover so we'd feel sorry for you and not kill you outright?"

Idiots. Werewolves had no brains, just fur and fangs. Why would anyone want West By-God Virginia? There was nothing here. "No! I swear to you I've been punished and exiled. We've always had an uneasy peace with the Kincaids, and my family wants as much intel as they can get. Look, this may be my only chance to get back to my family, and you said yourself that I need to get out of here."

The woman before her suddenly looked fierce, gray eyes nearly silver as they bore through Kelly. "No, this is different. Tensions have been increasing between the two vampire clans, and we're sandwiched right in the middle. There's been an increase in scouts from both sides crossing the borders, and vampire shell corporations have been trying hostile takeovers on some of our companies. Don't give me this crap about 'business as usual'."

Kelly caught her breath. What was it with this crazy

werewolf? The vampire was no weakling, but Jaq gave her pause.

"Look, it's an internal thing. Not werewolf business. We've got one Born too many, up north – a Prince who has come of age. I'm not privy to his plans, but I'm assuming the Master is thinking a raid on Kincaid lands is safer than a power-hungry son in his own territory."

"Yeah, not our business at all. We're smack in between you two — how can you think that's not our business? Do you expect them to do this raid across the DC metro borders, where security is high? No, they'll tear through our state and sneak into each other's lands in the rural areas. And why are vampires trying to take over the major corporations here?"

"I've got no idea," Kelly insisted. "I can't imagine the vampires being interested in any businesses here. Outside of the racetrack, they're not our usual businesses. I'm sure you're mistaken."

Jaq snarled. "We're *not* mistaken. These companies will be vampire owned by the end of next month, and there's nothing we can do to stop them. We don't have the kind of money to defend against multiple hostile takeovers, and it's not technically against the contract the vampires have with us. Once they control all the money, they'll starve us out. Is that what you have planned?"

Kelly crossed her arms defiantly in front of her. "We don't want your state, or your stupid businesses, and I'm sure the Kincaids' don't either. Look, I'll pass along any information I get from my vampire family that concerns your territories if you share information on the scouts you've caught to date, and any future info."

Jaq's eyes narrowed. "Why do I have a feeling the knowledge you have to share is slim to none? They beat you and tossed you out here to die. You're expendable. I can't imagine that they'd divulge anything worthwhile to a disgraced vampire whose life has no value."

The werewolf's words were like a punch in her gut. Expendable. Was this really a way for her to earn the trust of her family again, or a chance for them to drain whatever usefulness they could from her before she died? The whole idea was too depressing to dwell on. Equally cutting was the idea that she had no information that would be worth anything to the werewolves. It was true.

She could happily tell the pack about the ins and outs of running a casino resort, or how to navigate vampire politics, but she really *hadn't* been privy to anything beyond her own specialized role in the family. All she knew was gossip, but gossip was more than what these werewolves had right now.

"The northern family is facing civil war if they can't find a territory for their Prince. The Kincaids down south have always had a target on their back. The only thing that's saved them from an attack in the last century is that their territory isn't all that profitable. That's starting to turn around, and given the situation up north, even a less-profitable territory is tempting, especially one that's run by a Made."

Jaq leaned forward, donut forgotten. "You're losing me here. Why would it matter whether your Alpha is Born or Made?"

The coffeemaker beeped, and Kelly poured two cups, handing one to Jaq. "It matters. Back before the humans walked upright, there were vampires. They were the original, the pure of our species. Thousands of years later, when they began to turn humans, the Made ones were slaves. We're not slaves any longer, but preference is still given to those who are Born vampires, especially those who have come from the pure line. Blood and family ties command great loyalty, but lineage trumps it all."

"Seriously? You all would ditch a good Alpha and follow a complete stranger, who may be a terrible leader, because of the circumstances of his birth."

"Yep." Kelly sipped her coffee, choosing her next words carefully. "It's more complicated than you think. We don't fall under any scrutiny from the angels, because we're considered a separate species. If the original line dies out, and we become just a group of turned humans, that might change. And we *really* don't want a bunch of angels all up in our business."

The werewolf shivered, her hands tightening on her coffee mug. "On that, we're in total agreement."

"I'm sure you see why the Kincaid lands are so tempting. Kyle Fournier, our Prince, is a Born from the original, non-human line. Up north he has a sizable following of those who think a younger, more dynamic vampire would better our financial interests. Overthrowing the current Master would be near impossible — he's ancient, and although he may be out of touch with modern businesses and the culture that surrounds us, he's powerful. The Prince would need the whole family behind him to take his father down. It's easier to snatch Kincaid's territory, and then let any world-domination plans wait until he gains power and resources. Probably a few hundred years."

Jaq cradled her coffee and leaned back in the chair, considering Kelly's words. "When? When can we expect a war on our doorstep? Given the amount of vampires we've seen, I'm assuming soon."

Kelly shrugged. "Could be a few years, could be a few centuries. The good news is, vampires don't do anything in haste. All this intensive spying could go on for fifty years while they formulate a very detailed plan."

The werewolf raised her eyebrows and took a sip of

coffee. "Then we have a deal as long as you continue to provide us with information, even if you're brought back into your family. I'll guarantee your safety from the werewolves as long as you don't prey on any humans or attack us, and I'll assist you and supply you with the information we have on the southern clan, but you need to tell us everything you know about this war as soon as you find out."

"Deal." Not that she'd have much to report if she wound up shelling shrimp in the kitchen back in Atlantic City. Still, it wouldn't be much of a hardship to send an occasional stealth message with some gossip to appease the werewolves. She owed this woman at least that much.

"If we get blindsided, "Jaq warned with narrowed eyes. "If our borders get swarmed and you didn't give us a heads-up, the angels will be the least of your worries."

Kelly bristled. "I swear I'll send you everything I know, but I'm not exactly high up in our family, especially since my disgrace. It won't be my fault if they move on the Kincaid lands and I'm not aware of it."

"Don't care. You all are supposed to be sneaky and smart. Maybe this will give you incentive to actually dig for information instead of sitting on your butt and letting us fend for ourselves."

Sneaky had always been one of Kelly's great skills. She resented that she'd need to work for the werewolves for an indefinite period of time, but if that's what she needed to do to get back into her family, then she'd do it.

"I said 'deal'. Now it's your turn — tell me what you know about the scouts and spies coming into West Virginia."

"Okay, okay, keep your britches on." Jaq took a long drink of coffee. "Used to be scouts would come through either the northern or southern borders, moving quickly. Sometimes we'd catch them, but plenty of times they'd be gone and out of range. From what we could tell, it was about fifty-fifty from your clan and the southern folks. Last six months, the vampire presence has increased ten-fold. Southern vampires tend to cross from Winchester and Leesburg. They primarily come through here and up near Martinsburg then exit out anywhere along the Maryland border, although quite a few exit near Hagerstown where interstate human traffic covers their tracks. Rarely are they in vehicles. They tend to travel on foot, which makes me think they're not just passing through, but are checking along the way."

That made sense. Traveling on foot was often just as quick as using a vehicle, given vampire speed and the ability to cut a straight line. Foot travel also afforded a vampire the chance to check key areas, sneak in and out to talk to informants, and smell for any enemy that might be in the border lands.

"How long are they out before they come back through — the one's you don't kill, I mean."

"A few days, not much. I really don't understand why they don't cross at other points. It's always the same three or four spots, and it's becoming rather easy to catch vampire scouts."

"The DC area crossings are heavily guarded," Kelly explained. "Besides the ferry or the few bridges, the Potomac River is an issue. Vampires don't swim, so large bodies of water make for a great barrier on territories."

The other woman tilted her head, intrigued. "Don't swim? Seriously? Can't you just walk along the bottom then? I mean, you don't need to breathe, do you?"

Stupid stereotypes. "Do you see me breathing?" Kelly snapped, instantly regretting her tone. "Sorry. The younger vampires all still need to breathe. We can walk in daylight. We still need solid food. The Ancients are a different story, but they're not likely to be on the front lines of any battles."

Actually it was kind of amusing to imagine the Master wading through the depths of the Potomac River. Would his illusion appear sodden when he came out the other side? Or would it disappear altogether, leaving a grayish monster crawling from the water's edge?

"That's good to know," Jaq mused. "Not all the scouts we've caught are low-level spies though. Two traveling together managed to kill one of our wolves, even with the element of surprise on our side. We got their scent and captured one alive next time he came through."

"What did you learn?" This could be the very info her family needed. Kelly sat on the edge of the sofa, leaning toward Jaq.

"The information I told you about the business take-overs — two large medical centers, a power company, and the racetrack and casino near here in Charles Town. Other vampires were doing the due diligence from the business end; these guys were checking out suitable areas for setting up a long-term vampire population. Stuff like availability of humans to feed from and law enforcement that wouldn't notice any suspicious deaths."

Kelly frowned. West Virginia wasn't viable for vampire occupation — no huge urban areas with enough crime and gang activity to cover up human deaths, and the businesses weren't the type of industry vampires specialized in. Biomedical and pharmaceutical, maybe. Hospitals and power companies? No way. At least they weren't stupid enough to look into coal or retail, which were West Virginia's biggest employers. They'd proven to be hopeless at running those kinds of businesses profitably.

"Why would Kincaid possibly be interested in West Virginia? No offense, but he's got enough poor states with struggling businesses. Why spread himself thin by adding one more, especially when he'd have to fight his way through a bunch of werewolves to take and hold the territory?"

A smile flitted across Jaq's face. "They weren't Kincaid scouts; they were yours. It's your family that's plotting a raid on us. With your southern enemies, it's just business as usual."

Kelly felt a surge of anger. This wasn't anything she could barter for her return. "I don't care about my family, I need to know what Kincaid is planning."

Jaq stood, towering over the smaller woman. "You should care. Your family killed one of ours, is threatening to take our lands. Trust me, if there is a war on our doorstep, the pack would be more sympathetic at this point with your enemies to the south than your own family."

"Let me get this straight — vampires passing through your territory get ambushed and killed. Two manage to take down one of your own. One as compared to the dozens or so you werewolves have killed, and you're ready to jump in bed with the Kincaids? I'm sure their scouts fought back too; we just got lucky, or maybe we're better fighters. Either way, I can't see how you're taking the highroad here. Trespassing surely doesn't warrant a death sentence."

"This is our territory," Jaq rasped out, curling her lip slightly. "Ours. We won't have you all feeding on our neighbors, buying up our businesses, drawing attention to us and putting us at risk. We've fought to keep you out this long, and we'll continue to fight as long as we live. You signed an agreement with us. You know the risks each time you step foot over the border."

Kelly opened her mouth to argue then realized she would have done the same. A trespasser in their territory was as good as dead. "So why let me live? I'm of the same family that killed one of your own. It would have been easy enough to kill me when they dumped me here."

Jaq's expression was unreadable as she stared at Kelly. "Because I'm an idiot. You looked so helpless, and the vampires who left you were horrible, throwing you around and kicking you like you were a play toy. There were too many for me to kill, so I let them go. But I just couldn't kill you."

"Instead you fed me." Kelly mused. Fed her. Like she was a wounded bird and not a dangerous predator encroaching on another's territory.

The tall woman glared. "Yeah. I helped you. You were dying, and like I said, I'm an idiot."

And with that, the vampire made a decision. "I need to do anything I can to get back. I can't stay here — vampires don't live solitary lives, and your pack wouldn't tolerate me here on a permanent basis. I appreciate what you've done for me. I'm sure most of your pack would rather I was dead. I'll not only let you know what's going on as far as any raids on the Kincaid lands, I'll dig up what's going on with my family and their interest in your businesses."

The other woman smiled faintly. "That would go a long way toward convincing my pack you're to be trusted."

Kelly took a deep breath. "And hopefully I'll be leaving soon."

The werewolf looked oddly unsettled at the idea. "I patrol this area each night. Are you interested in any rival vampires I catch? Maybe you'd like to join in my hunts."

Normally Kelly would be interested, especially with the need to provide information to her family, but given her injured state, and the fact she was unlikely to get a regular source of human blood in the heart of werewolf territory, she doubted she could keep up. Her pride swelled, choking her slightly. "No. This is your land. You go ahead; just let me know if you find anything out from those you catch, or bring them to me if you can."

Jaq's eyes glowed, reminding Kelly that she was not the only predator in the room. "Do you want them alive and talking, or just the heads?"

This werewolf was downright nuts. "Umm, alive and talking, but severely disabled would be best. Better dead than escaped, though."

Jaq grinned, picking up her donut. "I agree."

CHAPTER 12

Kyle frowned down at his tumbler of gin. He had more pressing matters to worry about than some cast-off New starving and going insane in the werewolf territories. *You're not ready*, a nagging voice inside his head reminded him. He wasn't. Haste was unseemly in a vampire, but he chafed under his father's increasingly condescending rule.

Would it really be more advantageous to wait than to act now? In another fifty years, some other vampire might have snatched Kincaid's territory, and he'd wind up stuck between two losing options. He was Born of a Born of a Born. From the moment of his birth he'd been shepherded toward his destiny. Already at three-hundred years, he had more power than most of his father's top advisors. Those with greater power bowed before him because of his lineage. It was good to be Prince, although it would be better to be Master. If he passed up the opportunity before him, would he find himself regretting it?

But instead of concentrating on getting his finances and alliances in order for a possible takeover, he was listening to one of his staff complain about the stupid girl. He'd dumped her in the werewolf territory expecting her to be dead within a few days, and he'd put a silver knife on the table beside her just in case she wanted to take the easy way out. He wouldn't condemn her for using the knife. No one would. In fact, his man Rube was incensed that she hadn't used it.

"She's drinking blood from wildlife," Rube repeated in outrage. "A bunny."

"And this matters to me why?" Kyle asked in monotone voice. "I didn't ask you to go check on her. I know you all still have bets on the table, but we have more pressing things to do. Instead, you're tormenting an exile and critiquing her dining habits."

"Juan was trying to collect," Rube protested. "He was sure she was dead by now. I don't have her killing herself until next week. Besides, she's right next to the Kincaid border. I figured if she's still alive she could prove of some use to us."

Kyle sighed. "She's a business manager, not a spy. She'll never survive long enough to get us information. If some Kincaid scout doesn't kill her, the werewolves or the humans will."

"They haven't yet. I'm sticking with my wager that she'll last another week. She might as well be valuable for that week."

Kyle ran a hand through his dark hair, tugging it in frustration. "Fine. Go back tonight and see what she's managed to find out. I don't care what you threatened, don't kill her yourself. Her fate is in her own hands now. And besides, you'd be disqualified from the betting pool."

"She should be dead," Rube asserted. "What self-respecting vampire eats cute little bunnies? Meat from the grocery store is one thing, but blood from an animal? It was the most disgusting thing I've ever seen in my life."

"We've never been a day away from starvation," Kyle said,

amusement coloring his voice. "It's hard for us to know what we'd do in that position."

"I'd never eat a bunny," Rube insisted vehemently. "She doesn't have any fangs, and she practically gnawed the thing's head off. You should have seen it, Sir. Wager aside, if I see her eating a raccoon or a groundhog, I'm going to kill her."

Kyle shook his head. "I said no, and I mean no. Kill her without my permission, and you'll find yourself taking her place in that trailer. Understood?"

Rube swallowed hard and nodded.

"Good. But just to show you I'm not a complete stick-in-the-mud, let's have a little side bet. If she dies in the next thirty days, you win. If she lives, I win."

"Even if she's insane?" Rube asked doubtfully.

"If she's insane and tearing the heads off animals now, she'll hardly live another month," Kyle replied dryly.

"Ok," Rube agreed. "If I win, I get my pick of the humans at the next private staff party."

"And if I win," Kyle said in amusement. "I get to watch you eat a rabbit."

CHAPTER 13

The moonlight through the naked trees cast faint shadows along the ground. Kelly's night vision highlighted the warm patches where animals had recently passed, as well as the shape of a rabbit hiding in a patch of briar. Wind stirred her short black hair, but she didn't notice. Her focus was on listening for the vampire she was to meet tonight, hoping he'd bring more blood. The small bag she'd consumed the night before only highlighted her desperate need. The boost it had given her reminded her of how many skills she'd lost, and how close to death she'd been. Her body ached with hunger, and she felt dizzy and weak.

Kelly shifted slightly and heard the crunch of leaves beneath her feet. Presumably he was to meet her in the same spot as before. He'd given her no instructions otherwise, so she'd just have to assume he'd manage to find her.

As if on cue, a shadow disengaged itself from behind an oak and moved towards her, gliding on silent feet. The wave of his aura was sharp against her skin. Family. The very feel of him brought her a sense of relief, easing the tension she experienced in this desolate place. It felt so good to have another vampire near. Even the hated Pierre would be welcome right now. Any vampire from her family helped her feel more settled, more in control.

"At least you're not eating a bunny this time," he sneered.

She was hungry enough to, but she'd hoped he had something better with him. Some kind of reward to keep her going.

"I have information." She wanted to get right to the point, so she could feed. There was no way she'd be going home right away. It would probably take a few times before she proved herself enough to be allowed back home.

"Speak."

"There are Kincaid spies and scouts that frequent the area. They move through fast and tend to exit into our territory in Hagerstown and along the Maryland border near Martinsburg. They stay a few days then pass back through on their way to Virginia. I doubt they're planning any large-scale attack. Most likely they're just taking preventative measures."

"Or planning a pre-emptive strike." The other vampire rubbed his ear, lost in thought. "How many? Are they increasing the frequency of their scouting missions, or just following a routine schedule."

"They've increased, but I don't know how many." Kelly faltered, not wanting to give enough information away that her source would be questioned. "I've only been here nine days, and most of that I was unconscious. Not much time for me to see any patterns in movement or judge the frequency."

"So catch one and interrogate him."

Right. In her condition? Jaq had offered to assist her, to bring in the next vampire she caught so they could question him or her. Good thing, otherwise she'd really be stuck. She was a casino manager, not a spy, not a warrior. This sneaking around the woods wasn't her strong suit. But "no" wasn't exactly an option.

"What information does the Master wish me to obtain, specifically?" she asked.

"What Kincaid is doing in the border lands, and what he is planning."

Kelly nodded, her heart sinking. She hated to keep going back to Jaq for help, but this wasn't something she could do herself. "When do you need this information? I don't really have any way of knowing when they'll be sending more scouts over. Is there some way to contact you?"

"Nope." The vampire seemed almost gleeful. "I'll be back in three days."

Three days. Let's hope he had a bag of blood or she'd starve before he returned. "Okay." She watched the vampire grin before breaking the silence. "Can I have some blood now? I got you the information you wanted."

"What? Lost your taste for rabbit?"

Kelly swallowed her pride. "Please. I won't be any good to you dead."

His grin grew wider until he appeared eerily like the Cheshire cat in the moonlight. "Yes you will. I've got a sizable sum of money on you only making it one more week. Personally I care more about that than if you manage to collect any further information. You're New. You'll be killed by the first Kincaid scout that gets downwind of you if the werewolves don't take you out first. Since you'll be dead either way, I might as well profit from it."

The vampire vanished in a burst of speed, but not before his laugh rang out through the forest.

Kelly felt anger bubble up. They ripped her fangs out, dumped her in some backwater without even a fucking toothbrush, then took odds on her survival and made a game out of her struggle. This was her *life!* Everything had been stripped from her; she was fighting to survive, and this jerk was treating it like a sweet sixteen college playoff. Screw them.

Running on adrenaline-fueled fury, she moved with vampire speed to Dale's. It was only about midnight, and activities were in full swing. Country music pounded from the tavern, and she could hear the clink of glass and the shouts of the humans enjoying their evening. She prowled around the woods behind the bar, keeping downwind as much as possible and watching carefully for a suitable victim. Sober people going in were ruled out, and those leaving weren't drunk enough yet to consider. It was possible she'd need to wait a few hours for a truly inebriated patron to leave.

"Scott!" a man yelled into the parking lot after a guy climbing into an old sedan. "You going to the strip club?"

A strip club? Where was the strip club?

"Yeah," the guy yelled back. "Meet you there?"

"Gotta finish our drinks and we'll be there," the first guy promised, stepping back into the doorway.

Kelly walked casually by the car, identifying the particular smell of Scott as well as his vehicle then blended into a bush by the road to see which way he went. The car turned left and Kelly ran after it, keeping in the shadows. A short two miles down the road, the car pulled into another establishment advertising exotic dancers. That was it? Two friggen miles? Less than three miles from her trailer? There had to be a God and he had to be smiling on her tonight.

Bars, strip clubs, casinos were all businesses that vampires had a hand in. Kelly hadn't been old enough or high enough to be privy to all the operations of the family, but she'd managed a lot of the accounting for the various holding corporations. Strip clubs weren't just good business, they were easy hunting grounds. Drunk men were plenty, and the frequent drug activity made it easy to feed from the dancers too. Blood laced with cocaine had a certain spicy flavor, a quick rush. It was very nice.

Kelly prowled the outer edges of the club and planned a strategy. She'd look for a dancer or a customer drunk or high to the point of losing consciousness, and then she'd make her move. Grabbing an empty beer bottle from the parking lot, she smashed it against the curb and held the neck, testing the sharp edge with a finger. It would look like a drunken fight, a barroom brawl gone wrong, and a victim that was drunk or high would likely not remember enough to tell the police.

It took great patience. She squelched down the anger and the hunger inside her and waited. Man after man left the strip club. Two o'clock came and went. Finally, around four o'clock, a single man staggered out the door and made his way to the far edge of the parking lot. He fumbled for his keys and dropped them on the ground. Weaving side to side, the guy reached for the keys and lost his balance, face planting on the dirt.

Well, this one should be easy, she thought, tying her overly large t-shirt in a knot under her breasts before staggering up to him as if drunk. Not that it probably mattered. This guy was so far gone, she could have been a donkey-faced leper and he'd have hit on her.

"Hey," she slurred. It wasn't hard with her missing teeth. "Got a cigarette I can borrow?"

The guy stumbled getting to his feet, and Kelly thought for a moment that he would go face down in the dirt again. He stared at her with huge bleary eyes.

"Cigarette?" she asked again.

He stared at her and patted clumsily at his pockets.

Oh, for Christ sake, she thought. What did she need to do to get this guy in the car so everyone coming and going wouldn't be witness to a bloody mess?

"Wanna screw?" That might work. He was at a strip club, after all.

The man's eyes bugged out in surprise. He nodded, looking down her body and swaying against the car. Picking up his keys, Kelly beeped off the car alarm and helped him in the driver's side where he slumped against the steering wheel. At least she wouldn't need to worry about him actually trying to take her up on her offer.

Carefully closing the driver's door, Kelly glanced around, scenting the air and listening carefully for any sound that might indicate her werewolf minders had caught up with her. Mike always made a racket, as if he didn't care that she knew he was following her, but Jaq was nearly impossible to detect. The only werewolf smell that she caught was old and faint, and she got none of Jaq's distinctive icy pine scent. Clear sailing — for now, but she'd better make quick work of this and get back.

Kelly slid into the passenger side, carefully keeping one eye on the club's door to make sure she was not observed. The man made a snoring noise and lurched to the right, collapsing on top of her in a heap, and crushing her at an awkward angle against the car door. The overwhelming odor of alcohol fumes crashed over her senses.

"Ugh. Get off me."

He snored in response. Just lovely. The guy felt like he weighed a million pounds. As a vampire, Kelly should have been able to easily move him, but for some reason this was difficult — another indication of her weakened state. Finally she managed to shove him aside and scoot herself into position. Again ensuring no one was in view around the parking lot, she sliced his wrist with the broken beer bottle. The guy didn't even grunt.

It was hard and messy work. The blood spilled out across the man's wrist and Kelly found herself frantically chasing every drop, cutting him again and again as it clotted and slowed. The blood hit her starved system like a hammer, making her feel oddly weak and giddy. Or maybe it was the alcohol rushing to her head. Wow, this guy was drunk, drunk drunk.

More. She needed more. It wasn't just the alcohol in the man's veins seizing her control and making her greedy and reckless, it was her body taking over her common sense — demanding what she'd been without for too long. The taste pushed her over the edge. Warm, like sweet silk on her tongue, the burn of alcohol a nice compliment to the rich flavor. Some small part of her brain screamed at her to take only a pint and walk away, to be cautious, but she ignored it. There may not be another chance — not for a long time. She battled with her conscience, starvation getting the upper hand. So what if she killed him? This was just a human. He didn't matter, and she desperately needed every drop he had to give.

Again and again she sliced the unconscious man as each wound started to clot. She should stop. She needed to stop, but her body had a will of its own, and she just couldn't pull away. It was getting more and more difficult to suck blood from the man, and she felt his cool flesh against hers, heard his heart stutter.

"Stop it! Stop!"

Strong hands grabbed her shoulders and ripped her from the car as if she were a rag doll, tossing her aside to the gravel. Gripping the bottle defensively, Kelly looked up into silver eyes in a freckled face.

Jaq loomed over her, but instead of attacking Kelly, she

began to berate her brother for his carelessness. "I swear he *wants* you to do something like this so he has an excuse to kill you. I'm going to kick his ass for this — off playing poker when he's supposed to be watching you. Worthless cur."

Kelly waved the bottle at her in what she hoped was a menacing fashion. Sometimes there was one Jaq, and sometimes there were two, fuzzy and blurring together. How much alcohol had been in that guy's blood?

"And you!" Kelly cringed as both indistinct Jaq's pointed a finger at her. "What do you think you're doing? I warned you not to go after any of the humans. The pack will have your head when they find out what you've done." The werewolf looked at the man in the car and uttered a soft oath. "Stay there. Don't move."

Surprisingly, Kelly obeyed while Jaq crawled into the bloody car with what she was sure was a dead body. In a daze, she looked down at herself. Blood coated her hands and her shirt, splotches darkened her sweatpants. She felt the sticky texture of it down her chin and neck and guiltily licked her lips. Oh God, she'd killed him. She'd lost control and killed someone. She needed to run. Get as far away as possible before Jaq called the police. Or worse, called in the other werewolves. She should run.

Where would you go? The little voice in her head taunted. She had nothing. A vampire wandering another's territory, covered in bloody too-large clothing wouldn't exactly blend into her surroundings. Plus there was that annoying lack of cash. Her only hope to get back to her family was doing this spy job for the Master. If she left, there would go her only chance of redemption. If she stayed, the werewolves would kill her. The little voice laughed. Either way, she was dead. Dead like the man in the car. Horror gripped her. She'd killed someone – someone whose only crime was being drunk at a strip club.

Power danced through her as her body absorbed the blood. Kelly breathed out and stretched her hands in front of her, dropping the broken bottle to the ground. How much of her sensation of invincibility came from the large infusion of blood after near starvation and how much was from the alcohol her victim had been swimming in? She was invigorated. Ready to eat a decent meal of solid food, rest a bit and begin looking for Kincaid scouts. *Or fight for her life*, she thought, eyeing Jaq's shadowed form inside the car.

A strange light filled the vehicle, almost as if the werewolf had turned on one of the interior lights, then it faded, and Kelly saw the woman's long legs as she awkwardly backed out of the vehicle.

"What were you doing?" Jaq's voice was barely controlled fury, and Kelly stared up at her, dazed. The werewolf practically glowed, her eyes shifting from silver to gold in the moonlight. She should be scared. She should be bounding to her feet ready to run or battle, but all Kelly could do was gawk drunkenly at the woman looming over her.

"Dinner. Was hungry." The words slurred from her in an incoherent ramble. "I didn't mean to kill him. Didn't want to kill him."

Jaq moved her hands as if she'd like to wrap them around Kelly's neck. "I *fed* you. I brought you food, gallons of blood. Are you insane, attacking a human like this? Do you want to die?"

No, she didn't want to die. Kelly struggled to clear her head, realizing that if she had any hope of making it through the night, she would need to get this werewolf to understand.

"I was starving. Blood has to be human. Live prey. Too long without human supply and we die. Animals are only good for a day or so."

The other woman put her hands to her face, and Kelly

saw something sparkle in her eyes and on her cheek. Was she crying?

"Why didn't you tell me? *Why*? I could have let the others know about your needs, taken up some kind of collection from the human neighbors — a blood donation or something."

"No! Less humans who know, the better," Kelly slurred. "Need live prey, but I've got no fangs. People will know. It will hurt them and they'll kill me, so I thought this drunken man would be best, but I was too hungry. Or maybe he was too drunk. Wow was he drunk. I don't think I can stand up."

"If you don't want anyone else to know, fine, but I can't have you slicing up humans like this. That guy nearly died. He would have if I hadn't helped him. You can't do this anymore. Others will find out, and I won't be able to protect you. No more humans. You'll have to figure out something else that will work. Do you understand? I won't be able to protect you from either my pack or the humans if you keep doing this."

Kelly tried to stagger to her feet only to fall back onto her rump in the gravel. "I'll be outta your territory soon. Just gotta find a Kincaid spy and interrogate him." She collapsed in a fit of giggles at the idea. "I do it and my family takes me back. Two weeks tops. If I can make it that long, I'll be back home with my family."

Jaq did not seem to find the idea as amusing as Kelly did. "You're kidding me. They're just toying with you. They're not going to take you back, no matter how many hoops you jump through for them."

"It's the vampire way," Kelly announced, again trying to stand. "I prove my worth, and they take me back."

Jaq moved forward and helped her up, stooping to support the vampire's weight with her arm. "Then I'll figure something out. I told you I'd help you with the vampire scouts. I'll help you find and interrogate this spy, and we'll find a way to get you enough blood to stay alive. Just no more feeding on humans. No more."

"Can't promise that." Kelly stumbled forward, leaning heavily on Jaq. "It's like trying to fast while standing next to a buffet. Death by starving, death by werewolves — I'll take my chance with the werewolves."

"Well, you're going to have to figure out a way to restrain yourself. Actually, how about werewolves? We've got a pretty high pain tolerance, and we heal fast. Maybe you could use us instead?"

The whole idea was bizarre. Werewolf blood. Would it taste like it smelled? Dogs and old ham wasn't very appealing, but if it kept her alive it might be worth trying to choke down. "Don't know. I could try, but I can't feed from you. Can't do it."

"Why not?" Jaq sounded offended.

Kelly patted her shoulder. "Friends aren't food. Don't eat friends."

Kelly could have sworn she heard a quickly muffled snort from the woman beside her. "Well, that's nice, but you need to eat. Don't you vampires drink each other's blood sometimes?"

"Oh. My. God. No." If anything sobered Kelly up it was the idea of drinking another vampire's blood. "That's disgusting. Why would we do that?"

"Well, I thought during sex, or when you turn humans?" Jaq seemed rather amused at Kelly's reaction.

"Ugh, no way. You watch too much television. Or porn. There's a gland connected to our fangs for turning. And drinking a vampire's blood? Ugh. Just . . . yuck."

Jaq laughed softly. "Okay. Good to know. Come on, Toothless, let's get you home."

The tall woman half supported Kelly as they moved toward the shelter of the woods.

"Did I kill him? He going to be okay?" Kelly nodded at the car.

Jaq sighed. "Yeah. He'll wake up perfectly healthy, just covered in blood. Not even a hangover, which I can't say for you. You're going to be sick as a dog tomorrow."

"No, seriously, Jonah. We need to figure out a way to get her some human blood or she's going to die."

The Alpha snorted, hanging up a pheasant and a brace of quail on a rack inside the pole barn. Early-morning sun streamed through the gaps in the siding, hitting the red and gold plumage on the pheasant. Jaq had met Jonah coming in from his hunt. As usual, he was without gun or a bow. Running down a deer took skill, but the dexterity it took to catch birds with only teeth and claw wasn't lost on Jaq. Jonah may look like every other human in West Virginia, but even among werewolves his hunting skills were legendary.

"I'd rather she die. It would make it all a lot easier. No, Jaq. No exceptions. I'm not having anyone preying on our human neighbors, let alone some skanky New Jersey vampire."

Jaq bristled, but held her temper. "Well then, how about we let her have werewolf blood? Just a pint a day. We could run it like a blood donation clinic."

Jonah examined his catch before turning a stern eye on

the other werewolf. "Jaq, my girl, you have surely lost your mind. Imagine that for a moment — werewolves sittin in a chair all nice and quiet like while some vampire chews on their arm. No one is gonna be a blood donor for your pet monster. I'm doin all I can to keep them from ripping her into little bitty pieces. Kill her or drive her out of our territory, because I can't hold them all back for much longer."

The image flashed before Jaq's eyes, and it wasn't a pretty one. No werewolf would willingly let another bite them. The whole thing would dissolve into a nasty, probably deadly, fight. But what was the alternative?

"We *need* her; everyone is just too blind to see it. She may be young, but she's smart, and she can help us defend our territory. And she's not a monster. She's actually nice. And funny."

"She's not your pet, Jaq. She's a rival predator, and nice or not, she's going to turn on you. We can't trust her. I promised you a week, and I'll stand by that. Help her get in good with her family then let her go back with them. It's for the best."

Jaq squirmed. "They're not going to let her back. I can tell. They're using her. Even if she does what they say, I've got a feeling they'll just leave her here and laugh while she starves to death."

"Well then, the best thing is to kill her now. You can't let an animal starve to death, even a monster. Put her down."

"No! She's not a monster. I've talked to her, and she's no different than us, just with some odd dietary requirements. Why can't she stay? She'll never be able to return to her family, and the vampire group won't accept her. If we figure out a way to get her blood, then why can't she just stay here?"

Jonah snarled, his eyes golden. "Jaq, you overstep your bounds. I won't have a vampire in our territory."

"It's not just our territory; it's the humans' territory too. What do you think is going to happen if the vampires move in here? What do you think will happen to us? You can piss on the borders all you want, pretend that we're the big bad in the woods, but at the end of the day we're just a bunch of wolves hiding from the outside world."

"And one vampire, some young, barely turned thing, is going to make all the difference?"

"One vampire and me. We just need forewarning, and with a big show of force, they'll leave us alone. It worked once, centuries ago, it can work again."

Jonah shook his head, his eyes dimming to warm brown. "It's too risky, Jaq. We're pledged to protect you, and we can't do that if you don't lay low. Besides, it's not just you at risk; it's the whole pack, and it's werewolves as an entire species."

She nodded. "I know. I'm thinking of a way we can pull it off without revealing too much, but we need this vampire."

Jaq winced slightly at Jonah's wry expression. He turned to tend to his quail, and she let the silence stretch on. One. Two. Three.

"All right. I don't see how some vampire girl is going to get us out of this, but I'll give you a few extra weeks. Just keep a tight leash on her."

Relief washed over her. "I think we can make this work. I've already talked Dale into giving her a job at the bar. She'll feed us information on what the other vampire groups are doing. She can be a valuable asset to us. We just have to figure out how to keep her from starving to death."

"Not my problem," Jonah growled. "I'm trusting you on this one, Jaq. Don't screw up."

The werewolf dipped her head in respect and took her leave, striding into the chill morning breeze. There was no plan. She had no idea how Kelly could be of help beyond supplying information, and even that might be worthless. Jaq's main goal should be to protect the pack, to keep their territory intact, but she needed to be able to sleep at night.

Kelly's face flashed before her — pale skin with a silky cap of black hair and equally dark eyes. But it wasn't the vampire's features that hung in Jaq's memory; it was the desperation behind her eyes. The girl had no options right now, no road that didn't lead to her death. She could talk all she wanted about reinstatement with her family, but Jaq saw deep inside that the vampire feared her end was near. That wasn't the look of a monster.

Kelly might be a ruthless predator, sneaky, conniving, and untrustworthy, but she was *not* a monster. Jaq wasn't about to toss her out of the state into the clutches of those who would like nothing more than to rip her apart. If their territory was big enough for humans, werewolves, and her, then it would surely be big enough for one small vampire.

CHAPTER 15

"I don't know, Elizabeth." George's voice was thick with doubt and fear. His hand reached for hers and gripped. She felt the cold sweat on his palm. It sent a feeling of unease through her that she couldn't manage to shake.

This was a different George than the lanky, sixteen-year-old butcher's apprentice she'd run away with. That one had blown into the frozen emptiness of her life like a breath of warm summer air. He'd wooed her with his quick smile, and his promises of riches and power. She'd abandoned everything in a heartbeat, less interested in riches and power than the promise of something different in the boy's sparkling blue eyes. Unlike the other men, he hadn't smelled like onions, and his hands awoke a fire beneath her skin. She'd followed him into the dank dark of the catacombs and had happily talked to these intense strangers with him. George was her sunshine, the only happiness she'd ever known.

"Don't be silly. So you saw one of them feeding. I've seen worse things in back alleys late at night."

Her voice came out strong, confident, but inside she wasn't. Why should she care? People did horrible things to each other all *the time. These strangers might treat her with the same cool detachment as nearly every human she'd met in her life, but at least it didn't concern them that she was a girl — or that she was a bastard.*

"I'm not going through with it." George looked around him nervously, clearly worried that someone might overhear. "They said we could say 'no' at any point if we wanted to. Let's leave. We're not locked in, and I know the way out. Let's go now."

And go back to the kitchens to peel vegetables? Cook would never let her return after she had run off with the butcher's boy. How long would they survive on the streets? How long before George abandoned her and she wound up lifting her skirts for anyone that would have her, just to put a bit of food in her belly? She looked over at the boy, and his brightness dimmed.

Pulling her up by her hand, he stood and guided her to the doorway, his other hand firm on her lower back. He hadn't even waited for her decision, just assumed she'd come with him. Should she? He was her sunshine. Fear gripped her at the thought of remaining in these dark stone rooms without him, surrounded by cold, emotionless beings that drank blood. George opened the door and a damp breeze stirred the loose strands of dark hair at her neck. She hesitated, hearing a thumping from far away, and a sound — as if someone was calling.

Kelly woke up to her door banging and the now familiar "Heloooo" of her neighbor Melody. For a moment, she tightened her hand and felt nothing. *Where was George?* Panic gripped her. Gone. They'd said he had moved on, forgotten her, and she'd been crushed. Years later she'd learned the truth, but by then it was too late to change her course. Far too late.

George. The pain was like a knife of silver through her chest, even after nearly two centuries. It was too long ago to still hurt this bad. George had belonged to another person —

Elizabeth, the human. She was Kelly, the vampire, and there was someone banging persistently at her door.

"Helooo!" The loud knocking thankfully stopped, but the slam of the door alerted Kelly to the fact that Melody was no longer on her front step, but *inside* the trailer. Opening her eyes, she winced at the light and struggled to rise from the lumpy bed. Her head throbbed, and she felt an odd combination of peppy and ready to puke. Why couldn't the dratted woman let her sleep? Why didn't they respect the fact that she was nocturnal? She'd put old newspaper all over her bedroom windows, but it wouldn't help her sleep during the day if the darned humans kept forcing her to keep to their schedule.

"Wake up, sweetie. Jaq and I are here with some food. I'm making coffee."

Kelly buried her head under a pillow. It was no use. Melody was relentless. If she didn't get up, the woman would be in her bedroom to 'check' on her. At least she'd brought food. That was one good point.

Kelly shuffled out in the borrowed oversized sweatpants and t-shirt, already smelling the coffee. Melody bustled about the little kitchen area, and Jaq looked up at her, snickering before turning her gaze away.

"How are you feeling this morning, *sweetie*?"

Dratted werewolf. Kelly rubbed her throbbing head and glared at the tall woman. "As good as can be expected."

Melody chuckled. "Did you go out and tie one on last night? Don't you worry one bit. Auntie Melody has the perfect hangover cure. I'll just get breakfast going here and run over to my place and get it. I always keep it handy for Joe. He sometimes has a few too many beers at poker night, you know?"

What Kelly did know was that she'd need to watch this

neighbor of hers. Jaq wasn't the only sharp one around here. In spite of her appearance, Melody was pretty quick on the uptake.

"You are so thin," Melody continued, looking Kelly over. "And I can't believe how much food you go through. Didn't that horrible man of yours ever feed you? No, don't answer that. We're not going to speak of him at all. I saw you went out last night, and I'm glad you're starting to have some fun, but you need to be very careful. You're just a tiny thing, and there are some pretty rough places around here."

Kelly wasn't sure whether to be amused that Melody thought her incapable of protecting herself, or alarmed that she was apparently keeping an eye on her comings and goings just as closely as the werewolves were.

"Early this morning, some man was found passed out in his car, all bloody from a fight at that titty bar down the road." She giggled. "Did I say titty? Oh, I shouldn't laugh. That poor man. He's okay, but that's what he gets, drunk and lusting after those loose women. You should be very careful. It's not safe for a woman to be out alone at night. Next time take Jaq with you, or maybe Tanya. No, not Tanya; she's liable to leave you stranded the moment some cute guy offers her a beer."

Kelly stiffened and exchanged a quick, anxious glance with Jaq. It didn't sound like the man had died, thank God. She'd taken so much blood from him that she hadn't been sure, despite Jaq's reassurances. She did need to be more careful, although not in the way Melody meant.

"I brought more food," Jaq told her with a rather peculiar look. "I know you're hungry. I'll do the best I can to make sure you have what you need."

The tall woman took an armful of ziplock bags from a sack and sat them on the counter, then reached back for more.

"Goodness Jaq," Melody scolded. "Drain some of the blood out of those things before you put them in the fridge. That's just gross."

"No," Jaq said sharply as she grabbed the bags. "They need that. Gives the meat flavor. Makes it tender." She shot Kelly a stern look and stuffed the bags quickly into the refrigerator.

"Well, you're the expert, dear," Melody said cheerfully. "Jaq is such a good hunter," she told Kelly. "She's always giving us bologna, ground venison, and other stuff. She brought us squab a few weeks back. It was very good. I like it much better than that squirrel stew from the other week."

Jaq smiled fondly at the plump woman. "If you run out, I've got more. I'm working this afternoon, but Mike's home and he can get a few for you out of the ice box."

Kelly looked at her fridge bursting with bags of meat floating in blood. There was no way she was going to force more cow blood down her throat. No way.

The fresh human blood she'd had last night should hold her for a few days. After that, she'd be back to living on the edge. Perhaps if she didn't wait so long this time, she'd have better control trying to feed from a human. Where could she go that Jaq wouldn't know? The woman probably wouldn't let her out of her sight after what happened last night.

"I'll definitely take you up on that, Jaq," Melody replied. It took Kelly a moment to realize they were still talking about the squabs. "Not tonight though. We're having pre-Thanksgiving Thanksgiving. Turkey and all the works. Joe loves it so much that we can never wait for the actual holiday. You're coming over for dinner."

Kelly started, realizing the command was directed at her. No! She had to hunt for Kincaid spies tonight. The vampire glanced out the window, quickly calculating sunset to be just before seven in the evening.

"How early?" Hopefully this whole dinner obligation

would be over before nightfall. It's not like she could say "no" after all the woman had done for her. It just wouldn't be polite.

"Five. Come over at three, though. You can help me cook while Joe watches his game." The woman dashed over to Kelly, and before she could flinch, wrapped her arms around her in a crushing hug and planted a wet kiss on her cheek. "See you soon!"

Kelly stared in shock as the woman darted out the door. Jaq made a choking sound then lost control and bent over laughing. "Your face; if only you could have seen your face," she gasped.

"How in the world do you stand her? She's so cheerful. I just want to rip her head clean off her body."

Jaq wiped her eyes. "I know, I know. But she's sincere. There's never an ulterior motive with Melody."

"That's the only thing keeping her alive right now. That and her tuna casserole."

Jaq laughed again. It came out as a snort, and Kelly couldn't help but grin. "Just remember that when you're suffering through hours of turkey and mashed potatoes tonight. You've got to refrain from killing her, otherwise no more tuna casserole."

Kelly groaned. "And that couldn't come at a worse time! I need to find a Kincaid scout to interrogate. How am I going to do that when I'm helping her stuff a turkey? Not that I know how to stuff a turkey. Or how to interrogate a vampire."

With an easy jump, Jaq sat on the counter edge, tucking her legs up in an impressive show of agility and balance. "I'll do the vampire search and then meet up with you after your dinner. How fast are you?"

The vampire couldn't help the little noise of superiority. "Faster than you."

"I doubt that." Jaq grinned. "Will you be strong enough for a dash to Martinsburg? He or she may be pretty far ahead of us by the time you're taking that last bite of pumpkin pie."

Kelly hesitated. She felt fine now, but needed to conserve energy if the prospect of human blood was a week or so away. If she raced full speed to Martinsburg, she may not be strong enough to capture and interrogate the scout. By the time she got back to her trailer, she'd be weak and dizzy once again.

Jaq's expression softened. "Or I can just catch and interrogate the guy for you. Save your strength."

Ah, the mighty werewolf saves the day. Still, Kelly shook her head. She needed to do this on her own. Or at least as much of it on her own as she could manage. "No. I'll be okay. I'd appreciate the help in tracking and apprehending him though."

It felt strange to depend on someone else. She'd spent her whole vampire life working as a giant team, but underneath the cooperation, it had always been each vampire for him or herself. This felt . . . weird. Jaq had her back, could be relied upon. They were a team. The thought made her uneasy. *You can't trust anyone but yourself, girl. Don't go getting any foolish ideas that this woman is going to catch you if you fall.*

The werewolf hopped from her perch on the countertop, landing lightly and walking a few steps towards Kelly. Jaq's gate was smooth and light, her movements more like that of a cat than a wolf. Kelly's eyes traced up from the woman's feet, taking in the spotted skin that led from the neckline of her t-shirt to her angular face and startling gray eyes. Could she really trust Jaq? Those silver-gray eyes always seemed so kind, so warm when they looked at her. Maybe . . . just maybe she could.

"And with that out of the way, we need to talk about last night."

The werewolf's gaze was still gentle as she met Kelly's eyes, but there was a steely note in her voice the vampire didn't like. Tentative thoughts of trust fled, and Kelly stiffened. Last night . . . she'd broken the rules. Remembrance of what happened the last time she got caught breaking the rules twisted in her gut. And she'd almost killed someone, too. It shouldn't bother her, but the thought halted her instinctive defensive reaction transforming it into guilt.

"Is that man really going to pull through? I don't want you to think I'm one of those vampires who routinely kills their dinner. It won't happen again."

Jaq sighed, placing a hand briefly on Kelly's shoulder in reassurance. "Yes, he'll be fine, but I'm pretty sure it *will* happen again. You were drunk as a skunk off that guy last night, so let me say it again: we need to confide in the neighbors and get a regular source of fresh blood for you. They know about us werewolves, they'll be more understanding than you think about living side by side with a vampire."

"No!" Visions of a lynch mob skittered across Kelly's mind. "I can't let them know what I am. Promise me you won't tell them!"

"Promise me you won't try last night's stunt again."

Both women stood silent. Finally Jaq sighed. "Seems we're locking horns on this one. All right. I understand the need to keep some things secret. Let's figure out a temporary blood supply that's acceptable to us both until we can come up with a long-term solution."

There was no alternative. Bagged human blood might hold her off, but even that wouldn't work for long. Twenty-four-hours old was really the maximum it could go and still be effective.

"Fresh animal blood would be okay," Kelly lied.

Jaq narrowed her eyes as if she knew. "Okay. We'll work

this afternoon in setting up snares and traps for both small and large animal prey in the woods. I'll teach you."

Great. Now she was some kind of Davey Crockett. Kelly glanced over to the chairs with the skirt and blouse she'd washed over and over, trying to get the bloodstains out, then down at her Italian leather flats. Setting animal traps, tracking and interrogating members of a rival vampire family, what next?

"And you need to get a job."

Kelly made a strangled sound deep in her throat and stared at the other woman. "Tired of supporting your freeloader neighbor? You worried I'll end up living in your basement playing video games all day?"

She'd contemplated getting a job. It was one of her first keys to survival when she suspected she'd been cast out for good. But now it seemed her family would be bringing her back into the fold sooner than expected. Besides, how was she supposed to hold down a job while gathering intel? Add to that the fact that working for humans would be problematic. That first day when she was numb and in pain, it seemed like the only alternative, but now that she felt like a vampire again, it struck her as demeaning.

"I don't have a basement. I live in a trailer, remember? I already got you a waitress job down at Dale's. He's an old friend. Likes my venison jerky. You start tomorrow."

Kelly's mind screeched to a halt. Not working for humans, working for werewolves. Oh. My. God. "I can't . . . how dare you . . . there's no way I'm going to. . . ."

Jaq quelled her with a stern look. How could the woman *do* that? "No arguments. I'm going to get some supplies to make traps. Meet you in the woods in ten."

She didn't have the time for a job — wouldn't be here long enough for a job if things went her way. Dratted bossy woman was like a long-legged, freckled steamroller. Kelly sighed, looking again at her shoes. They were the only ones she had. "I doubt Donald Pliner, whoever the heck he is, had high-speed running and wilderness trekking in mind when he designed you. Let's hope you hold up or I'm going to be barefoot for my first day of work."

Kelly stared down at the index card. She'd managed to rip the stale bread into chunks, but did she need to melt butter next or add the nuts and apple? And how small were the apple pieces supposed to be? She peered again at the card and looked up at Melody helplessly.

"I'm sorry. I don't really understand what I'm supposed to do next."

Melody's trailer was different than the one Kelly occupied — a luxury model by comparison. The kitchen and living area were equally cramped, but a small door to the back led to a screen-enclosed deck that had been skillfully added on. The longer length of the building allowed for a second bedroom —— barely bigger than the bathroom beside it. When Melody had given her the obligatory tour, Kelly had seen it had been turned into a cramped office, complete with shelves that made the room even smaller. She wondered how the woman could possibly turn around in there without knocking something over.

"Dear, we really need to teach you to cook." Melody said

with a sympathetic noise. "Jaq told me you burn everything you make."

Dratted freckled werewolf. She did *not* burn everything. Just the liver. And the chicken. And those grilled cheese sandwiches the other day. Kelly scowled and looked over at Joe, Melody's husband, who was sprawled on the couch watching football and wished that she could just go join him. She never cooked at the Casino. She'd never cooked as a vampire. She hadn't cooked much as a human either — just peeled and chopped and diced. Endlessly peeled, and chopped, and diced.

"I haven't ever really cooked," she confessed. "I worked in a kitchen when I was a child, but I only did certain things."

Melody sniffed. "I'm sure that violated all sorts of child labor laws, even if you were working for your own parents."

Labor laws were non-existent when Kelly was a child, and she'd never known her parents, but there was no sense correcting Melody and getting into a difficult explanation. No, she didn't want to go there. Or here. She'd rather be out with Jaq, tracking trespassing vampire scouts.

"Well, what *did* you do when you worked in a kitchen?" Melody asked. "Maybe you can put the rolls on the baking sheet? I'll watch the timer so you don't burn them."

With her luck, they'd still come out of the oven blackened lumps. Kelly looked around. This was what human women did in this century — they cooked big elaborate meals. But she wasn't a human. She was a vampire with no cooking skills whatsoever, lost in a mess of turkey, stuffing, and pota-toes. Potatoes.

"I used to peel vegetables. I can do that."

Most of her human life had revolved around cleaning pots and prepping food. It hadn't been so terrible compared to the life some children had. She'd had a warm box with a blanket behind the stove. Work to keep her hands busy, if not her mind. She'd quickly figured out who was kind, and who would take out any frustrations on a little girl with no last name.

Things had changed as she'd gotten older. She'd no longer fit in the warm box behind the stove, and suddenly there were all sorts of offers for other overnight accommodations. The men and boys who had ignored her before now wanted to shove her in a dark corner and feel her up.

Options had been limited given the circumstances of her birth, but she had been pretty. There was a good chance she could have caught the fancy of a groom, or possibly the younger son of a merchant. If she were lucky, passion would overcome the social disadvantages of a marriage with her. Kelly felt tears sting behind her eyes. Her life as a human had completely depended on attracting a man. It didn't matter if she was smart. It didn't matter what her skills were. She just needed to be pretty enough to snare a man.

George. That stupid dream had once again brought him out of the dark recesses of her memories. Like yesterday, she saw him in her mind, tall and deceptively skinny. There were muscles under his rough muslin shirt. His hands were calloused, but the rest of his skin was soft and warm. *I love you,* he'd told her, blue eyes dancing with mischief. He was trouble, but he'd meant it when he said he loved her.

Guilt flooded her. It wasn't her fault. It couldn't be her fault. She'd made the only decision she could. Love didn't buy you food or give you a warm, safe place to put your head at night.

Life was supposed to be different as a vampire, but it wasn't. Not really. Smarts mattered over looks, but in the end a Made, especially a Made female, could only go so far. She'd made her decision — walked away from sunshine and chosen a life of darkness, and what had it really gotten her?

"Wow, you *can* peel potatoes," Melody said in amazement.

Kelly had flown through five pounds with vampire speed, too lost in thought to pay any attention to what she was doing.

"What do I do now?" Kelly smiled at the older woman, forcing the unwelcome memories back. She might as well try to learn to cook. Maybe she could surprise Jaq and actually make her a dinner that didn't look like something that fell off the coal truck. A vision of the werewolf came to mind — blond and lanky with her freckled face and unusual gray eyes. Kelly chuckled, imagining the look on the werewolf's face if she presented her with a reasonably well-cooked turkey — one that wasn't charred on the outside and raw on the inside.

It was actually fun, making the mashed potatoes, the dressing, and the pumpkin pies. Joe continuously came in to poke at the turkey and test it, snagging little bites where he could. Melody would scold him affectionately, and he'd kiss her with his mouth full of food and laughingly pat her rear. Then Melody would wave her spatula menacingly at him and banish him back to the football game. Kelly's chest tightened painfully at the sight. Maybe her future as a human would have been more like this than the dismal hell she'd imagined. Maybe if she and George . . . but there was no sense in going down that path. George was long dead, and she'd never be a human again. Never.

They ate until Kelly felt like she'd burst. If only she'd been able to drink some blood, it would have been perfect. Joe did the dishes, while Melody took her into the bedroom to show her a bunch of knitting. Kelly followed reluctantly, glancing at the darkness outside the trailer. It had to have been after nine o'clock. How much longer would they expect her to stay? Would it be rude to dash out right after dinner, or would she be stuck admiring this human's handicrafts for the next three hours?

"I have an internet group," Melody told Kelly proudly as she pulled out box after box of brightly colored items. "We make hats for preemies, prayer shawls for cancer patients, and socks for our troops overseas. There are over five hundred of us on the east coast alone."

Kelly looked at a box of small blankets. When could she leave? She really needed to leave.

"Those are lap afghans. Our church is putting a box of them together for the local nursing home. Those people really appreciate a hand-made blanket."

"Wow. That's really impressive." It was, actually. She couldn't imagine coordinating the efforts of five hundred people from a distance. The casino had been one thing. She'd been able to dominate with the force of her personality and physical presence. But the Internet?

"Yes. I feel like they're all my best friends, although I've never personally met any of them. We chat; I see pictures of their grandkids and families, and I organize which charities we're knitting for, and the schedule. Everyone sends their donations to me, and I send it out to the charity."

She showed Kelly a calendar with a schedule of charities and due dates as Kelly snuck glances through the window, trying to see the small alarm clock beside the bed.

"Come on; I'll teach you."

What? She'd completely been ignoring the conversation. Melody had grabbed her arm and was dragging her back into the living room, a bag in her other hand. Kelly once again glanced at the door as the other woman shoved her down on the couch and thrust two large metal sticks into her hands before plopping down beside her.

Two hours later Kelly walked home, feeling a flurry of snow on her cheeks. Her trailer was dark and silent after the warmth and bustle of Melody's. Jaq was nowhere to be found, so she put her stash of leftovers in the fridge and deposited the rest of her bundles on the couch before heading out. She'd check their traps first then hopefully meet up with Jaq.

They'd put down six rat traps and rigged up a box trap with the milk crate and a stick. Kelly remembered seeing something like it on a TV show once and was really impressed that Jaq knew how to do it. The other woman had assured her it would work, but it seemed that the animal would knock the stick out and only be half in, easily backing out of the trap. Perhaps she was supposed to sit quietly by with a string and pull it shut on the animal? That would be a totally impractical use of her time.

Kelly felt the hair rise on the back of her neck as she checked five traps. There was a faint, old smell of vampire, and not one from her family either. The light dusting of snow had diluted the scent, though, and she couldn't tell if it was carried on the wind from a distance, or just faded from the weather. She paused, closing her eyes and inhaling deeply, but finally gave up trying to pinpoint the smell. Hopefully Jaq was having better luck.

It was disheartening to find the five traps untouched. She sucked at this. She was trained as a business manager, not a survivalist. The closest she'd come to this skill was as a human when one of the footmen had taught her to steal, and pick locks.

Going to the location of the sixth rat trap, Kelly frowned. It was gone. Leaves had been scraped to the side leaving a patch of cleared dirt; branches were broken as if there had been some sort of struggle where she and Jaq had placed the trap. Looking for the trap in an expanding circular search grid, she finally found it smashed to small bits a few feet from where it had been placed. She shook her head as she examined the broken splinters of wood and twisted metal wires. This didn't look like a large animal had been caught and thrown the trap off. It looked like a large animal had been caught and smashed the trap in a fit of rage. Human? How embarrassing it would be if one of her neighbors had gotten caught in her trap.

Carefully she picked up the wood and metal pieces, easily visible to her night vision. One had a spot of blood. She scrutinized the spot and licked it. Not that she thought she'd recognize the victim. As soon as the wood touched her tongue, she recoiled in surprise, spitting to rid her mouth of the taste. It wasn't human: it was vampire. And whoever this vampire was, he wasn't her family. His smell matched the faint odor she'd picked up at the first trap. Kelly held still, every muscle tense as she searched the woods carefully. This was dangerously close to her trailer. She'd hoped to take a scout by surprise, but could it be that her presence had been discovered? Was *she* now the hunted?

Concentrating, she sniffed around, specifically on the area that had been disturbed. There was nothing to reveal where the vampire had gone, or how long ago he'd passed through. The most telling thing she discovered was the lack of an aura. Whoever this was, he was a New, and most likely a scout.

A spy. A scout. Right near her trailer. How long had they been coming here? How long had they known about her? When did they plan to ambush her? To kill her? Damn. First she lost her method of feeding, and now this. What a night this turned out to be. Heading back toward her trailer, she once again thought through her options. She could leave. Take the twenty she had to her name, and a duffle bag of her scant belongings, and move in further from the border. Hope that her family didn't take exception to her move.

Kelly shook her head, willing the paranoia to go away. Jaq lived here too. If this scout had been watching her, the other woman would have known and most likely would have already taken his head off. No, this had to have been a coincidence. Or if not, the vampire had only just discovered her. She still had time, as long as she could catch him before he alerted his entire family.

He'd managed to get caught in a rat trap. She chuckled at the thought. The vampire had clearly lost his temper, too. No control at all. Idiot. She could take him. If she could catch him, that is, especially if she had Jaq the Mighty Werewolf by her side.

A twig snapped, and Kelly whirled about, jumping as she saw Jaq standing two feet behind her, arms crossed. Sheesh, that woman was quiet.

"Sheesh, you're deaf. A herd of elephants could have plowed you over and you wouldn't have noticed."

That was a gross exaggeration. Her hearing and all of her other senses were exceptional. She'd just been momentarily lost in thought, slightly panicked at the idea of an enemy vampire so near her home.

"Did you see this?" Kelly shoved the damaged trap at Jaq. The other woman took it, sniffing it before nodding.

"He was gone by the time I got here. I tracked him to the Virginia border, but he'd already crossed."

Even in the dark, Kelly could see Jaq was worried. "Do you think he knows I'm here?"

"If you could smell him, then he sure as heck could smell you. I'm just hoping with the snow, he wasn't able to pinpoint exactly where you've been staying, or if you're still here or not."

"Plus you said he went straight back to Virginia. Not toward Maryland like the others?"

Jaq nodded. "Fast too."

Kelly felt a twinge of panic. She should leave — move somewhere else in case the vampire came back with reinforcements, but then could her family find her to collect the information? She had no way of contacting them to let them know.

"You know, this guy's a bit of a moron getting himself caught in a rat trap," Jaq commented, turning the damaged piece of wood over in her hands. "I'm thinking we put something a bit bigger out here and we might catch him. It's easier to have him come to us than try and run him down across the state."

Kelly was doubtful. "I don't know. Unless you've got a bunch of silver weapons around, it's not likely to work. Box traps or snares, no matter how big or strong they are, aren't going to hold a vampire,."

Jaq grinned, pocketing the damaged trap. "Well, it's a good thing I'm not too attached to my jewelry then, is it?"

Kelly crawled out of bed in the late afternoon and showered to get ready for her first day of waitressing at Dale's, cursing Jaq under her breath the whole time. They'd both been out in the forest until past dawn setting up a variety of traps to hopefully injure and slow down any vampires approaching near the trailers. Kelly had been concerned the neighbors might get caught in them, but the other woman quickly assured her that no one but her or Mike entered the woods — and Mike would recognize the traps before he got close enough to set one off.

So now the vampire faced an evening of waitressing, followed by more trap setting and hunting enemy scouts. There'd been no time to iron the black skirt and pink-stained shirt, and her expensive shoes were a wreck. With any luck, this Dale guy would toss her out for improper clothing and she could spend the day doing something useful — something that would expedite her acceptance back into her family. Kelly frowned as she pulled on the skirt, a fresh wave of irritation at her friend washing over her. What was Jaq *thinking* getting this job for her? She had no time for this.

And the ever-present gnawing hunger deep inside was becoming insistent.

At least there was one good thing about this ridiculous job. She'd get tips. Hopefully enough for a bus fare somewhere where she could accost a human and take what she desperately needed without the neighborhood werewolf watch patrol being any wiser. Bus fare, a meal, and maybe some clothing that actually fit, as well as more appropriate footwear for her new, hopefully temporary, lifestyle.

Kelly looked at herself in the tiny bathroom mirror, smoothing the skirt and checking her hair. She was thinner than when she'd been in Atlantic City, and the skirt was in danger of spinning around her hips. She'd never been busty, but the shirt hung on her like she was an adolescent. People would begin to wonder if she kept losing weight in spite of the huge quantities of food she consumed. If things didn't change soon, that Melody woman would probably drag her off for an intervention, accuse her of having some eating disorder. Which she did, sort of.

At least her face and body had healed. Kelly opened her mouth and examined the spots where her fangs should have been. They were still empty sockets. It wasn't like she'd expected any different.

"Hurry up in there. You'll be late," Jaq called, rapping on the trailer door before barging in.

Kelly grumbled, glaring at the other woman as she walked right on into the bathroom. There was no privacy with anyone around here. She could have been taking a number two on the toilet and Melody would have no qualms about walking right on in and discussing a recipe for baked chicken. Jaq was just the same.

"I *am* hurrying." This was a good as she was going to get — blood-stained shirt, loose skirt, and shoes that were beginning to look like she'd stolen them off a hobo.

"Here." Jaq thrust a folded ten dollar bill into Kelly's hand. "Dale doesn't provide his staff with free meals, so you'll need lunch money. Well, supper money actually. It's too late for lunch, isn't it?"

Kelly stared down at the money, once again thinking how surreal the last few days had been. This conversation was no exception.

"I don't . . . I can pack something. Here, take this back."

She shouldn't care. Jaq and the humans had already given her so much that ten dollars shouldn't matter, but it bothered her. Jaq refused to take the money, waving Kelly's hands aside, and blocking them when she tried to put the folded bill in her pocket.

"Call it a loan, then. You can pay me back in a few weeks, or once you're back on your feet. It's no big deal."

The werewolf turned to leave, and Kelly chased after her, half running to keep up with Jaq's long stride.

"It *is* a big deal," she insisted. "I don't borrow money."

Jaq opened the door and turned to her with a grin. "You do now. Look, you'll need stuff like underwear and make-up. You wear make-up, don't you? You seem like the kind of girl who would wear make-up, but maybe vampires don't. And you definitely need underwear. Anyway, just let me know and I'll loan you more. Bank of Jaq, that's me."

Kelly's mouth dropped open and she stood like an idiot, ten dollar bill in her hand, staring at Jaq. Yes, she wore make-up sometimes. And underwear? She'd been commando after realizing that none of her loaner clothing included undergarments. How had Jaq known that?

"See you tonight after work," Jaq said, ruffling Kelly's hair before disappearing through the doorway.

Crazy. They were all crazy here. Kelly smoothed down her dark locks and pocketed the ten dollars. It was a loan. If she made anything in tips tonight, it would go to pay the werewolf back. There was no way she was going to be beholden to anybody.

* * *

DALE'S WAS a typical roadside tavern, heavy on the wood décor and beer signs. There was a pool table, a dart board off to the side, and thirty or so tables in addition to a bar that spanned half the width of the restaurant. The door chimed as she walked in, and the man she'd seen in the truck the first day looked up from behind the bar. He glanced at her from head to toe, frowning as if he was just as displeased by her presence as she was.

"There's a locker in back for your purse. Tomorrow you need black slacks. There are two Dales' t-shirts on the desk. If you need more than that, you gotta buy extras at twenty a piece."

Wow. What a welcome. Kelly had no purse but changed into one of the t-shirts, stuffing the other one and her stained blouse into one of the open lockers. So much for hunting tonight. She was going to have to squeeze in a late-night bus trip to a Walmart for black pants. Fingering the ten Jaq had given her, Kelly frowned. The twenty she had back at the trailer plus any tips she earned should be enough for the bus fare and one pair of pants. Hopefully. Otherwise, there went her vow to pay Jaq back this evening.

Shutting the locker, Kelly walked out, perplexed to see that she and the man were the only ones still there. Where were the other wait staff? The bartender? The cook, for crying out loud? She'd always insisted on promptness from her employees. What was with these werewolves?

The man ignored her and flipped a page on the catalogue. Should she ask him if he was Dale? Or would that make her look even more like an idiot? Shrugging, Kelly walked over and began grabbing ketchup bottles from a shelf under the bar, lining them up on top. A bit of searching revealed an industrial-sized jug of ketchup on a wire rack in the kitchen. Kelly flicked on the grills to warm as she went by and began filling the ketchup containers, wiping them carefully with a clean rag.

"What do ya think you're doing?" The man asked gruffly, his eyes never leaving the catalog.

"Getting ready to open. I assume you're Dale. Thank you for giving me a job here." He *had* taken a chance on her — a vampire of all things in a werewolf establishment. Plush she had no references, no verifiable job experience, nothing beyond Jaq's recommendation. It was more than Kelly would have done, which made her wonder about how much pull Jaq actually had around here.

Dale grunted. He was a big beefy guy with a red nose and balding head. Kelly bet his cheeks shook when he laughed, although from the look of him right now, she wondered if he ever cracked a smile.

"You looking at new grills?" Kelly asked, leaning over to see the catalog as she lined the saltshakers up on the bar to fill. She knew she was annoying her new boss, but couldn't help it. The werewolf's surly silence just begged for idle chit chat.

Dale made a noise somewhere between a laugh and a snort. "Wish I could afford a new grill. I'm looking at security cameras, although those seem to be out of my price range too. Chip down the road just put some in yesterday after that that guy got sliced up in his parking lot. He'll get a bad reputation with those kinds of fights going on.

Kelly knocked over a salt shaker, catching it in a rush of speed before it hit the floor. Well, there went any further opportunity for her to grab another human outside the strip club. She'd not even thought to look for security cameras. If she wasn't more careful, she'd be exposed.

Although she might already have been. Had Jaq reported her activity at the strip club to the rest of her pack? Was that what was behind Dale's comment on the security cameras. She wiped up the spilled salt, and eyed him suspiciously.

Dale had raised his eyebrows at her lightning-quick grab at the saltshaker and scowled. "Luckily the guy lived. Funny that. Broken bottle and a whole lot of blood, but he seemed fine outside a few shallow cuts. And the blood was all his, too. Couldn't remember a thing beyond some prostitute accosting him outside of his car."

Kelly carefully controlled her breathing and continued filling the shakers. She felt Dale's eyes on her, saw him close the catalog and roll it, tapping it lightly on the bar as he turned to face her.

"I don't like you being here one bit," he growled. "Jaq should have killed you the moment she saw you. I got no idea why she's helping you out like this, but out of respect for her, I'll go along with it. Just know that if you lay one fang, one broken bottle, on anyone within a hundred miles, I'll know it. And I'll kill you myself."

Kelly steadied her hand as she screwed on the tops of the shakers. Werewolves seemed to be a pretty violent bunch if Dale was any example. Besides Jaq, they were all just waiting for her to make one wrong move so they could kill her. Kelly got the feeling she was in far more danger from them then any Kincaid scout. She could probably take Dale, but how many others were there? Jaq had said over a thousand, and Kelly began to think she hadn't been exaggerating. One vampire would never be able to wade through a mob of determined, pissed-off werewolves. They'd easily overpower her. She had to make things right with her family and get the heck out of here before she wound up dead one way or another.

"Yes, Sir." It seemed the right thing to say. The only thing to say.

The door chimed again, breaking the tension as three women walked in — all werewolves. Great — as if working with one wasn't bad enough. The real icing on the cake would be if all the patrons were werewolves too. There would go any tips. She'd be lucky if she finished her shift alive.

Dale stalked off to the back without introducing her. Kelly stared at three sets of surprised eyes that traveled from her face to the saltshakers and back.

"Hi I'm Kelly . . . the new waitress."

There was a thick, tense silence as the three women stared at her. This was going to be the worst job ever. She'd take that jerk Stephen and the malicious Pierre any day over this.

"Nan's the cook. Elaine and Jen — bartender and waitress."

Kelly nodded and the others finally turned from her to begin their opening routine. "I turned the grill on for you," she told Nan as the woman shouldered by her.

"Overachiever," she snarled back. "Stay outta my kitchen."

It was going to be a long evening.

Kelly watched Elaine and Jen, and they, in turn, scowled at her and wrinkled their noses, occasionally whispering together. Finally Kelly had enough. "Look, what is wrong with you people? Did I take someone else's job or something?"

Elaine stalked over to her, towering over the tiny vampire. Kelly fantasized about putting her fist through the woman's face. She might be small, but she was still a vampire.

Of course, if she did that, the other three would beat her to a pulp before she managed five steps toward the door.

"You better not bite any of the customers, or I'll rip your fangs out."

"Too late," Kelly responded, opening wide to show the gaping holes. She was furious. Stupid fricken werewolves. It's not like she wanted this job. It's not like she even wanted to be in the same state as them.

Elaine's fierce expression turned to one of horror. "Saint's alive. Did Jaq do that to keep us safe from you? Why didn't she just kill you instead?"

Jaq? How in the world could they have thought Jaq would have done that to her? "*No!* I was punished by my family and exiled here."

"Jen, come here and look at this! Your own people did this to you? You guys *are* a bunch of bloodthirsty monsters. What did you do? Did you fight back? How do you suck blood? Will they grow back, or can you get fake ones?"

This wasn't much better than when they were threatening her. She'd turned into some kind of vampire freak show. Kelly avoided the questions about her feeding and decided to steer them towards the questions less likely to get her killed or arrested.

"I lost my temper and yelled at a prominent guest in public."

Jen sucked in a breath. "And they did this? Wow, I wouldn't have made it two days as a vampire."

"Was it another vampire you yelled at?" Elaine asked excitedly. "Did she challenge you? Did you beat the snot out of her?"

"No it was a demon."

That brought a look of respect to both the women's faces.

"Did you kill the demon?" Elaine asked. "I've never seen

one, but I've heard they're vile. I can't imagine one of them letting you live after you offended it."

"She wasn't mad. Actually she thought the whole thing was funny. But we have rules, and I broke them. We need the demons, need their favors and their alliance. My behavior could have damaged that alliance, so they made an example of me."

Jen made a sympathetic clucking noise. "This is an awful sorta punishment. If they was any sort of civilized, they would have just killed you."

"I won't be here long. Jaq's helping me and soon I'll be back in Atlantic City with my family."

The two women exchanged skeptical looks. "Girlfriend, people that do this sort of thing don't welcome you back with open arms. Better find a new family."

Girlfriend. That was a big change from five minutes ago. "It doesn't work like that. When you change families, you start at the bottom, and you're always regarded as an outsider. This is how things work in vampire societies. They'll let me back in."

She hoped. Part of her was beginning to think what the women were saying had a higher probability of truth. But the faint hope of redemption was better than imagining a short, painful life in exile.

Customers started coming in at that point, and they all hustled to get ready for the dinner rush. Kelly lost herself in the familiar routine of work. She hadn't realized how much she missed the casino, the satisfaction in organizing everything so it all fell together like pieces of a puzzle. This wasn't so bad, and for a few moments she indulged in a daydream that it could last forever. Tolerated, if not welcomed by the werewolves, comforting and familiar work, and a magical supply of blood that would sustain her without getting her killed by her furry hosts — it was such a pleasant fantasy.

CHAPTER 18

Midnight came quickly. Kelly counted out the fifteen dollars in tips as she walked home then stuffed it into her pocket with the two phone numbers written on napkins. Jen and Elaine had gotten nervous as the men slipped her the phone numbers, once again threatening her with bodily harm if she dared lay a hand on any of the locals. Not that they had anything to worry about. Between Jaq and Dale, there was no way she'd be able to feed on any human within a ten mile radius, and the very idea of dating one was revolting. She'd had quite a dry spell with her long hours at the casino and the odd interplay of status in vampire relationships, but she was hardly desperate enough to consider even a fling with a human. Don't date your food — it was an unspoken rule among vampires. Even so, she'd pocked the numbers with a wink, just to annoy Elaine and Jen.

Jaq was waiting for her on the steps to the trailer, and Kelly felt her temper flare once again.

"That place is crawling with werewolves. Everyone there is a hair's width from ripping my heart out with their claws.

How many werewolves have you run your mouth to? Do you realize what a danger this is for me? They've already made it clear they don't like me, and threatened to harm me if I so much as look at a customer wrong."

Jaq stood, towering over the vampire. "I had to tell them, you idiot. Besides, you might as well have a sign on your forehead announcing you're a vampire. Anyone a hundred yards downwind could tell."

Kelly gaped. This was worse than she'd thought. *Over a thousand* Jaq had said before. The idea made her shiver. "How many are there in the trailer park? Did you tell the humans too? Melody and Joe? Barbara? Margaret and Shanna?"

Jaq waved an irritated hand in front of her. "No, I haven't told the humans. Of course they don't know. Just the pack. Mike and I are the only werewolves on Briar Lane, but there are a few hundred around Ranson and Charles Town. More once you get up towards Martinsburg."

Kelly suddenly felt dizzy, and for once it had nothing to do with her slow starvation. How in the world was she ever going to feed from a human again? Everywhere she went, she was in danger of coming across a werewolf — and they all knew. They'd all be watching for her, scenting the air. Her plans to take a bus into Charles Town derailed. She'd slowly starve, and there was nothing she could do about it. "Were-wolves," she said slowly, as if she couldn't quite believe it. "I'm surrounded by werewolves."

Jaq scowled. "Well, yeah. I told you there were a couple thousand of us here. Did you think I was lying?"

Yes, she had. Or at the very least exaggerating to make it seem to Kelly that she would be up against a formidable army. She'd never truly believed there were that many of them in the state.

"Crap." She needed to get out of here. It was bad enough when she'd thought she was exiled among a bunch of humans and a handful of werewolves, but now she was surrounded by enemies. Kincaid to the south, and now a couple thousand of these predators whose territory she'd invaded.

"Tell me about it," Jaq muttered cryptically. "You're fine. Really. No one will mess with you as long as you don't go attacking any humans. Or werewolves."

The gnawing in Kelly's middle grew more insistent at Jaq's words. How would she survive? She had to get out of here. Get back to her family and home.

"Come on then." Jaq motioned with one hand toward the woods. "Let's go check your traps and see if we can pick up any scents. If we move quick enough, we may be able to cover a good bit of territory before dawn."

Kelly threw up her hands in frustration. She didn't have enough strength to go racing all over the countryside, and no matter what was in those traps, nothing was going to help at this point.

"I can't. I need to find a bus into town and go buy pants for this stupid job. My priority should be finding and interrogating a Kincaid scout so my family will reinstate me and get me out of this hellhole, but no. Instead, I have to go buy a pair of black pants for a job I'll have all of a week max."

"Are all vampires this ungrateful?" Jaq snarled. "I help you when you're dying in a trailer, dumped by this so-called family who you're so desperate to get back to. I bust my tail bringing you food, protecting you from the local pack-members. I give you information on other vampires, help you set traps, offer to help you track and catch one. I get you a job. This is the thanks I get?"

She was right, and Kelly felt guilty, but she also felt hungry and at the end of her rope. "Thank you, I really *do* appreciate all you've done for me, but I don't need a job. It's wasting my time and I'll be home in a few weeks."

"You'll be lucky if you're not dead in a few weeks," Jaq shouted. "Stupid fool. Do you really think they'll take you back? They ripped out your fangs, beat you worse than I've ever seen and left you for dead in that trailer. They're using you, and if you don't get killed by that rival vampire group, they'll finish you off themselves."

Kelly felt tears sting her eyes. All she could do was shake her head. It was true, but she just couldn't face the alternative.

"I got you the job because I want you to stay." Jaq's voice turned soft, with an edge of hurt in it. "Forget the vampires. You can have a home here, with us."

Kelly choked on a sob. "With werewolves? With humans?" That wasn't home; it was a kind of hell. She'd go crazy. Vampires didn't live outside their family units. Ever.

Jaq winced. "Yes. It's that or death, and I'd hoped you'd find us preferable to dying."

Kelly gaped, unable to come up with any response. Couldn't Jaq understand that life here *would* be death? Forbidden from feeding from the humans? Starvation would kill her long before the insanity of loneliness set in.

Jaq made a frustrated noise. "Fine. Go have fun at Walmart buying pants. Or quit the job and go hunt vampires on your own. I don't care anymore."

The blond woman spun about and stalked off down the lane as Kelly watched after her, feeling like she'd just made yet another in a long line of terrible decisions.

CHAPTER 19

Kelly looked at the set of darts on the table before her. She'd gone on a shoplifting spree at Walmart once she'd realized how little forty-five dollars actually bought her. There was still a twenty under her mattress that she'd managed to keep, but the rest was spent — including the ten that Jaq had "loaned" her. Shame reddened her cheeks, and Kelly bit her lip. She'd pay the werewolf back soon. If she ever saw her again. Their argument gnawed at her insides just as painfully as her hunger, but she couldn't think about that now. She had too much to do.

Jaq's traps, carefully placed in the woods and around the trailer, would serve as an early warning system, but Kelly was far too weak to fight vampires in any kind of hand-to-hand combat. It was time to create some weapons.

Covering her hand with a washcloth, she took the silver chains Jaq had brought over the night before and cut the links into small bits. With a pair of tweezers, Kelly carefully placed a bit of the silver on the tip of the dart and melted it in place with a crème brulee torch she'd borrowed from

Melody. Why Melody had a crème brulee torch, she had no idea. The human seemed more like a cake and pie person. Kelly didn't even think the woman had the foggiest idea how to make the custard, let alone caramelize the sugar on top. Not that she had any room to criticize. Even a box cake would be beyond *her* skills.

In a few hours, she'd covered the metal of the darts with a thin coating of silver. It wouldn't kill a vampire, but it would hurt like crazy and give her the few seconds she'd need to rush in and finish him or her off.

Vampires weren't as hard to kill as legend said. Yes, they could re-grow limbs and organs given enough time, and could heal an amazing amount of damage. Remove their head, destroy or remove their heart, slice them into little bits, blow them up or burn them sufficiently, though, and they'd be dead. Even a fall from a great height, like from an airplane, would most likely kill them. Slicing them in half worked. The key was to inflict such massive damage that their body couldn't cope.

Silver helped as it burned, and the pain it caused distracted a vampire enough to gain an edge over him. Everything else would work only if you were fast enough and strong enough to reduce them to small chunks before they could kill you. With modern technology, even a human could kill a vampire. In fact, a human mob could take one out with axes and guns as long as the vampire didn't escape and run for safety. And Kelly was pretty sure werewolves could kill them too. She thought of Jaq with a twinge of guilt then shook her head. No. She'd apologize later. Right now, she had work to do.

Finished with darts, Kelly eyed the remaining bits of silver. Inspired, she took out the large metal washers and melted silver onto the rims. It was tricky work, and the silver slopped over onto the sides of the washers. She'd need to either use a slingshot, or be very careful if she pitched them with her hands so as to not burn her fingertips. Looking out the window, she eyed the rising sun. She could catch a few hours of sleep and check the traps before donning her new black pants and heading to Dale's, or she could just get it out of the way now.

Kelly was dragging, but it was better to push on and sleep later. She hadn't had a decent amount of human blood since the incident at the strip joint. The feeling of deprivation was starting to become familiar, even manageable, as if she could carry on at the edge of starvation forever. Shaking her head, she gathered her supplies and headed into the woods. She'd just need to push on and hope some caffeine during her shift at Dale's would help her make it through the night.

Kelly surveyed each trap. They were all empty.

On one of the paths, Jaq had constructed a drag noose and used sticks to create a fence that would hopefully channel her prey into the noose. They'd attached small wire nooses at short intervals along its length. Jaq had called it a squirrel pole, but there were no dangling, hanged squirrels ready for consumption.

Kelly also checked the deadfall trap before heading back to her trailer and crawling into bed. Nothing.

No human blood, and the prospect of any in the near future was bleak. No fresh animal blood, either. Kelly just couldn't face any more of the old cow blood Jaq had stuffed into her fridge. With her head throbbing and hands shaking, she shivered in her blankets and slept fitfully until it was time to get ready for her new job.

* * *

"YOU LOOK LIKE SHIT," Dale told her as she walked through

the door. It chimed merrily, causing Kelly to rub her head. "You got that stomach thing going around?"

"Insomnia," she told him. "I didn't sleep at all last night."

With a dozen cups of coffee, she managed to make it through the night, depleting her meager tips to buy a rare burger to eat on her way home. There was no Jaq on her doorstep, nothing inside her trailer to indicate the woman had been there at all since she'd last seen her.

She practically cried with relief when she saw a small groundhog caught in one of her traps. Slicing its throat, she drank, being careful not to spill any of the precious blood. It didn't do any good. She was just too far gone for animal blood. A wave of depression crashed over her. Was this going to be the last night of her life? Even if she managed to find a way to get a small bit of human blood before dawn, this was the future she faced. Existing day to day, always worried about where her next meal would come from, and getting the majority of her blood from animals. Living in exile away from other vampires, trying to fit into a human world and surrounded by werewolves. Kelly imagined decades of this existence, centuries actually, and thought again about the fillet knife. Was there any joy, any satisfaction in this kind of life? Maybe Jaq and the others were wrong. Maybe her family would send for her. Maybe they would eventually take her back if she proved useful.

Shaking her head, she walked back to her trailer. She was so exhausted. And hungry, and depressed. It was still early, but if she went to sleep now, it might help her mood.

As soon as she approached the trailer, she realized that sleep would need to wait. A vampire was inside. A vampire with an aura. Drat. Rube was here. Here for information she didn't have. Kelly hesitated. Would he kill her? Give her more time? Either way, she had to find out.

The aura grew stronger as she neared her front door. The

asshole was back. Let's hope this time he brought some blood.

She walked inside and instinctively assumed a respectful position. It was like forcing rusty bolts to turn to lower her head and place her hands behind her when she really wanted to rip his head off. Not that she could even open a jar of pickles at this point.

"Hello, Kelly," Rube said. His tone seemed uninterested, as if he'd had a chance encounter with her on the street. "Everyone is quite surprised you're still alive, myself included. Not that I'm particularly displeased about it. You've won me quite a bit of money with your dogged survival."

Well at least he wasn't planning on killing her in a fit of pique for having lost a bet.

"Personally, if you were to croak in three days, I'd be a rich man, but it's not up to me. Boss wants to see if you can still be of value to us or not. Let's see what you can do."

Rube reached in the pocket of his black cashmere coat and pulled out a bag. It was full of blood. Kelly's eyes shot to it, and her mouth watered. Struggling, she pulled her eyes away and tried to keep from trembling with desire. He was either intending on teasing her with the food only to deny her, or she would need to earn it in some way. Either scenario sucked. And either way, she wasn't about to let him see how much she wanted the contents of that bag. As if sensing her inner struggle, the vampire squeezed and rolled the bag in his hand, molding it in an almost sensuous way. She fought to keep her eyes averted and swallowed heavily.

"Been eating any more bunnies?" His tone relayed amusement and disgust, as if he were enjoying a particularly gruesome horror movie with her in the leading role. She felt her temper snap to the surface.

"You should try them sometime; they're quite good."

Her reply was beyond rude, and she regretted it the

moment it left her mouth. They were hardly going to think she'd learned her lesson and bring her back into the fold if she continued to act like this. Maybe it was the hunger and lack of sleep fueling her recklessness. *Or maybe I've just had enough of being jerked around by these entitled assholes*, she thought.

His aura flared. It felt like a whip across her.

"Watch your tone," he warned.

A few moments passed while he continued to tempt her with the bag of blood.

"What additional information do you have for me?" he finally asked. "The Master was pleased with your information on the movements of scouts probing our borders, but now I need more. Did you find and interrogate one of their scouts as requested?"

"There was one a few nights ago, but he was across the border before I could capture him." Well, before Jaq could catch him. Still, it sounded like she was at least making progress.

Rube made a tsk noise. "You must not fail, Kelly. You do understand what's at stake here?"

She nodded, although she wasn't sure if he was referring to the family or her own personal future. Although in her particular situation, they were kind of one and the same.

"The Master would also like you to gather information on Kincaid strongholds over the border in Virginia, as well as the names of any spies they've placed in our territory. Probe the border and find out." He rolled the bag of blood between his palms. The red of it caught in the moonlight, and she couldn't help but glance longingly at the bag. How could she possibly do what he asked? Kelly felt like that woman in the fairy tale, commanded to spin wheat into gold. Where was Rumplestiltskin when she needed him?

"I'm a casino manager," she said, unable to keep the frustration from her voice. "Not James Bond. Surely you have someone more qualified than me to do your spy work, or does this particular job require a defanged vampire skilled in eating rabbits?"

She found herself instantly pinned against the fridge, his hand gripping her jaw, and his aura a flame against her skin.

"You are very insolent for someone on the verge of starving to death," he snarled. "You should be begging me for a way to prove your value, to show me a good reason we should bring you back into the family."

His words were like a cold splash of sanity on her pride.

"Please, Sir. I do want a way I can earn your trust again. But I'm not skilled to do this. I can't do this task," she said, hating the desperation in her voice.

"Then perhaps you should learn some skills. You're a smart girl." His fingers tightened again on her jaw, and he smacked her head against the refrigerator door. "I suggest you consider how you can perform this task while hunger eats at your sanity."

Letting her go, he tore open the bag of blood and poured it down the sink drain, rinsing the basin then leaving the trailer.

She knew better than to check the sink for any stray blood, but she did anyway, climbing onto the counter and licking the stainless steel. After she'd covered every inch, she wept and curled up on the counter in a shaking ball. If anything, the few tastes she'd gotten had made her hunger worse. Muscles cramped deep inside her body, desperate for more.

Finally she wiped her eyes and climbed down, holding the edge of the countertop for support as a dizzy spell hit hard. This was the worst she'd ever been. Even if a human walked through her door right now she doubted she could catch him. Would she wake up in the morning? Maybe that was for the best; a peaceful passing in her sleep as opposed to thrashing on the floor as her body attempted to devour itself.

Shaking from hunger, Kelly walked to the back of the trailer and collapsed into her bed fully clothed. The Master was insane. He couldn't possibly want her to spy, to capture and interrogate other vampires. That was like telling a baker he needed to sail a ship across the ocean. What in the world gave him the idea she could do this? She'd be killed instantly. She wasn't a warrior, wasn't a fighter — she was a casino manager! And by denying her even that small packet of blood, Rube had pretty much ensured she wouldn't live long enough to do as he asked.

Maybe that's what he wants, Kelly thought as she drifted to sleep.

* * *

BIRDS SANG OUTSIDE HER WINDOW, and light pouring through a gap in the cardboard window coverings, hitting Kelly right in the eye. For a moment, she thought she was dead and this was the proverbial light at the end of the tunnel, but the severe cramping in her legs and arms told her otherwise. Besides, there probably weren't birds in heaven, or itchy polyester comforters. Blinking in the sunlight, Kelly heard her door slam and groaned. It had to be her neighborhood alarm clock. Or maybe Jaq?

The thought got her to climb out of bed, only to have her hopes dashed as she heard Melody's cheerful greeting. Kelly staggered into the main room of the trailer to see her neighbor sliding a plate of muffins onto her kitchen counter. This time, however, Melody had brought most of the neigh-borhood with her. Four women were crammed in her little trailer, all looking at her with resolute faces.

"What?" Kelly asked with trepidation. Had the humans

discovered there was a vampire in their midst? That she was devouring cute woodland animals and had attacked a guy at a strip club? It was bad enough that she was surrounded by werewolves that wanted her dead without the humans joining in too.

"We're here for an intervention," Melody told her, taking Kelly firmly by the shoulders and pushing her down onto the couch.

Kelly looked around at their faces. Barbara still had on her nurse uniform from her graveyard shift. Shanna yawned and ran a hand through her sleep-rumpled hair. Margaret looked longingly at the empty coffee pot. Melody stood before her, arms crossed and a determined look on her face. They didn't look like a lynch mob, but that word 'intervention' was disturbing.

"We know he was here," Margaret accused, before succumbing to her need and starting a pot of coffee. "Did he try and convince you to come back home? Tell you he was sorry and beg you to come back?"

"Did he threaten you?" Barbara asked sympathetically. "Is he going to keep all the money from you? Hurt your family if you don't come back?"

Oh no. They'd seen Rube. And they were under the crazy idea that he was her abusive ex-boyfriend. Immediately, Kelly's thoughts turned to Jaq. Had she seen too? She must have. What did Jaq think of her? Just one more thing to drive a wedge between them. Kelly hadn't even had a chance to apologize and make things right, and now this.

"He was pretty hot," Shanna admitted. "Did you see the coat he had on? That thing probably cost more than every trailer here combined. He can't be that bad. I'd go back to him."

"Shanna!" everyone shrieked, glaring at the young woman.

"You are not going back to him," Melody commanded, her eyes fierce. "Over my dead body will I let that man drag you off. I don't care how hot he is, or how sorry he says he is, he's going to kill you."

Yes. He probably was.

"He's not my boyfriend," Kelly said, desperately trying to think of something. "He's a family member. He just came by to check on me."

Melody made a disapproving clucking noise. "Sweetie, Barbara saw him smack you around. She saw him push you up against the fridge and threaten you."

Kelly frowned at Barbara, who was studiously ignoring her and helping fill the coffee maker. The woman had been peering through her windows! Everyone in this state was downright insane, humans and werewolves alike.

"Don't you blame Barbara," Melody scolded. "I made her look in the window and tell us. No way I could get my round butt up there to see what was going on."

Melody could be very forceful, Kelly thought. She would be a difficult person to say no to.

"That man is not welcome here," Melody insisted. Kelly had never heard her sound so determined. "We are your family now. And we are not going to let him hurt you ever again."

We are your family now. Hadn't Jaq said something similar? The whole idea was absurd. Werewolves, humans, they were crazy. Kelly looked around. The women all smiled warmly at her. Barbara nodded, and Margaret handed her a cup of coffee.

"Well," Melody said cheerfully. "Now that that is decided, let's all have some coffee and those muffins I brought."

Everyone bustled about, chatting cheerfully and serving up coffee and muffins. Kelly sat on her sofa, numbly holding her coffee cup. She'd been adopted by a bunch of humans.

They considered her family. What would they think if they really knew what she was? Oddly, she was beginning to like the safety of their care, actually enjoy their friendship, but they'd never be her family. These humans would cast her out, try to kill her, if they knew. No one wanted someone in their family who was liable to grab them and drink their blood, who was likely to kill them. She didn't belong here. She needed to find a way to do this thing her family wanted and get back with her own people where she truly belonged.

CHAPTER 20

*K*yle spread a map out on the shipping table. It was late. Only he and Juan were in the warehouse. Still, every noise, every disturbance in the air set him on edge. This was treason. He may be a Born but it wouldn't matter much if he were caught. He doubted his father would be lenient on his only son for what he was about to do.

"We snatch West Virginia from the werewolves, no one will even notice that, then we make our move."

Juan curled his lip, leaning forward to see the map. "I hate those things. The whole state smells like them, even the humans. It will take us centuries to get rid of the stink."

"I really don't care what it smells like. There's enough industry there to give us a steady inflow of cash. It's a perfect launching pad for our next move, especially since neither my father nor Kincaid will even notice we've taken the state. When we proceed with our next phase, no one will suspect a thing."

"And then?" Juan's voice held a barely suppressed note of excitement. Kyle smiled. Second to a Prince was one thing, second to a Master another. He could completely count on

Juan's support and discretion, as long as the odds were in his favor.

"Here and here," Kyle indicated to the other vampire. "Southern Pennsylvania just waits for our word and they're ours, western and southern Maryland too. Baltimore will be a fight, but we can grab it if we hold off until Durand is out of town. DC and the Maryland suburbs are going to be difficult. I'll have to wait until the last moment to decide on them; they could go either way."

"How about here," Juan asked, pointing to the cluster of counties around the city of Frederick.

"I'm not going head-to-head with a demon, especially that one. Those lands are off limits."

Juan nodded. "And the Kincaid territories?"

"I need to have a base before I can move on them," Kyle said. "I'll have to hit them right away, though, because once I grab our lower states, not only will Kincaid know I'm on my way, but my father will be coming down on me like a hammer. He'll back off if I have Kincaid's territory. If not, we're in for a big fight."

A losing fight, Kyle thought grimly. He could just go for Kincaid's territory from West Virginia, and that was still an alternate plan in his arsenal, but the southern section of his own territory would give him might and much needed financial resources. With those states, the Kincaid lands would fall quickly to him, without and he'd be facing a bloody few years. Kyle wasn't averse to getting his hands dirty, but if a clean and quick surgical strike would do the job, why try to bludgeon his way through the southeast?

"When?" Juan asked.

"That's the million-dollar question," Kyle mused. "If I'm not back in New York next week, my father will begin to suspect something. Two weeks and he'll send a crew to drag me back by my hair. I'm thinking we take West Virginia now, while I'm still here, and wait on the rest for a couple of years while I work things from up in New York."

"I can have everyone on the border ready to move on the werewolves in two nights. We should have them all cleaned out by sunrise."

"Good," Kyle said, folding the map. "Do it."

* * *

KELLY KNOCKED on Melody's door, hesitant to walk right in. Everyone else did. She wasn't sure how they avoided walking in on a private moment, or a spouse walking around naked. She shuddered at the thought. Ick.

"Come in, dear!" Melody called. "Do you need to borrow something?"

"Yes," Kelly said walking into the trailer. "Can I use your computer for a few hours? I need to look some stuff up over the Internet."

"Of course," Melody said, pouring her a cup of coffee from the pot that seemed to be full and fresh twenty-four hours a day. "I'm heading in to work, but you can stay and use the computer as much as you like."

"Are you sure?" She felt awkward being in the woman's home while she was gone. "I can always come back later."

If she wasn't dead later. Her legs had not stopped cramping on the way over, and she had nearly fallen walking through the door. Hopefully she wouldn't die face down on Melody's computer.

"No, no. You go right ahead. Are you okay, sweetie? You look really sick. Do you have that flu that's going around?"

"Yes. The flu," Kelly assured her.

Melody looked alarmed, backing up somewhat. "Oh, you poor thing! Let me get you something to take. Be sure to use the hand wipes too. I've got some here in the kitchen and some beside the computer."

"I'm fine, really," she assured the woman. "I'll make sure I wipe down the computer before I leave. I won't be here long; I promise."

Within minutes, Kelly was alone, a packet of cold medicine in one hand and hand sanitizer in the other. It felt good to be sitting in front of a computer again, even if she was in a trailer surrounded by colorful knitting projects and plates of cookies.

Opening a browser window, Kelly quickly began navigating through companies in Virginia. Not all vampires knew the markers, but she'd managed the Casino, the drug trade, and several other businesses for the family and had picked up on the identifiers. The Kincaid ones would be different, but would follow the same patterns as her family's.

Within an hour, she had over five hundred businesses identified and their information pasted onto a spreadsheet. She printed the information out then unfolded a map of Virginia she'd picked up from the tourist-information shelf at Dale's. Grabbing one of Melody's highlighters, she began to note the concentrations of Kincaid businesses throughout the state and wasn't surprised to see most of them clustered around the northern section, near the DC area. There. That and the list should help her gain favor with her family, and all from the safety of a trailer in West Virginia. There's no need for any of them to know she didn't gain this knowledge from dangerous scouting missions or capturing and interrogating the enemy.

Kelly was just about to get up and leave, when, on a whim, she began to scan West Virginia, focusing on the casino in Charles Town. *Oakwood Entertainment Enterprises expands their gambling division by acquiring a controlling interest in local racetrack and casino.*

Oakwood. That was one of the Master's companies. That vampire Jaq had interrogated had been telling the truth after all. She clicked on the article and read through it. The heading was a bit deceptive. Oakwood had about ten percent of the shares and had been making a bid to buy more, but they'd been rebuffed. Instead, they were continuing to buy from individual investors in a long-term hostile takeover move. Typical business, but why would the Master suddenly be interested in West Virginia?

Kelly continued searching, noticing lots of businesses on the verge of acquisition by corporations she recognized. Industrial complexes, manufacturing, energy industry, along with some large medical centers. Plus there appeared to be a good-sized drug market from the newspaper articles and arrest reports. Nothing huge, but still some profitable investments for any vampire family that managed to toss out the werewolves. Of course, nothing here would be worth the bloodshed that kind of war would cause.

Kelly frowned in concentration. Oakwood. Kings Green, Snyder and Sons, Marwick Incorporated — they were all Fournier companies, but they were all companies under the management of the Prince. The Master was always careful to spread acquisition activity around to keep his powerful elite from gaining too much of the pie. Doing so fostered ugly competition, and vampires fighting each other and jockeying for position were unlikely to be trying to stick a knife in their Master's back. So why the sudden change in a strategy that had worked for thousands of years? According to the rumors, the Prince was beginning to be a threat — why make him even more of one by basically giving him West Virginia?

Of course there would be that pesky little problem of the werewolves. Not that vampires had ever considered werewolves to be a problem. In spite of whatever contract they'd signed centuries ago, none of her family would bat an eye at killing them all and snatching the state if they thought it had any value. So why, after centuries of being a worthless buffer zone, would the Prince suddenly take interest in West Virginia? He'd be the weakest Master on the continent if he thought to rule over only West Virginia. No, there had to be some other significance to the state, some other reason to risk aggravating over a thousand werewolves and ejecting them from their homes. Unless her family didn't realize how many were here, or how strong they really were. It wasn't improbable. Vampires regarded every other species on the planet as a speck of dirt on their shoe. Wipe them off and move on.

Perplexed, Kelly made note of the companies and printed out a list of targeted businesses. While she was here, she might as well continue her search to any Maryland and Pennsylvania companies along the West Virginia border.

Oakwood. Kings Green, Snyder and Sons, Marwick Incorporated. What the heck? She knew those areas were managed by the Prince, but why would they all be held by the same shell corporation? Oakwood alone had enough revenue to support a family on its own. What was the Master's son up to? Clearly there was more on his mind than a raid on Kincaid lands. Was he possibly foolish enough to attempt to seize territory from his own father?

Kelly carefully noted them down and printed out the information, deciding to keep this bit of data to herself. She was trading in information with her own family, but there might come a day when she'd need to barter with someone else — either the Kincaids or the werewolves.

Glancing up at the clock, she realized that she had plenty of time before her shift began at Dale's. With some trepidation, she typed in the web address of a bank in New Jersey and stared at the login screen. Had they found the money?

Probably not. If they'd been able to trace it to her, she'd be dead. What if they were just monitoring the account, waiting for someone to access it so they could determine who the culprit was? If she transferred it to a West Virginia account, it would leave the equivalent of a big neon flashing paper trail.

She needed that money. Jaq's cooperation had ended with their argument; her family was probably as likely to kill her as the Kincaids were, and the werewolves would be happy to see her decapitated at the bottom of a ditch. This money could buy her safety. She'd heard the Rochelle family in Vegas was open to refugees if they saw an advantage to taking them in. As an outsider, she'd always be at the bottom of their hierarchy, but the money could guarantee that another family would at least bring her in and protect her.

She'd not planned on accessing it for a few-hundred years — enough time to move it around in various accounts and hide the transactions. Hundreds of years was no longer a viable plan. If she didn't dig herself out of this hole, she'd be lucky to see tomorrow's sunrise. Money would make everything easier.

Her finger hovered over the enter key, wanting to just check and see if the money was still even in the account. Could they trace the IP address? If it led back to Melody, they'd know it was her. She was the only vampire in West Virginia.

If they found out, any faint chance she had of being accepted back into the family would be gone. Better to wait than ruin her slim chance of ending this exile. Sighing, she closed the web browser and headed back to her trailer to change for her shift.

CHAPTER 21

The tall vampire seemed bored as he leaned against the tree by the fence line. Kelly saw him check his phone twice, sending brief text messages before snapping it shut with a click and looking around impatiently.

"Come on Wes," he muttered under his breath.

They were only about a mile from Kelly's trailer as the crow flies. She had snuck through the woods behind the trailer park, carefully avoiding Jaq's traps, and skirted the hedgerows and fences to this spot. The trees were bare, leaving only the briar bushes to use as cover. The heavy carpet of dry, brown leaves on the ground seemed to amplify each step.

It had been slow going. Agonizing muscle cramps had tapered into an occasional spasm before disappearing as she left Dale's. Their absence worried her. Was this some final stage? Nothing hurt, but she did feel oddly lightheaded. The temperature had dropped dramatically in the last few hours, and she shivered. It was below freezing, but she shouldn't be so chilled. She hadn't felt the cold this keenly since she'd been human.

Dropping to a crouch, Kelly used rotted deadfall as cover and edged closer to the vampire. One. There was only this one, and hopefully the guy he was supposed to meet would be coming alone. That was one more than she wanted to face solo. If only Jaq were here. Sniffing the air, she tried to scent the werewolf, and once again came up empty. There were no werewolves within a mile. No humans either. In this weather, she would have been able to tell. The cold, sharp air brought every scent to Kelly's nose, and when she'd first caught the faint whiff of vampire, she was positive it was no mistake.

She'd been right to trust her nose. The scent had grown stronger as she'd worked her way through the woods. It was unmistakable now that she stood downwind next to the field.

The vampire paced back and forth at the edge of a small wooded area between two fields, freshly sowed with cover crops for the winter. This guy was clearly a Kincaid scout. He had a faint aura, putting him at fifty to a hundred years older than Kelly. That was information she could give her family.

Maybe it would be worth a bag of blood, she thought, immediately feeling ashamed. Pride fell when it clashed with survival. *I don't want to die. I don't want to die.* Not that chanting it would do her any good. Maybe a bleeding human would drop from the sky into her lap? Maybe some kind of blood fairy would appear from nowhere with wings and a tutu, granting her wish. Maybe she was going insane. Surely that had to be the case, sitting here with an enemy twenty feet away and daydreaming about fairies.

This vampire posed a direct threat, and she needed to get her head out of the clouds and concentrate. Starvation wouldn't be her only problem if they smelled her. Was it this one who had sprung the rat trap, or the guy he was meeting, Wes? Or was it some other vampire?

A shadow moved in the woods, and Kelly's eyes fixed on

the area, carefully trying to separate any heat signature from the trees and shapes surrounding her. It wasn't easy — vampires could dramatically lower their body temperature to blend in, as well as still their heartbeats to a bare flutter. Again she saw a movement, and a man came from behind a large oak to approach the other. *This must be Wes*, she thought, admiring how silently he moved among the leaves.

"About time," the other man said, irritated.

"Does she hunt out this far?" Wes asked, looking around nervously. "We're only a mile or so away from her trailer. What if she has some kind of surveillance?"

"Idiot," the tall one said. "I've been watching her. She's just some scout Fournier planted out here on the border and forgot about. They've abandoned her to the humans."

"So, no need to capture and interrogate her?" Wes asked hopefully. "I'll just report she's an abandoned spy, and you can kill her."

"Where's your sense of adventure?" the other asked. "She gets off work at midnight tonight. She'll check her animal traps around two in the morning. We'll grab her then and see if she knows anything before we kill her. Should make for a fun evening."

Kelly felt cold. They'd somehow been following her without her knowing, and although Wes seemed to be a scout, his companion had skills beyond that. How had he managed to avoid getting killed by Jaq? Were there far more scouts in and out of West Virginia than Jaq and her pack of werewolves realized?

There was no way she could take these two out on her own, weak and with nothing more than a set of silver-tipped darts and a fillet knife, but she'd have to do something. They planned on capturing and killing her tonight. It was a good thing it had been so slow at Dale's that he'd let her go early.

Not that he needed much excuse to tell her to go home.

Her schedule for the week appeared to be slowly dwindling to a few hours here and there — not worth spending the money on those cheap Walmart pants. More alarming was how Dale didn't have her scheduled at all past the end of the week, as if he expected her to be dead by then. Kelly was sure that was his dearest wish — either dead by his or someone else's hand. But now was not the time to ponder unfair workplace practices with two vampires practically under her nose.

Hopefully, if she had the element of surprise on her side, she could kill these two before they could do the same to her. Kelly gripped her hands together as she fought off a wave of dizziness. Who was she kidding? They'd kill her regardless. She wasn't trained for this sort of thing. She was a business manager, not an action hero. And all the training in the world wouldn't help her in a battle against two healthy, well-fed vampires. She'd go down fighting, but Kelly was reconciling herself to the fact that she'd most likely be the one dead at sun-up.

A few flakes of snow drifted down as Kelly snuck back along the hedgerow and into the woods, careful to keep an eye on the vampires as she retreated as silently as possible. She made her way back to her trailer, changed her clothing and waited until two o'clock before she went out to pretend to check her traps.

It was a weeknight, and the trailers all along Briar Lane were dark and quiet, the humans either sleeping, or off working a third shift. Kelly made her way around past Jaq's trailer, lingering by the door a brief moment. Was the werewolf at work? Or maybe she just didn't care anymore. A sense of loneliness and loss washed over her. Jaq was the closest thing she'd ever had to a friend. She missed their partnership, the quick smile that lit up the other woman's face, the freckles that seemed to cover every square inch of the werewolf's skin.

With a sigh, she circled around behind Jaq's trailer, entering the woods from a different trail than she normally took. Although she moved carefully, trying to catch the other vampires' scents to see if they'd left any trace along the trails, she saw nothing. They were good. She would have doubted they were anywhere near, but when the wind changed directions, she caught a faint hint of their scent.

Wes was a scout, familiar with moving silently and without a trace, but he wasn't a fighter. That other guy . . . he was the one Kelly worried about. That was the guy she needed to take out first, as quickly as possible. If he managed to get his hands on her, it would be all over. She hesitated, sorting out the smells on the wind so she could move herself toward her appropriate target. What she wouldn't give for Jaq right now. The woman's woodland skills, hunting ability, and sense of smell were far superior to Kelly's, and she wasn't ashamed to admit it.

Instead of starting with the snares as she usually did, Kelly went about fifty feet away, to the rattraps. There. He was nearby, about twenty feet behind a stand of saplings, if her nose could be trusted. He had to have smelled her by now, but just in case, she rustled about to make some noise.

She caught a small movement out of the corner of her eye. Kelly bent to examine the ropes tying the traps to a tree, her entire body tense in anticipation.

A branch moved. A twig snapped, and she jumped to the side, throwing herself to the ground just beside the snare trap. The movement saved her life. She barely avoided the vampire who dove past, missing her and clothes-lining himself on the nearly invisible trip wire.

A huge log dropped, and Kelly held her breath, springing to her feet, ready to either run or finish the guy off. The vampire hadn't been going fast enough to decapitate himself on the wire, and the deadfall trap completely missed him, but Kelly smelled the rush of blood and heard his choked off curse. She made a quick choice and ran.

The injured vampire raced after her, and Kelly heard a second set of footsteps crunch through the leaves. Wes, she guessed, was heading up the rear, and quickly gaining on his companion. The scout was either the faster of the pair, or more confident moving at speed through the woods. Either way, Kelly knew she had to hurry. Ignoring the sharp pains shooting down her legs, she put on a burst of speed.

A few seconds later, she began to slow. Her legs felt like dead stumps attached to her torso, and a buzzing filled her ears, drowning out the sound of her pursuers. She was weak from lack of blood, but she knew these woods better than the vampires did and the first one was probably losing blood at an alarming rate. He'd heal, but not while running flat out. She still had a chance.

Kelly felt herself slow even further and heard the pair gaining. Heart pounding, she pushed harder. *Come on, just a little bit further.* Rounding a corner, she saw her goal up ahead — a huge root from a black locust tree jutting up in the path. *One, two, three,* she counted her steps, shoving her foot a bit too far forward on the last step. Her toes slammed into the root and Kelly sprawled head first, sliding a good ten feet along the ground. It wasn't the most graceful move of her life. Sticks and rocks scraped along her arms and chest as the smell of dirt and leaves filled her nose.

The vampire behind her laughed in triumph. "Gotcha."

As if in slow motion, Kelly rolled to watch him avoid the root that had brought her down, hopping lightly over it as he ran toward her. There was a crack, a sharp whip-like sound, then a flash as something flew between the trees toward the vampire. His eyes widened, and he threw his hands forward, but he was too late. The next sound Kelly heard was a gurgle as the silver-tipped arrow impaled him to a tree. *Wow, just like in the movies,* she thought in amazement.

Unfortunately the vampire was taller than the deer the trap had originally been set for, and, instead of his head, the arrow had buried deep in his stomach. Kelly felt a moment of panic as he grabbed the arrow and tugged violently, trying to free himself. Jumping to her feet, she grabbed for the first weapon she could reach from her belt. Before the vampire could manage to pull it out, Kelly was on him, slicing through his breastbone and into his heart with the silver filet knife. She worked fast, well aware that Wes was not far behind him.

Confident that this assailant was dead, she whipped around and saw Wes, frozen and wide-eyed right at the spot where the trip wire had ended his friend. Kelly wished briefly that she'd set up a second trip wire, but it didn't prove necessary as Wes turned tail and ran. Kelly hesitated, undecided as to whether she should give chase. She was exhausted, but she couldn't let him get away. The next guy, or guys, he brought back would be stronger than this one. Her only hope was to get him before he crossed the border.

Leaving the other vampire dead and pinned to the tree, Kelly took off after Wes. Her head pounded, and her legs screamed in pain as she pushed past exhaustion. Wes was a scout, but he'd slowed his retreat to avoid setting off any traps that might land him in the same situation as his companion. Kelly saw him jump a small stone wall that separated a dirt lane from the woods, then leap over its match on the other side. She followed, having to scramble over the wall instead of jumping it cleanly.

An eerie silence greeted her on the other side. In the lane, Kelly hesitated, no longer seeing her quarry. There was no sign of him in the woods on the other side, but she clambered over the other wall, determined to check just in case. Listening, she could hear nothing but the rasp of her own breath, the pounding of her heart, and the persistent buzzing in her ears. Her hands shook as she lowered herself to the other side of the wall and stared into the thick woods. Where had he gone? There was no path, no way for him to get through the dense brambles without leaving a trail of crushed foliage. Kelly turned to climb back over the wall, completely surprised by the fist that smashed into her side.

She doubled over, gasping for air and unable to avoid the second fist that slammed into the back of her head. Wes kicked her a few times, ensuring she stayed face-down on the ground.

"Think I'll take you back home to interrogate rather than do it here," Wes said, bending down to twist one of her arms up behind her back. "That way we won't be disturbed by any other rabbit-eating scum Fournier might have in the area."

For God's sake, did every vampire on the continent know about that? Eat one bunny, and no one would ever let you forget it. Kelly snarled, arching her back as she struggled to pull free from Wes. The vampire twisted her arm, and she felt the sharp burn of something against the skin of her stomach. The darts! And she still had one hand trapped under her chest. Wiggling and pulling against Wes' hold, she edged her arm downward, toward her waistband.

"Besides, some of the others might want to have a little fun with you in revenge for killing Derrick."

Kelly's arm twisted further. Wes' weight shifted as he straddled her and reached for her other arm. Almost there. She touched the feathered edge of the dart, felt the silver tip drag agonizingly along her flesh.

Wes slammed a knee into her back, trapping her arm once again and causing the silver tip of the dart to dig into her stomach. Kelly winced in pain, unable to do anything.

Fortunately, Wes found himself unable to pull her arm around to the back of her body with all his weight pressing down. Cursing softly, he shifted, moving his knee and planting his foot beside her hip to hold her steady. Yanking her left arm further upward, he grabbed the elbow of her right and moved to pull it from under her body. Kelly turned slightly and struck backwards, hearing his scream as the silver-tipped dart slammed into his shin.

It wouldn't kill him, but it did what she'd hoped. Wes released her arm and jumped back, bending over to pull the dart from his leg. Kelly rolled and launched herself upward, aiming another dart for the back of his neck, but Wes must have seen her move. He shifted to the side, and Kelly found her dart embedded in a tree trunk.

What to do now? She had two more darts, but had lost the advantage. All Wes had to do was keep her fighting or running, and wear her down until she collapsed. At this point, it was a matter of making her death count, of dying honorably rather than killing or even evading this other vampire. They circled, eyeing each other warily in the narrow space between the low stone wall and the wild forest. Wes grinned, sensing he had the advantage, and Kelly gripped her two remaining darts, determined to go out fighting. At the same time, both vampires heard a sound, clearly something large in the woods on the other side of the lane. Kelly tried to take advantage of the moment by lunging for him, but Wes easily threw her aside. She crouched, waiting for his attack, but he hesitated, looking back and forth between her and the trees on the other side of the road.

There was another noise. A snap of a large branch and something that sounded like a crash. Wes snarled at her and spun about, racing at top speed beside the stone wall before vanishing into the forest.

Kelly leaned against the sharp, cool edges of the wall and

tried to gather her strength. She wasn't badly hurt — some bruised ribs and a concussion, but those wouldn't heal. Not unless a human with an open wound just happened to stroll down the lane. She could just lie here, let the scents of the forest comfort her as she drifted into whatever afterlife awaited vampires. Or maybe whatever had been on the other side of the woods would come and finish her off. It didn't matter anymore.

A damp flake of snow hit her nose, followed by another. Nothing vaulted the stone wall to kill her. Kelly began to realize that although she might die tonight, it wouldn't be in the next ten minutes, and the prospect of sitting here on the damp, chill ground covered in heavy, wet snow as she waited hours to die wasn't appealing. Struggling to her feet, she stuffed the silver-tipped darts back into her belt loops and crawled over the wall. If she was going to die tonight, she'd do it in her trailer, curled up on the couch with a blanket and a plate of Melody's tuna casserole. That would be a good way to go out.

Blind instinct alone led Kelly back to the trailer. Her mind wandered, thinking of her childhood, the years when she was a Candidate hoping to be chosen to turn, busy days at the casino. Awareness would return, and she'd find herself wondering how long she'd been tramping through the leaves, and how she'd even gotten to where she was. Snow started to fall in earnest, masking the heat signatures from the animals and casting the moonless night into dark shadows. The patch of maples came into view, as well as the dead vampire impaled to a tree.

Kelly paused beside the corpse. She couldn't exactly leave him here for the neighbors to find. Jaq had said she was the only one that ventured into the woods, but this was danger-ously close to the tree line. A sharp-eyed human might see the outline of a body against a tree and investigate. Blanket and tuna casserole would have to wait. First, she needed to do something with this body.

Bracing her foot against the tree, she tugged at the arrow. Wedged firmly in the tree, she was unable to pull it loose. Kelly yanked and twisted, each effort adding to the gore that coated her and the ground under the dead vampire. Finally she picked up a good-sized rock and broke the arrow off, sliding the body from it and onto the ground.

Sorry, Jaq. You've got one less arrow, she though ruefully. The vampire's body was splayed in a wet mess on the forest floor. At this point she doubted she could carry the thing. Perhaps she should just drag it further into the woods and leave it there. It's not like it really mattered anymore, and her blanket and tuna casserole were calling. Lost in thought, she was startled to hear someone clearing their throat only a few feet away.

"You looked like you needed a hand," Jaq said gruffly. "Sorry I killed him. He wasn't very cooperative when I tried to bring him back alive, and I didn't have much choice in the matter."

Kelly stared her mouth open. She was here. In spite of everything she'd said, in spite of not seeing her at all for the last few days, Jaq had come through for her. The werewolf stood before her, a pick axe in one hand and a body slung over her shoulder. With a shrug, she dumped the body face up onto the ground. Wes stared up at her, his face a mask of surprise and horror, his chest nothing but a bloody hole.

"Next one I'll manage to keep alive for you to question," the woman said confidently. "I'm sure these guys let someone know you were here before they set out. There will be more soon enough."

Kelly made a noise, unable to speak. She leaned over, trying to clear her head of the dizziness. She was dying. It wouldn't matter if Jaq killed the next one or not; she wouldn't be alive to question it.

"Should we dig a hole?" Jaq asked, her voice sounding like it was coming from inside a tunnel. "It will go faster with the two of us."

Kelly shook her head and stood straight, trying to focus her fuzzy eyesight on the woman before her. She was too weak to dig anything. After her mad dash through the forest and the fight with Wes, she was barely strong enough to stand. But she had an idea, something preferable to a blanket and comfort food.

Her family didn't want her back. Facing her death had brought that home loud and clear. They were just toying with her. The Kincaids were the enemy, and even if she could access the money, she'd never make it to Vegas alive in time to beg the Rochelle family for asylum. She'd die tonight, but maybe she could at least feel like she had died in her own land.

"Is that offer of home still open?" she asked, gritting her teeth as a wave of pain nearly doubled her over. "Cause I could really use one about now."

Jaq dropped the pickaxe and threw her arms around Kelly. "Yes, that offer is always open. I'm sorry, honey. So sorry."

"I'm the one that's sorry," Kelly mumbled against the other woman's shirt. She felt herself relax, her weight collapsing into the werewolf. It was nice to rest there for a moment, to know she'd die at home where at least one person cared about her. *More than one*, she thought, remembering the humans who'd invaded her trailer. Still, she wasn't dead yet, and there was one more thing she wanted to do before she left this life behind.

"How far is it to the Virginia state line?"

Jaq pulled away to look at her, holding her shoulders for a

moment before letting go. "Probably eight miles. It's about fifteen miles to Berryville."

Eight miles was too far to walk carrying two dead bodies.

"Is there a strip club in Berryville?"

"I don't know." Jaq looked at her curiously. "It's about twenty-five miles to Winchester. I'll bet there's one there."

Kelly thought for a moment. "Do you have access to a car?"

"I have a truck we can use." Jaq reached down and tossed Wes' body across her shoulder, then walked over and effortlessly did the same with the other vampire. Balancing their weight, she bent down and retrieved her pick axe.

"You change out of those bloody clothes and meet me at my house. I'll put these two in my truck and grab some supplies." Jaq paused, a faint smile at the corner of her mouth. "Are we going to a strip club after we take care of these guys? I've never been to one, and I don't know what to wear."

She'd missed that smile. Really, really missed that smile.

"No." Kelly couldn't help but laugh. This whole situation was absurd, but the feeling of joy she had at having Jaq by her side once again was indescribable. When the werewolf was around, Kelly felt more like fighting and less like dying. "We're going to dump the bodies at a strip club and head back. I've got a promising evening ahead of me with a blanket and tuna casserole."

"Sounds good to me. I might join you." Jaq strode off as if the two vampires on her shoulder weighed nothing, while Kelly stared after her. Werewolves were downright scary. No, *Jaq* was scary. Wonderful scary. Killing vampires like she was swatting flies, completely nonchalant about the idea of body disposal. Where had Jaq been dumping all those vampire bodies? Kelly giggled, thinking of all the deer bologna in the other woman's freezer. Jaq wasn't *that* scary.

CHAPTER 22

Kelly rode shotgun in Jaq's old truck; the vampire bodies in huge garbage bags rode in the back, weighted down with tools and bricks. Jaq told her they were taking back roads to avoid the highway.

"It's early morning, and there'll be lots of police catching drunks," she explained. "Better to be on the safe side."

Kelly nodded. They sat in silence, the only noise the whirring of the truck's tires on the road. *Tired. So very tired.* Kelly leaned her head against the truck window, feeling strangely disconnected. Her body seemed to be filled with lead weights. It had taken every ounce of strength to pull herself up into Jaq's lifted truck. But it was her head, floating above her like a helium balloon that was the strangest of sensations. Head here. Body there. What would happen if she floated right out above the truck and drifted away? Already she felt a blurry sense of peace at the idea.

Jaq stirred in the driver's seat, taking her eyes from the road to cast a concerned glance Kelly's way. "You look like complete and total crap."

"Thanks." She couldn't manage a smile let alone make a

witty comeback about her lack of make-up. Head, floating away.

"I didn't realize . . . I mean the last two days you've really gone downhill."

There were all kinds of witty rejoinders to make, but even if she'd been able to put words together in her head, Kelly doubted she could manage to get them out of her mouth.

"You're getting weaker, and I can tell you don't have much longer. I don't know what to do. I don't know what to do." The werewolf pounded the steering wheel with a fist. It bent slightly. She must do this a lot, because the steering wheel looked like it hadn't been completely round in several years.

"Screw it. I'm getting you a human. Just this one time, that's all. I'll grab him or her, and hold them down while you cut them up and drink. I'll heal them. I'll deny everything; claim that they're some psycho that imagined the whole thing."

"Then in three days I'm back to this," Kelly forced out.

"Then we'll do it again in three days." There was terrible pain in the werewolf's voice, and Kelly knew she would be breaking every moral she held dear.

"No. Won't let you betray your pack's trust."

It wouldn't work anyway, and she saw that same realization in Jaq's eyes. They could get away with it maybe once, but over and over again? Humans with the same bizarre story of being attacked by a blood-sucking girl in a dark alley, with an accomplice that healed? Kelly didn't think the werewolves would overlook it the first time it happened.

The truck abruptly pulled over to the side of the road in a spray of gravel, and Jaq slammed it into park, turning to face Kelly.

"We've got to tell them," Jaq said, her voice catching. "Margaret is a nurse at the VA hospital in Martinsburg. She could probably sneak some human blood out for you. They all care about you, but they can't help you if they don't know. I'm not gonna tell them your secret. I know what it's like to need to hide what you are, but sometimes you got to trust people to help you."

Kelly stared out the window. She'd broken a lot of rules, but she'd never betrayed her people to the humans. How could they tolerate her presence if they knew she needed to feed on them to survive? A predator. A parasite. Cue the doom music and fire up the torches.

"Ok," Jaq said, wiping her eyes with her sleeve. "Drink those dead vampires then. They still have some blood left in them. Enough to get you by. I know you said you don't do that sort of thing, but if it will help you live, you need to."

Kelly gagged. Gross. She couldn't drink vampire blood, even that of her enemy. Her stomach rebelled at the thought.

The woman beside her took a deep breath. "Then drink from me. I have a knife, and you don't have to worry about hurting me. I'm not sure my blood will be okay. It might make you sick or kill you, but a little bit will probably be fine. Besides, the odds are better than what you're facing now."

Kelly shook her head.

"You stupid, stubborn vampire!" Jaq slammed her hands on the steering wheel, cracking it with the force of the blow. "Just take my blood."

Kelly again shook her head. Jaq was a friend — her only friend. She didn't eat friends. Besides, the balloon-head feeling was beginning to be rather nice.

"It's okay," Jaq said, a carefully contrived note of hurt in her voice. "I know I'm not human, that I'm not what you like when it comes to blood type."

Kelly almost laughed. Werewolves were also manipulative. Who knew? She pulled her floating mind back and forced herself to focus. She at least owed Jaq a reason.

"No." The glass of the truck window was cool on her cheek. "You're my best friend. The only friend I've ever had." Thoughts of George crossed her mind, but that had been different — a flurry of reckless passion and desperation. He'd been a ray of sunshine, but Jaq was like her right arm. "Friends aren't food. I can't do that to you."

Jaq reached under the seat for something. Suddenly the scent of blood filled the air. Strange blood. Sharp as ice, with cloves and the bite of exotic black and red pepper. "Best friends help each other. Please. I don't want you to die," she begged Kelly.

Jaq *was* her best friend. Caring for her after her own family left her for dead, filling her fridge with cow blood, watching out for her, helping her, defending her when she had no one else in the world to turn to. Kelly couldn't recall anyone ever drinking werewolf blood before. What would it taste like? Would it kill her, or do nothing, leaving her just as weak and on the edge of starvation as she was now? Kelly struggled to lift her head and put her lips over Jaq's spotted wrist, determined to take only a mouthful.

It tasted of honey on the coldest snow, numbing the sides of her throat as she swallowed. An explosion hit behind Kelly's eyes, sending sparks racing down through her nervous system. There was a wash of color and noise over-whelming her senses. Her heart froze in place and then galloped out of control.

Gasping for air, Kelly pulled her mouth away. Sound roared in her ears, like she'd had too much oxygen, like she was on sensory overload. Her night vision crashed as her pupils dilated to their full diameter. She'd drunk from crack addicts and never had such a rush. For a moment she thought she'd die, that every cell in her body would rupture. Then gradually her heart resumed its normal rhythm; her breathing slowed. Kelly stared at her hands. It was as if every nerve ending was lit up and alive.

"Are you okay?" Jaq asked, her voice rising in panic. The werewolf gripped her arm, and gently shook her. "Kelly, speak to me."

"What *are* you?" Kelly stared at her hands in amazement, flexing the fingers. She was powerful, invincible. Nothing could harm her. Not even the Master with all his ancient power. There's no way werewolves had blood like this. Vampires would have drained them all dry centuries ago if they had.

"I'm a First," Jaq whispered. "No one can know. No one."

"First what?" Kelly rubbed her fingers along the dashboard of the truck, marveling at the feel.

Jaq shifted in her seat, looking around as if there were someone to hear them on the deserted road. "First. A Nephilim. The offspring of an angel and a human."

Kelly turned her attention from her hands to the woman beside her. "Wait. I thought you said you were a werewolf."

"I am. My children will be like the other werewolves, but Firsts are different. That's why no one can ever know. If the angels catch me, our whole species is at risk."

Well, yeah. Angels were not supposed to be making naughty with humans, and any offspring would have a death sentence hanging over their heads. A link between Nephilim and the werewolves would lead to their genocide. The whole heavy-handed existence contract was due to their undecided status — either a quirk of human evolution or the product of illicit passion. But that wasn't what grabbed hold of Kelly's thoughts.

"Children? Who are you having children with? Is this a duty? An obligation that you have to further the werewolf race?" Her hands sparked against the dashboard of the car, or maybe it was just her screwed up vision. Either way, the thought of Jaq married to the highest bidder and surrounded by a dozen pups filled her with anxiety and a slow burn of anger.

There was a soft snort of laughter that smoothed her worry. "Silly. What do you think we are? I mate with who I choose, when I choose, and I'll have offspring only if I wish to. But Firsts don't have the fertility problems that plague latter generations of werewolves, and we have a broader range of abilities so we're coveted as a potential mate. We're also granted special status in the Pack."

"I wondered. I mean, you don't smell the same as Dale and his crew. I thought maybe my sense of smell was off because I've been so hungry."

She saw Jaq's faint smile. "Are you saying I smell bad?"

"Werewolves smell bad," Kelly confessed. "Like dogs and old ham. You don't smell bad. You smell like ice and pepper, cloves and pine trees."

Jaq choked back a laugh. "*Ham*? Old ham? If you value your life, don't ever tell a werewolf that to their face."

"Wait," Kelly said, suddenly facing the other woman. "Is Mike a Nephilim too? How many of you half angels are there?"

Jaq shook her head. "No. He's my step-brother. My father brought me to the Pack when I was an infant. I'm the only one in West Virginia at the moment. It's really not that common."

"You never knew your parents?" Kelly asked softly. Maybe she and Jaq had more in common than she'd thought.

"Well, I consider the werewolf couple that raised me to be my parents, but no, I never knew my angel father or my human mother. It was for the best. I would have been a danger to both of them if they'd kept me — proof of an angel's sin."

Kelly squashed a wave of jealousy. What she wouldn't

have given for a pair of loving foster parents, and a step brother. All she'd had was a box behind the stove and a slap if she daydreamed and didn't work fast enough. But that life was behind her, and she should be thankful that Jaq didn't suffer the same bleak childhood as hers.

"I worked with an angel back in Atlantic City — our liaison. He was alright for an angel, but I can't see him having reproductive organs, let alone allowing passion to sway him into sex with a human."

Jaq laughed, clapping a hand over her mouth. "I *know*. Seriously. I've never met an angel, obviously, but from what I've heard I just can't imagine it."

"You blood is a total rush. I can't tell if I've got enhanced abilities or I'm just on some delusional high. Good thing you aren't a full angel. I think I my head might have blown right off my body."

"What does it feel like?" Jaq peered at her curiously, waving a hand in front of Kelly's face.

"I can feel everything in such detail. My whole body is tingly. I'm still hungry, but not starving. It doesn't seem to bother me as much. I'm not as weak."

"Do you need more?" Jaq asked, indicating her arm.

"Good lord, no. I think it would kill me. Just that mouthful and I felt like I was going to explode out from the inside. I've never heard of any of us drinking from a werewolf before, let alone a Nephilim. If they did, I can only assume it didn't end well. If I hadn't been holding back, I'd probably have taken too much and stroked out."

"I'm not sure werewolves would have the same effect," Jaq confessed. "My make-up is really different. I'm probably more potent."

"I'll say. Super potent. Super-duper potent." Kelly looked at her fingers again. Could she shoot laser beams from them? It sure felt like she could.

"Will it wear off?" Jaq asked, peering at her. "Your pupils are huge, like you're drugged."

"I'm sure it will. I just don't know how long it will take."

Jaq put the truck back in gear. "I'm going to keep driving. Let me know if you need me to pull over so you can puke or something."

They headed on to Winchester as Kelly marveled at the stars and the scenery that seemed in such incredible detail. She felt like she could recall every leaf on every tree they passed. It was like being on a hallucinogenic. As they pulled into town, Kelly suddenly smelled vampire. Kincaid vampire.

"There," she told Jaq. "Turn there."

"The pawn shop?" Jaq asked.

"Yeah, pull around back and we'll throw the bodies in front of the dumpster."

They got out and dropped the tailgate to pull out the bodies when Jaq froze, looking at Kelly with an eerie intensity.

"There's one here. I smell one," she whispered.

Kelly didn't have time to react before she was knocked to the ground and straddled by a male vampire.

"Fournier scum. What are you doing in our lands?" he snarled, his hands at her throat.

A roar split the air and massive claws slapped the vampire from her, sending him skidding ten feet across the asphalt parking lot. Jaq had become an enormous wolf, her tawny fur covered in unusual brown spots.

Unfortunately the intimidating effect of the werewolf's fierce roar was negated by the lacy panties dangling from one rear leg and the t-shirt and bra twisted around her middle. Kelly couldn't help a snort of laughter.

The wolf paused just a moment to glare at Kelly before leaping after the vampire. Jaq no longer had the element of surprise on her side, and the vampire had taken advantage of her inattention to jump to his feet and charge. They collided. He grabbed Jaq, tossing her into the side of the dumpster.

"No," Kelly shouted, scrambling to her feet. She reached out her hand, and the shovel from the truck flew into her open palm. Instinctively, she swung the tool, impacting the side of the vampire's head with strength far beyond her years, breaking the wooden handle in half and sending the vampire sprawling backwards.

Knowing the blow wouldn't do more than slow him, she tossed the splintered handle aside and grabbed the vampire, heaving him into the air and slamming him against the side of the dumpster. He hit the thick metal rods used to lift and empty the garbage with force, and they slid through him, impaling the vampire right through the heart. He was dead. Jaq stared at her, the werewolf's form returning to human with a flash of light.

"I've never done that before," Kelly marveled, looking at the broken shovel on the ground, then at her hands. Telekinesis. Vampires began to acquire the skill at around two-thousand years of age. "I think it may be a side effect of your blood. I'm guessing that will wear off eventually too. Pity, because that would be a really nifty skill to have."

"Do it again," Jaq urged. The werewolf was mostly naked, her pants on the ground beside the truck, and her shirt and bra still an awkward tangle around her midsection. Who knew where the woman's underwear had gone.

Kelly bit back a smile and reached out a hand. The broken handle flew into her palm without her even looking at it. "Yeah, I could get used to this."

The werewolf nodded then began to look around the pavement, no doubt searching for her underwear. "Me too. I don't think you should make a habit out of drinking my blood, though. I have a bad feeling it could have some terrible long-term side effects."

"You werewolves must go through a lot of clothing," Kelly commented, picking up Jaq's pants and shaking gravel from them.

"Not normally." Jaq picked up a tiny scrap of fabric and examined it, making a disgusted noise. "It takes most were-wolves ten to twenty minutes to change. With today's effective human weaponry, we usually only use the wolf form for organized social occasions, like hunts, so there's plenty of time to disrobe."

"But you're different." Kelly handed her the pants, and Jaq gave one last annoyed look at the underwear before shoving them in a pocket.

"Yeah, I can change immediately. I can be other animals besides a wolf, and in animal form I'm pretty indestructible. I don't usually do it, for the obvious, clothing-destroying reasons, but when I don't know what I'm up against, it's worth ruining fifty-dollar lingerie."

Kelly whistled. "That's some expensive lacy stuff under your Carhartt overalls, girl. I never would have guessed it."

Jaq frowned, hopping as she put the pants on, commando. "I'd really prefer if you didn't tell anyone. No one in the pack would ever let me live it down."

"Two secrets," Kelly teased. "Nephilim and girly under-clothes. Hmmm, such blackmail potential."

Jaq hesitated, a flash of distrust flitting over her face.

"I'm teasing, you know," Kelly told her softly. "Best friends don't betray each other."

Jaq's smile returned, her shoulders relaxing in relief. "Help me get these dead guys out of the truck. I want to get out of here before more vampires show up and I have to ruin what's left of my clothing."

It was good to have a friend to joke with, one to rely on when you needed help. This whole thing — exile, starving, enemy scouts trying to kill her — it was a horrible situation, but with Jaq by her side, it all seemed manageable. More than manageable, actually. With Jaq, it felt like she could conquer the world, and *that* had nothing to do with the half-angel blood coursing through her system.

"I'm so glad you're with me, but I feel kind of guilty. I dragged you into this whole thing."

Jaq shrugged. "I was killing vampires before you came along. It's a whole lot more fun when there's someone else by your side."

Kelly nodded and looked at the two corpses in the bed of Jaq's truck. "We probably should have just buried these bodies, but I wanted to make a statement. I wanted to send a message to Kincaid to keep off my land and leave us alone."

My land. Somehow it had become her land. Yes, it was also werewolf land — a worthless buffer zone between two vampire territories. Could she manage to survive being squashed between two powerful families, living in the company of werewolves? Jaq wanted her to stay, but would the others? And how could she ever manage it with their ban on human blood?

Jaq grinned. "I think the guy dangling from the dumpster will get your message across."

Kelly looked at the gruesome sight.

"I understand territory," Jaq added. "I want to keep these guys out of our lands as much as you do."

Kelly considered her words then climbed into the back of the truck to shove out the two vampire bodies. Jaq grabbed them off the bed gate and easily tossed them over her shoulders before striding to the dumpster and pitching them to the ground.

"You're right — we need to get out of here," Kelly muttered, keeping a sharp eye turned to the pawnshop and dark buildings down the road. "We're not usually out alone. I don't know where that guy's buddy is, but he's bound to be back soon, and I'd like us across the border when he gets here."

Jaq nodded, shutting the tailgate with a bang and gesturing for Kelly to get into the car. "Yeah, I've got to get ready for work too. Early shift this morning."

Some friend she was, dragging Jaq all over the place fighting vampires and ruining her clothing when the woman had to work.

"Sorry. I really appreciate your help." In more ways than one — with Wes, with the vampire drooping from the dumpster, and even her rocket-fuel blood. Which she was *not* about to have any more of.

Jaq smirked at her as she climbed into the truck. "Don't mention it. I'd call in sick, but I've got a vampire I'm supporting and I need the hours."

"Ha ha. I'd be a lot cheaper to support if you had a basement in your trailer for me to live in."

Jaq started the car and turned to Kelly, a serious expression on her face. "And as much as I hate to bring up a prickly subject when we seem to be on speaking terms again, we need to talk about blood."

Kelly knew what the woman meant, but she just didn't want to go there. "So you need laundry advice on how to remove it from your clothing? Well, you've turned to the right vampire. I'd suggest soda water, or baking soda. Or you could just dye your t-shirt pink and be done with it."

Jaq pulled the truck out onto the main road, but not before shooting her a stern, one-eyebrow-raised kind of look. "Don't. I didn't work my butt off that night they dumped you half-dead in the trailer only to have you starve to death out of stubbornness. The cow and deer blood isn't working for you, or the fresh blood from the animals we're trapping. Human blood — how much and how often do you need it to keep you alive and in tip-top shape?"

It was time to be truthful. Kelly sighed. "At the casino I got three meals a day. A pint each, fresh from a human. That's a privileged modern life, though. It wasn't always that way. We have the ability to gorge and store, but I haven't even been able to do that. I would have been dead days ago if it hadn't been for that guy outside the strip club. And if I hadn't been so injured and weak from blood loss, what I took from him would normally have held me a week."

"Draining someone dry is going to get you killed before sun-up," Jaq commented, her tone deceptively casual. Kelly could see the tension in her shoulders, hear the strain in the very back of her voice. "What's the minimum you can have? We'll work up from there."

"I . . . I really don't know." She didn't. She'd always been fed. Fournier vampires didn't go hungry, whether it was a shared meal from an expendable human out of the slums when she was first turned, or the civilized delivered meals in the casino.

Jaq threw up her hands in frustration, momentarily leaving the truck's steering unattended. "Give me a ballpark here, Kelly. I can't let you run around like some fangless Dracula, stabbing strippers and drunken guys."

"How far does your pack's mandate extend? Maybe I can borrow your truck and run in a few times a week to Martinsburg for drunks and strippers."

"Not gonna happen." Jaq's voice was firm, her profile grim. "Thousands of us, remember? The pack *owns* this state. You start killing or assaulting humans anywhere in West Virginia and there's not much I can do to save you."

Kelly frowned, realizing that the fact Jaq was a Nephilim wasn't the only thing the werewolves were hiding. There was no way the angels would have allowed thousands of them in one state under the existence contract. No way.

As if reading her mind, Jaq shot her a perceptive look.

"And no, the angels don't know. We've got a huge number of werewolves under the radar here. For some reason, we've managed to keep it under wraps. No angels, no demons."

"No vampires," Kelly added softly. "Until me."

"There were plenty of vampires nosing around and passing through before you. We killed every one we got our paws on. Makes them think twice about sending people into our territory." Jaq's voice turned gentle. "You're the only one that's lived here. Our very own token vampire."

Her words tugged at something deep inside Kelly. The staff at Dale's was still wary of her, but Jaq appeared to carry some weight in the pack. For a moment, she had a fantasy of life here, as the token vampire surrounded by others. The panicked feeling at the thought of being so far from her vampire family had dulled to a throb over the last few days. Would it go away eventually? Could she find some kind of peace, or maybe even happiness here? Kelly stared at Jaq with her disheveled blond hair and freckles, which were clearly visible even in the dim dashboard light. It was such a silly, ridiculous idea, but somehow it seemed far more appealing than the harsh reception she'd get even if she *was* reinstated into her family.

"I couldn't." Cold reality crashed down on her. She had no fangs, and the werewolves would never tolerate what she would have to do to survive. The humans either. It was a lovely fantasy, though. One to dream about while curled up alone in her bed as dawn colored the horizon. "I know I said I wanted this to be home, but I'd starve. The werewolves won't compromise on this issue, and I *can't*."

Jaq's face momentarily betrayed her disappointment before her eyes shuttered, closing the emotion off. "So we're back to the original topic. If I'm robbing an American Red Cross blood donation site, how new does the blood have to be and how much should I steal?"

She was clearly serious. Kelly closed her eyes. This was more than she'd ever been given; a gesture of real friendship. "No more than twenty-four hours old. I could probably drink eight pints one night, and eight the next before it loses its effectiveness. Which means you'd be robbing blood banks on a weekly basis."

She and Jaq, the Bonnie and Clyde of blood donation facilities. Once a week, breaking and entering to run off with a cooler full of ruby liquid. It was the stuff Hollywood movies were made of, and it would get them incarcerated within a month.

From her sigh, Jaq realized it too. "This would be a lot simpler if you just let me talk to our friends about a system of donation."

"This would be a lot simpler if you'd just let me stab a drunk guy behind a strip club," Kelly replied. Humor was the only way she could combat the grim situation. It was the only thing left in what had become a stalemate between her and the ruling werewolves.

"Consent," Jaq snapped out. "What part of consent don't you understand?"

"Vampire," Kelly retorted. "What part of vampire don't you understand?"

The drove for a while, Jaq grinding her teeth in rhythm with the engine noise of the old truck.

"Is it a secrecy thing?" she finally asked. "Because they're eventually going to find out. They'll spot you doing something vampire-like, or notice how they're all getting old and you don't look a day over twenty."

They wouldn't, because she wasn't going to stay, although her options seemed to be getting narrower with each passing day.

"It's not just secrecy; it's not done. There are the Candidates and everyone else is food. You don't talk with your food. You don't borrow their crème brulee torch to melt silver for weapons, and you don't eat their tuna casserole."

Somehow all the neighboring humans had become off-limits to her, fallen into the Candidate category although she had no intentions of turning them, even if she was able to.

"I'm not asking you to chomp down on their arm or suck on their necks. Barbara is a nurse. She can draw blood and bag it for you, so you don't have to get all squeamish about eating your friends. You don't even have to know where it came from."

"No."

Kelly made sure the word sounded final. Jaq glared at her and mumbled comments as she drove. The effects of Jaq's rocket-fuel blood were starting to wear off, and Kelly felt hunger creep through her. Didn't matter how much it would piss off her friend or the werewolves that seemed to constantly be peering over her shoulder, she was going to have to find fresh human blood in the next twenty-four hours. She just had to make sure to cover her tracks.

Jaq glanced her way with a quick sigh. "If you ever need to borrow my truck, the keys are under the floor mat. Winchester is the biggest city in Virginia that's close to the border. Leesburg is a bit further out. I'd prefer if you take me along. I can guard while you're taking care of things and make sure you don't get carried away. You kill someone, even out of state, and nothing I can do will protect you. Plus, the Kincaid vampires are now going to put some kind of bounty on your head."

Kelly's mind spun. That Jaq was willing to bend her personal ethics for Kelly was something she'd never expected.

"I don't want you to feel like you have to be involved in this," Kelly said earnestly. "I know I'm attacking humans and this bothers you. It's not something you should get involved in."

"I need to go with you," Jaq said with more firmness in her voice then Kelly had ever heard. "It's safer; you'll have a better chance of success and of remaining undetected if we work together. We'll travel across state lines, and if the pack suspects you of any attacks in West Virginia, I can assure them you weren't involved."

Kelly watched the scenery pass by as they drove — long stretches of fields dusted with snow, broken by the occasional appearance of a farmhouse set far back from the road. The mountains rose in the distance, hidden by the night and low cloud cover.

"I'm so sorry, Jaq. I wish the cow blood had worked. I wish I didn't need to do this." She wished she'd kept a tighter leash on her temper back at the casino, or that her family had somehow found her useful and brought her back.

Farmland gave way to thick groupings of trees, shielding housing developments and smaller farms from the road as they crossed the state line. Kelly felt the tension leave her shoulders.

"You need to feed on human blood," Jaq said softly. "It's who you are. There's nothing wrong with doing what you have to do to survive."

Kelly was surprised when Jaq reached out and took her hand, squeezing it. She looked down at the long fingers intertwined with hers in wonder.

"You're not a monster," Jaq added. "You're just a carnivore. Nobody blames a lion for what he is."

"Yes, until the lion starts attacking humans. Then he's killed. They won't even let lions live close to villages. They'll kill them, or catch and relocate them. It's too risky. I'm the same way. I prey on humans. They'll kill me or drive me away if they know. It's hard enough being an outcast from my family; if I had no contact with any sentient beings at all, I'd go insane."

"All right," Jaq replied doubtfully. "I don't think you're giving the humans enough credit though."

She pulled her hand away, and Kelly peered at her face in the dim light, trying to read the werewolf's expression. Was she angry? Jaq was her only friend. Even in her vampire family, she'd never been close to anyone. She'd been safe, sheltered, but without any kind of individual personal connection. Kelly's hand felt suddenly cold, and empty.

CHAPTER 23

Gideon Kincaid scowled as he looked down at the dead vampires lined up before him. Wes and Derrick, dead, their bodies dumped behind a pawnshop. Literally dumped, as if they were no more than an empty fast-food bag.

And Bruce. The vampire had been lifted and thrown with force great enough to impale him on the side of the dumpster. Gideon shook his head thinking of the power it must have taken to perform that feat. No New scout could have done that, or taken out two experienced scouts. This had to have been someone Old.

"The scouts were not killed here. Their bodies smell of Fournier, and the scent is also on Bruce as well as here and there along the ground," the female vampire next to him said. "I'm assuming from the scent patterns that one of our enemy trespassed to bring these two to us as a sort of message."

"One?" Gideon asked. This was a lot for one vampire, but he trusted Monica's analysis. It just confirmed that whoever did this wasn't some lightweight.

"One. The deaths don't concern me as much as the confrontational method of their return."

True. Vampire scouts and spies generally did not live more than a few centuries. The lousy ones even less. Sometimes it was a dumping-ground job for those Turns that didn't quite live up to a Master's expectations. Generally they just disappeared. Monica was right to be anxious. Throwing the dead at their doorstep was a rudeness that could be considered an act of war.

"What about Bruce?" Gideon asked, gesturing angrily at the body. "What's your counsel on this?"

"I'm thinking this one was a defensive kill," she said reluctantly. "They were trespassing to return the bodies. Saul said he went out for a quick bite while Bruce was finishing up the month-end paperwork, and when he came back, this is what he found. Bruce probably smelled an enemy and attacked him."

Idiot. Anything this strong would have had an aura — Bruce should have noticed and waited for backup. Better to hide and gain valuable information, than die from foolish bravery.

"There's another trace smell here too," Monica added, tilting her head and inhaling deeply. "Cold and sharp, sort of a pine note."

Gideon frowned. "Was the enemy vampire accompanied by someone else? Do you think this unknown creature assisted?" That's all he needed. Enemy breathing down his neck, and now some pine-forest-fresh monster sniffing around his territory.

The woman shrugged. "For all I know it could be some odd new human perfume from Saul's late-night snack. Or a genetically modified animal — they always smell a bit off."

She was lying. It hurt that she was suddenly keeping things from him, but it was to be expected. Someday soon he'd find her gone, off to partner with a vampire more her equal.

"That's the least of our worries right now," she added.

It was, as was the inevitable departure of his Consort. How should he deal with this insult from Fournier? He'd felt the young Prince closing in for a few years now. Was this the first shot fired in what would probably be a very bloody war?

Gideon stalked over to the dead vampire and bent to examine him. "He's got gashes across his back and side. Did Fournier's man hit him with some multi-bladed weapon before impaling him on the dumpster?"

Monica strode over to look curiously at the gashes. "I've never seen a weapon like that. Something with a handle, like a type of old threshing tool perhaps? One of the scouts took a silver-tipped projectile through the stomach and probably a silver knife removed his heart. I can't tell what kind of weapon killed the other. It looks like a sharp digging implement removed his heart, and pretty much everything from his chest cavity, but I don't know if he that caused his death, or was done afterwards."

"Wes had some crazy tale about an insane Fournier vampire right over the border," Gideon confessed, a bit embarrassed to even mention it. "A spy living among the humans. I sent him and Derrick to interrogate and kill her. You don't think?" His voice trailed off. It was absurd to even ask.

Monica shook her head. "I can't see Fournier allowing an insane vampire to exist, even as a solitary in West Virginia. Too risky, too difficult to control. It's not in keeping with what I've gathered about the young Born either."

The Prince. Gideon winced. His time was running out. Any day now he expected vampires to surge across his borders and attempt to rip his head off. He glanced over at the angular face of the brunette next to him, seeing beyond the illusion to the ancient vampire beneath. It would be dawn soon, and she needed to be safely underground. Monica. His Consort. He'd hoped by aligning himself with a Born he'd stave off this sort of attack. How long would she stay by his side? One word from the younger Fournier and she'd betray him for the chance to rise in the ranks, to rule as the Consort of another Born. He needed her. She leant a noble legitimacy to his rule. She was old, powerful, and highly intelligent.

Gideon glanced at her again; a longer look, to take in the illusion of warm golden skin and the puffs of black hair that escaped her tight braids, hugging the nape of her long, elegant neck. It had been a long time since she truly appeared that way — long before he'd been turned, long before he'd been born of his human mother. Some might see the gray, sinewy creature under the illusion as horrific, but to him, she was beautiful. When had she become more than a political ally, more than a partner? She was a part of him, and losing her would be worse than losing a limb.

"What?" She smiled, her eyes dancing with rare humor. "You're staring. Is my illusion slipping?"

"Perfect as always, dear."

Gideon needed one of the Fournier leaders dead, but that sort of assassination took time. With the Prince dead, there was no threat. If the old Master died, the young one would have his hands full taking over his father's territories. The last scenario was more unlikely to happen than the untimely demise of the Prince himself. But he had no time for assassinations. He had no time at all. Tomorrow was as good a time to die as any.

"This is an affront. A grievous insult," he told the woman, ensuring the others heard him as well. "Fournier vampires crossed our border and sent us this clear message of their intent to take our lands. We can't just hand over our territory to a young Born barely weaned from his mother. We must show them that the Kincaid family won't allow such a thing to happen."

Monica nodded in understanding, a look of sorrow in her eyes. She knew — knew his reign was almost over. Gideon took a deep breath and steeled himself to continue.

"Call in my leads in Virginia, and my seconds. We advance into DC and Maryland by tomorrow nightfall."

"Who are we attacking?" Monica asked with mild curiosity. "The elder or the younger?"

"Doesn't matter. Right now they're one in the same. Declare war."

She smiled. "With pleasure, darling."

* * *

MONICA SAT in the diner waiting. Two hours until dawn. She'd raced from Gideon's side in Winchester to this location, and would need to hurry to ensure she was underground before the first deadly rays crested the horizon. This was such an irritation, being confined to business only during the dark hours. At least the winter afforded her more time to get things done before she slept like the dead.

The vampire was risking a lot with this meeting, but she needed to make a decision, and she hated making decisions based on hearsay. It was always best to evaluate others face to face and judge their worth without the filter of another's perceptions.

This was a decent diner, right on their border. She was here alone, assuming that Fournier would be hesitant to initiate a bloodbath in a human public place. In the off chance of an attack, she was fairly sure she could take him. She was a Born too, and had five-thousand years on him. She smiled, more actually, but a lady never admitted her true age.

Out of habit, Monica glanced at her reflection in the chrome of the music-selection device in the booth and saw . . . nothing. It was still a shock. It had been at least two-thousand years since she'd been able to see her reflection, and even before that it had become hazy and faded as she aged. She actually missed it more than she missed the sunlight.

Not that she'd been particularly attractive, even when she'd had human characteristics. Her hair had always been a tight mess of frizz, exploding out in a pyramid shape from her skull unless oiled and tamed into snug braids. Her nose had been a sharp beak, her dark eyes deep set, and lips thin. Her best asset; her skin, the color of dark honey, smooth over high cheekbones and an angled jaw. She knew what she'd become, what her body and face morphed into as her reflection faded away and the vampire inside revealed itself. Ah well, she was what she'd been born to be. Part of her hoped she was an attractive vampire, that somehow her milky eyes and gray skin, stretched tight over lean muscle and bone, were more appealing than most. She hoped, but she was too vain to ask anyone, and Gideon for all his honest affection, never commented on her appearance.

Maybe she did miss sunshine more. It had been hard watching Gideon's enjoyment of the intense heat all those years. He'd get up long before she was capable and sweat out on the beach. She loved the smell of it on him when she awoke at dusk, the way the sun and the warmth combined with his perspiration. Still, she was secretly glad when he'd begun to feel pain, begun to blister at exposure. She hated being jealous.

The bell rang on the diner door, and two vampires walked in. Monica felt a twinge of irritation. He'd brought back-up. Prudent, given her age, but still a mark against him.

Gideon had come alone when she'd negotiated with him. Warmth spread through her as she remembered the meeting.

Her previous Master, a Born, had been killed in the struggle to take over as head of the family. She'd been the only Born left. The fact that she was female had spared her a preemptive execution. Gideon had come to offer her an alliance — she would become his Consort to lend status to his claim as Master, and she would live.

She'd been prepared to fight to the death at that meeting. She could not imagine suffering the humiliation of being a Consort to a Made, especially for one of her age, of her lineage. All those plans fled the moment he'd walked into the room. He had been so young, but there had been something about him. There still was. Gideon Kincaid had the raw power of a self-made man, a vampire who had earned by shrewdness and strength every step up the ladder he'd taken. One look at him and she'd changed her mind completely. One look at him, and she'd lost her heart.

She still loved him. Almost two-hundred-and-fifty years they'd been together. He treated her as an equal, valued her intelligence and relied upon her counsel. They worked as partners. Even as a Born, there was a glass ceiling for female vampires. Gideon had always acted as if that barrier never existed. Her word carried the same authority as his. And there was passion — then and now. A consort relationship seldom included intimacy, and many were strictly a contract on paper. Theirs wasn't. It amazed Monica to think of how desire flared between them. Gideon was gorgeous, by human or vampire terms, and she . . . she was not. Still, a vampire's life was a long one and love was a fleeting thing. She needed to put emotion aside and evaluate her options. She needed to ignore that part deep within her that protested and begged her to walk out of the diner right now.

Monica observed the two vampires that approached. The Fournier Prince was obviously the young man with the ridiculously expensive suit. He resembled his father, whom

Monica knew from many millennia back. Another good-looking man. She grimaced slightly, thinking that this one was unlikely to desire a sexual relationship with her. Her status and power were a heady attraction, but it was clear from his glance that he'd not want more. It wouldn't be a problem. He was so young; it would have been like having sex with a child.

His aura was solid and strong, but it had a sharp bite to it — a sensation of inexperience. Some found that attractive; she did not. Another mark against him. If he had been a thousand years older, she might have jumped sides right away, but he was just too darned young to be going up against either Gideon or his own father for territory. Youth. They were so impatient. They thought they knew all the answers at three hundred.

"Revered Ancient," Kyle said as the Latin-looking vampire with him took a seat at a distant table. Close enough to rush to the Prince's aid if need be, but far enough away to not offend. Monica hid her annoyance at his greeting. He'd pointedly not called her 'Consort'.

"Young Born," she greeted him, insulting him slightly with the minimal title. He didn't react at all, his face a bland mask of pleasantry. A point in his favor.

He sat down and got right to the topic without unnecessary pleasantries. Another point in his favor.

"I know I'm young, but I'm prepared to offer you Consort status if you assist, and if we are successful in our goals. I appreciate the power and knowledge you hold, and find those traits valuable assets in a Consort. In return, I would grant you an active role in the management of the family and territory. Your influence would not lessen. In fact, it would expand with greater territory and a larger population."

Monica considered his words. "What if you're only partially successful? I could end up with a smaller piece of the pie than I have now. Even if you take Kincaid's entire territory, what advantage would there be to me if you were unable to grab at least a section of your father's holdings?"

"My ultimate goal is to consolidate both territories. Achieving that would be quicker with you by my side."

The amusement she felt didn't show on her face. "Quite ambitious of you, but my question still stands. I'm not convinced the odds of your success are favorable enough for me to align myself with you."

"I can't reveal details to you at this point in our negotiation," Kyle replied smoothly. Another point in his favor. "The speed and size of each acquisition relies on many fluid events. I have plans in place to accommodate each changing variable in the situation."

She nodded. Even if he had outlined his take-over plan to her, ultimately her assessment of his success would hinge on her assessment of his character. So far she was impressed. If only he wasn't so darned young.

"What's to stop me from using your activities to seize control of the Kincaid territories myself? I'm a Born with a far stronger aura than you. Between the two of us, I'd exert more influence."

It was a leading question, and it paid off. There. She saw it deep in his eyes, although he hid it immediately — the same look his father had, the same look her own father had, the same look every male vampire except for Gideon had. The Prince was absolutely confident that in a contest between them for loyalty, he would triumph because he was male and vampires would not follow a woman. Perhaps she was wrong. Perhaps it was because his lineage traced slightly father than hers. She doubted it. Women were equals until the very top, and then they were not. At that point, the best they could be were partners, Consorts.

"Vampires work in groups for the good of the entire

family," Kyle said smoothly. "Together we are much stronger than alone. Together we can combine two families and territories and rule the largest vampire holding in the world. Wouldn't that be far more satisfying than trying to maintain a financially struggling territory against a very persistent foe?"

The threat was there in his words, but not in his tone. He knew she was smart. He knew she realized all this. It was a little reminder, an acknowledgement between them of what constituted reality. Another point in his favor. Monica rose. This was enough for a first meeting. She had much to think about, and she was sure he did too. Besides, she had to get underground before dawn.

* * *

"WHAT DO YOU THINK?" Kyle asked Juan as they drove back to Baltimore. He'd already made up his mind, but knew how important it was to solicit other's opinions. It helped tighten their bond to him, and they often had interesting views that caused him to alter his position.

"She's so old," Juan said in a reverential tone. "She reminds me of the Master. It kind of scares me," he admitted.

Kyle nodded. He, too, felt a little uncomfortable around her, like he was a naughty, presumptuous little boy. It would be difficult to have her as a Consort. He'd constantly need to be on guard that she not overshadow him. He didn't want to end up second fiddle to her. Before the meeting, he'd thought of proposing a simple alliance on paper. They'd join forces, then when the battle was won, go their separate ways. He was beginning to rethink that.

"I might truly give her an active role in managing the family. We'd have a huge territory, and she could mean the difference between spending a century gaining solid control or gaining control straight away. I just worry about her upstaging me."

Juan looked curious. "She's a woman. She wouldn't want to single-handedly run a huge territory."

Kyle agreed that she didn't seem particularly driven to rule alone. He knew his own prejudices, knew how dangerous it was to make assumptions based on them. Yes, women never ruled unless as a Consort, and even then with less authority then the Master. That didn't mean it would never happen. Didn't mean that someday a smart, powerful woman wouldn't unexpectedly seize a territory and lop their heads off while they looked at her in surprise,

"Stereotypes can get you killed, Juan," he warned. "With proper motivation, there's nothing stopping a dominant female vampire from taking and holding a territory. I'm hoping this one doesn't have the motivation."

CHAPTER 24

It was closing time when Jaq staggered into Dale's, barely making it to the end of the bar before dropping heavily onto one of the stools. She hadn't slept in nearly two days, but instead of catching some much-needed shut-eye after work, she'd headed straight out to repair the damaged traps. Once Kelly got off work, they'd put out additional traps and wait for the inevitable retaliation from last night.

Good thing it was Sunday and Dale closed early, because she wasn't sure how much longer she could keep her eyes open. Normally she'd do it herself, but Jaq didn't want to leave Kelly alone in her home in case the Kincaids came to deliver their revenge. Maybe the pair of them could take turns standing watch while the other slept on Kelly's hideous sofa.

Worry gnawed at her. It was one thing to pick off the occasional vampire, but the forays into West Virginia had increased beyond what she could manage. What if one or the other of the opposing families decided to take up residence? What if Kelly was right and vampires swarmed their lands in war? They'd never be able to share the state — it would be win or die, or flee into another area to live in one of the small spread-apart packs that survived in neighboring states.

Musing over the visions of a grim future, Jaq watched Kelly sweep empty glasses from a table, whirling to the kitchen in a graceful dance of movement. To every other eye in the bar, the vampire probably seemed fine, healthy and strong, but Jaq noticed little details, like the way her shoulders drooped, how she leaned on the bar for support as she rang up customer purchases on the cash register. She was so thin, and the dark circles under her eyes deepened each day. Could they skip the extra fortifications and try a dash across the border to get the blood she so desperately needed? Jaq winced. Given that they'd just dumped two vampire bodies behind a pawn shop and killed another, it probably wouldn't be a good time to be trespassing in Virginia. Although, they may have no choice. It didn't look like the vampire could wait for things to settle down.

Kelly scooped up a huge tray, effortlessly balancing the heavy load of dishes on her shoulder as she headed toward the kitchen. She looked delicate and fragile, breakable as a glass figurine, but Jaq knew better. The werewolf had known the moment she'd reached down and touched the vampire, bleeding and broken on the floor of her trailer, that the woman had the strength to endure. She had proven herself to be smart, adaptable, with an unexpected sense of humor.

A vampire is my closest friend. I'm trusting her with my life, with the lives of my pack-mates, with the lives of my human neighbors and friends.

The whole thing was unbelievable. Bloodsuckers had always been the enemy. Their snooty, superior attitude, their lack of compassion, and their willingness to sell out their own mother for gain — not exactly traits that made for a long-lasting friendship. What in the world was she doing trying to carve out a space for one in a werewolf world? How could she ever think this would work?

Idiot.

Jaq caught the reflection of herself in the mirror behind the rows of liquor bottles. If she was wrong, she'd put her whole pack in danger. The devil on her shoulder prodded her with a pitchfork of doubt. What if Kelly was lying, setting them all up for a fall? What if her helplessness hid a scheme to open the doors and let the northern vampires take what had belonged to the werewolves for centuries? Was Kelly some kind of Trojan horse, and she the fool at the gate?

"Idiot," she told her reflection firmly.

"I'm constantly reminding the rail liquor of that fact, but they still overestimate their IQ. Especially the gin," a teasing voice said. Jaq glanced over at Kelly, suspicion still clouding her mind. The vampire walked so fast, moved so quietly that Jaq hadn't even heard her.

"What's up?" Kelly asked. The warmth in her voice was mirrored in her eyes as she smiled at the other woman. "Do you need a menu? Can I get you a beer?"

Jaq shifted on the bar stool and pushed her doubts aside. Kelly wasn't a monster. She wasn't like the others. It was time to stop worrying over these things and worry over the retaliation that was surely coming their way.

"Nah. Just wanted to see how you wanted to handle this evening. Should we set up an ambush? Or do you need to make a quick run across the border first?"

"I'd like to borrow your truck," the vampire said, her face reddening. "And . . . uh . . . maybe some money for gas. Tips haven't been too good. I'll pay you back; I promise."

Jaq bit back a smile. Sheesh, the woman was still fretting over ten dollars here and ten dollars there. She'd probably rather ask for a kidney than borrow money. She dug a folded bill out of her pants pocket and slid it across the bar.

"Of course you can borrow money. I just filled it up though, so we should be okay. Do you want to leave right after work?"

Kelly made herself suddenly busy, scrubbing what appeared to be an imaginary spot off the bar as she took the money and stuffed it into a pocket. "No, you stay here. I'll meet up with you later. It shouldn't take me long."

A chill ran through Jaq. She couldn't let the vampire do this alone. There was too much risk that the Kincaids would catch her and overpower her. She shuddered to think what they'd do to Kelly if they found her poaching across the border.

"I really think I need to come with you. Someone to watch your back."

The vampire's dark eyes met hers, and she reached out a hand to Jaq's arm, squeezing gently. "I thought about things a bit this morning, and I just can't let you do this. You can say what you want about me being a lion, a predator, but attacking humans is wrong in your mind. I'm not going to let you bend your ethics like a pretzel. I'll be quick. I'll be careful. And I'll be back in an hour."

As if on cue, Dale locked the door, turning to face them. Besides Nan banging around in the kitchen, they were the only ones left in the bar.

"I'm going to run the trash out to the dumpster and start pulling together the deposit. Go ahead and close out the register, then you can leave."

Kelly nodded, walking away from Jaq to perform the closing routine as Dale disappeared through the swinging door into the kitchen. She was still counting and sorting bills when Nan came out of the kitchen, purse over her shoulder. She gave Jaq a sharp look, but a respectful nod.

Darn straight. None of the wolves might approve of her protecting the vampire, but none of them would challenge their First, especially with the Alpha backing her up. Nan wouldn't be much of a threat, but others might, and Jaq reminded herself that she'd need to watch carefully, in case anyone planned an "accident".

"Night, Nan," Kelly called cheerfully after the cook. Jaq hid a smile, realizing that the vampire was baiting the werewolf with her unwelcome friendliness.

Nan grunted and turned the deadbolt. "Jaq, will you lock this after me?"

Jaq slid off her stool. Not that anyone with half a brain would rob a werewolf-owned establishment, but there were a few humans with more bravado then sense.

The door chimed as Nan opened it. Then all hell broke loose.

There was an explosion of red, and Nan's head hit the floor, her body slumping as the door slammed open. Jaq instinctively shifted into her wolf form, grateful it didn't take her twenty minutes like other werewolves. Taking a split second to shake off any loose clothing, she launched herself toward the door, preparing to intercept the vampire that shot through it in a blur of speed. They collided mid-room, crashing to the floor. The cloying, sweet taste of thick vampire blood filled Jaq's mouth as her teeth sank deep into his arm. It tasted horrible. No wonder Kelly refused to drink their blood.

The vampire cursed, shaking her like a doll as he rose to his feet. Jaq's four paws dangled off the ground, and she felt her teeth slip on his arm as he whipped her about. The vampire's free arm grabbed her neck and squeezed. Biting harder, she flailed all four legs in an attempt to connect somewhere. Her head throbbed as his grip tightened, and she felt her teeth slip further. Just as spots were beginning to float in her vision, there was a loud crash. Jaq fell to the floor, gasping and spitting out the foul blood as she rolled away.

She heard a string of curses as she rose unsteadily to her feet, shaking her head to clear her vision.

Kelly had pitched the cash register at the vampire, complete with a tangle of electronic cable. He had staggered backward, dark blood pouring from his head. The ten-pound, sharp-edged piece of equipment hadn't knocked him out, but he was tangled in the mess of wires and furiously trying to get free.

Kelly vaulted the bar. Before the vampire could attack again, she snatched up one of the round tables, wielding it like a giant club. He ducked and dodged, backing up to avoid the round end of the table; their actions like a movie on fast forward.

Jaq hesitated, uncertain how to place herself in between the two vampires without Kelly accidently smacking her with the table. The woman was sure to tire soon. With Kelly's lack of blood, she was probably running on adrenaline alone. And where the heck was Dale? He must have heard the commotion, even if he'd been out putting trash in the dumpster. Jaq caught her breath, worried that another vampire might have been sent around back to enter that way. Dale was her pack-mate, and she should be racing to assist him, but her heart was with Kelly, who was swinging a table like it was no heavier than a fencing foil.

The vampire grabbed the round end of the table and Kelly staggered, her momentum throwing her off balance. Twisting the table, Kelly lost her footing entirely, and let go of the metal feet as she fell. It was the moment she'd been waiting for. Jaq leaped at the vampire's back, digging her claws into his shoulders and waist and biting down on his head. Bone cracked, but before Jaq could finish the job, he whirled about and began smacking her into the wall.

Pain lanced through Jaq's back and her breath whooshed out. Dale had lovely brick walls, a good eighteen inches thick, and the vampire had slammed her into it with all his strength. Mortar and brick chunks rained around her. She struggled to take a breath as he smashed her against the wall. The vampire's movements became more frantic. Jaq realized that Kelly had attached herself to his front, her hands around his neck. Jaq wasn't sure whether her friend was attempting to strangle the other vampire or rip his head off, but it was becoming quite clear she didn't have the strength for either.

Another slam against the brick and Jaq felt her limbs grow numb. Her hold on his head slipped, and he tossed her aside, spinning around to do the same maneuver on Kelly. Jaq slid across the floor, trying to force her numb legs to obey her commands. He bashed Kelly into the wall, and Jaq saw blood trickle from her mouth and nose, her hands losing their grip on his neck.

The roar of an explosion deafened her, and all Jaq saw was red. The mangled flesh that had been the vampire slid to the ground, and Jaq glimpsed Dale from the corner of her eye, bloody as he racked the shotgun and took aim for a second blast.

Kelly! Jaq howled, a piercing noise of grief and warning as she managed to put herself between the vampire and Dale's shotgun. Was she okay? Had the shells blown clean through the other vampire to kill her?

"Jaq! Move aside!" Dale commanded.

She snarled, exerting her status as First to disobey the older werewolf. He cursed, transferring the shotgun to one hand and pointing the barrel toward the ceiling.

"Fine. But even you gotta admit that this vampire of yours is trouble. She brought this on us tonight. If you don't end her, you're jeopardizing the pack."

Probably. But what Dale didn't understand was even without Kelly, the pack was in danger. And Jaq was not about to choose between the vampire that had become her friend and the pack she owed her life to. There had to be a way she could protect them both.

Jaq turned from Dale and panicked when she saw the condition of the attacking vampire close up. He had been shredded — the silver shot in Dale's gun keeping him from regenerating as the pellets tore through him. Silver shot wasn't enough to kill a vampire. He stirred, and Jaq knew that even though it would take him days to heal from the silver damage, he'd still be up and mobile in a few moments. She should take his head off. She should dig his heart out with her claws. But all she could do was shove him aside, her own heart in her mouth as she examined the other vampire he'd been laying on.

With a flash, she'd transformed back into her human form, her hands roving over Kelly as she frantically tried to determine what blood was hers and what belonged to the other vampire. Relief flooded her as Kelly opened her eyes.

"Where are you hurt?"

"I'm okay," Kelly grimaced, obviously lying. "Make sure you kill him. Take care of him first."

Assured that Kelly wasn't on the edge of death, Jaq complied, pulling the knife from her pocket and slicing through the vampire's neck. With a twist, she'd separated it from the body and turned her attention back to Kelly.

"Dale's gun was loaded with silver. Did any of it hit you?"

Kelly winced, raising her arms and shifting her legs. "Mostly in my extremities. I've got some surface burns from slugs that went all the way through the other guy."

"How's your back and head?" The other vampire had bashed Kelly hard against the wall. Hard enough for her to bleed from her mouth and nose.

"Bruised. Concussion. Nothing that can't heal."

Nothing that couldn't heal if Kelly had not been at the

edge of starvation. Jaq sighed, tears burning the back of her eyes. This had to stop. Now.

"Romantic as all this is, I really want to know what's going on here," Dale growled, placing the shotgun on a nearby table as he approached. "I get jumped taking the trash out and come in here to find you two doing tag-team wrestling maneuvers with another of these jerks. Think I deserve some explanation."

Jaq exchanged a glance with Kelly and helped the vampire to a sitting position. "There's a war brewing. We'll need to get ready for a lot of vampires tromping through our territory. If we're lucky, we can manage to keep them out at the end of it all, but the odds aren't good."

Dale's expression darkened. He shook his head slowly and looked at the bodies on the floor. "The guy killed Nan. And he didn't come here passing through on his way to a battle field. Your little friend brought him on us. What cha gotta say about that, Jaq?"

Kelly winced, like she'd been hit. Jaq moved to protect her from the other werewolf. "Let her be, Dale, or you'll face me in challenge."

The other wolf snarled, but he dipped his head, retreating slightly. "Fine. But she's fired. I don't want her around here no more. I'm not putting my employees at risk for a disgusting vampire. I'm not putting her before the safety of my pack mates."

The implication stung, but it was honest. Jaq stood, helping Kelly up. Everyone was on edge with the aftermath of adrenaline and violence. She didn't trust herself to reply.

"I gotta get my clothes," she told Kelly. "Can you stand, or do you need to sit down."

The vampire glanced over at Dale. "I can stand." Her voice was defiant, although from her shaking legs, it clearly took effort to remain upright.

Jaq snatched up the clothes, yanking on pants and tossing a shirt over her head before looking around for the rest.

"Underwear is over there," Kelly laughed weakly.

It was. The tiny scrap of black lace hung from the top of a chair with the matching bra on the floor. These were her favorite pair. Worry over whether they'd been ruined warred with worry over Dale seeing the sexy underthings. Embarrassment won over, and she snatched them, shoving them in a pocket of her cargo pants to examine later.

Kelly needed her help to walk out the door and into her truck. But no sooner was the vampire in the truck than she began laughing.

"I'm sorry; I can't help it. The look on your face when you saw your lace thong hanging over a chair in full view of Dale — so funny."

"Oh God," Jaq groaned. "Do you think he saw? At least he didn't get a good look at the bra, too. It's a demi-cup push-up. I'd never live it down."

"No, I think he was too distracted and upset to notice your underwear."

Kelly's reply sobered them both. Nan had been killed. A vampire had attacked them in a werewolf-owned establishment. Jaq realized that everyone around them was in danger. These vampires wouldn't think twice about taking out their neighbors. They'd use any means necessary to have their revenge. What had they done? And Kelly . . . she had probably used up her last strength fighting that guy. There's no way she could face another vampire in her current condition. No way they could spare the time for a blood-run across the border either.

They drove the short distance to Briar Lane in silence, Jaq finally speaking as they pulled up in front of Kelly's trailer.

"Do you need me to help you remove any of that silver?"

Kelly laughed, the sound a faint noise in the truck cab.

"Can you? I thought this stuff was worse for you than it is for us. I'm surprised Dale has it in his shotgun. Heck, I'm surprised you kept those necklaces."

Human friends had given her the necklaces, and she'd endured the pain just to keep from offending them, only to shove them in a box once back at her trailer.

"Dale likes to keep silver in case there are any fights. They work for vampires too, but y'all don't stand still long enough to shoot most of the time. If we can't take you by surprise, then it's hand to hand. I swell up every time I have to load silver shot in my gun. Look like a raspberry with red blisters and burns all over me. It's hard to breathe if I've been touching it too much. I could help you if I wear gloves, though."

Kelly shook her head. "I got it. I've probably only got a dozen or so slugs in my legs and arms. Once I dig them out, I'll be able to start healing. Give me half an hour, then we can head out to check the traps and plan some kind of ambush. I doubt that guy was the only one they're sending tonight.

Jaq nodded, watching the vampire stagger from her truck to the door of her trailer. Half an hour. She'd be back, but not to check traps with Kelly. There was something else far more important that they needed to do first.

CHAPTER 25

Kyle waited impatiently in his car. He would have been a lot more comfortable waiting for Juan in the human diner down the street, but it was too risky. Vampires always did their subversive business, their clandestine meetings, in human diners, and his father was too smart not to know trouble was brewing. Diners were out.

Everything stood on a razor's edge. Tonight they'd take West Virginia. He had his vampires poised at the border, ready to move. And tomorrow, his corporate business would move in, sealing the deal on the largest money makers in the state.

Everything else needed to wait until he heard from the Kincaid female, and he knew she was watching to see him prove himself. It was the waiting that was the hardest. He pushed the need for action down deep within himself and practiced calm. Patience was a critical trait for a vampire, although the high level of self-control he desired would not be his for many centuries. Seeing his second walking briskly towards him, he was finally able to relax the tension from his shoulders.

"Sorry I'm late, Sir," Juan said with barely concealed excitement. Juan always had difficulty hiding his emotions. If he hadn't been so loyal, so capable, that trait would have stalled his career a hundred years ago.

"Do you have the information?"

Juan spread a map out before him. Red circles dotted the paper like chicken pox. "I've got the addresses for two-hundred werewolves in the state, most clustered towards the east. Should we move house to house? Send groups of two or three to take down a section of them at a time?"

Kyle frowned. "Two hundred?" That couldn't be right. The angels would never allow that many werewolves to congregate in one area. The most he'd ever seen in a twenty-mile radius was fifty, and that was rare.

"My source insists that he's correct."

That would require a change of plans. Kyle didn't have enough vampires to attack two hundred werewolves at the same time, and success required surprise. Once those things had time to transform and take to the woods, they were a pain to catch.

"Then we need to draw them together so we can hit them fast and hard, all at once. It would need to be something urgent enough that they'd come without taking the time to change form. They're easier to kill on two legs."

Juan chewed thoughtfully on the end of a pen as he scanned the map. "Then we probably need to attack a group of humans. They've got some kind of agreement with them and will run to defend them. "Maybe Martinsburg, at the veteran's hospital?"

"A hospital?" Kyle shuddered at the thought. Ill humans had a horrible aftertaste. "How about the racetrack/casino here, in Charles Town?"

"It's Sunday night. Live racing is only Saturday through Wednesday, and only the die-hard gamblers will be at the casino late on a Sunday. We'll have more humans to threaten at the hospital."

Ugh. He could wait. Should wait. Friday or Saturday night would be better, and vampires never did anything in haste. Kyle looked at the map, his eyes tracing the distance to Charles Town. Martinsburg was closer to the Maryland border. They could be in and seize the hospital before the werewolves even knew they were in the state.

"There are fifteen buildings at the VA hospital, though. We'll be too spread out."

"That is a drawback," Juan admitted. "We could take the main building and the community center — they're liable to have the most humans."

True, but Kyle didn't like the way the other buildings crowded in close, or the one that stood between the main building and the center. It would split them into two groups, and even with the big parking areas, there were plenty of tall buildings and tree-lined walkways for the werewolves to sneak up on them. He didn't want his trap to turn into a siege. But the casino. . . he *should* wait. One week, or maybe a few months when warmer weather tempted more humans to visit.

"We're taking the casino. Are we ready to move tonight?"

West Virginia. It might be slim pickings, but it would be his — a territory of his own, no matter how small.

"Yes, but we need to be elsewhere tonight," Juan replied with barely concealed excitement. "Kincaid has crossed the border into DC and attacked. Durand has ramped up his fighters in the suburban Maryland areas. You and your staff are to provide back up in Potomac in an hour to flank Kincaid as the Master pushes him north-west."

"Kincaid what?" Kyle asked in shock.

Maybe he didn't need to wait for the Kincaid Consort to pick sides. If Kyle stood with his father, they'd push Kincaid back in a matter of weeks and have the justification and outrage to take at least three states. Of course, once his father got his hands on those states, he'd be unlikely to gift them to Kyle.

The vampire mulled over the situation. This changed everything. He could proceed as planned, but ignoring his father's summons would bring unwelcome notice to his West Virginia project. Plus he'd have to face the old man's wrath. Forget New York — for that, he'd probably be shipped off to France.

"Why in the world would Kincaid attack *us*?" Kyle wondered. There had to be a catch, something he was missing. It just didn't make sense.

"Kincaid claims the Fournier family has declared war on him by killing two of his vampires then trespassing into his lands to deliver the insult. Once there, the Fournier agent killed another of his vampires, displaying his body in a clear declaration of war."

Juan recited all of this as if reading from a paper. The man practically danced with excitement. All this intrigue in his own backyard was clearly too much for a young vampire to take.

Kyle frowned. Could Kincaid be lying? It was inconceivable that his father, who had never shown interest in the southern lands, would have done such a thing. And besides motive, it wasn't his style. That sort of message was arrogant and flashy, the act of someone who let unseemly emotion rule their actions.

"Who? I didn't do that, and my father wouldn't have bothered. If he wanted their territory, he would have poisoned them all, or had Kincaid knifed in the back. Is this possibly a ploy of Kincaid's to turn my father against me, to somehow implicate me in a sloppy incident?"

Because this would be blamed on him. He was the caretaker for the lower states. These events would land right on his doorstep. His responsibility; any protests of innocence would fall on disbelieving ears. The whole family would think he screwed up and started a war without adequate planning.

Kyle thought furiously. What would Kincaid gain from this? Did that Consort of his set this up? He couldn't see an advantage to her if Kincaid was killed. She'd be forced to immediately become Kyle's Consort and hand the whole lot over as a sort of dowry. No, the most likely result from this move would be a split between him and his father, and a significant delay of his plans for seizing the lower states. If his father thought he'd been carelessly assassinating vampires, risking the family and acting without permission, he'd be kept in New York for centuries. Kincaid would have bought himself time.

Of course, there was another possibility nagging at his mind. The one who truly gained the most advantage from this was the old man himself. Kyle had allies, but support for him would be weak if his family thought he'd been so rash and impulsive as to whack the Kincaid wasp's nest without an adequate plan in place. They'd all think he wasn't ready. His Father's lands would be safe from him for centuries while he rebuilt support. It would be the perfect thing to put him in his place, and the whole time his father could appear the disappointed Master, lovingly holding his son back until he was ready.

"I wouldn't put it past the Master to do this," Kyle thought out loud. He'd normally never say this sort of thing, but Juan was the only vampire in his family he could trust enough to speak candidly around. "I'm implicated. It will turn some against me and might force me back into his fold. I won't have the backing to move forward with this hanging over my head."

"A temporary setback," Juan commented. "We'll assist him, protest that you're innocent, and wait for better timing."

"But what about West Virginia? We're ready — everything is in place." Kyle asked, more to himself than to Juan.

The best move he could make would be to join his father and push back Kincaid. That's what every reasonably intelligent vampire would do. Leaving the Master to his own devices and taking West Virginia would give Kyle nothing but a tiny, poor territory. He'd not have the time to wait on the other parts of his plans. He'd need to strike right away, or risk being sent off by his father and losing his newly won territory after holding it a scant few weeks. It was madness.

Juan shook his head. "You should be conservative in your plans, cautious. Wait until you're completely ready to make a move; don't jump ahead and lock yourself into a course of action that might lead to exile. There will be another opportunity."

Kyle thought for a moment. His starting territory would be miniscule. Once his father's forces repelled Kincaid, either or both groups would squash him in a matter of weeks. He wasn't ready. The smart, mature plan would be to support his father, push back Kincaid, head to New York like a dutiful son and wait for a better chance. He was young. He could wait hundreds of years for the right moment. It was what an Old would have done, what any intelligent vampire would have done.

"Tell my vampires to advance as planned," he told Juan. "Tonight. Then pull together a meeting at sunup to plan phase two. We need to think of all the scenarios that could result from this little war and have plans in place to take advantage of any of them. I want more than West Virginia in my hands before the blood dries."

Juan's face was tight, but he nodded. "Yes, my Master."

Not yet, Kyle thought. *But soon. Very soon.*

CHAPTER 26

At least Jaq gave a perfunctory knock before she barged into the trailer, unlike Melody and the other neighbors. It still didn't give Kelly much time to clean up the mess. Jaq halted abruptly on the doorstep, her eyes sweeping over Kelly with alarm before she shuttered them back into calm friendliness.

"Give me a moment to wash up," Kelly grumbled, sponging herself off with paper towels. There was already a pile of bloody ones on the counter and in the sink, but she was still bleeding, gaping holes and gashes unhealed from where she'd dug out the silver. It wouldn't get any worse, but it sure as heck wasn't going to get any better. Not that it mattered. She just needed to run on adrenaline until they'd safeguarded the neighborhood from any more vampire intruders. Perhaps after that, Jaq could keep watch while she rested. Rested for all eternity.

"What's this?"

Kelly glanced over her shoulder to see Jaq holding up a tangled mess of yarn.

"It's supposed to be a scarf. I'm not having much luck with it though."

"Vampires knit?"

"No, humans knit. Vampires make a big knotted mess and pretend they know what they're doing. Maybe I can use it as a tourniquet. I can't seem to stop bleeding."

The werewolf dropped the yarn back onto the sofa and walked to Kelly, gently examining her arm. "Should we tear up sheets and bandage it? Probably wouldn't be a good idea for you to be leaving blood trails everywhere."

Kelly pulled up her shirt, showing her the taped gauze at her waist. "That was the worst. These have almost stopped bleeding." Stopped bleeding, but not even scabbed over. If she needed to run or fight, she'd be covered in fresh blood as the fragile clotting broke open.

Jaq's jaw set into a hard line. "Come on then. We've got a lot to do and we need to make a brief detour first."

Kelly didn't protest as the werewolf led her out the door and down the lane. Her mind whirled as they climbed the step to Melody's house. Were they collecting supplies? More silver chains? One of Joe's carving knives?

Bright fluorescent light greeted the vampire as Jaq flung open the door and half dragged her into the trailer. Inside were Melody, Barbara, Margaret, Shanna, and Kristen. They stood with arms crossed, regarding her with somber expressions. Kelly's eyes strayed around the room and froze as she saw a chair. It was padded, with arms that hinged out to the sides. Everything else faded into a blur except that chair. It was eerily similar to one from her memory. She felt the panic race through her veins, remembered the feel of metal on her fangs, the pain that had collapsed her surroundings to white.

"I know you're pissed, but I had to tell them." Jaq's voice jolted her out of the nightmare, and she reached out, clinging to the werewolf's thin arms.

"Oh, I can't *believe* we've got our very own vampire, right here in the neighborhood!" Margaret squealed, hopping from foot to foot in excitement. "I'm A positive and so is Barbara. Melody and Kristen are O negative, and Shanna is O positive. Which would you like today?"

Kelly's head spun with relief. The chair wasn't for her; it was for them. Jaq had told them, and strangely enough they seemed excited by the prospect of having a vampire living down the street. How could she explain this to them? It wasn't like they saw in the movies, all sex and pretty drops of red — especially since she had no fangs.

"I . . . I can't. You're my friends, my neighbors, not a source of food."

Melody shook a finger at Kelly. "You eat my tuna casserole, don't you?"

Kelly couldn't help but grin. "Every chance I get."

"Well then, feeding you tuna casserole isn't any different in my book then giving you some of my blood. It's the neighborly thing to do."

Kelly felt this went far beyond neighborly care. "But without my fangs it would hurt horribly. I'd need to cut you over and over again to get enough blood."

"Nonsense," Barbara announced, waving a thick bag wrapped in plastic tubing. "I do this every single day. Thirty minutes tops and you'll have a pint. See these tubes? You can drink it right from here, like one of those juice pouches."

"There's ten of us, including the husbands," Melody chimed in. "Barbara says we can donate every eight weeks, so that's a little more than a pint a week until we can get some other people on board."

"And I can smuggle out expired blood from the hospital if that will do you any good," Barbara added. "It might not be as beneficial as fresh, but it might work as a supplement."

"How old?" This conversation was surreal.

"We have to dispose of it after forty-two days." Barbara paused, an apologetic expression on her face. "Of course, our supplies are chronically low. I might not always have expired blood available."

Kelly shook her head. "Forty-two days is too old, even if it's been refrigerated. It's not worth you risking your job over."

Barbara looked relieved. "So which shall it be tonight?"

One pint per week would take the edge off, keep her just this side of starvation. It wouldn't be enough, though, if she was going to fight. Kelly hesitated before making her decision. She wasn't likely to live past the end of the week if the assassins kept coming, or if the war brewing between the two families sparked into flame. Might as well go into it as strong as possible.

"Would it be possible to have three tonight and two tomorrow?"

Jaq shook her arm slightly, leaning over to whisper. "That's half your available supply, and you'll need to go seven weeks on five pints if we can't line up any more. Can you do that?"

A twinge of guilt went through Kelly. "Yeah. Once I'm up to full strength, it shouldn't be a problem," she lied.

It shouldn't if she lounged around in bed for seven weeks. Racing through forests, fighting vampires, and healing injuries was another thing entirely. With all that, she'd go through her available supply by next week. Kelly put the thoughts in a corner of her mind. She'd deal with that later, if she survived long enough to worry about it. What mattered now was making sure she could protect her new friends.

"Yep. Do you want A and A, or O and O, or mix it up?"

"All three O's tonight."

It was easier than she ever dreamed it would be. The girls chatted as Kristin, Shanna, and then Melody's blood steadily filled the plastic bags, like they were getting manicures and not giving blood to feed a starving vampire.

"Here." Barbara handed over the three bags, and Kelly rolled them in her hands. Oh God, they were still warm. Her ears buzzed, and she felt weak at the thought.

"Hold the bag like this, then push this needle in through the seal of this tube. Make sure you stick the other end of the tube in your mouth first, because it's going to flow out right away."

"Thanks." Kelly looked around at all the expectant faces, hesitant to do this right in front of them.

"You can use my bedroom, dear," Melody beamed. "Or the bathroom if you're worried about spilling anything. When you're done, we'll have some of these lovely brownies that Margaret made."

Bathroom it was, because it would be mortifying for Melody to walk in and find her frantically trying to suck blood off her comforter.

The tub actually was ideal. Kelly sat on the edge and stuck the tube in her mouth like a straw, following Barbara's instructions. The blood flowed almost as quickly as it did with her fangs, so warm and sweet that she almost cried. She never thought she'd experience this again. She'd truly thought that she'd spend her remaining days trying to ineffectually lap blood from messy razor-blade cuts.

Finishing the first bag, Kelly set it aside and started on the second one. Already she felt better, strength flowing through her limbs. The wounds from the silver shot granulated, the edges beginning to close as she watched. Her skin lost its gray tone, taking on a faint golden hue — a remnant from her human past that would remain for another few centuries before fading away.

With the second bag gone, Kelly moved on to the third. She felt full for the first time since she'd nearly killed that drunk outside the strip club. Her body had quickly absorbed the blood and its nutrients, and now her stomach growled, reminding her that she was still young enough to require other food. Brownies would be good right now, and maybe some of Melody's tuna casserole.

There was no time for tuna casserole. Kelly had barely made it out of the bathroom when the door to Melody's trailer burst open, and a burly man in a heavy tan jacket filled the doorway.

"They're swarming the state," Mike said, his expression grim as he faced Jaq. "There's fighting in DC and Virginia, but a group crossed the border and they've seized that race-track/casino in Charles Town."

"What?" Jaq rose to her feet. "They can't expect to hold one business in our territory. Have they made demands? Are they holding hostages?"

"Don't know. Jonah wants us all there to assist. And if that's not bad enough, the other battle might drag through here as they surge north."

"What's swarming?" Melody asked, her voice barely more than a whisper.

Mike turned to glare at Kelly. "Vampires," he spat.

It was one thing for two families to battle it out, but why were they grabbing the casino and holding hostages? *Oakwood.* Kelly remembered the peculiar hostile takeover attempts from vampire companies into West Virginia businesses. They had been the Prince's domain. The Master would never lower himself to bother with a small werewolf-held state, but the Prince. . . .

"I don't trust this," she told him. "There's no reason for them to physically take the casino — they're on the verge of buying it out anyway. You've got nothing to negotiate against human hostages. I doubt you all would vacate the state and turn it over for a few-hundred humans."

"No way," Mike exploded. "This is our land. I'm not letting a bunch of stinking blood-suckers tromp all over my home. We'll storm the place and take them out. Rescue the humans. I don't care what they're asking for, they're not getting it."

"How many vampires are in there?" Jaq asked.

"Jonah said maybe ten or fifteen. We'll have a few hundred of the pack in Charles Town in less than half an hour. It's overkill, but they'll think twice about trying this again once we send a truckload of body parts back to them."

"Ten or fifteen," Kelly mused. "It's not enough. This whole thing doesn't make sense. Is the fight in the southeast vampire on vampire? Or are they gathering a force to attack you from the east?"

"It's those north and south families, fighting it out," Mike told her. "So far, they're pretty busy with each other, but there's a good chance it will spill over our border."

"Crap. Should we head there in case they cross the border, or to Charles Town?" Jaq asked.

"Jonah says Charles Town. He wants a show of force there."

"Wait," Kelly urged. "Why? If two families are fighting to the east, why would they send a handful of vampires to grab a casino? It doesn't make any sense. They've got enough to worry about without trying to snatch one out-of-territory business. No, there has to be a reason for this."

"Would they want us to head to Charles Town and give them an opening to come in from the southeast, through Berryville?" Mike frowned. "That doesn't make sense either. It's only fifteen miles away. They wouldn't make much progress before we'd be on their backs."

"Or maybe someone is using the fight to the east as a cover while he makes a move on the state," Kelly mused.

Jaq slowly shook her head. "Then they should have us all

run to Leesburg while they make a grab behind us and push us into Virginia. Ten or fifteen vampires taking a casino and making a big deal about it? Reminds me of a prank — something just to get us riled up."

It was a small number of vampires. If they'd wanted to annoy the werewolves, they would have just popped in and randomly killed humans here and there, or attacked werewolf-owned establishments. This was too big a move to be a thorn in their side, but too small to be more than a half-hearted attack. And vampires never did anything half-heartedly.

"The casino — it's to get you all in one location," Kelly said. "It's a trap. He knows you'll come out in a big group. It would be much easier than trying to pick you all off one at a time across the state. A few-hundred werewolves dead in one evening would make the rest think seriously about leaving the state — especially if he managed to kill your Alpha."

"Who is 'he'?" Jaq's tone was suspicious. "Did you know about this? We had a deal. You were supposed to let us know in advance."

"The Prince. I told you he might make a move to raid Kincaid lands across your territory. You told me about your businesses being bought up. I suspected he might make a play for your state, but couldn't believe it. Seems he is."

"We've got to warn Jonah," Mike said. "If we hurry, we can get to Charles Town before he does."

Kelly threw her hands up in frustration. "Doesn't anyone around here use cell phones? Can't we just text him?"

Jaq shook her head. "In a situation like this, we'd take wolf form. No pockets, no fingers to push the buttons. Everyone just leaves their phones at home or in their cars so they don't get lost or trampled."

Great. Suddenly they were all back in the Middle Ages.

"By the time we drive there, it may be too late," Mike said, his brow creasing in worry. "We don't have time."

Kelly saw a look pass between Mike and his sister, and then Jaq turned to her, eyes full of indecision.

"I need to run ahead. I can change in a blink, and I'm faster than Mike. I'll warn Jonah."

Mike nodded. "I'll catch up. Save a few for me. It's been three months since I've ripped the head off of a vampire."

Kelly winced. Jaq running ahead left her and Mike going together in the truck. Maybe she should go with Jaq. Anything but being trapped in a truck beside this werewolf who would like nothing more than to gnaw a vampire's head off.

"You drive." Jaq tossed Kelly the truck keys. "That way, Mike can change into wolf form in the bed and be ready for fighting."

Ugh. Her worst nightmare. But Mike would be less likely to lop her head off from the bed of the truck. "Let's go, then. Time's a-wasting."

"She's not coming with me," Mike snarled. "I'm not changing into wolf form in a truck while a vampire drives, and I'm most definitely *not* fighting beside one."

"Fine." Kelly tossed the keys over to Mike. "I'll just run along with Jaq then. Have fun driving."

"She's not coming at all. No one wants to fight beside a vampire, Jaq. She'll betray you to get in good with her family. If you're lucky, one of the pack will kill her before she turns on us."

Kelly caught her breath, but held silent, waiting for Jaq to defend her.

"He's right," Jaq said, trying for a gentle tone. "Mike, you change form a few miles out where you can be safe, then join us from there. Just leave the keys under the mat. Kelly, you stay here with Melody, and we'll touch base with you when we get back."

That hurt more than anything ever had in her life. Even more than George. "What do you mean? Don't you trust me to fight beside you?"

Doubt flashed across Jaq's face, and Kelly felt the knife twist further. "It's not that. My pack won't be able to tell if you're friend or foe. Most of them don't know you to tell you apart from the other vampires. Plus, these people we're fighting are most likely your own family. I know you still have hopes that they'll take you back. I can't put you in a position that would jeopardize your ever being able to return to them."

Oh, it hurt. "You mean you wouldn't trust me to side with you out in the battlefield, don't you? Isn't that what you're really saying? Because let me tell you right now, I made my choice the moment I tossed those two dead vampires in the back of your truck. I'm offering to come with you knowing that every vampire I kill tonight used to be one of my own."

Melody looked back and forth between them, her face pale. "What should *we* do? Vampires can't come into our house without invitations, right? So we're safe if we stay here. I've got Joe's rifle, and a jar of minced garlic. My rosary is in the nightstand."

Kelly bit her lip, uncertain what to say to the five women frozen with fear in the trailer's small kitchen. Vampires could come into any home they wanted, invitation notwithstanding. "Stay inside. I doubt any will be out this far, but, just in case, stay inside. Turn off the lights and be as quiet as possible. If anyone tries to get in, shoot them."

"I'll send one of us back to stay with you," Jaq promised. "And we'll come by to let you know when it's all clear. As for you," she turned to Kelly. "I do trust you to fight with us, but I also worry about you. Tonight is the first time you've had a decent amount of blood in five days. One skirmish and you'll be right back where you started. What's going to happen when your body can't heal?"

"I'm going," Kelly insisted, crossing her arms in front of her chest.

"We don't have time for this," Mike snapped. He threw the keys back at Kelly. "It's time for you to prove whose side you're really on. Time for you to earn your keep, to repay the kindness my sister has shown you. Get your butt out there and kill some vampires. And if you dare try anything while I'm changing in the back of the truck, I'll hang your head above my doorway."

Gross, but pretty much what she'd come to expect from Mike. This was probably as close to acceptance she'd ever get from him or any of the werewolves.

"We'll be okay," Melody chimed in. I've got a whole bunch of silver bullets for the rifle, and silver-coated slugs for the shotgun."

Jaq looked at her in surprise. Melody's expression turned defensive. "What? We're surrounded by a bunch of werewolves, and as nice you, Mike and Dale are, some are not so nice. Best to be safe."

Kelly hid a grin. "That should do it. Don't answer the door. Act like no one's home, and if someone tries to get in, open fire."

"Got it," Melody replied, saluting before hauling a rifle out from under the sofa.

Kelly turned to meet Jaq's worried eyes. "Let's go."

CHAPTER 27

The bitter November air was sharp in Jaq's nose. It smelled of snow, even though the moon and stars shone clear above. Avoiding the main roads, she'd run through the woods, familiar as the fur on her paw, before cutting through long stretches of open fields. The only sound was her breath. Animals hid and held silent, forewarned by the thud of her paws on frozen ground. It wasn't time for stealth; it was time for speed.

As she approached the railroad tracks, the werewolf slowed. It wouldn't do to barge in head-on. If this was a trap, she wasn't sure where the other vampires would be positioned. Crossing the tracks and heading a bit east would bring her to the practice track and the rows of stables below. It would allow her to get close to the casino building under their cover, but her instincts told her there would be vampire guards placed there to ensure werewolves didn't sneak into the main building undetected.

Straight down the railroad tracks would take her to the parking lot, but she'd be exposed the whole way. Veering west, Jaq hopped a wooden stockade fence and, instead, made her way weaving in and out of the manicured lawns of a residential subdivision. At the last house she paused, sniffing the air to get her bearings. There was no avoiding it; she'd need to expose herself in a dash across the parking lot to reach the line of tour busses that Jonah had positioned himself behind.

The fur on the back of her neck rose as she streaked across the nearly empty parking lot, belly close to the ground. It was too quiet. Sunday midnight and the humans were all settling in for the night. The air smelled of wolves from her pack, of grease from the fast-food joints that lined the highway ahead, of auto fuel and human sweat. It didn't smell of vampire — not even a faint trace from the ten or so that were inside. It worried her. Where were they all hiding?

Jonah looked up as she approached. He was still in his human form, outlining strategy to a mixed group of twenty werewolves — most on four feet, although a few were still on two. Twenty. Mike had said there would be about two hundred. Hopefully she'd made it here before them.

Skidding to a stop, Jaq transformed into her human self. She was always a bit uncomfortable with her nudity, even though the pack routinely saw each other without clothing. *No one cares*, she told herself, and sure enough, not one of the werewolves looked below her face. That somehow bothered her even more. *Idiot*, she thought. Now wasn't the time to question her attractiveness, or angst over the size of her breasts or the freckles that covered every inch of her skin.

"Jonah, Kelly fears this is a trap, and I agree."

The alpha frowned. "Your pet vampire? Please tell me you didn't bring her. I've got enough to worry about without fussing over whether one of us 'accidently' kills her in battle."

Jaq winced, ignoring the question. "She has information to suggest that the northern prince may be making a play for the state, trying to drive us out and take over."

"By seizing a casino full of humans?" Jonah looked at her as if she were insane. "That's just going to piss us off, not drive us out of the state. No, this is just a rowdy group that came here to chow down on a bunch of humans safely out of their own territory. Once everyone else arrives, we're going to distract them and send in three teams to take care of the situation."

"Since when have vampires ever been a 'rowdy group'?" Jaq argued. "They would have snuck in, drained half the gamblers and been back across the state line before we even knew. Come on, Jonah, you know better than that!"

He scowled, and Jaq cringed, realizing she wasn't taking the best tactic with her alpha in front of twenty other pack members. "I mean no disrespect, Sir. I fear that this is a trap, that the vampires are gathering us all in one area hoping to kill enough of us that it encourages the rest to flee the state when they take over."

"What trap? I don't smell any vampires in the outlying areas. There will be almost two hundred of us — that's more than enough to take on a bunch of vampires. Unless . . . you don't think they mean to blow up the casino?"

Jaq shook her head. "They're trying to buy it out. I doubt they'd destroy one of the better investments in the state. I don't smell any vampires either — but I also don't smell the ones in the casino. Could they be using some kind of olfactory camouflage? Or working with a witch to provide a masking spell?"

Jonah glanced toward the mish-mash of connected buildings that made up the racetrack and casino. "No witch in West Virginia would work with a vampire, but I guess they might have paid one of those New York ones to do it. So, Jaq, as our pack's First, I'm asking your counsel."

She caught her breath. "Sir. I'd suggest we move now. They'll wait for the rest to arrive before they attack us.

They'll also expect us to storm in, in a huge show of force. Instead, let's send a few individuals in through the back to rescue the human hostages. If they loop around by the stables, and go in on the lower level where the horses enter the track, they can sneak up the service stairs to the dining room, then down back into the casino."

"We make a big show out front here to keep their attention in the meantime." Jonah tapped his chin thoughtfully. "I'll send my best hunters to locate the ambush party and report back."

"What would you like me to do, Sir?"

Jonah grinned. "Why, Jaq, you're my best hunter. I expect you to hunt."

CHAPTER 28

Kelly couldn't help the occasional peek backward as she rocketed down the road in Jaq's pick-up. It took every bit of strength to keep from being tossed around the bench seat. Jaq had stripped in Melody's bathroom, the poorly hidden periwinkle bra peeking out from under the folded Levis as she placed them on the sofa and popped into her wolf form with a flash of light. It was disconcerting to see her race off through the trees, leaving Kelly behind with a werewolf that hated her, and an old pick-up with bad shocks.

She glanced back, feeling vaguely like a peeping tom, to see a shape twisting as it bounced around the rear of the truck. "If I don't slow down, he's liable to fly out," she muttered, half hoping he would. Of course, that would make for an awkward conversation later, when she had to explain to Jaq why she'd driven off and left Mike beside the road, a horrific mixture of fur and flesh.

Ten minutes to the casino, even with the crazy back roads Mike had insisted she take before starting his revolting transformation in the back of the truck. Kelly hoped he'd be fully wolf before she arrived, otherwise he wouldn't be much good in a fight. A huge pothole sent the truck lurching to the left, headlights bouncing around uselessly on the road. They were screwing up Kelly's night vision. She'd contemplated turning them off and just driving in the dark, but at this speed, she was worried she'd plow into a deer before she could stop. Shocks weren't the only thing barely functional on Jaq's truck.

"Holy shit!" Something darted across the road, a blur in the headlights. Too fast for a deer, and too tall.

With a thump, the road disappeared and a face took its place on the windshield. Instinct took over, and Kelly jerked the wheel, sending the vampire sliding off to the side, hanging on to the light rack on the roof and scrambling with his feet to regain balance.

There was another thump, this time toward the rear of the vehicle. Kelly felt herself flung forward as the truck jerked backward. The wheels skidded on the gravel road and she shouted again, twisting the wheel. The truck spun around, slamming to a stop and flinging her onto the floor in a heap. If Mike hadn't fallen out before, there was a good chance he had now.

"Vampires," she shouted, hoping Mike could hear from the rear of the truck, and that he was in a position to do something about the attack.

The truck shook as the vampires jumped onto the hood and roof. A hand smashed through the window beside her and Kelly reached up from her position on the floor to grab it and pull. There was a shriek as the vampire's arm raked across the jagged glass, spraying red onto the truck's worn upholstery. With one hand, Kelly twisted and pulled to break the vampire's arm. With her other hand, she yanked the door handle, kicking the door as hard as she could. There was a satisfying thump, and another yell of pain.

She repeated the action a few times, gaining momentum to spring up and out of the truck when the door flung open. Keeping his arm trapped through the window, Kelly spun around to face him.

The vampire stared at her with shocked eyes. "You're not. . . ."

"No, I'm not," she assured him as she rammed the silver filet knife into his heart, twisting while it smoked.

Thanks, Prince. This knife sure has come in handy, she thought as she yanked it from the vampire's torn chest before giving it a quick wipe on her pants leg.

The truck rocked with impact, and Kelly jumped into the bed, slipping on the blood coating the floor. The tailgate was a torn chunk of metal dangling from broken hinges, and just past the end of the truck, two figures rolled across the frozen gravel — one on two legs and the other a strange, furry two-legged creature — half man and half wolf.

"Mike!" Kelly shouted, jumping from the truck and running to his aid.

The vampire pulled his head up to see her, and took a swipe across the face with a sharp set of claws. Turning his attention back, he grabbed Mike by the front leg and picked him up, spinning to fling him into the woods. Kelly heard a dreadful "crack" and saw a tree shudder just as she plowed headfirst into the vampire.

The momentum drove them both backwards, and the vampire hit the ground hard with Kelly on top. Once again, she stabbed for the heart, but this one had full use of both his arms. He grabbed each of her arms then lurched forward to smack his head against hers.

Everything blurred with pain, and Kelly's grip loosened on the knife. Before she could react, the other vampire shifted his weight, rolling her over and snatching the knife from her hands.

"Hold still, you traitorous bitch," he snarled, stabbing her repeatedly as she thrashed around, trying to get free, or at the very least keep the silver blade from her heart.

Wiggling an arm loose, she reached up and grabbed the vampire's hair, yanking his head in a futile effort to throw him aside. As he shifted to the side, Kelly found herself looking into a pair of golden wolf-eyes and a massive jaw of razor sharp teeth in a human face. The teeth closed on the male vampire's neck, slicing cleaning through muscle and bone, and blinding Kelly with a spray of red.

She panicked. There was a silver knife burning its way through her stomach, a decapitated vampire weighing her down, and Mike looming over her. Would he take this chance to kill her? Tell Jaq the vampires had done the job before he could save her? She frantically tried to push the corpse off her and wipe the blood from her eyes. Any moment, she expected those teeth to be slicing through her neck. Instead, she felt a soft paw patting against her cheek. When she looked up again, she saw through a red haze that the wolf-man was staring down at her, a look of wary respect on his grotesque face.

"Fanks for helpin," Mike said, spittle spraying her from his misshapen snout. "Didn't expect...."

"I know. That's okay. No thanks necessary." Anything to keep him from trying to talk. Those fangs, inches from her face and shiny with drool, the foul spray with every word – Kelly was never so grateful that Jaq's transformation with quick and elegant. Mike's breath stank.

The werewolf shoved at the headless vampire still pinning Kelly to the ground, embedding the knife even further into her gut. "No. Don't. He's got a knife in me. Just move off me to the left. I've got this."

Mike shifted, and Kelly gasped, pain lancing through her

middle. "No, your left. Your other left. The other way, other way."

He obliged, and Kelly breathed in relief at the reduced pressure. "I'm going to lift up. Can you grab him with your hands . . . er, claws, and pull him toward you? Easy — his weight is pushing this knife into my gut. I don't want any more damage than I've already got."

Kelly struggled, lifting the vampire up and off the knife while Mike jammed sharp, furred claws into the body to pull it free.

"Hate silver. Hate it, hate it."

"Me too. Hate the stuff," Mike agreed, a line of drool extending from one fang to dangle a few inches above Kelly's arm. She eased the knife slowly out of her stomach, and the burning subsided as her body began to heal. Two dead vampires– the one by the car, and the other decapitated between her and Mike. The woods rustled with noise of the battle only a few miles away, but Kelly could scent no other vampires nearby.

"North or South?" Mike spat out, waving a sharp claw at the dead vampire by his side.

It took her a second to realize he was asking which family the dead vampires were from. "Fournier. They're from the north."

Which meant they weren't assassins sent to take her out, but part of the Prince's trap. One had been surprised to see her, expecting another werewolf. If she was careful, she could use that to her advantage. They'd never suspect another vampire, especially one that clearly bore the scent mark from their own family.

A long, mournful howl carried faintly on the wind. Kelly raised her eyebrows as Mike turned toward the sound.

"We're kicking 'pire ass." He grinned, and Kelly shuddered

at the sight. "Driving them out toward Harpers Ferry. They're almost to Halltown."

Right where Virginia, Maryland and West Virginia joined in a line of jagged mountain cliffs and churning rivers. It was a good place to make a stand — as long as you didn't have the river at your back. Another cry rent the night, taken up by a dozen other voices. Mike joined in, his howl echoing through the trees.

"More." The werewolf took a deep breath. "Two families fighting crossed the border and are almost to Blair."

Crap. Blair was just south of Halltown. If the other battle continued north, there was a chance they'd sandwich the werewolves in the middle as they drove the Fournier vampires east to Harpers Ferry.

"The werewolves are going to hold back at Halltown so they don't get flanked?"

Mike nodded. It was the only solution: wait until both battles converged, then attack the whole lot of them. Of course, that would mean hundreds of vampires to fight instead of just the Prince's followers. The only good news was that the vampires would be just as busy fighting each other as the werewolves.

"Shall we go on foot?" They were almost to Route 9; then it would be fields and a golf course between them and Halltown.

Mike shook his head. "Truck. Want to get a bit ahead of everyone. Make sure I get a few kills in before they all drown in the river."

Lovely image. Jaq must have told her brother about the vampires' inability to swim. She'd need to remember never to stand next to a pool with Mike around.

"Only if we can take 340. These dirt roads are killing my back, and I think Jaq's truck is about ready to lose an axle."

Mike tilted his head. Was that his doubtful look? It was

hard to tell with his patches of fur and elongated snout. "Highway cuts between Halltown and Blair. We might run into them."

Kelly smiled. "I hope so. I've been wanting to see what Jaq's truck will do in ramming mode. Three quarter tons should be enough to kill vampires, especially if I put it in four wheel drive."

CHAPTER 29

The ride was much smoother down the highway, but Kelly was seriously concerned about the noises coming from Jaq's truck. The front grill had been smashed in from the tree one of the vampires had pitched at it, and the other vampire had ripped the light bar loose. It banged against the hood of the car with catchy rhythm that went well with the roar from the newly departed exhaust and rather alarming high-pitched screaming under the hood.

Please make it, please make it, Kelly chanted. Hopefully Jaq wouldn't be pissed. It's not like she could pay for repairs having just been fired from Dale's, and with no job prospects in the near future. Maybe she could knit the werewolf a scarf.

She slowed as she saw the signs for the casino, shouting into the rear of the truck through the open sliding window. Mike made a series of unintelligible noises that were of no help whatsoever. He'd originally said he wanted to head off the group near Halltown, so Kelly accelerated, smiling slightly as she heard Mike thump in the back. *Paybacks, buddy.* They might have declared a temporary truce, but that didn't stop her from taking advantage of any opportunity to stick it to the werewolf.

Roaring past the golf course, Kelly made the turn onto Shepherdstown Pike, wondering if Mike wanted her to go this far, or if they were supposed to head all the way to Halltown or not. She could smell nothing beyond diesel fumes, and could hear nothing except for the truck. It would be a miracle if she could ever hear properly after this ride. Something moved in her peripheral vision, and Kelly nearly wrecked as a paw came from the back of the truck to swat her in the face.

"Okay, okay! Sheesh, you could have said something. I nearly crashed."

A growl answered her, and she turned to see a huge wolf head pressed against the dividing glass. Guessing this meant "pull over" she did, swinging into the empty parking lot of a paper mill. She'd barely stepped outside before Mike launched himself from the bed with a powerful leap. In seconds, he'd vanished into the woods opposite the railroad tracks, leaving Kelly standing on a rural road, beside a battered pick-up truck, alone.

A sharp wind flung the vampire's short hair around. Now that the noisy truck was silent, her hearing was slowly returning to normal. Snarling, shouting, and crashing seemed miles away, but Kelly knew the fighting was closer. She peered through the woods, but the security lights from the paper mill reduced her night vision, and she could see only shadows.

What was she thinking coming out here? It was one thing to take out solo vampires in the woods behind her trailer when she was desperate and on the defensive. Business manager, not warrior. This was a battle, and she hadn't the foggiest idea what to do. Should she just run into the woods, grab the nearest vampire and start killing? What if one of the werewolves attacked her? Suddenly Jaq's words came back to her. She shivered. With Jaq gone, she had no one to protect her from the other wolves. As untrustworthy as Mike was, he was better than nothing, but he'd taken off and left her as soon as they'd stopped. *Paybacks are hell*, she thought with dark humor. Maybe she shouldn't have bounced him around in the back of the truck quite as much.

With one hand on the door handle, she contemplated getting back into the truck. Having a few inches of steel between herself and any attacking vampires and werewolves sounded like a good idea. *Coward*. Kelly shook her head, cramming her hands resolutely in her pockets and turning her back to the truck. The werewolves would never respect her — heck, never *accept* her, if she didn't take an active role in this fight. Once again she needed to prove her worth, this time to a different kind of family.

Taking a deep breath, she broke into a jog and skirted the woods, heading down Halltown Road. The noise was getting louder, and Kelly wasn't sure if it was her hearing returning to full sensitivity, or if the battle was truly moving east — directly toward her.

Abandoned houses flanked the paper mill. They gave way to homes in slightly better repair before wide-open farm fields were the only sight along either side of the road. There wasn't much cover, and the moonlight shone bright. Hopping a fence, Kelly raced along, taking shelter in the tree-lined division between fields. The fighting sounded as if it were coming her way. Maybe if she climbed a tree, she could jump down on a vampire from above and take him by surprise. It would be better than just standing there and waiting for one to run into her.

Snap.

Kelly turned slowly and looked into the golden eyes of a

huge wolf slowly advancing along the edge of the field. It paused as it saw her then charged.

"I'm on your side. I'm with you. I'm with you," she shouted, whirling about and scrambling up the nearest tree.

Breath warmed her ankle, and she felt teeth tearing at her pants hem. Yanking her leg free, she made her way to the first large branch and perched where it joined the trunk. The werewolf below was on hind legs, digging sharp claws into the tree in an effort to follow her up. It wasn't the biggest of trees, and it swayed with the added weight. Kelly clung to a branch, praying she wouldn't fall off.

"Stop. I'm with Jaq. I'm her vampire friend. I'm not one of the enemy."

This guy clearly didn't care. Or girl. Kelly couldn't really tell from this viewpoint and wasn't about to climb down and look. The werewolf gave up trying to climb and, with a snarl, shook the tree violently. Kelly screamed, wrapping her legs around the larger branch and grabbing anything within reach to help her hold on. The tree pitched back and forth. Even if she managed to stay on, she'd probably end up with whiplash.

Crack. The tree continued to shake, but at an increased angle. Kelly's hands slipped, and she spun around, hanging off the branch by her legs. The tree jerked downward again with another loud noise.

It didn't matter how tightly she held on, this werewolf was going to eventually break the tree. Then she'd have to deal with a fall, and potentially being crushed by a branch, as well as having her head bit off. Kelly swung herself forward and used the momentum of the swinging tree to launch herself off the branch away from the werewolf. She rolled as she landed, sprang to her feet, and ran.

* * *

KELLY. Ross had her pinned against a tree. Jaq could see her arms shake as she struggled to hold the werewolf's massive jaws away from her throat. Claws dug into the vampire's sides, and blood ran in red rivulets down her shirt and jeans. Jaq dove at them from the side, knocking Ross to the ground where they tumbled, a blur of fur and snapping teeth.

With a sideways roll, Ross came free and sprang to his feet, facing Jaq. Careful to keep her body between him and Kelly, she bared her teeth and snapped — a clear warning to back off. His eyes were defiant as they met hers, and Jaq realized that he meant to challenge her for the right to kill the vampire behind her.

I don't have time for this shit. The battle was quickly moving east and she was tasked with taking out any enemy that lagged behind the main group. Getting into a pissing contest with a fellow pack-mate wasn't on her agenda.

Ross darted to the side to pass Jaq, and she blocked him with a swipe of her paw. *Enough.* Summoning the power deep within her, she shifted, adding nearly a foot to her size and doubling her muscle mass. Not exactly pretty, but it should get the message across. Ross blinked, a brief flash of uncertainty crossing his face before he locked his eyes on hers and snarled.

Clearly not the smartest wolf in the pack. Losing her patience, Jaq once again reached down deep within to the gifts of her father and brought it humming to the surface. Fur stood on end with the force of it, and the werewolf *glowed*. Ross winced, hesitating a moment before lowering his head in submission.

Good. Now get out of here. Jaq snapped her jaws at the other werewolf, and he raced away. The moment he was gone, she dropped the energy into her core and transformed into her human form.

"Impressive stuff. What's with the glowing, though?"

She turned to face the vampire, relieved that she'd apparently healed and seemed merely curious about Jaq's unusual abilities.

"I have no idea. It happens when I heal, but not to that extent. Whatever it's supposed to do, it seems to scare the bejesus out of werewolves."

"Scared the bejesus out of me," Kelly commented, looking in the direction Ross had run. "Thought you were going nuclear for a second there."

The vampire moved closer to her. "Thank goodness you found me. I wasn't sure how long I could hold him off."

She'd been looking for Kelly, trying to track her by scent through the hundreds of vampires and chaotic smells of battle from the moment she'd heard Mike's reply to Jonah's howl. And Mike — she should have known better than to trust him to look after Kelly.

"Where's my good-for-nothing brother? He was supposed to stick with you."

Kelly shrugged. "He did until we hit Shepherdstown Road. Don't be too hard on him — he had vampires that needed killing. I'm just glad I wasn't one of them."

"It's almost over," Jaq assured her. "They're on the run to the border. I'm supposed to bring up the rear and catch any stragglers. Wanna join me?"

"Count me in." Kelly watched as Jaq shifted back into her wolf form and took off. Without hesitating, she followed her friend into the woods.

* * *

"Sir, there are more than we thought, and they were ready for us."

Kyle frowned down at the city lights before him. The view of Harper's Ferry was breathtaking from Maryland

Heights. He'd parked his car down past the ruins of an old tavern and scaled the cliff face, enjoying the rare physical exertion. Right about now, he should be surveying the start of his little kingdom, looking out as his new family seized control of the eastern part of the state. Instead, he was watching a slaughter and an embarrassing retreat.

His ten vampires inside the casino had been surprised by an early sneak attack, and his groups hidden around the perimeter had been taken down one by one. By the time the other werewolves had arrived and their planned attack took place, he'd lost four strategic groups, giving the werewolves an escape and a way to circle around and take the advantage. The human hostages were safe in werewolf hands, and his fighters were on the run. It was mortifying. He could try again, or drive them out through business acquisitions. It would just take longer, and time was no longer a luxury he had.

"Faulty information is no excuse for failure, Rube."

The other vampire paled, his hands shaking. "We can succeed on the western side of the state, Sir. If we shift our forces, we should be able to hold that section by dawn."

And a lot of good it would do him. All the viable business interests were here, in the east. This is where he could launch into the key sections of Virginia. This is where he could spread out to snatch sections of his father's holdings — not the west.

"How many have we lost?"

Rube shuffled his feet, looking down. "A third, Sir. Mostly to werewolves, but we did lose five to humans."

"What?" Kyle stared at him in astonishment.

"The humans here are surprisingly well armed. Every one of them has a gun of some sort, and their bullets are silver coated. They're not as tractable as the humans in our territory. Xavier saw them run one of his guys over with a huge truck until he wasn't more than a stain on the road. The humans here are as crazy as the werewolves."

Great. Maybe he didn't want this state after all. Not that he had much choice at this point. Once a plan was set in motion, it was nearly impossible to retreat — especially now that he'd disobeyed his father's summons to pursue his own goals.

"I have news, my Master."

It was Juan, his second. Kyle smiled at the title. It may have been premature, but having Juan refer to him as such gave him hope.

"Speak."

"The battle between your father and the Kincaids has drifted west. They are outside of Brunswick and closing fast."

Rube made an agitated gesture. "Oh no. Should I call everyone back? Get out of here before they see us?"

Such short-sightedness wasn't boding well for Rube's future. Kyle smiled, and Juan grinned back. "No. Rube, tell them to head east and flank the Kincaid forces. We had intel that Kincaid meant to rush a force through West Virginia to trap my father in the middle and have been busy repelling their advance. Now that we've succeeded, we're racing to support him and defeat Kincaid."

"You are a loyal son, my Master," Juan smirked.

"Of course. And, Rube? Get your butt down there on the front lines and fight. Once the battle is over, go see if that little outcast you've been tormenting has anything on those Virginia businesses. If I can't defeat them physically, I'll drive them out financially — both Kincaid and the stupid werewolves."

Wind howled down the mountains, picking up speed and force as the cliffs channeled it down along the Potomac. Kelly paused a moment to catch her breath and admire the way the moonlight danced along the waters of the Shenandoah, lighting the rocky rapids with flecks of silver. It seemed like they'd been fighting forever, but a glance at the stars told her it was at least three hours until dawn.

"You okay?"

Jaq had remained close the entire night. Kelly wasn't sure if it was to ensure the werewolves didn't attack her by mistake again, or to act as back-up. Either way, the vampire was grateful. Jaq was a tireless fighter, snapping back and forth between wolf and human forms in a blink, and completely unfazed about fighting completely naked when she was on two legs. Kelly chuckled, wondering what the humans would think to see a tall, freckled naked woman racing through the woods.

The humans hadn't been spared this night. She'd seen the bodies with the familiar puncture wounds — victims of injured vampires in need of blood. Some looked as though they'd been shared by several. There was a time when Kelly wouldn't have concerned herself with the thought of their terror as vampires grabbed them from their houses and cars, but now she shuddered to think of it.

"I'm fine. Just a quick rest."

Concern flashed across her friend's gray eyes. The Kincaid force had collided with the other group just outside Harpers Ferry. The werewolves had managed to push the Kincaid vampires over the border toward Loudoun Heights, and a good bit of the Fournier forces had followed them to drive them further into their territory — but some had remained. And those who had were hammering the werewolves as if they had a visceral need to see every last one of them dead.

"You don't look fine."

No, she was positive she didn't. It was the price a vampire paid when they were under two-hundred years old and had been on the edge of starvation for two weeks. The donated human blood she'd drunk earlier had gone to healing a multitude of injuries, and now Kelly found herself weak once again.

"Let me have a bit of your blood." It was risky. Who knows what repeated exposure to the stuff would do to her, but the alternative was falling to the next vampire she faced. Jaq had enough to do without needing to bail her out repeatedly through the night.

The werewolf hesitated. "Let me drive you back home instead. You can get more blood from our neighbors, and heal up while I come back here."

Kelly felt a wave of shame. "You don't have time to drive me home — you've got a fight going on, or didn't you notice? Besides, your pack will never accept me if I have to go home and rest in the middle of a battle.

Jaq tilted her head, a smile teasing the corner of her mouth. "Since when are you worried about my pack accepting you? And I'm worried what my blood will do to you. I've worked too hard to keep you alive only to have you stroke out right before my eyes."

"I'll be fine. I was fine before, and, as I recall, your blood had some pretty awesome side effects. And yes, I'm worried about your pack accepting me. It's not like my family would ever take me back after tonight. Kincaids aren't going to want me either. Might as well put my fate in the hands of a bunch of smelly, old werewolves."

"I, for one, will welcome a skanky New Jersey vampire into my pack."

Skanky? It's not like she could be offended after claiming they smelled like old ham, though. "Then bite yourself for me, would you? I don't have any fangs, and I doubt you'd appreciate me cutting you with a silver knife."

"Unless you want to be drinking from a wolf, I've got a better idea." Jaq pulled a small knife from her jeans pocket and flipped it open, expertly slicing her arm. Blood welled up in a line of red beads against the freckled skin. She extended her arm toward Kelly, as if she were offering a tray of hors d'oeuvres.

The few drops were like a sledgehammer to her head the moment they hit her tongue. This time it was worse. Her heart went supersonic, and her brain felt like someone had lit a torch to it. She couldn't breathe, couldn't think, all she felt was pain. Inescapable pain.

"Kelly!"

Someone was whacking her chest and screaming her name. The blurred shape before her coalesced into a freckled face framed in blond hair, inches from her own.

"Oh my God! Oh my God. I am *not* doing this again. I don't care how much you beg me, I am not doing this again *ever*. You were having convulsions. Your heart stopped, and I'm not really sure if that's an okay thing for a vampire or not."

Kelly traced the freckles with her eyes. They were like arcane symbols, their meaning just outside her grasp. If only she could decipher them, she'd know the answers to all the questions in the universe.

Jaq swore. "I'm taking you home. Right now. Taking you home and getting you some human blood. Hang in there."

"I'm fine." Kelly raised a hand and was momentarily distracted by the sight of it. Bones and veins, muscles that flexed and relaxed. "There are three vampires closing in about a hundred yards to the west. Fournier. They don't recognize me. They're waiting for you to finish me off before they attack, so they only have to deal with one opponent instead of two."

"So are you psychic now too?" Jaq asked, rising to her feet. "Cause if you can read the future, please tell me that this ends well."

Kelly stood up, too, weaving slightly on her feet. "I have no idea. My head is killing me. I'm just hoping I'm not worse off than I was before."

There was no time for the werewolf to respond. Two vampires burst through the trees, one grabbing Jaq, before she could transform, and throwing her across the clearing. The other plowed into Kelly, knocking her against a tree as he tried to twist her head off. It all seemed to proceed in slow motion — the vampire's face as he scowled down at her, the feel of his hands against her cheeks and neck, his weight pinning her to the tree. She could hear the nearby rush of the river as it churned over rocky ground. Rocks everywhere. Mountains so close they were like castle walls on the other side of a white-water moat.

"Kelly! Snap out of it!"

Ow, her neck hurt, like someone was trying to rip her head off. Reaching up, Kelly placed a hand against the face looming over her and pushed. Hands wrenched painfully from her neck and the vampire flew across the clearing, his head bouncing on a rock. Kelly looked about her at the rocks that littered the ground. Pretty. Limestone, quartz, and shale. Streaks of pink and green among black and white. She picked one up, as big as her head, and admired it.

"Kelly!"

The vampire was almost upon her. She raised the rock and extended her arm forward, pushing it into him as if his face were cookie dough. He fell to the ground, clawing at the huge stone, and Kelly stared down at him, a coldness creeping into her mind and snapping parts of it together like puzzle pieces. This was an enemy, and she needed to kill him. So she did, reaching down and yanking his head from his body, carefully removing the pretty rock from his smashed face and wiping the gore from it onto the brown grass.

A hand grabbed her arm, and once again Kelly looked up into Jaq's freckled face. There was blood on it, and down her arms and chest. It wasn't vampire blood. Kelly could smell the sharp icy scent of it, thick and sweet. Her stomach heaved, and she forced back the urge to vomit.

"You took on the other two?" Kelly panted.

Jaq rubbed Kelly's back, the werewolf's eyes full of concern. "Yeah, and now I'm taking you home. No arguments."

"There are two more vampires half a mile out. They are wondering what's taking their three friends so long, and they're heading this way."

Jaq threw her hands up in disbelief. "You're scaring the hell out of me, Kelly. You stay here, and I'll take care of them."

"No, I'm fine. Really." Kelly got to her feet and tilted her head, hearing her neck crack into joint. "I think it just takes a while for your blood to settle in. That first hit is a doozy."

Hands grabbed her shoulders, and gray eyes searched her own. "Well, you're pupils aren't as big, and you seem semi-coherent at least. But if you pull one more stunt like you did with this last guy, I really am taking you home."

Kelly nodded, not trusting her words, and followed Jaq into the tree line. They split up, Jaq motioning her to the south along the river as she headed north. Kelly felt the vampires shift, following the werewolf. With a smile, she edged around behind them. This close to the river, and with all the vampires that had passed through here, there was a good chance they'd never notice her. One of the good things in being young enough not to have an aura.

They were right ahead. A woman, she saw with surprise, and a broad-shouldered man in a black coat. Women vampires weren't often allowed into the fighting ranks. They usually wound up running the business interests, and some-times acted as informants, but it was the male vampire that made Kelly pause. He was old, over five hundred, with an aura that was disgustingly familiar. Rube.

Kelly circled around to the north, farther away from the river and closer to the railroad tracks that bordered the edge of town. It was slow going, her path littered with not only the natural rocks, but ballast from the railroad. The woman sprang ahead, attacking Jaq, while Rube edged closer to Kelly, awaiting an opportunity to jump in and grab the were-wolf from behind.

"Nice evening we're having, Sir."

Rube whirled around in surprise as Kelly plunged her silver knife into his chest, missing his heart by a fraction of an inch.

"You!"

"Yes, me."

She twisted the knife, but he'd reached up to grab her hands, slowly easing it out. Jaq's blood gave her an edge, but she was still no match for the strength of a five-hundred-year-old vampire.

"Traitor. Who has offered you protection, starving waif? Kincaid? The werewolves? They'll kill you the moment your usefulness has ended."

His grip tightened on her wrists. Bones creaked in protest, and Kelly gritted her teeth, trying to force the knife back in.

"Like you? Like my own family? It's one thing to cast me out, but to taunt me with promises of redemption that you had no intention of keeping? I can hardly be a traitor if I'm no longer part of the family."

Rube snarled, and the knife slipped free of his chest. With a quick roll of his shoulders, he twisted Kelly's arm to the side, and the knife dropped to the ground. Still holding her wrists, he pushed her backward, toward the railroad tracks.

What did he intend to do? He'd need to release one or both of her wrists if he wanted to take her head off, or go for her heart, and that would give her a split second to evade or strike. Kelly kept moving backwards, stumbling as her feet hit the rocky ballast of the train tracks. In a smooth motion, Rube crossed her arms in front of her chest, spinning her around so her back was to him. She was truly trapped now, pressed against his chest with her arms immobile in front, like a straitjacket.

Tar-covered railway ties with a neat pile of spikes sat alongside the tracks, awaiting future maintenance crews, but it was what was beside them that caught and held her eye. Her blood ran cold as she saw a stack of railway pieces before her, chest high. Kelly struggled as he edged her toward them.

"I'll lose my bet, and the new Master will never get those

reports on the Virginia businesses, but it will all be worth it to see you impaled on a railway iron."

Kelly dug in her heels and focused on the metal spikes, willing them to move. *My hands, reaching out beyond my body to grab them.* They stirred, and rose in the air, turning in a line. Rube pushed her forward, all his attention on the long sections of track jutting out from the stack.

"Rot in hell, little bunny eater," he laughed, kicking her feet from under her and edging her forward.

"You first."

She flung the spikes at him, thankful that she was barely above five-feet tall and that Rube towered over her. He gave a grunt of surprise, and shoved her, his hands leaving her wrists. Kelly dove for the pile, snatching up a spike in each hand as she whirled about. Two of the four spikes she'd tele-kinetically thrown had hit — one in the vampire's neck, the other in his shoulder. Not bad for a blind attack, although Kelly winced to think how close one had come to her head.

"Bitch."

The word was almost a whistle as Rube pulled the spike from his throat and air rushed into his windpipe before it closed and healed. Kelly held back, realizing that the metal spikes in her hand would do no good against a vampire this old. She needed silver.

He dove at her, and she scampered aside, throwing her spikes as she clambered up the stack of railroad ties and hopped to the other side. Rube batted the projectiles away, as though they were flies, and smashed through the ties, grab-bing a six-foot piece of track to swing at her head. Kelly ducked and rolled, coming up on the other side of him.

Something hard crashed against her hip. A glancing blow, but enough to spin her off balance and send her flying into the grass. She rolled, feeling the rush of air as the section of track dented a chunk of ground right where her head had been. Scrambling to regain her feet, her hand pressed against something hard. Something that burned like the fires of Hades. Her knife.

Curling her fist around the blade, Kelly ignored the searing pain and smell of burnt flesh. She turned, flipping it around, with a skill born of decades in the kitchen, to clasp the hilt in her palm. The long piece of metal arched in a return swing, and she dove, praying her aim this time would be true.

The knife slid in with a hiss. Rube gasped. The momentum of his swing crashed his arm against Kelly's shoulder, slicing the silver blade in a diagonal line through his heart. Blood sprayed, and he fell forward, taking Kelly down with him. Using his weight to her advantage, she squirmed, shredding his heart with the silver blade. The acrid smell of burning flesh filled her nose, and for once, she gloried in the odor.

"You done with that guy?"

"Yep. Could use a hand getting him off me, though. Sucker weighs a ton."

Jaq pulled Rube's lifeless body from her and tossed it aside, extending a hand to help Kelly to her feet.

"Do your newfound psychic abilities reveal any other vampires near here?"

Kelly closed her eyes and reached out, extending her awareness past the railroad tracks and down along the river. The area was filled with werewolves, but there were only ten vampires in a mile radius. They were toward the east, all heading toward one specific spot.

"In the town of Harpers Ferry. I think they're retreating. We've won."

Furred shapes raced by, through the trees, heading east into Harpers Ferry. A series of yips filled the air followed by a long howl. Close.

"The werewolves are tightening ranks and herding the remaining vampires toward the river."

Once there, they'd have a choice of taking the train bridge across the Potomac into Maryland, or following the highway through a short stretch of Virginia before crossing. Kelly sighed in relief. It *was* over. They'd ensure the vampires retreated into Maryland, and then go home to regroup. She thought of her future. What would life be like, a solitary vampire among werewolves? She'd lost her job at Dales, but maybe she could get one somewhere else. With the humans donating blood, and the vampires out of their territory, the future suddenly didn't look so bleak.

Jaq smiled. "Excellent. We'll corner them down on High street, at the fork in the rivers. It's fight or swim. We'll kill the remaining ones, then they'll know to never mess with us again."

"Wait . . . no."

But it was too late. Jaq had morphed into her wolf form and took off through the trees. Kelly cursed, racing after her. Foolish werewolves. Cornered vampires who'd lost all hope of survival were dangerous. It would have been better to let them escape. They'd sent their message. It would be a long time before the vampires attacked again — if ever. West Virginia wouldn't be worth the trouble. This last stand would only result in more losses.

They ran down the streets of Harpers Ferry toward the Potomac, steadily joined by other wolves who made clear their dislike of Kelly. Jaq held back to run by her side, snapping at any who came close.

A railroad bridge gave access across the Potomac River, but the werewolves carefully guarded it. Kelly could see figures darting here and there among the buildings and along the rooftops as the wolves attempted to herd them into a group.

"Just let them cross the railroad bridges," she told Jaq.

The werewolf snarled in response. This was going to get bloody, and all for nothing.

"It won't gain you anything. You'll wind up with more dead, and there's a good chance most of them will escape anyway."

Jaq shot her an exasperated look and slowed to a walk. The scene ahead of them broke into chaos as vampires used their ability to leap and climb to avoid the werewolves who threatened from below. Like monkeys, they hopped across rooftops and scaled up railroad tresses to cross the river. In the end, the werewolves watched, frustrated, as their quarry escaped.

"It's for the best," Kelly told Jaq. "Enough have died, and the vampires aren't going to risk this again. The goal was to secure your territory. You've done that. Don't put yourselves in further danger for nothing."

Jaq flashed back into her human form. "I get the feeling this isn't over."

Exhaustion overcame Kelly. Her shoulders drooped. All she wanted was her bed.

"Well it's over for tonight. Let's go home. I want to check on Melody and the humans, and get a hot shower. Then I truly want to be in bed by dawn. It will be nice, for once, to sleep the day away."

Jaq took one last look at the retreating vampires darting across the railroad bridges. "You're probably right. And I could use some sleep too."

CHAPTER 31

"I'm sorry about the truck," Kelly repeated once more as she and Jaq shuffled along the empty road. The thing had sputtered to a stop a mile from their home, and no amount of Jaq's tinkering and cursing had managed to get it running again. Finally she'd given up, declaring herself too tired to work on it. She wasn't the only one. Kelly had that weird sensation of being high and completely exhausted at the same time. They were the lucky ones. Mike had stayed behind with the other werewolves to clean up. There were bodies to bury, lost pack-members to find and mourn, and families to notify.

Bed, bed, bed. It was the only thing that had kept Kelly going, although she knew there would be no bed until she checked on the neighbors and cleaned the filth and gore from her skin. Tomorrow they'd help with burial, relieving the others. But what would tomorrow bring? What kind of backlash would face her after this-evening's activities? The prospect of more Kincaid assassins depressed her, but not as much as the knowledge that she'd probably added Fournier assassins to her list. And there was no guarantee the werewolves would ever accept her, let alone defend her against two vampire clans. She hoped the word hadn't gotten back to her previous family that she'd fought against them.

And there it was, absurdly noticeable on the quiet rural roadway — a big black Mercedes parked right off the shoulder by the turn onto Briar Lane.

Jaq bristled. "It's that asshole with the silk suit from the night they dumped you here. I'd recognize that car anywhere."

Maybe. Or maybe someone just borrowed it for the evening. Although who would have the gall to borrow the Prince's Mercedes?

Kelly's heart quickened as they carefully walked towards the line of trailers. They'd just rounded the corner by Melody's when the familiar aura washed across her.

"He's in your house," Jaq hissed, pulling at Kelly's arm to drag her behind an unkempt hedge.

Yes, and I'm exhausted, still high as a kite, and covered in vampire blood, Kelly thought.

Why was the Prince here? Kelly's first panicked thoughts were that he'd seen her during the fight and was here to deliver the ultimate punishment for her betrayal of the family.

"It's the Prince," she told Jaq. "You go check on Melody, and I'll go see him." There was no sense in getting Jaq involved in this. Better to make sure she was safe and face whatever was inside that trailer alone.

"No, you're not going to see him! Let's kill him and be done with this whole thing. No Prince; no more raids on our territory, and no more vampires tromping through on their way to take out the southern group. Problem solved."

"No, problem just beginning. Let's just say the pair of us get lucky and manage to kill a Born vampire of his age. The Master will turn the whole east coast upside down searching for him, and when he finds out what happened — because he *will* find out — every werewolf on the planet will suffer an agonizingly long death."

"We could do it," Jaq insisted. "We're strong enough, and we can use the battle to cover it up — let your master-guy think the southern group did it."

"First, we're not going to be able to kill him. Maybe if I had more of your blood, but I'm terrified that even a little more will kill me — I'm still high from what I took earlier. Even if we manage to kill him, and successfully blame it on Kincaid, you'll still have the entire Fournier family pouring through the border to avenge their prince. He's the Master's *only* offspring. If the Prince dies, the whole area is going to become a bloodbath."

Jaq waved her hands in agitation. "He's going to kill you. You betrayed your family, remember? They betrayed you first, but I doubt they'll see it that way. I'm not letting you walk in there to your death."

Deep breath. He wasn't here to kill her. It was all going to be okay.

"Princes don't do their own dirty work. He didn't even stand close enough to get blood on his suit when they were walloping me. I think the only reason he helped when they were pulling my fangs was to save time. I'm not sure why he's here, but I doubt it's to kill me. He would have brought a couple of helpers, otherwise."

Jaq sighed, glancing once again toward the trailer. "Fine, but I'm sticking around, in case you need back-up."

"Just don't get too close. I don't want him to recognize your smell as anything out of the ordinary, or think there's someone spying on us."

The Prince was arrogantly leaning against the kitchen table, his arms crossed. Kelly felt a wave of irritation. She was just a tool to him. He didn't care about her; none of them did.

Dispensing with the respectful vampire posture, Kelly nodded curtly at her visitor and went to put on a pot of coffee. It was what she'd gotten in the habit of doing every time she had human guests. Funny, to be making a pot of coffee that the Prince would most probably not drink.

"Where exactly does your alliance lie, I wonder?" Kyle mused, shifting slightly to better stare at her profile as she scooped grounds into the filter. "You were supposed to interrogate spies and report back to my man, Rube, but instead I get the feeling you're playing both sides of this game."

Kelly ignored the first question. "I have the list of Kincaid holdings in Virginia. I wasn't able to interrogate their spy, although I did kill several Kincaid scouts tonight. There were quite a few passing through here earlier."

His face darkened. "Yes, there was a bit of a skirmish. We prevailed, of course."

She knew it was wrong to bait him, but just couldn't help it. "Prevailed? And yet you're here to collect my findings instead of Rube? Since when does a Born, a Prince, run his own errands."

Her tone was beyond rude. She felt Kyle's glare on her back, felt his aura flare against her in anger.

"Rube is busy doing something else for me tonight, and I wanted to check up on you myself. You're looking mighty fit for a vampire without fangs. Last I'd heard, you were gnawing the heads off rabbits and were on the edge of starvation, but you look reasonably well fed to me. And clearly well fed enough to 'kill several Kincaid scouts tonight.'"

Crap. Why couldn't she just keep her head down, her mouth shut, and hand over the information like a good newly-turned vampire? Anger was once again going to be her downfall.

"The werewolves would never tolerate a vampire in their midst." Kyle continued. "Who is protecting you? Who is feeding you? Who are you working with?"

No sarcastic comments, no taunts; for once, just keep a rein on my temper. Kelly kept him in the corner of her vision as she pulled mugs and the little jar of sugar from the cabinet. The silence grew uncomfortably heavy.

"Who, Kelly? Is it Stockinger trying to make a play for some eastern territory?"

He was pissed. Unable to ignore him further, she took a deep breath and turned around to face him.

"So do you still want the list of holdings or not? I have them. Rube expressed some urgency in my obtaining them for the Master."

The Master's name was like a magic word. She saw him hesitate, hunger in his eyes at the prospect of getting a detailed list of Kincaid-owned businesses.

"Let's see what you've got." Kyle relaxed slightly, and Kelly realized for the first time how tense he'd been.

Turning back around, Kelly grabbed the sheets of notebook paper covered in handwriting out of the lower drawer under the oven, thrusting them at Kyle. "I was a bit surprised by Rube's request. Isn't it a bad time to plot an incursion into Kincaid territory when he's alert and prepared for war?"

Kyle looked through the sheets, pausing to frown at a few of the names. "That's the Master's business, not yours."

Kelly hid a wince. For a second, she'd forgotten how things worked in vampire families. She'd become used to discussing things openly with Jaq, to having her opinion count for something. Hopefully she wouldn't be dealing with these vampires much longer.

Kyle looked at the sheets, his face registering surprise. "Where are the rest? I'm sure there are more than this," the vampire said slowly.

Yes, there were. And she would be a total fool to give him a complete and detailed list.

"I'm not trained in interrogation, and I don't have a computer or internet access. This was the most I could obtain given the short timeframe I was given."

"Shame that. There could be a regular source of fresh human blood if you happened to find more in that little drawer under your stove. I can't imagine how difficult it is for you to continue, with that desperate need facing you every waking moment."

A day ago he would have been right, but now she had a small but steady supply of fresh blood. Let him think she was still desperate for blood. Let him underestimate her as everyone else had done her whole life.

"How would that work? I have no fangs. How would I possibly be able to obtain a consistent supply of fresh human blood?"

Kyle looked down at the papers in a mannerism that echoed his father's. "We could arrange for regular deliveries of fresh blood. Less than twenty-four hours old."

Although that would certainly be a nice benefit, Kelly didn't like the idea of a Fournier vampire trotting across the border every day or two. He'd eventually catch her doing something she wasn't supposed to be doing —– like working with the werewolves. How to get out of this without the Prince suspecting anything? A vampire on the edge of starvation, as she was supposed to be, would eagerly accept this deal.

"How regular is regular delivery?" she asked.

Kyle shrugged. "We wouldn't want you to lose that edge. I think it's important for you to remain hungry. After all, you are banished. This is your punishment."

Jerk. Kelly remembered Rube pouring the bag of blood down the sink and had an idea.

"Why do I get the impression you'll never let me back? If eternal exile is my punishment, then I might as well die of starvation now and not jump through hoops like your little trained dog."

The Prince didn't quite have the temper that Rube did. His grey eyes grew cold, but beyond a tightening around his mouth, there was no indication he'd found her rudeness anything worthy of a response.

"Oh, I don't mean to push you quite that far. You've proven to be very resourceful, ruthless even, about staying alive. I think if what else you have for me proves equally of value, we could place an end-date to your punishment, as a reward and an encouragement to continue to serve."

Liar. Kelly was beginning to hate this guy with a passion. Stupid, arrogant, entitled snob.

"I don't have anything more for you." Two could play the lying game.

Kyle looked at the papers for another moment before folding them and putting them into an inside jacket pocket.

"That's a terrible shame. If you were to find more, there might be some blood in it for you. If not, well, I hope your death is quick and painless."

Yeah, I hope your death is quick and painless, too, Kelly thought. Jaq's idea was starting to sound rather appealing.

"Walk with me to the road," the Prince said, abruptly heading out the door, leaving Kelly trailing behind.

They walked down the lane, to his huge black sedan. Either he hadn't been in the battle, or if he had, he'd driven there. Others fought and died, and their Prince drove through it all in his Mercedes.

Reaching into the back seat, he handed her a bag of blood. It was still warm. Kelly stared at the bag for a moment in shock. She'd not expected to be paid for tonight's information and guessed that he hadn't originally intended to give her this. He must really want further info if he was resorting to the carrot method.

"There's more where that came from. Let me know if you have any further information, and I'll have a bag at your doorstep," he said as he climbed into his car without backward a glance.

Kelly watched him pull away and promptly heard a rustle behind her. She felt Jaq's warmth, smelled her ice and forest smell.

"You're smiling. Must have been good news?" the werewolf asked.

"Nah, just having a pleasant fantasy about ripping his head off."

"What a coincidence. I was having the same fantasy."

Kelly turned to walk with Jaq to Melody's. "I have no idea why he wants this state so badly. I would have thought he'd beat a strategic retreat for a few decades, but I'm getting the feeling he's going to press on — both in West Virginia and for the Kincaid lands."

Jaq shrugged. "I really don't care about anything south of here, but he's not getting our land."

"Thankfully he didn't seem to know Rube was dead, or that I played any part in what went down tonight. I'm not sure whether the best plan would be to string him along and see what information I can gather from him, or cut him completely off and try to keep him out of the state."

"Do you really think he'll leave us alone? He seems pretty desperate."

"Well, he's about to get more desperate." Kelly turned toward Melody's trailer.

CHAPTER 32

Melody's leopard-print tights and lilac ruffled shirt were a startling contrast to her shotgun. She answered the door with it in hand, and ushered both Kelly and Jaq into the cozy trailer. Joe and Dale were slumped on the couch, as far apart from each other as possible. Both looked ready to nod off at any moment.

"All clear," Jaq told them. "Vampires are out of the state — well, except for Kelly and her recent visitor who is probably almost to the border by now."

"Good." Dale struggled to his feet and rubbed his eyes. "We had a quiet night. Joe got home from work a few hours ago, but I didn't want to leave until relieved of my duty."

He glared at Jaq as he said the last words then turned his scowl on Kelly. "Glad to see you got some blood on you, although from the look of you, it's probably mostly your blood."

"She held her own," Jaq bristled.

"Goodness!" Melody exclaimed, shoving Dale aside to examine the vampire. "You are a mess. Do you need some more blood? I'm afraid Margaret and Kristen left once their husbands got home, but Barbara and Shanna are asleep on my bed. I can have them get you a pint, if you need, from Barbara."

"Thanks, I brought some." Kelly showed her the bag. "I could use a mug to put it in though, and I really need to use your computer for a moment. It won't take long — I know you and Joe want to get to bed."

It was to Melody's credit that she didn't ask any questions about how Kelly was in possession of a bag of blood.

"Of course, dear."

Melody bustled about getting a mug and setting out snacks for her and Jaq, while the others took their leave, Barbara and Shanna stumbling to their own trailers half asleep. Kelly grabbed her mug and bag of blood and headed back to the spare bedroom that housed Melody's computer, leaving Jaq to discuss the battle with Joe.

With shaking hands, Kelly typed in the url then hesitated. Taking any excuse to procrastinate this momentous decision, she sipped her blood and perused Melody's knitting projects until she could delay no more. Login. Password. The spinning cursor seemed to take forever, but just as panic threatened to overtake her, the screen loaded showing her the account balance. There was no turning back now. With a few clicks, the money had transferred, but it wasn't enough.

This part was even more dangerous and sealed her fate to a degree the other transaction hadn't. With a few clicks, she'd hidden her IP address through a software program then used an offshore VPN service to further mask her trail. There. The program she'd paid dearly for in case of an emergency. There was no looking back now. Either move forward or die. She hovered a finger over the mouse button for a brief second then depressed it, watching the numbers spiral across the screen.

Five in the morning. She was exhausted and still flying

from Jaq's crazy blood, but she needed to do one more thing. One more login screen. One more transaction. One more hacker software program to run. That Lowry guy had cost a fortune, but his work was untouchable. Worth every penny. The numbers spiraled once again, and Kelly found herself looking at a banking account balance of eleven dollars and twelve cents. Done.

When she walked out, Melody was dozing on the sofa, and Joe was huddled over coffee with Jaq, whispering.

"Sorry that took a while. I'll leave you all to get some sleep. Please tell Melody 'thank you' and that I'll have that scarf to her in a few days."

If she was lucky. She ended up tearing out more rows than she knitted most nights. Craft work was clearly not her calling.

"What were you doing?" Jaq asked, rising to walk with Kelly to the door.

"Transferring money." She handed the werewolf the print out.

"Eleven dollars and twelve cents. Wow. You should be paying *my* bills. I'd have charged you for the deer bologna if I'd have known you were so rich."

If only she knew. But Kelly didn't want to get into a huge discussion with Jaq about her moral justifications for embezzlement. She'd figure it out soon enough, but that was an argument for another day. Hopefully one where she'd had enough sleep and wasn't high on Nephilim blood.

Kelly glanced over to Jaq's trailer and saw the light on. "Mike's home."

Surprisingly, Jaq followed her in through her own door rather than continue on home. "He likes you, you know."

Well, she certainly couldn't mean her brother. The vampire ran through a mental checklist of the males she'd encountered recently and came up blank. "Who?"

"Mike, silly. He says you saved his life."

Now that was a gross overstatement. "Uh, more like he saved mine." An unpleasant thought crossed Kelly's mind. "Wait, you don't mean like-like, do you? I'm not the most perceptive woman in the world when it comes to romantic interest, but unless you werewolves are *really* different, I don't think he's suddenly taken with the urge to send me flowers and put on the Barry White."

Jaq snorted. "Hardly. He'd sooner cut off his arm. I mean, he's less inclined to kill you than he was yesterday."

Well, that was an improvement.

"So I'm assuming you have a boyfriend back in New Jersey?" Jaq continued, her voice full of curiosity. "Does he know what happened to you?"

She'd put all that aside long ago. "Vampires aren't known for their romantic relationships. I've had one boyfriend in my life — only one, back when I was human. His name was George. I stayed with the vampires. He didn't."

It all sounded so wooden when she said it, so unlike the giddy rush of passion and hope George had brought into her life. Jaq must have sensed there was more behind the stilted words. With a sympathetic noise, she put a hand on Kelly's shoulder.

"It must have hurt when he left."

"He didn't leave; I did." It all came out in a rush of emotion. "We'd run away together, but after a few weeks in the catacombs, he changed his mind. We left together, but as soon as the daylight hit my face, I got scared. Isn't that ridiculous? I was more afraid of putting my future in the hands of love than a bunch of ruthless killers. We'd curled up to sleep in an empty horse stall at some inn, and I snuck out. Didn't wait to say 'goodbye'. Didn't even leave a note — it's not like I knew how to write at that point in my life anyway. I just left him the little silver ring he'd given me when we ran away together. A part of me died the night I left him, but I was too scared to stay."

Jaq rubbed her shoulder, but Kelly couldn't stop the flood of words. "I always figured he'd moved on, that he eventually married some nice girl and they had a great life — kids and everything. A few decades after I'd been turned, I found him. The catacombs are good at preserving bodies, but I wouldn't have known it was him if it hadn't been for the ring."

She choked on a sob and forced it back down. "He came back for me. He came for me, and they killed him — just dumped him there in the catacombs. That's when the rest of me died."

"Is that the little silver ring that was on the table? The one you didn't want me to touch?"

Kelly nodded, pulling it from her pocket and showing Jaq. Silver scorched her fingertips, but she held it as long as she could before sliding it back.

"I carry it everywhere. It's my reminder of a time when I wasn't dead, when I wasn't a monster." This time she couldn't hold back her tears.

Thin, strong arms encircled her, and she felt her head rest against Jaq's shoulder. "I'm sorry, Kelly." The words whispered into her hair. "Nothing I say is going to make you feel any better. You're not dead, though. And you're not a monster. You're funny, smart, strong, capable. Not dead at all."

She'd become resigned to her choice, but seeing George's body, his twisted skeleton crumpled against the wall — it had made her rethink every choice she'd ever made. She'd cried then locked it all away, taking the silver ring from his finger when she left. At that point, she truly became Kelly Demir.

But who was Kelly Demir now? Not the calculating, hardened vampire putting self-advancement before everything else. Not the scared, street-wise teenage girl either. Whoever she'd become, she really liked the feel of Jaq's arms around her, knowing that the werewolf would always be there to stand by her side.

Kelly pulled back, smiling in gratitude as she wiped away the stray tears. "Thanks. So, your turn. Tell me about the hot wolf-boy you really wear those undies for."

Jaq turned as pink as her underwear. "There's some things even lacy bra and panty sets can't fix. I wear them for me now, proof that under the fur and fangs I'm more than just one of the boys."

"Well, he's an idiot. You're beautiful and sexy, even when the underwear is hanging on the end of your tail."

The werewolf laughed. "Beautiful? I've been called a lot of things, but never beautiful. I can alter my form in less than a second. You'd think I could at least manage to rid myself of these hideous freckles. They're always there, no matter what shape I take."

On impulse Kelly reached out a finger and traced the marks, like connect the dots, from the other woman's brow, along her cheekbone and down to the edge of her lip.

"They're like spots on an orchid, pied beauty."

Silver eyes met hers, surprised and confused. The air seemed heavy and charged, but Kelly left her finger on the werewolf's face. Was this . . . something, or was she still tripping on Jaq's crazy blood?

"Are you still high?" Jaq echoed her thoughts. The words moved the corner of her lips against Kelly's finger and she resisted the urge to lean in.

"I don't know. Probably."

The werewolf pulled back. "Then I should go."

Kelly dropped her hand to her side, searching Jaq's face for reassurance that all was okay, that she hadn't somehow screwed up the only friendship she'd ever had.

"Don't look so worried." The werewolf leaned over and planted a quick kiss on her forehead. "We're good."

Kelly watched her walk to the door. "Then I'll see you tomorrow?"

Idiot. It was tomorrow. The sky had already lightened to a glorious pink outside her trailer windows. And what was with that weird fissure of fear in her voice?

Jaq turned toward her, the open door letting a gust of morning cold sweep through the room. "Yes. Tonight, and tomorrow, and the next day, and the next. You're not getting rid of me so easy." She smiled, and her silver eyes danced. "I meant it. We're good."

Kelly sat back down on the lumpy sofa cushions as the door closed. *Good.* Suddenly that word meant a whole lot more than it ever had before.

CHAPTER 33

Kyle glanced at Juan before returning his gaze back to the paperwork before him. The other vampire had a tense look to his face that foretold bad news. Of course, bad news was all that seemed to be coming his way the last few days. The disaster in West Virginia, the loss of many good vampires, including Rube — the only good thing was the information on Kincaid's businesses in Virginia. Hopefully that was a sign of better things to come.

"My Master, Durand gave me this message for you from your father."

Fear rolled over him with an icy touch. There was hesitancy in Juan's voice as he pronounced Master, as if he had doubts about the truth in the title. But that was nothing compared to the dread of what might be in that message. Kyle had returned to Baltimore an hour before dawn and was surprised to see his father waiting for him. A vampire as old as the Master needed to be sheltered and asleep before sunup, and it was unlike his father to cut things so close.

The meeting between them had been agonizing — full of

carefully worded questions and accusation hiding behind false affection. Kyle had held his ground in insisting he'd backed his father the entire battle, but the old man was unconvinced. Decades of small rebellions had made his father suspicious. This was the one time he desperately wanted the Master to believe in his loyalty, but Kyle was sure his father did not. In the end, the Master had no proof of treasonous intent or actions, only disobedience. It should have ended with a minor slap on the wrist, but Kyle wasn't so sure his father would be lenient this time.

Schooling his face to show nothing beyond bland interest, Kyle took the envelope and tossed it casually on his desk. "Thank you, Juan. I have this list of Virginia businesses that we should target in the Kincaid takeover. Please give them to Abigail and have her begin diverting funds for their take-over. Let's run this one through Kings Green."

Juan's took on a decidedly green tinge. He extended a stack of papers toward Kyle, his hand shaking slightly.

"Sir, I'm sorry, but Kings Green was drained of its funds early this morning. So was Snyder and Sons, and Marwick. They were all stripped, and their corporate identities dissolved."

"How. . .?" Kyle leafed through the papers in astonish-ment. Was this his father's doing? "Where were the funds transferred? To the main Fournier account? To Rensalver Enterprises?"

"Abigail says they went to an offshore account, were transferred to a Swiss bank account then out again to an undisclosed location."

Breathe. Breathe. Kyle's chest felt like someone had applied a giant vice to it. Those three companies held funds neces-sary for operation of three Fournier states. He'd need to go begging to his father for emergency cash or watch those businesses fold within the month. Was this another way to keep Kyle under his thumb? Such an involved series of transactions didn't seem like his father, but the old man could have employed one of his close staff in the scheme. And now his father would not only get to see Kyle humble himself before him, but would get to berate him on his irresponsible loss of three companies.

"Okay. Let's use Oakwood for the Virginia companies while I try and make sense of what happened with the other three."

Juan was definitely green, and this time he shoved his shaking hands in his pants pockets before speaking.

"Oakwood no longer belongs to us. The articles of incorporation were somehow changed last night, and the entire business was acquired by a company called Alchemy. Abigail thinks they may be a foreign-owned company. Privately held, and no way to trace ownership. They're managed through an offshore fund in Nassau."

Kyle's eyes drifted to the envelope on his desk, but he refused to open it in front of Juan. Everything was falling apart. Everything.

"I don't suppose you've heard any decision from the Kincaid Consort?"

Juan shook his head.

That wasn't a good sign. After they'd pushed Kincaid back across the Virginia state line last night, she should be ready to accept his proposal. Her silence indicated the opposite.

"Then let's prepare to move on the Kincaid lands tomorrow night. We'll take Leesburg and the Northern Virginia cities."

"Is that enough? I mean, without West Virginia, and with the loss of your revenue base in Maryland, will you have enough to hold that sliver of territory?"

"I'll challenge Kincaid directly for the entire territory." It was the quickest way to gain the territory, much faster than a protracted war or financial sabotage. Of course it meant he'd have to win against a vampire two thousand years his senior. He was a Born, with enhanced skills for his age, but that was still quite a gap.

Once again, Kyle glanced at the envelope from his father. This was probably his last chance for a long, long time, but he couldn't let Juan see that. If Kyle showed any cracks in his confidence, he'd lose all his supporters. No one wanted to be on the losing side. It would be a risky gamble, but anything was better than cooling his heels in Manhattan for another century. Anything was better than failure, than looking like an inept fool in front of his entire family.

"I'll make sure everything is in place, Sir." Juan said, bowing as he left.

Sir. The change in title didn't escape Kyle's notice. This *would* probably be a failure, but he was hardly going to crawl back to New York with his tail between his legs. Might as well go out with a bang. At the very least, he'd give Kincaid a world of hurt, show him what the future held for him and his struggling territory. And if he succeeded — well, all the better. Miracles did sometimes occur. His own birth was proof of that.

The envelope taunted him from the desktop — he could resist no longer. It wasn't his father's usual missive — elegant embossed cardstock, nor was it the more ominous skin parchment. A plain, legal-sized, business envelope, such as one somebody would mail a bill payment or a collection notice in. The detached nature of it chilled him.

Grasping the brass letter opener lightly in one hand, Kyle sliced through the top of the envelope in one smooth motion. The inside was just as impersonal. No note, no letter, nothing to indicate the contents came from the Master at all.

But Kyle knew, and a leaden resignation gripped his chest. Tomorrow night would be his last chance — a hail Mary seconds before the whistle. Upending the envelope, Kyle watched the paper inside slide onto his desk. An airline ticket — one way to France. General seating.

good morning, sunshine! I brought you something."

It wasn't exactly morning, and Jaq's "something" was a blood-covered vampire with a large knife protruding from his chest. A Kincaid vampire. Kelly wrinkled her nose in distaste. Noon was far too early to be dealing with this, but she could hardly tell Jaq to come back at sunset.

"A present? For me? How thoughtful. And I thought you only brought me deer bologna and liver. What's next? Flowers? Candy?"

Jaq strode through the door, vampire clasped to her with one hand, the other firmly gripping the knife embedded in his chest. It was a bit to the left of his heart. Close though, from the panicked look on the man's face. He was young — nearly as young as Kelly, with blue eyes that begged her for help. A Kincaid begging a Fournier, well former Fournier, for assistance. It would have been funny had it not been so stinking early in the day.

"He's not the present; this is." The werewolf wiggled a

small envelope from between her fingers, clearly reluctant to let go of the vampire.

It was a thing of beauty — cream colored cardstock with her name in lovely ornate script. Kelly edged it out from between Jaq's fingers, eying the vampire curiously. A messenger then, not an assassin at all.

"Mike caught him late morning, sneaking around the woods," Jaq continued. " When the guy begged for his life, saying he had an important note to deliver, Mike brought him back. He says it took great restraint on his part not to kill him. See? I told you he liked you."

Kelly stared at the note, deciding to reserve judgment in the matter of Mike's affections. The seal at the back of the envelope was in blood. The smell of it curled through her, and she wrinkled her nose in a combination of attraction and repulsion. If the vampire Jaq had dragged half a mile through the forest hadn't reeked of Kincaid, she wouldn't have believed it. She could see the Prince sending her a note, especially after last night, but Kincaid? Breaking the seal, Kelly pulled out the saffron-hued note inside.

"It's an invitation," she mused. "From Kincaid's Consort."

Jaq sniffed, wiggling the knife deeper in the vampire's chest. He whimpered, eyes pleading at Kelly for mercy. "An invitation to what? Their annual Christmas party?"

"A meeting. What would the Consort want with me? She's ancient, as old as the Master, probably. She's also a Born and the foundation for Kincaid's rule. Vampires like that don't meet with an exiled, half-starved New."

"So how about I kill this guy, then we pitch his body over the border with her embossed invitation stapled to his forehead?"

The vampire's eyes grew wider. Kelly felt a bit sorry for him. He was just a messenger. Did the Consort expect him to come back alive? And what could the woman possibly want with her?

"No, I need him alive to deliver my response. I'm going to accept, and I don't think a stapled note on a dead vampire is the message I want to send — at least for now."

"Seriously?" Jaq wiggled the knife again, and the vampire let out a desperate whine. "Don't you guys ever use cell phones? Or e-mail?"

"Oh like you werewolves? Even if the Consort did have one, which I strongly doubt, I lost my cell phone when my family beat the crap out of me back in the casino."

JAQ HAD PARKED outside the gas station convenience store. Sleet coated the windshield and accumulated on the wipers. They looked like jagged teeth as they swept across the glass, clearing a narrow strip. They'd borrowed Mike's truck. After spending the afternoon assisting in burial and vampire body disposal, neither had time to repair Jaq's truck. Not that Kelly knew how.

"See, he likes you," Jaq teased, indicating the truck with a sweep of her hand.

"He's the only one then," Kelly grumbled.

It had been a nightmare working side by side with the other werewolves. The polite ones just declined to speak to her; others treated her with open hostility, refusing to allow her to touch any of the werewolf or human dead. She found herself assigned to cleaning up dismembered vampire corpses and loading them in a truck for a mass grave. It made her ill to think it would please most of them to see her in the back of the truck with the dead.

"Think she's arrived yet?" Jaq asked, nodding toward the entrance.

"Yes."

The Consort's aura flowed out through the parking lot and across the roadway like an ocean tide. Kelly had sensed it from a quarter mile away. Curiosity had initially prompted her to accept the invitation, but now she wondered if this could be a way out. The werewolves would never accept her. She'd burned all her bridges and now found herself terrified that no one would want her. Alone.

"Don't run off with her, okay?"

Jaq was pretending to tease, but Kelly could see worry in the werewolf's eyes. It soothed her panic. Those other werewolves didn't matter. Jaq was family enough. Jaq, her human neighbors, and possibly Mike. Although she wasn't sure if she could ever fully trust Mike.

"Not a chance." Kelly took a breath and opened the car door. Icy rain hit her face and arm. "Guess I better get this over with."

A few people milled around inside the store, paying for gas or selecting from the rows of snack foods. The Consort sat at one of the small tables beside a closed deli, staring intently at the contents of the Styrofoam cup before her.

"I'm honored by your request to meet with me, Born and Consort," Kelly said, walking over to stand awkwardly in front of the woman. She could sense Jaq lurking outside the building, but no vampires besides the one before her. Kelly was well aware that one as old as the Consort didn't really need back-up.

The woman's eyes traveled over her, shining with curiosity. Kelly returned her scrutiny with a more respectful gaze. At first glance, the Consort appeared a tall, angular, stork of a woman, her hair an explosion of long dark wool from her scalp. Like the Master, though, this woman had no aspect of human appearance behind the careful illusion. Her long fingers slid around the coffee cup with their extra joints, tapping the Styrofoam with golden-colored claws. Her aura was smooth and heavy, almost comforting in its weight, so unlike the snap and sharp bite of the Master's aura. Under the scent of Kincaid and another family, she smelled old — sweet, like dried decay.

The milky-white eyes lifted to meet Kelly's. "Your friend remains outside?"

Crap. She'd smelled Jaq and somehow managed to figure out that they were together. Hopefully she'd not know what Jaq was from her scent.

"I hear you have been taken in by wolves, just like that Tarzan story, no? And now you come to me with a Nephilim companion. Quite interesting company. I'm impressed that you have managed to ally yourselves with what are usually considered enemies."

She knew. She knew Jaq was a Nephilim. Kelly was speechless, her mind frantically worrying through the potential risk to her friend. Would the Consort blackmail her to keep the secret?

The woman waved her hand, as if shooing a fly. "No worries, little one. Those such as your friend used to be quite common, nine-thousand years ago. It's a shame the angels killed the majority and drove the rest into hiding. Fascinating creatures. Intelligent, unpredictable, with a lovely capacity for violence. When I was a girl, we always gave them a respectful distance."

That didn't sound much like Jaq. She was smart and could get the job done when it came to killing, but her soft-hearted, loyal friend wasn't one she'd describe as unpredictable or particularly fond of violence for its own sake. She'd deal with any threat to Jaq's well-being later; right now it was time to get down to business.

"I'm Kelly Demir, formerly of the Fournier family. Why did you want to see me?" There. Direct and crossing the line into rudeness. This was becoming a habit in her dealings with older vampires. She quite enjoyed it.

The other vampire didn't even raise an eyebrow.

"I am Monica Rasmuth, the Kincaid family Consort. You may sit," Monica said, her tone friendly. "You may also partake of this odious beverage if you feel the need for self-inflicted torture."

Kelly bit back a smile as she slid into the chair. She'd not expected humor. Kelly had pictured a snobby trophy wife who would make her wait for half the night then insult her and waste her time, not a tranquil yogi joking about the crappy coffee.

"And as to your rather blunt question, how could I not want to see the vampire who killed two of our skilled scouts then dumped them on our front porch, killing another in the process. At the time, I thought it was the young Fournier, but we were able to quickly trace it back to you. You kill our assassins, but are also seen fighting against your own family. Werewolves, Kelly? Was there no better choice? You turn against vampires for those . . . creatures?"

Kelly bit her lip. A lecture was not what she needed right now. "Those creatures helped me when no vampire would. We vampires have an agreement with them that West Virginia is theirs. I see no wrong in helping them defend what's rightfully theirs against those who only want me dead."

Monica chuckled, her illusion slipping as she revealed a smile of long, jagged fangs. "If that fool of a Fournier Prince had a brain in his head, he would have killed you last night. Although I'll give the poor boy credit — he's having a hard enough time keeping his father from packing him off to France."

"What do you want? This is a lovely conversation and all, but I've got vampires to kill. Those assassins you have prowling around my trailer aren't going to wait all day." Probably not the best move, but Kelly was losing patience.

"I wish to offer you protection and alliance with our family," the older vampire announced.

Kelly thought of Jaq back in the truck. *Don't run off with her, okay?* She'd made her decision; there was no turning back now.

"I have a family — werewolves, a Nephilim, and a bunch of humans."

"They are not vampires. You're useful to them right now, but they'll kill you as soon as they see fit."

"Like you? Like my former family? Seriously, if I really wanted to jump back into that frying pan, I'd take the Prince up on his offer and go back to my previous Master." Kelly replied with equal candor.

Monica eyed her steadily, her illusion gaining enough force that the disturbing vampire eyes were temporarily overlaid with dark bird-like ones.

"Your Prince is a traitor. Kyle Fournier intends to take a handful of counties in Maryland and Pennsylvania, along the border. How long do you think it will be before his father beheads every vampire affiliated with him?"

The room swirled before Kelly as she tried to retain an air of nonchalance. She'd suspected the Prince might have such a plan under consideration, but the odds were so tiny that he'd have to be insane to try it. He was better off making a play for the Kincaid lands. He was better off waiting a few centuries for his father to slip up and seize control.

"Right now I'm an outcast. I'd be a traitor if I aligned myself with him, a traitor if I aligned myself with you, and a traitor if I support the werewolves."

"Death faces you in three of those four options. And your Prince will hopefully have his head detached from his body before year's end."

Kelly laughed, but the sound came out shaky. "The Master would never kill his Born son, the only offspring he has ever sired. Would you?"

Monica winced. "I have never been blessed with any but Made children. And you overestimate the importance of Born. In time, you will see there is no difference between the Born and the Made."

"There should be no difference, but as long as vampires place value on lineage, as long as the angels watch to make sure our original species continues with unbroken lines, then there will be a huge gap between the Born and the Made."

Monica regarded her intently, her illusion rippling with a surge of power. Kelly briefly glimpsed the child the ancient vampire had been, racing barefoot along the reed-filled land-scape, waving at humans poling their barges down the river. The child's black braids were decorated with golden beads that clacked merrily as she ran. Her brown legs raced beneath a short tunic, and she shouted a phrase in an ancient language. Cranes took flight from the floodplain beside her.

"Don't you wonder, Kelly Demir, why the Born have a human form at birth? Why they appear as human without the need for illusion for millennia? Your own Prince is what . . . three-hundred years old? Yet he walks in the day, combs his hair with the aid of a mirror, and is nearly indistinguish-able from the humans around him. Don't you wonder?"

She had, but at less than two-hundred years, she'd just assumed that was the way vampire genetics worked. Perhaps it was an adaptation to allow them to blend in with the more numerous humans until their power reached a point where they could adequately defend themselves against a group attack. A baby that appeared as Monica now did would surely be killed on sight by any human it tried to feed from, and young vampires never had the power of illusion.

Monica leaned forward, her eyes bright and alert. "There

are no original vampires left. We're all Made at one point or another. It's just a lovely lie the Born tell to make us seem special. We build our society on the mythos of a race that died out almost ten-thousand years ago, and give it urgency by claiming this non-existent treaty with the angels. The Born must rule, and we must make nice with the demons in case our elven enemies attack or the angels move against us. All lies, my dear. All lies."

"But the angels. . . ." Kelly sputtered. She'd lost all ability to maintain a disinterested appearance. The Consort must be lying — although every sense Kelly had screamed that she told the truth.

"They've been a little self-obsessed the past few millennia. Angel politics make ours look like a playground negotiation. Yes, if they found out, they'd kill us all. It might take them ten-thousand years or so to get the execution order signed and out of committee, but they'd eventually kill us all."

Kelly stared at her, unable to speak. Monica smiled. "And now you have leverage. It would mean your death too if the secret got out, but I get the feeling you'd willingly sacrifice yourself for the safety of your furry friends, no?"

"Why are you telling me this?"

Something dark and sad flashed over the elder vampire's face. "Because I'm old, and I'm tired of this farce. I found something that really matters to me, and thankfully I wasn't stupid enough to throw it away. Gideon is a good man, the type of Master vampires need to have, not some vain, self-important fool in a silk suit. I will stand beside him and fight for what we've worked so hard to achieve over the centuries."

"Even if it means your death?" Kelly asked, stunned. "You could be Consort to a Born, eventually rule the entire east coast, and more, if rumors are true."

Monica leaned back in her chair. "Yes, even if it means my death. Would you take the Prince's offer? An empty title, an eternity filled with back-stabbing and intrigue? Given your reluctance to take my own offer, I think your answer would be 'no'."

Kelly opened her mouth to protest and shut it with a snap. No, she wouldn't take that offer, not after she'd seen how life could really be, even in a dilapidated trailer surrounded by humans and werewolves. There were things money and status couldn't buy — although money helped.

"So, I find I must amend my offer to you," Monica said, a faint smile on her thin lips. "I can see you already have a family, so I propose a revision to the treaty signed two-hundred years ago. Assist us in keeping the Fournier family out of our territory, and we will do the same for you. We'll also pledge no further illegal crossings — from now on, any of our vampires passing through your lands must have prior permission and abide by rules and restrictions you set forth. In return, we honor your claim as a new family and pledge assistance in both your business interests and any enforce-ment or protection you may need from others — vampires, humans . . . and angels."

Kelly couldn't help an involuntary glance at the doorway. It wasn't just the werewolves that needed protection from angels, Jaq did too.

"I can't commit them to this proposal without their Alpha's approval. He's the one running this show, not me. Why aren't you talking with him about this?"

Monica pushed the coffee cup aside. "Because vampires do not make deals with werewolves; we make deals with other vampires. If their Alpha has brains sharper than his teeth, he'll realize your value in this scenario." Monica stood, looking down at Kelly fondly. "And that, my dear, is my gift to you. Now, if you'll excuse me, I feel sunrise approaching, and I can tell that your Nephilim friend is reaching the end of her patience."

Kelly stood. "Uh, how shall I let you know the were-wolves' decision? You wouldn't happen to have a cell phone, would you?"

Monica laughed. It was an eerie noise, like a rasp on wood. "I will know. Young Fournier will attack us in Lees-burg tomorrow midnight. Either you will be there, or you won't."

She glided across the floor and through the glass double doors as if her feet didn't completely touch the ground. Before the door closed, she vanished in a burst of speed. Barely five seconds passed before the door opened again, and Jaq walked in. Kelly couldn't help but contrast the two — the Consort with her inhuman mannerisms and floating move-ments, and Jaq, who walked on the balls of her feet, silent and smooth as a panther.

"You heard?"

"Uh huh. She gives me the creeps. I mean, completely gives me the creeps. I still feel itchy from that aura-thing she's got going on. Her scent makes me want to sneeze. And rub baking soda up my nose. Ugh."

"Do you think your Alpha is going to go for it? This could solve a lot of your problems — mine too."

"Yeah, but can we trust her?" Jaq looked out through the door, but the other vampire was long gone and probably safely underground by now.

"I trust her more than the others. We may be a bunch of monsters, but we do respect a solid, well-crafted agreement."

Jaq tilted her head and shrugged. "Well then, let's go wake-up Jonah. What's the worst he can do? Say no?"

CHAPTER 35

*N*o."

The word was absurdly firm and final, coming from a muscled werewolf wearing pajamas covered in dancing penguins. He didn't even have the courtesy to look at them while uttering it, instead concentrating on some object he was whittling with a pocket knife.

Kelly held silent, letting Jaq take the lead. The Alpha for several thousand werewolves looked like any human she'd meet on the street in this state. A youthful ball cap covered his head, but the gray in his blond beard and the faint lines on his face put his age around mid-fifties.

"We're in the middle of two factions," Jaq argued. "The fight last night is only the start. The one tomorrow night will most definitely cross into our land."

"Maybe it will, maybe it won't. Vampire squabbles aren't any of our business. One of them will eventually win, and everything will go back to normal. We just need to hold our ground."

"And how many will die for us to hold our ground? We

can end this quickly, with minimal loss, if we take the Kincaids up on their offer."

"No." Jonah punctuated the word with a sharp jab to his carving.

"There won't be a return to normal," Kelly interjected. "No matter which group wins, you will all lose. The Prince to the north wants West Virginia. The early attack had nothing to do with the battle that followed. He's moving against us, either as a financial supplement, or as a preparatory move to take the Kincaid land, or a section of his father's lands. We could keep this war from our borders, but we'll still face direct attack from the Prince."

Jonah swore. "You vampires are worse than boils on a summer day. We have a contract that nobody seems willing to honor; what makes you think this Kincaid woman, or man, or whoever, is going to honor a new one?"

Kelly squirmed. How could she justify all this on gut feelings, or the strange affinity she felt for the ancient vampire? "They will continue to be vulnerable with a Made Master; they're pledging mutual support. The contract benefits them more than just this one battle. They'll honor it."

"This is our chance to experience a bit of freedom," Jaq added. "We're trapped in this state. This pack is in violation of so many stipulations from the angels that we don't dare venture forth. The vampires have offered us protection. If they can manage to keep visiting demons safe from angels, then they can do the same for us. Just think, Jonah, our pack can visit family in the southern states, maybe even participate in large hunts again without fear of reprisal from the angels."

Jonah snarled. "And what if it is all a trap? Some kind of long game to get us out of the state and in a place where the angels can get us? I can see it now: we're in Georgia on a hunt, and down drop three angels to administer their own special brand of justice. I don't trust vampires."

"They won't," Kelly insisted. She exchanged a quick look with Jaq. They'd wanted to keep this bit of information in their back pockets, but Jonah would never trust the vampires without it. "Vampires have just as much reason to fear the angels as you do. If their secrets got out, they'd be massacred. They won't betray us."

The alpha leaned forward, eyes narrowed. "So you know their secret, but you're a vampire too. How do I know this isn't all a lie for you to gain a lucrative position in this new family?"

"I know it too," Jaq said. "For God's sake, Jonah, put your prejudice behind you and think of the good of the pack."

"I am," he snapped. "We've had no reason to trust them. Your girl here has fought nicely on our side, but that's not enough to ease my worries. And this deal is all about physical trespass and attack, what about financial? Vampires have been making inroads into our business interests in the last year; who's to stop this Kincaid vampire, or your Prince, from crippling us financially? We'd have the land but nothing else. It would be like being smoked out in a siege."

"That won't happen." Kelly could feel Jaq's surprised gaze on her. "I can assure you there will be no further hostile take-over attempts on your businesses."

Jonah paused his whittling, the werewolf's eyes shrewd as he stared at Kelly. She held his gaze and was surprised to see him shrug and turn his attention back to the wooden object in his hand.

"Jaq, why don't you ask Ellen to bring out some hot tea for us all."

Jonah's voice was casual, but there was no mistaking the steel of command under the soft words. Jaq stiffened, her face pink. The Alpha didn't repeat himself, and with just enough hesitation to be defiant, Jaq stomped off for the house. Kelly watched her go then turned her attention to Jonah. Kelly observed him whittle in silence, just as she would a Master. It was uncomfortable standing here without Jaq's reassuring presence. Kelly decided to fall back on what she knew in terms of behavior. Don't speak unless spoken to; don't answer unless asked a question.

He held up what was shaping up to be a wooden peg and examined it, running a thumb along its smooth length. "It's to plug up a cask. I've taken up wine-making, you see. Ellen, my wife, tells me it's good for a man my age to have a hobby."

Well, that was an abrupt change of topic. Was their earlier conversation over? What was his decision on the Consort's proposal? Deciding to just go with it, Kelly made a noncommittal, what she hoped was approving, sound. Jonah turned to face her, waving the peg her way. *Screw it. Might as well live dangerously,* she thought.

"Is your wine any good?"

The werewolf made a noise somewhere between a snort and a hacking cough. "No. Tastes like shit. I'll break it out with great ceremony at the next pack event, and everyone will drink a few glasses and tell me how marvelous it is."

Where was he going with this?

"They'll lie to you." She understood lies. Kelly really understood lies. The important thing was to not get caught.

Jonah took his knife and smoothed out a rough spot on the peg. "We lie if it does us no good but benefits another. That's an honorable lie. A lie that benefits the liar but harms others is disgraceful."

Kelly raised an eyebrow. Sounded like a feel-good load of bologna to her. "So how does it benefit you if everyone lies about the quality of your wine? Wouldn't it be better if they told you it was wretched, so you could strive to improve?"

"I have no ambitions of being a professional. This is a

hobby, and hobbies are to bring joy and satisfaction to the creator, regardless of the quality of the work. It's important to know those you are lying to, to understand their hearts and desires, otherwise your lie may do harm."

Total bologna. The cheap kind, with the red plastic around the edges.

"I'm going to call bullshit on that one. The liars *do* benefit — by avoiding your anger, or toadying for your favor. They don't lie to spare your feelings; they lie to preserve their status, and possibly their lives."

The alpha sighed, lowering his knife to rest on his thigh. "And that's what worries me, little vampire. How long has it been since you were turned? A century? Hundred and fifty? You're bitter, and it colors everything you see. You'll never fit in here — not because you're a vampire, but because you'll never see the world as anything but a hostile place where the only thing that matters is your own survival. I suspect you were that way as a human too, but no matter. Old dogs can't learn new tricks, and I doubt you can either."

Kelly blinked back the tears that stung her eyes. She'd never been given a chance to trust anyone. It wasn't her fault she'd always lived in survival mode. Given the opportunity, she *would* put another first, would trust them. *George.* His face rose from her memories, sleep-tousled hair and mischief in his blue eyes. The image was quickly overlaid by another — a dusty corpse sprawled in a dank corner, silver ring on a bony finger. She'd not trusted him; she'd not put him first. She'd left and never looked back. Maybe this werewolf was right.

Jonah turned sharp eyes to her. "Vampires. From what I've been told, you all live in tight-knit family units with clearly defined roles and responsibilities. You work to serve the greater good of the family, and especially your Master. It's kind of like bees in a hive, isn't it? Each doing the job best suited to him or her. Each sacrificing personal gain for the good of the group. Sacrifice of the self, all striving toward bettering the family, the Master orchestrating every move with an eye to the long term. How on earth did you fit in there, Kelly?"

Screw it. She was dead anyway. Might as well go out with a bang. "I fit in just fine. It looks like a great social collective from the outside, but it's not. We all hedge our bets. Every single one of us plots to rise in favor by well-placed knives in the backs of our brothers and sisters. We scheme; we lie; we plot; we embezzle money — all while smiling and pretending we're serving the Master."

"And does he know this? Your Master?"

"Of course. We're not a hive; we're a coliseum with gladiatorial games twenty four seven. There's enough forward momentum to get things done — competition does have some benefit to the family as a whole — but those at the top do enjoy watching the soap-opera of Machiavellian intrigue that's right under their noses."

"Humph." The werewolf tossed the knife in the air, catching it by the handle as it rotated, all the while never taking his eyes from Kelly. "What do you think qualifies me to be Alpha, young vampire?"

She had no freaking idea. This stupid werewolf jumped topics with the speed of light. All Kelly knew was that she was pissed. She'd sacrificed everything, had nowhere else to go. If these werewolves didn't accept her, she was as good as dead, but she still couldn't bring herself to grovel. Waiting for her death in that horrible casino hallway had her frozen in fear, but this time facing her death was liberating. If he killed her here and now, or if she fell to a knife in the back, it didn't matter. She was free, and this werewolf wasn't going to intimidate her.

"You're old? The most powerful? You defeated all your

opponents in hand-to-hand combat? You're the best Tiddly Wink player in the northeast region?"

The werewolf glared. "I'm not *that* old. Power, yes, but there are probably a few werewolves in the pack that could take me one-on-one. Jaq could wipe the floor with me, but she's special. It's power in numbers, my girl. We don't vote or nothing, but the pack backs the person they feel will best serve their interests. I'd give my life protecting each and every one of my wolves, and one day I probably will. I never put my own safety above the needs of others, and my own children don't rate higher than any wolf in this pack. That's a hard thing to say, but it's what makes an Alpha."

"Mmmm." All this talk of self-sacrifice was getting old. Lovely rhetoric, but who knows what this guy would do when faced with a choice. Whatever. She wasn't about to get into a pissing match over it. Let the old guy believe what he wanted.

"That's why Jaq will never be an Alpha."

What? Kelly's brain screeched to a halt, and adrenaline rushed through her body. Every cell was on high alert. "Jaq is kind and generous. Just because she doesn't have some screwed up martyr complex doesn't mean she's not Alpha material."

"She sheltered a vampire, risked the safety of both werewolves and the humans we call our friends to satisfy her own personal wishes. Then, she not only shares her blood with you, but she tells you what she is. She tells you secrets that endanger our entire species."

Kelly's temper snapped. "Well there goes all that lovely talk about trust. And how do you know if her actions will work to the pack's benefit better than your isolationist dogma, you hypocritical, short-sighted, racist prick?"

Jonah snarled, stabbing the pocket knife halfway through

the wooden bench. "Because you are not just a vampire; you're selfish and immoral. You'll sell us out the moment it's to your advantage."

Kelly tried to rein in her temper. It's what got her in this mess in the first place. It was no use. "Oh yeah. I've got the angels on speed dial. They'll totally believe some barely turned, cast-off vampire and come rushing over here to exterminate every last one of you. And the rewards! Oh my, I'll be sitting high up on a throne with my own family to feed me peeled grapes and fan me with palm fronds. Are you insane? There is no advantage. None. And I don't care what you believe; I'd never betray Jaq."

Jonah puffed his cheeks out with air and let out a sound of disbelief. Then he turned and yanked the knife free from the bench, once again shaving bits off his cask plug.

"If it will make you feel any better, I'll share a secret with you. The vampires are all dead. They died out thousands of years ago. We're all turned humans, and the whole Born lineage stuff is bullshit."

The werewolf sliced clean through his thumb. He cursed and shook his hand, blood flying before he stuck it in his mouth.

"Yeah. None of the other vampires know. Well, maybe some of the Born Masters do, but they're not going to tell anyone. So how did I find out this juicy tidbit of gossip, you ask? Demons. I handled all the VIPs for the casino, and while they are the most boorish, rude, difficult customers I've ever had the misfortune of dealing with, they have an excellent ability to sense and trace DNA. I helped a thirty-thousand-year-old demon enjoy a vacation without an angel breathing down his neck, and he was happy to tell me all about my family's lineage and his long, close history with the vampire race."

It was a lie. Kelly paused to wonder for a moment whether the lie benefited her or the alpha, whether it met his definition of "excusable" or not. Associations with demons seemed to give her some street cred with the werewolves, so maybe it was to her benefit. Ah well, selfish habits die hard.

"And while we're discussing my immoral and selfish ways, here." She pulled a large envelope from the waistband of her oversized sweatpants and handed it to Jonah. "I've got a little gift here for you."

Jonah made a muffled noise, his thumb stuck firmly in his mouth as he took the packet with his other hand and shook the contents out on his lap. Papers spilled out across his thighs, some sliding to the ground. Picking one up, the alpha's eyes widened.

"Terrible, aren't I? Been embezzling from my own family for a century, then I top it all off with a huge hack job that stole millions in one click. And now you've got your own moral dilemma. All those businesses, that entire trust fund is for the pack. They'd never have to worry about being financially forced from their lands again. Of course, they'd be profiting from ill-gotten gains, accepting gifts from a horrid vampire."

Kelly leaned forward, letting all her vampire-self come to the forefront. Smooth and agile, quick with an inhuman flexibility; she edged in close and looked him directly in the eyes.

"Buying acceptance into a family is the vampire way. Taking a little off the top to ensure your own security is the vampire way. You could accept the Consort's proposal, welcome me into the pack. You could keep everything and slide a knife through my ribs. Or you could throw it all in my face and tell me to get out, knowing that the next vampire battle might signal the end for your pack. What a difficult set of choices, huh?"

For once Jonah was speechless, staring at the vampire

with his mouth open. Kelly smiled and backed up a few paces.

"We're even, old man. Now, if you'll excuse me, I'm going to leave with my friend, the not-Alpha-potential half-angel. Please let us know your decision."

Kelly stormed into the house. At least Jaq was in the kitchen and she didn't have to go wandering all over the place looking for her. Jaq looked up as she burst in the door, frowning when she saw Kelly's face.

"What happened?"

"We're leaving. Now," Kelly snapped. The woman next to Jaq backed slowly away from them, keeping her eyes on Kelly the whole time.

"What did he say?" Jaq demanded, hands on her hips.

"A lot of nonsense about his winemaking hobby and no clear answer on the Kincaid proposal." She wasn't about to tell Jaq about Jonah's hurtful words. The werewolf respected her alpha, spoke of him with great regard. Kelly didn't want to smash Jaq's opinion of him. The same with Jonah's opinion of her. Let the man make his decision. Either way, she'd made hers.

Jaq sighed, turning to the other woman. "I'm sorry, Ellen. I'll come back later."

"Sure, Jaq. No problem." The woman looked nervously at

Kelly, her face registering relief as the vampire moved toward the door.

Kelly fumed as they drove home. She'd not expected to be welcomed with open arms, but neither did she expect to be insulted and refused outright.

"You okay?" Jaq reached out to cover Kelly's hand with her own.

No, she wasn't okay, but she was going to make the best of what she had. *Keep moving forward, even if you find yourself standing alone.*

"I'm going to go to Leesburg tonight and help the Kincaids. I don't know if it will make any difference, but at least I'll feel like I held up my end of the bargain."

"I'll go with you." There was no hesitation in Jaq's response, and Kelly smiled, squeezing the werewolf's hand in hers.

"There's something I need to tell you before you go following me into the abyss. A confession of sorts."

"Shoot." The werewolf's tone was casual, but worry lines creased the corners of her eyes.

"Leaving George wasn't the only bad thing I've done. I'm not going to give you a bunch of excuses about my past to justify my actions. I'm not a good person."

Jaq shrugged. "You're a vampire. I didn't expect you to be a saint."

"But I don't think you really understand what that means. We routinely betray other members of our family, make them look bad so we get a coveted position or advance in some way. We embezzle money — I embezzle money. I've skimmed off the top of jobs for a century, taken pay offs, even diverted an entire shipment of illegal drugs then arranged to have my 'partners' killed. I've stolen from my family."

Jaq shook her head. "Kelly, I'm not going to judge you for

your past, only for who you are now — for your actions today."

"How about yesterday? Cause that's when I sabotaged four of my family's companies, stealing every dime from them."

"What, all eleven dollars and twelve cents?"

Kelly quoted a number. Her heart sank as Jaq's frown deepened.

"And now you're wondering if I'd do the same to the pack. Steal from them, set them up and frame them for stuff just to get ahead. You're wondering if I'd betray the whole lot of you the moment a better offer comes along."

"No, I'm wondering which island in the South Pacific you intend to buy with all that stinking money. And how I'm going to keep some really pissed off vampires from killing you once they trace this your way."

"Seriously, Jaq. Your Alpha doesn't trust me; the rest of the pack doesn't trust me. Be honest; deep down inside, you can't possibly trust me either."

The werewolf pulled over to the side of the road and turned to face Kelly. "I have no idea where you're going with all this so I'll play along. Will you steal from the pack, stab everyone in the back, and abandon us the moment the going gets tough?"

"Probably. Someday it will be me or them, and I'll pick me. I always pick me."

"Liar." Jaq let out a snort of a laugh and put the truck in gear, pulling back into the roadway. "You defended Mike when you could have run. You fought when you could have easily held back and stayed safe. No one would have known any different. You're knitting scarves for Melody! Don't give me this 'bad girl' crap. You're no more a monster than any of us are — humans included."

"I embezzled millions from my family. And I'd do it again if I could."

Jaq shrugged. "And how long did you work for those vampires without payment? Kelly, you're loyal, but only to those that deserve your loyalty. No one in your past gave a crap about you. You did what you had to do to survive."

"George." It was the one nightmare that haunted her. He was the one person in her life that didn't deserve to be abandoned, didn't deserve to be killed and tossed in an underground tunnel like a piece of trash.

"You were a child. You were scared, and you made a choice. I trust you. I trust you with my life. And in time, you'll earn the trust of the other werewolves too. Do you think I've had an easy time of it? Some of them still keep their distance when I'm around."

Kelly looked at her in surprise. Jaq? Kind and generous, quick to laugh and always willing to share what was hers? If they were wary about Jaq being in the pack, then there truly was no hope for her.

"Yeah, me. I hide a lot of my skills because I know many of them would feel threatened if they knew. Heck, some of them still feel threatened — Jonah included. Not that they have to worry. I've got no desire to be the Alpha — all that responsibility, everyone coming and whining because someone stepped on their tail or took their kill at the last hunt. No way. I'm happy to be on the fringes, a bit of a loner. Guess it's the rebellious streak I inherited from my father."

Her father, the angel. Kelly grinned. "What else did you inherit from your father? A lustful attraction toward other species? An inability to control your horny desires no matter the risk?"

Jaq glanced over, one eyebrow raised. "Yeah, that's me. The woman built like a beanpole, covered in freckles and wearing Carhartts."

"Pink, lacy underwear. Black thongs," Kelly teased. "I'm going to have to warn Melody in case you get an uncontrollable urge to have your way with Joe."

"I'm more likely to try and have my way with his neighbor."

Jaq's face was crimson. Kelly stared in surprise at her carefully averted gaze. Was that a come-on? How should she respond? She didn't want to assume . . . maybe she misunderstood?

"I'll come with you tonight to Leesburg and fight for that Kincaid woman," Jaq continued, still staring at the road ahead. "I'll even come with you to that island in the South Pacific, if you'll let me. And if you stay here, the pack will allow it. I can't force them to welcome you with open arms, but I can make quite clear the consequences to anyone that even thinks of harming you."

Watching the determined look on Jaq's face, Kelly felt a surge of affection. She didn't need a family, didn't need a pack. All she needed was one good friend by her side and everything else would work itself out.

CHAPTER 37

Gideon Kincaid stood on a rocky ledge overlooking the Potomac River. The setting sun felt warm against his back — too warm. It felt like someone was holding a lit match right next to his skin. Every nerve ending was hyper aware, stinging from the light that danced through the wind-tossed trees. He'd suffer for this later, but some things were worth the pain.

Leesburg at midnight was what their informant had revealed. There was no way to escape this sort of attack. The vampires would destroy businesses, kill whoever tried to face them then issue their challenge. Gideon had been through the same routine thousands of times, but not for a few centuries. It had been a lovely reprieve, but that was over. If not Fournier, then some other group would try to take his lands — perhaps even from within his own family. Monica was the only Born in their family, but he was certain other Made vampires were eyeing his spot, wondering if they'd be able to take him down. Monica would help him against internal threats — stability in the family was important, but he wasn't positive she'd assist in countering outside attacks.

She was the reason he was here so early, blistering his skin. When he'd seized the southern territory and Monica had agreed to stand by his side, Gideon had faced his remaining challenges alone. Yes, she'd supported him, silently doing what she could to ensure he came out the victor, but she'd not intervened. It was important for a Master to be seen as strong enough to rule. It was a difficult tightrope to walk when his Consort was most likely more powerful than he was. A Born, and so very ancient, Monica had never fully revealed the extent of her abilities, even to him.

Leesburg at midnight — it was just so wrong. The Prince didn't have his father's backing, so why would he issue his challenge when Gideon would be at his strongest? Unless he expected to have Monica by his side. His insides twisted at the thought, but he needed to face the harsh fact that she had everything to gain by aligning with the Prince. If no one advanced across the border until that magic hour, then his question would be answered, and Gideon would go to what would most likely be his death, already having lost the only thing of importance in his life. Wouldn't it be ironic for the young Prince to find that Gideon's heart was already ripped from his chest — shredded beyond repair?

His mouth twisted at the melancholy drama of his thoughts. The other explanation could be that the Prince didn't truly intend to wait until midnight, that he'd strike as the sun went down, before Monica had a chance to rise and gather her strength. It would be foolish for a three-hundred year old to face Gideon without the strength of his father or an ancient behind him. Did he have abilities the older vampire was unaware of?

Or maybe he was just a fool. Gideon didn't think so.

Route 15 stretched before him, cutting through the mountain pass and crossing the mighty Potomac into Maryland. He'd never been so pleased to see such wide and deep waterways. The Prince would take this route. Looping through West Virginia would be ill-advised with the werewolves riled up and ready to kill, and the only other route besides White's Ferry was the Capital Beltway. Gideon had never allowed that corridor to be unguarded. No, he'd take this bridge. The only question was when.

The burning at his back lessened, and he felt the shadows lengthen as they reached for him. Monica would be rising soon. He thought of her as she emerged from the dark of her space, her gray skin cool and smooth, her white eyes still heavily lidded with sleep. She always loved when he was there to greet her. He ached that he wasn't there now.

"Did you see that?" he asked the vampire beside him. Jared was only a few hundred years younger than him, but his second hadn't lost the acuity of his daytime vision . . . yet.

"Yep. Here they come."

Relief flooded Gideon. Facing a threat without Monica by his side was far preferable than seeing her stand by another. No matter what happened tonight, he'd won. She'd not left him for what was clearly a better opportunity. Surely that was a better proof of her love than any words they'd left unsaid over the last two centuries.

"Let's welcome them."

With a blur of speed, Gideon led the way down the mountainside, coming to a stop on the Virginia side of the bridge. Cars slowed as they passed him — humans on their evening commute eyeing the five figures standing on the shoulder. The movement on the Maryland side increased, and, with a rush, twenty vampires stood before him. Sweat beaded on Gideon's brow. The Prince had only brought nineteen with him. What was going on?

"Kincaid."

A young male vampire walked to the forefront. Even without the aura rolling off him, Gideon would have recognized the Fournier prince in an instant. The man in the expensive suit was a younger copy of his father's illusionary appearance. This was how the vampire would look for the next thousand years or so — attractive and un-aging with a human appearance.

"Kyle."

A muscle jerked in the younger vampire's jaw at the informal name. He might be a Made, but he was still a Master and many centuries this man's elder. There was no way Gideon was going to call the Prince by a name only his father had earned.

"I am laying claim to all the territory from Virginia south into the Caribbean, and west to Mississippi river."

That was definitely short and to the point. Yes, this prince would want to get things wrapped up quickly. The sun had edged halfway below the horizon, and Monica would be waking soon. Once she was informed he'd made his move, she'd be on her way. Twenty miles would only take her fifteen minutes if she hurried. Although, Gideon had no intention of dragging this out. He was no Master if he couldn't fight off this young, arrogant vampire on his own.

"I refute your claim. As Master of these lands, I command you and your staff to return and never cross into my family's area again."

"Then I challenge you for the right to be Master."

"Accepted."

This was an age-old ritual, but Gideon couldn't help think that the addition of cars whizzing by made a poor backdrop. Before it had always been the forests, the sea, or even an imposing castle — not a gas station fifty feet away and rush-hour traffic.

Jared walked forward to meet with the challenger's second. They examined the sharp knives each held on a cushion of velvet. The Prince's was a well-forged piece with the swirling, two-tone blade distinctive of Damascus steel. Its gleaming handle, accented with gold braid and precious stones was in sharp contrast to Gideon's. His iron blade had darkened with age to a deep gray-brown; the only embellishment a thin band of wirework at the top of the hilt. His ancestors had used this knife for war as well as tending their crops, and Gideon wouldn't have traded it for a dozen of the better-crafted one beside it. For this use, looks and quality wouldn't matter — it was the ability of the wielder that would decide who walked away and who lost their life.

With a quick motion, one of Gideon's staff vanished, only to appear a moment later carrying a large granite rock. It was the one he'd been sitting on just a few moments ago, and it would make a much nicer table than oil drums from the gas station down the road.

Gideon readied himself as the two seconds placed the knives on the stone, each contender's blade pointed toward his opponent. This is the way it had always been. They could use whatever skills they had — telekinesis, speed, strength, or even illusion, but at the end of the match, one of those knives would be buried in the other's chest.

With Jared by his side, Gideon nodded to the Prince. It began. The cars, the smell of auto exhaust, even the vampire by his side all faded into the background as Gideon focused. He felt his aura ignite and flare outward, all the strength of years pouring forth into this battle. Silently, he willed the knife to rise, feeling the pressure of Kyle's aura against his own. The Prince was stronger than he thought, although from the lack of movement of the other knife, he hadn't seemed to have developed the skill of telekinesis yet.

As the iron blade rose, it burst into twenty, and Gideon

felt their weight in his mind. The prince had created nineteen illusions, but they still bore all the heaviness of the original. If he let one drop, they would all fall and open a deadly gap in his aura. They danced and sparkled, the illusion blurring them and causing Gideon's hold to slip a fraction. Luckily the Prince didn't seem to notice his misstep. Hopefully that meant he was struggling just as much as Gideon was.

Picking one of the knives, Gideon managed to turn it and hurtle it toward the Prince. It was a one-in-twenty chance, and luck was not with him this time. The knife vanished as it struck the Prince's chest, and he heard a faint snicker along with what sounded like "Old Man."

True. But there were some advantages to age. Patience was one of them. Gideon pushed the external distractions further away and concentrated his full attention on his knife. Selecting another one, he spun it around and launched it at the Prince. Again, it turned to smoke, drifting away as it hit solid flesh. The action was smooth and easy, but Gideon felt his aura shake from the effort. His skin tickled with rolling drops of sweat that stung the sunburned skin along his back and shoulders. Eighteen more to go. One of them would strike true, and hopefully it wouldn't be the last one.

Why was the Prince's knife just lying there? The thought darted into his mind, and he struggled to section off another knife from the whirling mess above the stone. Did he hope to wear Gideon down first? Was the other vampire's power completely occupied on defense? Surely he should have made a move by now.

Another knife vanished on impact with the Prince's chest, and Gideon felt a wave of nausea. Seventeen left. If only he could break the illusion, but that had never been one of his abilities. Monica, now that woman could do anything. There were hints that she was so much more than she showed the world — like an iceberg below the surface of the water.

Again and again Gideon launched a knife at the Prince, only to see each one fail to hit its mark. Five remained. His clothing was drenched in sweat, but his aura held strong. The effort to continue occupied every ounce of his concentration. Nothing existed beyond the five knives before him.

Slowly one turned. He felt the pressure of the other vampire's aura against it. *This must be the one*, he thought in triumph as he pushed every bit of his will into moving the blade. With slow jerks, it inched forward. This was almost over. Gideon felt relief roll through him like a wave.

And then he felt a fiery pain rip along his back, penetrating flesh and searing a path into his heart. The knives fell, only one clattering as it hit the surface of the stone. His aura flickered and dimmed as he felt the silver knife twist in his back. *Jared.* He was the only one close enough. The only one he'd trusted to be close enough. It hurt more than the metal burning its way through his chest. As his vision cleared, he saw the Prince before him, saw the pretty, fancy knife move as if in slow motion toward his throat.

Monica, he thought as the pain in his neck mirrored the pain in his heart. *Monica, I love you.*

CHAPTER 38

The road twisted and turned its way through the hilly countryside. Visibility was limited to the pavement ahead and the few tattered houses that appeared here and there in the thick woods. Even with the bare winter trees, Kelly couldn't see more than a few feet past the narrow shoulder of the road. They'd crossed the Shenandoah river miles ago, yet Kelly could still smell it near. Were they just driving around in circles?

"Are we in Virginia yet?" she grumbled.

Jaq shot her a quick grin. "Yes. We're coming up on Leesburg in just a few miles. See? The city-limits sign is right there."

"But I still smell the river." Kelly frowned. Her insides felt like a rat was gnawing on them. Had she made a mistake? What if she got them all killed? Jonah had put his trust in her. *Jaq* had put her trust in her. So much could go wrong.

"Yes. You're smelling the Potomac River, and before that Sleeter Lake and Crooked Run. Don't you all have water in New Jersey?"

The ocean, which drowned out every other smell for

miles with its complexity. All this fresh water smell was usually confined to what came out of the tap in her manager's suite.

Farms gave way to rows of beautiful houses, surrounded by old-growth oaks and sweeping lawns. Jaq reached over and patted her hand as they led the line of trucks into downtown Leesburg.

"There's a lot of houses," the werewolf noted, an anxious edge to her voice. "I know it's not my place, but I'm a bit worried whether anything's going to remain standing after we're done."

Before Kelly could reply, a shriek hit her ears like a hammer, lancing pain through her skull. Jaq took her hands off the wheel and clutched them to the sides of her face, steering with her knees as she slowed and stopped in the middle of the street.

"What is that?"

Kelly couldn't even hear her friend. The sound went on and on, like a high-pitched air-raid siren. Jaq winced in pain, but the vampire felt something deeper, aching within her insides. It built, pressing against her chest until she was gasping. An aura. A really, really old aura. Was the Master here to back up his son? Had the Prince made his attack early? And what was that painful noise?

The noise ended as abruptly as it began, the aura vanishing with it. Kelly leaned her head against the dashboard and dragged a welcome breath into her lungs.

"What was that?" Jaq repeated. Her voice sounded far away with a faint echo to it.

"I don't know, but I think we need to scrap any early reconnaissance and find the vampires. I think there may have been an early attack."

Jaq slammed the truck into gear and spun the tires in gravel as she drove onward. Downtown was oddly silent.

Parked cars lined the road, but not a single person was seen walking the sidewalks or through the windows of the shops and brick row houses. Jaq's nose flared, and she moved her head side to side as she drove, casting about for vampire scent."

"Where is everyone?" Kelly wondered.

"Maybe they moved all the humans out to be safe from the attack? We do that sort of thing if we know ahead of time."

Kelly shook her head. "Humans don't know about vampires. And vampires certainly wouldn't care if humans got killed in any fighting. In fact, they'd want to keep some close by for convenient feeding."

The truck jerked to a stop as they rounded North Street. There, in front of a massive brick colonial-style building, was a large group of vampires — Fournier vampires.

"Shit!" Jaq went to put the truck in reverse only to see the line of vehicles behind her hindering her retreat.

Kelly felt the hair on the back of her neck rise. They weren't fighting. They were just standing and . . . waiting.

"It's over. Their intel must have been wrong because those are Fournier vampires, and although they look alert and ready to act, they're not attacking anyone."

"The humans," Jaq whispered.

Kelly didn't know what to say. She doubted they were *all* dead. That would be a terrible waste of resources, and if the Prince intended to keep this territory, he wouldn't be doing the equivalent of salting the earth.

The vampires turned and spotted them the moment they came around the corner, and one broke away to walk toward their truck. Kelly squirmed with indecision. Should they try and make a run for it, abandoning the vehicles? If the Prince had won, then all deals with the previous Master were off the table. She and the werewolves would be vulnerable once again. More vulnerable.

An idea wormed its way through her mind. They still didn't know she'd sided with the werewolves, or the Kincaid vampires. She still had a slim chance of redemption if she could work this in her favor. Jonah was in the truck behind them. Hand him over to the Prince and she'd surely be reinstated, perhaps even to her former position.

The thought made her sick. A few decades ago she wouldn't have thought twice. Heck, a few weeks ago she wouldn't have thought twice. But these werewolves trusted her — *Jaq* trusted her. They and the humans on Briar Lane were more family than these vampires in front of her ever had been. For the first time in her life, Kelly put aside her fear and summoned up her courage.

"Stay here," she told Jaq as she opened the truck door. "Don't come out until I say, and if things go bad, get everyone out of here fast. Especially Jonah."

Jaq's silvery eyes searched hers. "Be careful."

The vampire did a double take when he saw her, his eyes wide with disbelief as he took in Kelly and the line of werewolves behind her.

"I am Kelly Demir, formerly Fournier and now representing the werewolf pack in the West Virginia territories."

The vampire's mouth dropped open. "You're the castoff? The exile? The werewolves? Are you their lawyer or something?"

The guy was clearly not going to introduce himself, although Kelly was enjoying his shock. It helped her seize control of what was clearly a very lopsided situation.

"No. I'm their advisor and advocate when dealing with the adjoining territories."

Now there were huge incredulous eyes to accompany the

open mouth. He was a rather attractive Latino vampire, even with his tonsils clearly visible.

"But you . . . you should be dead. Or dying. Or . . . ."

Kelly waved his words away with an impatient hand. "Nonsense. Since I'd been unexpectedly dismissed from my former job, I found myself available for this interesting new opportunity. Back to the reason for my presence — I am acting on behalf of the werewolves, and we have a meeting with the Kincaid Master and Consort to discuss violations of the treaty and redress."

The vampire managed to pull himself together, although it seemed to take great effort. "I am Juan Manjarez, second to the Prince of the Fournier family. I regret to inform you that Gideon Kincaid is no longer the Master of these territories."

Kelly tensed. Her worst fears — Kincaid was dead, and the Prince had won. How to work this to her new family's advantage and keep them safe? She could see Juan's uncertainty. He would be wondering right now if it would be best for them to attack the werewolves, or to turn them away. She needed to make sure "attack" wasn't an option.

"Ah. How unfortunate. I can see you are quite busy here tying up loose ends, so I'll make a formal meeting request at a later, more convenient time."

The vampire nodded, his shoulders relaxing. It bolstered Kelly's confidence. If there was one thing she knew her way around, it was vampire politics and protocol. But there was one last thing she had to know before she turned everyone around to leave.

"May I ask — is the previous Consort no longer among the living? We had an open, unrelated matter with her concerning some money she was owed. I'd like to close that out if she is no longer alive to collect."

A flash of greed in Juan's eyes had Kelly biting back a smile. "She is now the Prince's Consort. If the werewolves owe any payments to her, you can address that through his staff."

The breath locked in Kelly's lungs. Still alive? The woman she'd met just the night before had been adamant about her refusal of the Prince's offer, yet she would have no other options if her current Master was dead. And Juan's statement — Monica would be a powerless figurehead, unable to even negotiate repayment of personal debt. An ancient vampire shuffled from Master to Master and locked away. Kelly shuddered at the thought.

She should walk away, just get into the truck with Jaq, turn the werewolf convoy around and head back across the border. Instead she hesitated. The werewolves needed allies, and the memory of her conversation with Monica haunted her.

"I'm afraid matters progressed to the point where we would need her to personally turn the matter over to another. I'm sure you understand."

"Of course. I'll have a power of attorney over to you within the week."

"If we could speak to her now, in person, it would save us all quite a bit of time."

The vampire gnawed on his lower lip, his eyes darting toward the group behind him.

"It's a considerable amount of money," Kelly added softly. "Due to confidentiality, I can't give the exact amount, but she seemed quite eager to collect."

Juan sighed, once again glancing nervously backward. "Okay. Wait here and I'll arrange for a quick meeting."

Kelly heard the car door gently open and close behind her. Knowing it was Jaq, she tried to wave the woman back only to see her move up beside her.

"I heard. I'm going in with you," she whispered.

And the other vampires probably heard it too. Kelly

winced, but was unable to reply before Juan was back. The vampire looked at Jaq with narrowed eyes then ignored her and turned to address Kelly.

"The Consort is able to see you for a brief moment."

"Thank you," Kelly tilted her head, giving Juan a brief, tight smile. "I do apologize for this, but I'm afraid a werewolf must accompany me as a witness."

Juan frowned. "I thought she was an offering for the Consort. She doesn't smell like a werewolf."

"I bathed today," Jaq told him. It was all Kelly could do to keep from laughing.

Thankfully Juan accepted the explanation and turned to lead. Kelly tensed as they walked through the group of vampires gathered in front of the brick building that announced it held the law offices of Stubben and Mercer. About twenty Fournier surrounded the fifty Kincaid. Normally the Kincaid vampires would have prevailed with greater numbers, but with the Master dead, they all held back, clearly waiting to see the outcome of the regime change. Kelly wondered if they'd fight against the Prince if another claimed the position of Master. Probably not.

"The humans. What happened to the humans?" Jaq asked.

Juan ignored her, so Kelly repeated the question. He turned to her, pausing briefly in surprise.

"Humans? No idea. We haven't seen any since we came into town. The Kincaids probably locked them away to starve us or something. We'll find them."

Jaq exchanged a relieved look with Kelly and continued on in silence as they walked past the last of the vampire group and up the front steps.

"Ten minutes," Juan told them as he ushered them through the door and closed it firmly behind them.

The sound echoed through the room. Plush carpet spread out before them into a large open entryway that extended up both stories and halfway through the house. A sweeping staircase at the end of the room led to a second story toward at the rear of the house, and on either side, doorways indicated offices. It was what lay in the middle of the floor that caused both Kelly and Jaq to gasp. A body was neatly arranged on the carpet, blood staining its ebony skin. Next to it sat a monstrous creature cradling a head in its arms and rocking to and fro.

Monica's illusion had vanished in her grief, and the woman before them was like something from a nightmare. Her body was skeleton thin, the bluish-gray skin tight over wiry sinew and bony joints. Hands with extra-long fingers clutched the head, caressing it with two-inch, yellowish talons. Her flesh was ripped in places, as if she'd clawed herself in grief, and black blood oozed sluggishly from the wounds. As she raised her bald head, milky-white eyes met Kelly's, and the woman's thin lips twisted, showing an entire mouth full of long fangs.

"Who? What?"

Kelly silenced her friend with a hand on her arm.

"Look what they did. How could they?"

With shaking hands, Monica loosened her tight hold on the head and placed it down against the corpse's neck, as if she could somehow reattach it. Three times it rolled a few inches away, and each time she grabbed it, trying to keep it against the neck's torn flesh. Finally she watched it roll and sighed, placing her hands on her knees and looking up at Jaq.

"Your kind, they often have the ability to heal, no? Angels do this. Some Nephilim do this. Please heal him. Please. I will do anything, give you anything. All my power, anything within my grasp will be yours if you do this for me. Please, I beg of you."

Jaq swallowed hard, her voice shaking. "Ma'am, my healing doesn't seem to work on vampires, and even if it did,

I can't do resurrection. I don't think anyone, even angels, can do that."

The woman seemed to crumple into a gray ball, her long fingers covering her face as she shook for a few moments in silence.

"They brought him back to me. At least they brought him back to me," she said, her voice muffled through her hands. "The others they left dead by the road. Only Jared was spared to carry his dead Master. I should be grateful that they brought his body back and didn't just pitch it into the water or throw it into the woods."

Kelly took a sharp breath. This was bad. Monica had lost herself in grief. They'd be on their own once more, fighting a Prince who would now be a Master. Their fate seemed to be set, yet she still had to see if there was any other option.

"The Prince waits for you outside. Once you compose yourself and stand by his side, he'll announce the transition and his assumption of the territory as Master."

Monica nodded, pulling her hands away from her face. Kelly looked at Jaq and saw the werewolf nod at her in approval. *Well, here goes nothing.*

"But before you go, I want you to know that I am here with eighty werewolves, including the Alpha to assist you. We came to accept your offer, to fight at your side. I hope that deal is still on the table."

Milk-white eyes rose to hers in surprise. "I thank you for your offer of alliance, but I am only a Consort and am unable to meet the terms of the contract I put forth."

Kelly shrugged. "Then be a Master. This territory seems to be lacking one at the moment."

The vampire slowly shook her head. "I'm a Consort, not a Master."

"I'm a vampire, not a werewolf and look where I am right now."

Monica laughed. It was a dry rasping sound that rubbed across Kelly's skin like sandpaper. Her shoulders straightened, and her mouth tightened into a firm line. "Thank you, Kelly Demir of the werewolves. I will meet with the Prince."

So much for her faint hope that this woman would step up to power. Their only chance now would be if the Prince saw some value in an alliance with them and honored their previous treaty as a favor to his new Consort. Either way, the future looked to be a difficult and bloody one.

"Would you please give us thirty minutes to cross back over the state line before you accept the Prince's offer?"

Monica raised her head, confusion in her eyes. "So you have changed your mind? You are declining my offer, then?"

"I thought. . . ." Kelly's voice trailed off, and she gestured at the body on the floor.

Monica followed her gaze and ran a hand down the front of Gideon's chest. "I never wanted to rule, but I won't see his hard work, his legacy, be handed over to his killer. He was my life. I won't let his death be for nothing, and for that I must face the Prince in challenge, and rule this territory as a Master."

"Then yes, we accept your offer. What do we need to do?"

The vampire shimmered as she rose, and where there had been a monster, stood a regal woman with hair like black wool, and golden skin.

"Just witness. And be ready to ensure none of the Prince's staff interfere with what should be a duel between the two of us."

Kelly nodded and she and Jaq left. The crowd of vampires watched them carefully as they descended the steps and made their way back to the line of trucks. Jonah and the others had gotten out by this point, but waited cautiously by their vehicles.

"So the deal's off?" Jonah asked Jaq.

She shook her head. "We need to wait while she and the challenger duke it out. Make sure no one interferes. We should have a plan to get out of here in case everything goes south, though. If she's killed, we won't find any diplomacy from the other group."

"Duke it out? What, like wrestling? Boxing? You guys do twenty paces with pistols or something?"

The door opened, and Monica walked slowly down the steps. Kelly watched as the crowd parted and the Prince came forward, a smile on his face, clearly expecting an acceptance.

"Not pistols," Kelly replied. "Knives."

MONICA WATCHED the young vampire approach the steps, standing with his hand slightly raised in welcome. She had to admit, he made a fine figure with his carefully disheveled hair and immaculate suit. There wasn't even a hint of triumph in his smile. Humiliating her, mocking her situation, would not benefit his cause in the slightest, and he was smart enough to put aside his elation in exchange for a humble attitude that would assist him in the long run. If only he were a few-thousand years older and she'd never met Gideon.

Gideon. The Prince's suit didn't even show a hint of the duel he'd fought, but in her mind, he was covered in blood and gore — a grotesque figure smiling at the bottom of a marble stairway. She'd never wanted this life, never wanted more than to walk by Gideon's side, but some things could not go unavenged.

"Greetings, my Consort," he said.

His voice was deep and pleasing, and Monica once again regretted that she would not be accepting his offer. Twenty-thousand years of tradition, and she was about to shatter it all. *Her*. The elegant and cultured Born. The little girl who always made her father proud. Daddy was no doubt spinning in his fiery grave right now.

She smiled at the Prince. "I am not, nor will I ever be, your Consort."

His shock was quickly masked, as was the scowl that creased his face. "I assume then that you will be returning to Egypt? My second will be honored to escort you to the airport for your flight."

The crowd of vampires behind him was so silent that she could hear the heartbeat of humans, safe a mile away, awaiting the all clear from the evacuation due to wide-spread gas leaks. Egypt. As if they would welcome her. She'd been gone three-hundred years after leaving for the new world. The fact that this Prince had offered his second as escort wasn't lost on her, either. That he'd declined to take her personally was a stinging insult. And she didn't care one bit.

"Why would I return to Egypt? I am Master of this territory."

There was a collective intake of breath from the vampires below. Monica stifled a smile. Yes, her. A Master. A thousand years ago she wouldn't have believed it herself. Actually, a few hours ago she wouldn't have believed it herself, but that feisty little exile had given her hope that maybe things could be different in this new, modern world.

The Prince stiffened, his posture rigid even though his facial expression remained calm and mild. "I am laying claim to all the territory from Virginia south into the Caribbean, and west to Mississippi river."

And here we go. Jared stepped from the crowd to stand next to her, his hands trembling as he clenched them by his side. He had every right to be afraid. His life depended on the outcome of this confrontation. Monica nodded at him, acknowledging his offer as a second, and turned toward the Prince.

"I refute your claim. As Master of these lands, I command you and your staff to return and never cross into my family's area again."

"But you don't . . . do you even have a knife?"

No, she didn't, but the fact she'd cracked his placid expression was worth the humiliation.

"I will use Gideon's — I mean, the former Master's. I'm assuming you have it and didn't leave it on the shoulder of the road."

He nodded stiffly, and another vampire came forward to hand Monica a simple iron blade. Bile rose in her throat as she took it, and she struggled to keep from collapsing into a sobbing ball on the steps. How many had Gideon faced with this blade? Its rough edges and simple hilt were so like the man she loved.

"Then I challenge you for the right to be Master."

Monica tore her gaze from the knife in her hands and straightened her spine. "Accepted. Jared, would you please get that little Louis XVI table from inside. There is no sense in doing this on something so crass as a stump or a rock."

Jared nodded and vanished through the door. Monica's lips twisted into a wry smile as she realized he'd not responded verbally, so as to not address her by title. Should he call her Consort, or Master, or just Ma'am? She was sure every vampire from Virginia south was wondering the same thing.

In a flash, he'd reappeared, placing the walnut table at the bottom of the steps. The vampire by the Prince's side stepped forward, and they examined the knives briefly before placing them on the marble top of the table. Monica walked down the few remaining steps to stand an equal distance from the table as her opponent.

"Shall we begin?"

The Prince inclined his head, and his aura flowed out to meet hers. It felt sharp and raw against her skin. The boy had potential. Monica edged open the gates deep inside her and allowed a trickle of power to release. It sliced through the Prince's aura like a black arrow and the iron knife slowly rose from the table. In a burst of light, it separated and twenty duplicates swirled and danced in the air.

The Prince seemed confident and composed before her, but Monica felt his aura tremble and sweat. The battle with Gideon must have taxed his resources, but she wasn't about to take an easy win. Her heart wanted to crush him, to tear his flesh to shreds while he screamed, to send his fangs back to his father in a box, but she held back. It was one thing to prove that she was a force to be respected, but one must always hide the true extent of one's strength — all the better to surprise any future enemies.

Holding her illusion tight, she reached deeper inside and twisted her neck in a serpentine motion. The knives glittered in a field of gold — all but one. Monica smiled and selecting one, she burst the illusion in an explosion of colorful confetti.

The crowd shifted, a low mutter penetrating her concentration. Another knife and another firework of colorful paper flew through the air. The Prince frowned. Sweat beaded his brow as he took a tiny step forward. He'd not yet mastered telekinesis; only illusion. That meant he'd need to physically grab the knife and shove it through her heart with his own hand. That wasn't necessarily a disadvantage. With enough speed, he could have her dead before she had time to react.

Another knife burst. Another step toward the pretty jeweled knife. This was a game she no longer had patience for. Her beloved grew cold in the building behind her, and all she wanted was an evening to grieve. Just one evening, then she'd assume her duties with all the grace and dignity she'd been raised to exhibit, leaving her aching heart for those daylight hours beneath the earth.

Ten knives popped, and the air was thick with tiny colored squares.

She would have missed it had she not been so very old. In spite of her concentration on her opponent, she felt something to her right — something sharp and deadly. At her age, Monica could feel silver from a block away. Even in sleep, she twitched and burned when it came within range. She refused to feast on humans who had worn the metal within the last month, knowing how even the faintest hints of it in their skin and blood caused agony throughout her body.

Splitting her concentration, and allowing more of her aura to roll from her core, she turned her face to the right. The silver knife stilled, less than an inch from her back. The hand holding it trembled as it tried to overcome the resistance and complete its forward momentum.

"Jared, darling, did you think I would not notice the wound in Gideon's back? My grief did not blind me to such an unorthodox injury. Treachery, and clearly from someone close and trusted — someone who would have been spared in the aftermath."

Three more knives burst in sparks of lavender. She'd tired of confetti, and her mercy was miles away, especially where a traitor was concerned.

"Give me a reason not to kill you, Jared. One reason."

The vampire stuttered and tried to jerk his hand away. Monica held him close, reaching out a bit of her aura to anchor him in place.

"I had no choice, my Master. Please. I beg your forgiveness."

She thought of the body lying in the building behind her.

Gideon. The smell of his skin at nightfall, when he'd been out in the sun all day. The heat in his brown eyes when he'd looked at her. The passion in his physical affection. If only she'd been able to have his child, to have something to cling to now that he was gone, but there was nothing except memories — memories that would fade as the centuries wore on. Rage consumed her. She reached out.

"I'm sorry, Jared, but forgiveness is beyond me at this moment."

Her aura flared. The vampires surrounding them cringed as a sound like glass scratching a chalkboard screeched across the street. Anger. Loss. Pain. Anguish that consumed her every cell. White light burst in a pulse, and Jared exploded into small chunks of flesh and bone. The silver knife fell to the pavement, clattering in loud protest. Monica smiled through her anger and turned her attention to the trembling, sweating Prince.

"Someday I hope you know my pain. Know what it means to love beyond every rational thought only to see it vanish before your eyes. Not because I wish for revenge, but because I wish you to see what truly matters in this life — not what your fool father has filled your head with, but what *truly* matters."

The Prince ground his teeth and muttered something unintelligible. His pretty knife trembled on the table. It was an improvement, and Monica couldn't help a smile. In five-thousand years or so, he'd be a force to reckon with.

Seven knives exploded into a spray of light, and one knife remained, spinning above the marble-topped table. Slowly it inched forward to hover within a few inches of Kyle's chest. He shook, his face determined and resigned. The bejeweled knife on the table shifted left, the hilt rising an inch.

Monica ignored it and concentrated on her own knife. She could feel it brush against the silk of his suit jacket, feel the acrid bite of his aura. It was the aura of a man who knew he was about to die. One move and it would be over — draw blood with the ceremonial knife to shatter his aura then leap forward to decapitate.

It played out in her head like a movie scene. With the Prince dead, she'd need to confront his father. The elder Fournier would be far more difficult to defeat. There would be centuries of spying, information gathering, assassination attempts and stealth attacks. All the things a Master vampire relished.

Gideon hadn't relished those things. He'd only wanted to make their territory a better place for the family, to grow their wealth and secure their safety.

She didn't want war and bloodshed. There'd been enough of that today. Monica's anger drained away, leaving her with only grief. With a jerk of her hand, the iron knife flashed forward and down, cutting a diagonal gash across the Prince's gray silk suit. As if from far away, she heard a gasp, the nervous mumble of the crowd. Reversing direction, she made another slash, drawing a line of red along the knife's path. The Prince's face grew white. He raised his chin, awaiting the move that would end his life.

"No." The knife plunged down, the blade stabbing the ground beside the Prince's foot, where it quivered with the force of impact. His eyes grew wide, and he staggered backwards, his aura cracking and falling away to leave him vulnerable.

She could feel them watching her. Waiting for her to make her move. Her eyes were on the Prince with his bloody, ruined clothing as he anticipated coming death. Not today. Maybe some other time, but not today.

"I don't kill children," Monica announced, her lip curled. "Go home to your father, and come back when you're out of diapers."

Spinning on her heel, she strode back into the building, and to the corpse of the only man she'd ever loved. This wasn't time for vengeance, it was time to mourn and build something new — something Gideon would have been proud of.

* * *

KYLE FELT HIS FACE REDDEN. She'd shamed him, called him a child and refused to kill him. Worse, he had nothing left. No power to launch a suicide strike and save his pride. His accounts had been hacked and drained; his attempts to take West Virginia had failed miserably, and now this. He'd thought with Kincaid out of the way, his path would be smooth. He'd never imagined . . . this.

Nineteen of his vampires stood next to him. Well, his father's vampires now. They'd only remained to escort him back into their territory and out of respect for his relationship with their Master. She'd spoken true when she called him a child. He'd entered as a conqueror, but he was leaving with no more than the newly turned.

Smoothing his hands down the sides of his tattered suit in an unconscious movement, he felt paper against his leg — the airline ticket in his pants pocket. This was a setback, but not a tragedy. He was a Born. His father was a Master, and ancient, a Fournier descended from the original line. Springtime in Paris was lovely, and he'd heard there were territories in Eastern Europe that were ripe for the picking. Next time, he'd succeed.

The door squawked, then shut with a smack of wood on metal. Kelly didn't need to turn around to know it was Jaq; she could smell her icy scent before the werewolf stepped foot in the trailer. The irritation she had always felt when the neighbors burst in without knocking was now a mild amusement. Besides, this was Jaq.

"Something smells good."

Kelly pivoted, angling herself so she could see the werewolf and keep an eye on her sauté. Jaq carried a wine bottle in one hand, and a bag of blood in the other. She must have stopped by Melody's on the way over. It was Joe's turn tonight. Kelly hoped he hadn't been overindulging on the donuts again. The last time he'd donated, she'd practically needed a shot of insulin to go with the blood.

"We're celebrating." Kelly waved the wooden spoon toward the pan.

Jaq grinned, setting down the wine to pick up a book from the table. "The Joy of Cooking. So I take it we're celebrating your new ability to cook something without burning it to a crisp?"

"Well, yeah, that too. But we're celebrating something else, too. Guess."

They had a lot to celebrate. There hadn't been a vampire besides her in the state for weeks. Jaq complained endlessly about how boring her evenings were becoming and had joked she'd need to take up knitting if things didn't liven up a bit.

"You getting invited to the pack Christmas party?"

Kelly scrunched up her face. That was *not* something she was looking forward to. The thought of a thousand were-wolves, all drunk on eggnog and dancing around, gave her cold chills. Jaq would drag her by her hair if she refused to go, and, besides, the werewolf had vowed to actually wear a dress. It was definitely worth tiptoeing around a bunch of werewolves if she got to see Jaq in something besides jeans or her trademark tan Carhartt overalls. It would give her teasing fodder for weeks.

"Nope. Guess again."

The werewolf blew out a puff of air that sent loose strands of blond hair bouncing upward. "I give up."

Kelly turned around and spread her arms to emphasize the importance of her announcement.

"I have a job."

Jaq squealed, nearly knocking Kelly over in a rush to hug her.

"Oh my God! Where? When?"

"The racetrack. I'm waitressing in their restaurant. It's a good start, and I can move up from there."

Dale had unexpectedly given her a reference, and knowing the owners hadn't hurt, although Jonah swore he didn't influence any hiring decisions. Soon she could finally get some decent clothing that fit, a sofa that didn't have stuffing coming out of it, and maybe even a cheap, second-hand television. Kelly smiled to think of the things that made her happy now.

Jaq gave her another quick hug then punched her playfully in the arm. "It's about time. Now you can stop borrowing money from me."

Kelly glanced over at the book on the table. "Uh, actually I'll need some bus fare. I spent my last twenty on The Joy of Cooking."

Jaq shook her head and laughed. It always transformed the werewolf, peeling away the fierce warrior to the playful woman beneath. On impulse, she reached a flour-covered finger out to touch the freckle at the end of Jaq's nose.

"I'll pay you back; I promise. For everything."

Kelly's heart skipped a beat at the warmth in the other woman's gray eyes.

"You already have."

Jaq pulled her in for another hug, and Kelly held her tight. She was surrounded by creatures that still didn't quite trust her, in a dilapidated trailer. Yeah, she was poor, but oh so rich. Richer than she'd ever been, even that brief time with George.

Jaq sniffed, her shoulder rubbing against Kelly's forehead as she pulled back slightly. "Umm, Kelly? Is whatever you're cooking supposed to smell like that?"

"Shit!" She'd burned dinner. Again.

Pushing the pan back further on the stove she turned around to see Jaq fighting back a grin.

"Can I borrow a twenty to order some pizza?"

ABOUT THE AUTHOR

Debra lives in a little house in the woods of Maryland with her sons and two slobbery bloodhounds. On a good day, she jogs and horseback rides, hopefully managing to keep the horse between herself and the ground. Her only known super power is 'Identify Roadkill'.

debradunbar.com

<u>IMP WORLD NOVELS</u>

<u>The Imp Series</u>
A Demon Bound
Satan's Sword
Elven Blood
Devil's Paw
Imp Forsaken
Angel of Chaos
Kingdom of Lies
Exodus
Queen of the Damned
The Morning Star
With This Ring (2020)

* * *

<u>Half-breed Series</u>
Demons of Desire
Sins of the Flesh
Cornucopia
Unholy Pleasures
City of Lust

* * *

<u>Imp World Novels</u>
No Man's Land
Stolen Souls
Three Wishes

Northern Lights

Far From Center

Penance

* * *

<u>Northern Wolves</u>

Juneau to Kenai

Rogue

Winter Fae

Bad Seed